A SPRING SURPRISE FOR THE CORNISH MIDWIFE

JO BARTLETT

Boldwood

First published in Great Britain in 2022 by Boldwood Books Ltd.

Copyright © Jo Bartlett, 2022

Cover Design by Debbie Clement Design

Cover photography: Shutterstock

Every effort has been made to obtain the necessary permissions with reference to copyright material, both illustrative and quoted. We apologise for any omissions in this respect and will be pleased to make the appropriate acknowledgements in any future edition.

A CIP catalogue record for this book is available from the British Library.

Paperback ISBN 978-1-80048-971-4

Large Print ISBN 978-1-80048-970-7

Hardback ISBN 978-1-80048-969-1

Ebook ISBN 978-1-80048-972-1

Kindle ISBN 978-1-80048-973-8

Audio CD ISBN 978-1-80048-964-6

MP3 CD ISBN 978-1-80048-965-3

Digital audio download ISBN 978-1-80048-967-7

Boldwood Books Ltd
23 Bowerdean Street
London SW6 3TN
www.boldwoodbooks.com

For Danni, the most amazing social worker I've ever met, who has shown me that the families which are striven for the hardest, are also the most beautiful

1

The view from Jess Kennedy's apartment, Puffin's Rest, which looked out across the harbour at Port Agnes, usually seemed to stretch on to infinity – or at least to the horizon far beyond the harbour walls. For once, though, February mists appeared to be shrouding the whole world in an invisibility cloak, making it much harder for Jess to drag herself out of the warmth of her bed. It would have been so easy to stay curled up under the covers. Luna, the once stray cat who now undoubtedly ruled every inch of Puffin's Rest, had other ideas. Sinking her claws into Jess's shoulder, the only bit of her body, apart from her head, visible above the covers, the little cat reminded Jess in no uncertain terms that it was time for breakfast.

'Okay, Luna, I get the picture.' Jess pulled herself into a sitting position. There was no need for an alarm clock when she had a hungry cat. Maybe it was just as well she'd had the rude awakening; she was due in clinic in just over an hour's time and the first patient on her list was Faith Baxter. It was one appointment she couldn't be late for and she still had her blonde bed hair to tame.

A hot shower and a happily fed cat later – or at least as happy as the notoriously hard-to-please Luna ever got – Jess was in one of the consultation rooms at the Port Agnes midwifery unit. She had a full day of antenatal appointments in clinic, but the next day she'd be out on home visits. Thankfully, the heavy snowfall that had made the winding country lanes in the Three Ports area almost impassable in January had now melted away. Snowdrops were now appearing at the base of some of the hedgerows and Jess was looking forward to spending some time out and about. The past six months or so seemed to have been consumed by the assessment she'd gone through to become a foster carer.

It had been a little over a month since the foster panel had recommended her for approval and her social worker had told her they were looking at lining up her first placement any day now. She'd be taking planned placements, for a week or so at a time, providing respite care that could fit around her job as a midwife. Anna, the manager of the midwifery unit, and one of the Jess's closest friends, had said they'd do whatever it took to make it work. As long as Jess could provide enough notice of when she'd have a placement, they could arrange agency cover for those times. There were three reasons she'd decided to do respite fostering, rather than full-time, but she'd only admitted two of them to her social worker. Jess was the only person in the world who knew about the third one.

Every time her phone rang, Jess's skin prickled in anticipation that this might be the call she was waiting for. She couldn't wait to welcome a child into her home, but part of her was terrified too. The weight of responsibility of making a child who'd already been uprooted from the life they'd known feel comfortable in another strange place made her heart race – the same way it had when she'd been in that position herself. But she desperately wanted to do it, and do it well, which meant excitement and anxiety collided every time she thought she was finally getting the call. For now, though, she was still waiting.

'Come in.' She looked up to see Faith coming in, her patient's bump seeming to enter the room a good ten seconds before the rest of her. She was at that stage of pregnancy where it was hard to get in and out of a chair without making a harrumphing sound. 'How are you doing?'

'I can't remember the last time I slept properly.' Faith gave her a watery smile. 'Everyone keeps telling me I should be using this time before the baby comes to get as much sleep as possible, but I've never found it harder to get a good night's sleep. It's been like this ever since I lost Archie.'

'Is that why you aren't sleeping?' With most patients Jess would have assumed that the lack of sleep was down to the uncomfortable final weeks of pregnancy, but Faith had been through so much. The placenta had stopped working late on in her first pregnancy and her son had been stillborn. Jess had given her as much support as possible throughout the pregnancy – agreeing with Anna that Faith needed more midwifery check-ups than most patients, in addition to the extra monitoring appointments she had with her consultant – but it was always going to be hard reaching the stage where her first baby, Archie, had died.

'I just keep picturing it happening again.' Faith sighed. 'I know I can't give birth here or at home, because I'm too high-risk, but being in the hospital just reminds me so much of losing Archie. Sometimes I just want to run away somewhere and hide until it's all over. I keep thinking that as long as I stay out of hospital somehow, there's no way the same thing can happen to Titus.'

'It's by far the safest place if you or Titus need any help at all.

You've got your consultant there with you too.' Jess reached out to squeeze Faith's hand. There were some patients she became closer to by virtue of how much they needed her, because the truth was Jess needed to be needed. Now more than ever. And Faith *did* need her. She'd told Jess about the reason she and her husband, Michael, had chosen the name Titus for their son. She'd said the reference to the name in the Bible was that Titus was a true son of faith, so it had seemed like the perfect choice to parents who so desperately wanted fate to allow them to keep their second child. Jess knew all about the power of second chances and the hope that came with them, but that always came hand in hand with fear too. When you'd been heartbroken once, there was no trying to pretend that it couldn't happen again.

'I just wish you were going to be there.' Faith's eyes were almost pleading and Jess decided it was time to impart something else she'd agreed with Anna. There were no guarantees, but it might help Faith to cope with the run up to the birth.

'I spoke to my manager and she's cleared it with a friend of hers who heads up the hospital maternity unit for me to be at the birth alongside Michael, if you'd like that? The hospital team will still be there, of course, and the only hitch will be if I'm already out on a home delivery when the call comes in. Otherwise I should be able to be with you.'

'Oh my God! *Really?*' Faith's face was transformed and she suddenly looked ten years younger, smiling as Jess nodded. 'I might actually be able to stop hiding my car keys to stop me heading for the hills when I go into labour if I know you're going to be there.'

'I wouldn't miss it for the world and I promise I'll be there if it's at all possible.'

'What about the fostering? I don't want to cause any problems for you if you're going to get a placement.' Faith's face had taken on a pinched look again, the slightest hurdle to her plans immediately sending her spiralling back downwards into fear.

'The paperwork takes a while.' Jess didn't want to tell Faith why she wasn't ready to take on her first placement yet, but she'd ask her social worker to wait until after Faith's due date before she started taking referrals. There was no way she wanted to add any kind of guilt trip to the load Faith was already carrying.

'I know it's selfish of me, but I'm so glad it doesn't move quickly enough to take you away from me before the baby's born.' Faith's shoulders seemed to slump with relief. 'What about the lovely Dexter? Will he still be involved?' Faith raised an eyebrow. She'd teased Jess about how often she mentioned her social worker's name when she had asked her for updates about how the assessment was going. Jess had shared some details of the process with Faith to try and put her at ease and make her check-ups focused on something other than the loss of her baby, but she'd done her best to brush off any comments about Dexter. He'd been really kind and had taken the assessment, which had raked up a lot of Jess's past, at a pace that worked for her. But he'd disappeared out of her life the moment the panel had recommended her for approval.

His job was done and that was clearly all it had been to him. He hadn't even turned up for the celebratory drinks the other midwives had thrown for her, even though he'd said he would. He'd texted her a couple of times since, but she hadn't replied. She'd liked him, but she wasn't going to repeat the mistakes she had made in the past and form attachments to people who didn't have them to her. It was the unspoken third reason for why she'd chosen respite fostering. When she'd been asked why she'd chosen that option, she'd told Dexter that the first reason was that she didn't want to give up the midwifery job she loved, and the second was because she was completely untested as a foster carer and there was a chance she might fall flat on her face. The third reason was the biggest, though. Jess's heart had been shattered for the first time when she was ten years old. When she'd finally decided to trust the whole of her patchwork heart to someone again – almost twenty years later – it had been ripped to pieces again. It was a miracle it was still beating at all, but she was never going to give the whole of her heart to anyone again because it wouldn't survive one more loss.

'He's working as a freelance social worker now, doing training and assessments, so he's not involved with supporting carers once they're approved.' Jess shrugged. 'I've got a new social worker, who said I should be able to take my first placement next month.'

'Are you excited about it? I was so pleased when you told me about getting approved. I went straight home and told Michael what a great mum you're going to make.' It seemed to be helping Faith to focus on something other than herself and even if it was making Jess feel a bit awkward, she was all for doing whatever it took to lower her patient's stress levels, whatever the cost to her own.

'I won't be anyone's mum, but I want to at least be a good memory for the kids who stay with me when they think back on their childhoods later on.' Jess tried to swallow down the lump which always seemed to settle in her throat when she thought back to her own childhood. 'I know what it feels like when these things are handled badly and part of me is terrified that if I get it wrong, I'll be making it worse for a child who's already been through so much. They all deserve to feel like they're the centre of someone's world and if I can help make them feel like that, even for a week at a time, I'll have achieved something worthwhile.'

'You'll be brilliant at it, but you've already achieved so much that's worthwhile and I couldn't have asked for a better midwife. I'm so glad the hospital has agreed you can be at my delivery because I don't think I could do it without you.'

'I'm really glad I'll be there too, but you've been so strong, you'll be absolutely fine with or without me.'

'I guess we're both stronger than we realise, then.' Faith smiled and Jess hoped she was right. She'd been let down so many times, by so many people, and she couldn't bear the thought of being responsible for making another child feel that way. She'd do whatever it took to make sure it didn't happen.

Two days after her appointment with Faith, Jess had spent the early part of the afternoon on home visits. When she'd checked her phone after she'd finished with her last patient, there were three missed calls from Ella and a message asking Jess to call her at the unit as soon as she could. Ella was the deputy manager of the midwifery unit and another of Jess's friends. Working in high-pressure situations together the way the team at the unit did, meant that deep friendships had grown between the midwives and they'd been through a lot together over the last few years.

'What's up?' Jess's mind was racing and she had everything crossed that Ella's calls had nothing to do with Anna or her pregnancy. Their friend, who was also head of the unit, was expecting twins after being told she might never have children, and it was turning out to be a challenging pregnancy. It meant they were all very protective of Anna and on high alert for any worrying signs that things might not be going according to plan.

'Faith Baxter has gone missing.' There was a definite note of panic in Ella's voice. 'She's been really anxious since yesterday apparently, and Michael just wanted to check that she hasn't been in touch with you.'

'Oh God! I haven't heard from her since her last check-up the day before yesterday. I wouldn't say she was any more anxious than any other time I've seen her recently, but there was always a chance if she's gone into labour, or even thinks she has, that it would send her into fight or flight mode and push her in the wrong direction because of what happened last time. I just hope she's okay.'

'Michael said she couldn't sleep last night and she got up at about four a.m. He went down at seven, expecting to see her, but she wasn't there. She's not answering her phone and he's tried all their family and friends.' Ella gave a shuddering sigh. 'The police and coastguard have already joined in the search, and there's a group heading off from the harbour in about ten minutes. Her husband sounded so desperate on the phone.'

'Poor Michael, he must be terrified. I'll try ringing Faith too, just in case she's willing to pick up my call, then I'm going to go down to the harbour and see what I can do to help.'

'Thanks, Jess, just let me know if you hear anything.'

'Of course I will and I know you'll do the same.' Ending the call, Jess scrolled down to Faith's number, but when she tried ringing her it went straight to voicemail. All she could do for now was join the search and pray that Faith just needed a bit of time on her own to get her head straight. She was desperately trying to believe that Faith wouldn't just disappear; there was no way she'd put her longed-for second son – her rainbow baby – at any sort of risk. Jess couldn't stop shivering though. People could make crazy decisions when they were terrified, but the baby wouldn't wait for Faith to come to her senses and Jess couldn't shake the feeling that something terrible was about to happen.

* * *

Almost twenty people had turned up by the time Jess got down to the harbour and Ella's father, Jago, who owned and ran Mehenicks' Bakery on the harbour, was heading up the search party, splitting the volunteers into four separate groups. Jess's group was tasked with searching the clifftop on the left-hand side of the harbour wall, where the coastal path stretched for several miles, eventually leading down to the road that headed in the direction of Padstow. There was no beach at all on that side of the harbour, just a cliff with a sheer drop into the sea.

The coastal path itself was about twenty feet from the edge of the cliff and could only be reached by a steep climb from the harbourside. There was just a handful of farmhouses dotted in the distance; it was a contrast to the centre of Port Agnes and the roads that led out from the other side of the harbour, towards Port Kara, where rows of cottages clung to the hillside and the hustle and bustle of village life was evident even in the depths of winter. If Faith had wanted some space to clear her head without interruption, and to breathe in the sea air, then she'd almost certainly have chosen the side of the harbour that Jess's group would be searching.

'Do you think a heavily pregnant woman could actually make it up this way?' Ella's mum, Ruth, was breathing hard as she walked with Jess up to the highest point of the coastal path. At barely half an inch over five feet tall, Jess was used to people towering over her, but Ruth wasn't all that much taller and they fell into an easy step, side by side.

'You'd be surprised what even a woman in labour can do with the right motivation. Let's face it, it's the only reason women manage to get through labour at all.' Jess gave Ruth a half-smile. 'Are you okay? Walking up here is definitely enough to take your breath away.'

'Just realising how unfit I am.' Ruth grimaced, her cheeks glowing with exertion. 'I think Jago put me in this group on purpose! I'm not complaining though, I just hope we find Faith.'

'Me too.' Jess pulled her phone out of her pocket again. There was still nothing from Faith, but there was another text from Dexter. She'd ignored the two he'd sent after he'd decided not to turn up to the wine bar. It was better if they called it quits on their burgeoning friendship now, because the fact it bothered her as much as it had that he hadn't turned up to her celebration drinks was a massive warning sign. Getting close to Dexter would be far too easy and far too painful when he let her down and she couldn't take the risk. Not again.

✉ Message from Dexter

Hi Jess. Hope you're okay? Not sure if you got my other messages or voicemail? I just wanted to explain why I didn't make your celebration drinks. A lot has happened since I last saw you. Can you give me a ring when you get a minute please? Thx.

Whatever the reason, it didn't matter; especially not when Faith was missing. It was almost a month ago now anyway and she'd assumed he'd given up trying after the first two texts – at least until now. She might have told him how much she liked him if he'd turned up that night when her defences were down. Thank God he hadn't; they'd both had a narrow escape.

Slipping her phone back into her pocket, she picked up the pace to catch up with Ruth again. The only call she wanted now was one to say that someone had found Faith. Jess knew only too well what it was like to feel like you were completely alone and that no one understood what you were going through. If Faith was feeling like that, they needed to find her fast.

* * *

The nights drew in quickly at this time of year and they'd been searching for almost two hours. A glorious sunset was lighting up the sky as Jess, Ruth and the rest of their group made their way back down the steep path to the harbour. They'd walked for miles looking for Faith and Jess's calves were aching from navigating the inclines and rutty patches on parts of the footpaths.

Some of the other search parties were heading back down to the harbour too, heads hanging low because Faith was still missing, and beyond them the lifeboat was being winched back into the station. At least there was one upside to that – Faith hadn't been discovered out at sea – but all the awful things that could have happened to her wouldn't be wiped out until she was found safe and well.

'Thank you all so much for your efforts to find Faith so far.' Jago stood on some upturned crates next to a pile of lobster pots on the side of harbour. 'Unfortunately, as you all know, we haven't been able to locate her yet. The police will be continuing their own search and for those of you who are able to join in, I'll be organising another search for us tomorrow.'

A rumble of conversation went through the small crowd in front of Jago, with most agreeing to join the search again the next day, including Jess. She wasn't scheduled to be working and there was no way she could sit around whilst Faith was still missing. There was always a strong sense of community in Port Agnes, but at times like this, Jess was all the more aware of it. When she'd transferred to the unit, not long after meeting her soon-to-be ex-husband at a mutual friend's party in Bristol, she'd fallen in love with Port Agnes almost as quickly as she'd convinced herself she'd fallen for Dom.

'Do you want to come back to our place for something to eat?' Ruth turned to Jess as the crowd began to disperse. 'Ella and Dan are coming over, as well as Anna and Brae, and we'd love to have you join us.'

'I don't want to make extra work for you.'

'Don't be daft, it feels more important than ever that we're all together at times like this.' Ruth linked her arm through Jess's. 'And you and Anna can help me persuade Ella that it would be a good idea to have a few fireworks at the end of the wedding.'

'A few?' Jess raised an eyebrow, enjoying the feel of Ruth leaning into her. Ella's mother might drive her daughter mad occasionally, trying to take over the plans for her wedding, but Jess would have given anything to have her own mother around.

Ella had reunited with her childhood sweetheart, Dan, after coming home to Port Agnes following an ugly break-up. Jess's relationship history might be a mess, but it was nothing compared with what Ella had been through. She'd been jilted on the steps of a London registry office in full view of a crowd waiting for a celebrity wedding, and the whole thing had been recorded in a video that had gone viral. No one deserved a fairy-tale ending more than Ella, so Jess was only too happy to tag along and help Ruth persuade her to have a few fireworks on her big day.

'Well, maybe more like a few hundred pounds' worth, if I'm honest.' Ruth laughed. 'I've only got the one daughter and I just want to give her everything I can.'

'She's lucky to have you and I'll do my best to help you persuade her. I'm just going to nip back and feed Luna first and I'll be over.'

'Okay, my love, it'll take me at least half an hour to sort

dinner anyway, so any time before seven thirty will be good with us.'

'Can I bring anything?'

'Just yourself, my love. See you in a bit.' Ruth unhooked her arm from Jess's and gave her a quick wave, before heading back around the harbour towards Mehenicks' Bakery. Ella's parents had the knack of making all of the midwives at the unit feel as if they were honorary members of the Mehenick family too, so Jess never felt like she was encroaching. It also meant she wouldn't be in if Dom decided to pop around again either. Ever since he'd been asked to give her a reference for fostering, he'd seemed to have accepted it as an invitation to be a part of her life again. He kept suggesting that they give things another try and no amount of her telling him that was never going to happen seemed to knock his confidence. He just seemed certain Jess would change her mind in time. In ordinary circumstances, she might have told him in the baldest possible terms that hell would freeze over first, but she worried that Dom could contact her social worker at any time and stir up trouble if he wanted to. She wanted to at least have one or two fostering experiences under her belt before she gave Dom the opportunity to rock the boat.

Being at the Mehenicks' would mean she had someone else to share her worries about Faith with too. Trying to remember if she had a bottle of wine in the fridge, and wishing she hadn't already eaten five chocolates out of a box that a grateful patient had dropped off for her the day before, Jess turned in the opposite direction towards Puffin's Rest, where Luna was no doubt already waiting impatiently for dinner.

'Jess!' She recognised Dexter's voice even before she turned back to look in the direction the shout had come from. He was sprinting along the side of the harbour, despite still being fully kitted out in his lifeboat uniform, minus the safety helmet. He was tall and dark-haired, and always seemed to have a slight grazing of stubble. His hair was slightly scruffy in a way that might have been deliberately styled to look sexy if he'd been the type, which he so obviously wasn't. A fact that would only have added to his appeal if Jess wasn't completely off the idea of men altogether.

'Do you usually wear that when you're off duty? You look like Mr September in the RNLI charity calendar.' Jess couldn't quite believe the words had popped straight out of her mouth. Thank God she hadn't added that her calendar would permanently be turned to September if he really had been that month's poster boy.

'I thought I saw you coming down the coastal path as we came back in, and I didn't want to miss you.' He was only a few feet in front of her now. 'I can drop the kit back off afterwards, but I wanted to make sure you'd got my messages. When you didn't answer the first couple of texts I sent, I wondered if you were trying to tell me something and it was nothing more than I deserved after I stood you up. But I kept finding myself wanting to talk to you about everything that was going on. So I thought I'd give it another shot.'

'Yes, sorry, I was going to reply when I got in.' Even Jess wasn't sure whether she was lying or not, so it was no wonder Dexter had wrinkled his brow. She was trying not to read too much into him saying he'd been finding himself wanting to talk to her, especially when she'd felt exactly the same every time the nerves about fostering had started to overtake the excitement, but she hadn't been able to stop the warm feeling from flooding her body. She could act casual, though, even if she didn't feel it. 'Don't worry about not making the drinks thing, it wasn't like it was a firm arrangement and it was ages ago now anyway.'

'I know, but I really wanted to be there.' He took a step

forward, sounding as though he meant it. 'But something came up.'

'It's okay, honestly. I know how busy you are.' Jess gave him a half-smile. Dexter had quit his full-time job as a social worker because of his stepson, Riley. The little boy's mother had died a couple of years earlier and his biological father was struggling with parenting him alone, so Dexter had stepped in. Jess understood how low down Dexter's list of priorities meeting up with her would be, but when he hadn't turned up it had still felt like a punch in the stomach.

'It's Riley's dad. He's gone from finding things tough to a complete relapse. He's drinking really heavily again and taking whatever drugs he can get his hands on.' Dexter sighed. 'It all kicked off a few hours before we were supposed to meet up, when Connor didn't do school pick up as arranged. By the time I'd tracked him down, it was obvious he was in no fit state to look after Riley. And I can't imagine him being able to do that again any time soon, either. I was ringing around everywhere, trying to get him into rehab, and there was no way I could leave Riley. By the time I had a chance to ring you I knew you'd already be out having fun, so I wanted to wait until things had settled down a bit.'

'Oh God, poor Riley.' Jess's chest ached at the thought of what the little boy was going through. Like her, he'd lost his mum in a car crash, but at a much younger age than Jess had. And now it seemed as though his dad was failing him in almost exactly the same way as her own had. Thank God Riley had Dexter.

'He doesn't really understand what's going on, but he was upset because Connor had promised to take him to a petting zoo near Boscastle after school. I took him the day after, but he kept asking when his dad was going to be coming back and it was so hard to know what to say.'

'He's lucky to have you.' Jess's fingers were itching to reach out and curl around Dexter's, but she told herself it was just a reflex action. It would have been stupid and Dexter would probably have been horrified. It was probably that she just felt guilty at ignoring his texts when he could have done with someone to talk to; that was the only reason she wanted to reach out to him.

'It's going to be tough, I'm not under any illusions about that. I'm going to be responsible for Riley 24/7 for as long as it takes, and with my freelance work and volunteering with the lifeboat, it'll be full-on. One of my sisters has got him for me now, but he needs the stability of being with me as much as possible when he's not in school.' Dexter held her gaze. 'So I'm going to need all the friends I can get, and you can tell me if I got it totally wrong, but I felt like we really formed a connection during your assessment in a way that doesn't often happen. I genuinely want to stay friends with you, Jess, and I've been kicking myself for not taking the time to message you on the night we were supposed to meet. Although for all I know you might have been relieved that the social worker from your assessment wasn't still hanging around!'

'I wasn't relieved.' It was as close as Jess would get to admitting, even to herself, just how gutted she'd been when he hadn't turned up. 'But you're not going to have time to stay friends with anyone and everyone you help out in your job. I understand that, I really do.' Jess had experienced the same thing as a midwife. The women she cared for often wanted her to stay a part of their lives and sometimes she did. But most of the time she moved on, she had to, or she'd never be able to do her job.

'You aren't just anybody, Jess.' Dexter was still looking straight at her. 'I miss talking to you.'

'I suppose I'm going to need all the friends I can get when I start fostering, too. Especially someone as experienced as you.' Jess fixed the smile on her face, ignoring the tightness in her chest that was warning her against taking a risk she'd promised to steer clear of. She should be worrying about Faith Baxter now, and poor little Riley – nothing else mattered. Feeling as uneasy as she did about letting Dexter into her life made no sense; they were only ever going to be friends. It was just her fight or flight instinct kicking in, that was all, and every child who'd been in foster care would understand exactly how she felt.

* * *

The first thing Jess did when she opened her eyes the next morning was to check her mobile phone, desperately hoping for a message to say that Faith had been found safe and well, or better still, that she'd returned to the family home of her own accord. Unfortunately, there was just an update from a Facebook group that had been set up, called *Bring Faith Home*, telling everyone who'd signed up that the search parties would be meeting at nine a.m. at the harbour to restart the search.

She still couldn't really imagine Faith doing anything crazy; her overriding motivation from the first time she'd come to see Jess had been to protect her unborn child and for everything to be okay this time round. But there was no way of knowing how she'd react when she went into labour and the trauma of losing baby Archie came flooding back. Jess just hoped by the end of today, Faith would be home again and they could help her prepare for her baby's birth. According to Michael, every other avenue they'd investigated to try and find Faith had led to a dead end. None of her friends or family had heard from her and she wasn't at any of the usual places she went to when she needed to clear her head. It was as if she'd disappeared, and every minute she was gone, there was more chance of her going into labour and ending up terrified and alone. Jess would do whatever it took to help get Faith home again.

With a nine o'clock meet-up to get to, she jumped into the shower and then grabbed a coffee and a slice of toast. If she was going to stick it out with the search party for as long as they continued to look for Faith, then she was going to need some energy.

'See you later, Luna, I've left you a big bowl of food in the kitchen,' Jess called out to the cat, who was stretched full-length along the sofa enjoying the morning sunshine and completely ignoring her owner. But despite Luna's nonchalance, as Jess put her key in the lock to open the front door, she could have sworn she heard the cat mewing. Except when she turned back round, Luna was still stretched out sleeping.

'I'm definitely losing the plot.' Jess was still muttering to herself as she pulled the door towards her, but if she hadn't been holding on to the handle, there was a good chance her legs would have given way beneath her. Because there, on the platform outside her front door, was a baby.

2

The baby lying on the platform outside Puffin's Rest was cradled in a wicker basket that wasn't really big enough and one chubby pink leg was already sticking out from the bottom of the blanket. Jess seemed to have forgotten how to breathe. She had to hold it together, despite the fact that goose pimples were already breaking out all over her skin. There was no one else around, so for now the baby was relying on her, even if she was terrified at what she might see when she peeled the blanket back.

As soon as Jess moved back the cover, it was immediately obvious to her that whoever had delivered him hadn't been a professional. The cord had been cut far too long and it had been clamped with the sort of clip meant for keeping a bag of open crisps fresh. Scooping up the baby boy, Jess's heart was galloping so quickly she wouldn't have been surprised if he could feel it too. 'It's going to be okay, sweetheart, I'll get you sorted out.'

Thankfully, despite the shock that was still making her hands shake, Jess seemed to have gone into some sort of autopilot, her midwifery instincts kicking in and taking over from the hundred or so other emotions reeling through her head. She had no idea what she was going to do about the baby, but one thing she could do was make sure he was kept safe and the first step was to get him indoors in the warmth. She also knew that if the cord wasn't properly clamped it could cause the baby to lose blood volume and risk infection so she had to move quickly. Taking everything she needed out of her delivery bag, Jess cleaned the baby up, checking him over and clamping his cord the way it should have been done – all the time feeling almost as though she was watching herself from above.

Once she'd dealt with the immediate emergency, the autopilot switched off and all the blood seemed to rush from her head to her feet, making her dizzy. She wanted to pick up the poor little baby who was lying in the middle of her bed, completely oblivious to the fact that he'd been abandoned, but she wasn't going to do it while she felt as if she might keel over at any moment. Instead, she sat next to him on the bed, running a finger down his soft downy cheek.

'Where's your mummy, sweetheart?' Whispering the words to him, she stared at his face. There was something strangely familiar about it. She'd seen hundreds of newborns, but while some people thought they all looked the same, they never had to Jess. There was something she recognised about this little boy and that could only mean one thing: he had to be Faith's son. She couldn't pinpoint exactly the resemblance with his mother, but it was the only thing that made sense. Why else would anyone leave their baby on Jess's doorstep and she'd talked to Faith about how much she loved living at Puffin's Rest with its view of the harbour, so she knew where Jess lived. And why would it feel as if she already knew him otherwise?

'Oh God, poor Faith.' Jess whispered the words, even though the baby had no idea what she was saying. She couldn't bear to imagine what his mother had been through and what state she must have been in to leave her longed-for son behind. It was almost impossible to believe that Faith would leave her new baby even for a second, or risk infection by clamping the cord herself. She must have been so distraught that she was incapable of thinking straight and Jess just hoped to God that Faith wouldn't do anything to put herself at risk, any more than giving birth alone already had. The trouble was anything seemed possible given what she'd already done. If there was any chance that Titus could be taken away from his mother, even for a few days, because of a decision she'd made when she'd been out of her mind with worry, Jess didn't want to be a part of that. But she had to keep the baby safe above all else, like his mother clearly wanted when she had left him outside her door. She just had to work out what the hell to do next and there was only one person she could think of who might know.

'Hey! I wasn't expecting a call, but it's lovely to hear from you.' Dexter's voice was warm and some of the tension immediately left Jess's spine. If anyone could sort this out, it was him.

'I've just found a newborn baby on my doorstep.'

'And I've just won the lottery!' When Jess didn't laugh, Dexter went quiet for a moment. 'You're joking right?'

'No. Although I can hardly believe it myself.' She looked down at the baby who was cradled in her other arm, just to make sure it really was true. Dexter was right, this sort of thing didn't happen in real life. He didn't even know how close to the truth his comment was. Someone giving Jess a baby really would have been like winning the lottery. Dom had ended their marriage when they'd discovered she was infertile and he'd blamed her for the reasons behind it. It was something she'd kept from Dexter during her fostering assessment and she would never be a mother without an intervention even more miraculous than a lottery win. 'He's obviously only a few hours old and it looks like a DIY delivery, but he seems perfectly healthy. He looks full-term, too, and Faith Baxter is the only patient I have at that stage.'

'Do you really think he could be hers?'

'It's the only reason I can imagine that anyone would leave a baby on *my* doorstep.'

'Do you know if she was expecting a baby boy?'

'Yes. But it's still almost impossible to believe she'd do this, although I struggle to understand how anyone could.' Jess bit her lip, as she looked down at the baby in her arms again. As a midwife she knew better than anyone else that not every new mother felt that overwhelming rush of love the moment they looked into their baby's eyes. But for someone to be so desperate they'd abandon their baby was something she couldn't get her head round, especially not when, like Faith, they'd already lost so much. Jess could still feel an almost primeval tug on her soul when she looked down at this little boy who might well belong to a woman who'd already lost one baby. He didn't belong to Jess, though, and he never could, so she had to get him back to his mother as quickly as possible – for both of their sakes. 'From some of the stuff Faith said, I could imagine her panicking and going into denial when she went into labour, but to give up the baby when he arrived? I would have bet she'd rather die.'

'I don't know her,' Dexter's tone was gentle, 'but I have known cases where a mother has left a much-wanted baby because they've convinced themselves that they're useless and can't keep the baby safe. Is there any chance Faith might feel like that?'

'She was so terrified of another hospital birth ending up like the first one, when her son, Archie, was stillborn. She wanted a home delivery to avoid all those comparisons, but the consultant thought it was too risky.' Jess shivered, she couldn't help thinking she must have missed the signs and that she'd let Faith down in some way. 'I suppose it's possible that she took things into her own hands and that even after delivering the baby safely, she's still convinced he's at risk by staying with her. I just really hope that isn't what's driven her to this.'

'There's a good chance that past trauma is at the bottom of all of this and it might be making her act completely out of character. It could well be that Faith doesn't trust herself and she wanted to leave her baby with the one person she believes will keep him safe instead. Her midwife.'

'Oh God!' Jess had never been the sort of person who'd worried about looking after someone else's baby, even before she'd trained as a midwife, but now the child in her arms felt as fragile as glass. Someone – almost certainly Faith – had trusted her with the most precious thing in the world. Suddenly Jess could imagine exactly how it felt to be so terrified of not being up to the job that you'd consider giving up a baby because of just how much you loved it. 'What the hell am I supposed to do now?'

'You're going to be fine, I promise, and whoever left the baby with you knew exactly what they were doing.' Dexter had a lot more faith in Jess than she had in herself, but there was nothing new about that, and just the tone of his voice was every bit as reassuring as it had been during her assessment. 'I've already dropped Riley off at school, so I'll phone social services and the police and then I'll be straight over. Just sit tight and trust your instincts and your training. He couldn't be in better hands.'

'Believe me, I'm not going anywhere.' The warm glow was back, the same one Jess got every time Dexter paid her a compliment. She didn't want it to mean as much as it did because she hated the idea of relying on anyone's approval, but knowing that Dexter had faith in her had made a huge difference from the moment she'd started the fostering assessment. 'He's been pretty content so far, but he's starting to get a bit restless and he's going to need some milk soon.'

'I'll grab some newborn formula, a couple of bottles and some other stuff you'll need on the way over. I'll be as quick as I can.' Even after Dexter ended the call, Jess stayed rooted to the spot. *This couldn't be happening.* There might have been times when she'd wanted a baby more than anything else in the world, but she'd never in a million years envisaged it happening like this. Either way she'd never be allowed to keep him and nor should she. He belonged to Faith. But just for a moment or two, as she rocked him in her arms, she let herself imagine that he was hers and that she could keep him forever. She tried not to think about the extra hairline crack that would almost certainly appear on her heart when she handed him over. Knowing he'd be back with his mum would override any sense of loss that she had no justification to feel anyway. She was almost sure of it.

* * *

Dexter knocked on the front door of the flat less than thirty minutes later. Jess had thought about calling Anna or Ella while she was waiting, but she didn't want to do anything until she'd spoken to him again first. She was sure her friends wouldn't want the baby to be removed from Faith's care any more than she did, but Dexter was the expert on how to play the situation so that there'd be the least risk possible of that happening. By the time he arrived, laden down with bottles and ready-made formula, the baby had just started to whimper.

'Can you just hold him for a minute please, while I sterilise the bottles and warm up his milk?' Jess didn't even wait for a response before handing the baby over, her arms shaking as she finally released her grip on him. Having Dexter there to share the responsibility was like a lead weight being lifted off her.

'He's beautiful and he feels like quite a good weight.' Dexter rocked the baby like a pro as he gazed down at him.

'I'd guess at close to eight pounds, but I haven't actually weighed him yet.' The truth was she'd barely been able to take her eyes off him, the sweep of dark lashes that rested on his cheeks when he closed his eyes and the tiny rosebud mouth which pursed when he started to whimper.

'Could you tell how big Faith's baby was likely to be?'

'At her last scan, a couple of weeks ago, they said the baby would be in the region of seven and a half to eight and a half pounds by the time she got to full term.' Jess put the water on to boil. Sterilising the bottles would be a bit of a makeshift operation, but before much longer the baby was going to be wailing for food and she didn't think she'd be able to bear to listen to him really crying. He'd already been through so much in his short life, the least he deserved was a full belly. 'Everything's pointing to Faith being his mother, isn't it?'

'At least if that is the case we know she's safely delivered her baby and there isn't an even worse reason she's missing. Hopefully it's just a case of tracking her down and getting her the help she needs.'

'I can't stand thinking about what she's been through, delivering him on her own like that. Let alone what she's going through now.' Jess shook her head. 'Do you think they'll give the baby to Michael while they wait for her to turn up?'

'Not without proving the baby is definitely his and Faith's first.'

'So what *will* happen to him?' Jess put the bottles into the boiling water, a sudden urge to snatch the baby back from Dexter almost overwhelming her – despite her relief at his arrival. If she could only have the baby for a little while; she didn't want to miss a second of holding him close to her and letting him know he was loved and wanted. His mother could do that herself once she'd got the help she needed, but in the meantime, even if it was just for an hour or so, it was down to Jess. Faith had chosen her, after all.

'The police will start an investigation to find his mum, most likely an appeal in the news and online to try and persuade her to come forward.' Dexter was still rocking the baby gently to and fro. 'And social services will look to place him with a foster carer in the meantime, once he's been seen at the hospital and they've made sure he's okay.'

'Do you think they'll let me go to the hospital with him when he gets checked over? At least until his foster carer shows up.' Tears burned at the back of Jess's eyes, knowing that Dexter would understand what she was about to say, even if it made no sense. 'I hate the thought of him being on his own, with no one there for him, and I know Faith would hate that too.'

'The social worker will go with him, but given that you're a midwife and that you've almost certainly got a connection to his mother, there's a pretty good chance they'll be more than happy for you to go too.'

'I hope so.' Cutting the top off the carton of formula, Jess offered up a silent prayer that Dexter was right. She was all the tiny baby boy had for now and there was no way she was going to let him down.

* * *

Jess came out of the examination room with the baby in her arms and a paediatrician at her side, which was just as well or she might have made a run for it. She'd already fallen in love with the little boy whose navy-blue eyes seemed to search her face every time he opened them, even if she knew full well he couldn't focus on anything at this stage.

'The good news is he looks to be absolutely perfect thanks to the swift action taken on his cord clamping. And as Jess suspected, he's definitely brand new.' The paediatrician, a jolly middle-aged woman with cheeks like ripe apples, laughed as she updated Dexter and the social worker from Children's Services on the baby's check-up. They'd been sitting waiting on the row of plastic chairs outside her consulting room, whilst Jess had been allowed in with the baby. 'So I'm more than happy to release him into your care.'

'Thanks, doctor, that's great.' Madeline, the social worker who, up until his resignation, had been a close friend and colleague of Dexter's, returned the paediatrician's smile. 'I think he was lucky he was left on Jess's doorstep by the sounds of things.'

'Yes, very lucky! Sorry, I've got to dash, I've got a clinic in twenty minutes, but you've got my details if you need me for anything.' The doctor was already turning back towards her consulting room and Jess was trying to prepare herself for Madeline saying it was time to hand the baby over. She'd never had lockjaw, but she imagined it must feel something like the rigidity she was currently experiencing in her arms – as though they might never come apart and allow her to hand the baby over. Faith had trusted her with her newborn son; that was the reason she was so desperate to keep hold of him. Nothing else made sense, she couldn't possibly have got this attached to the baby this quickly for any other reason. When she'd thought about fostering, what had worried her most was making sure that the children had a positive experience and felt wanted, even if they were only with her for a week. What hadn't kept her awake at night was just how attached she might get to the children and how hard it could be to say goodbye. Only a couple of hours of looking after Faith's baby had given her a whole new set of worries.

'You really were a lucky boy to end up on Jess's doorstep.' Madeline stood up and stroked the baby's cheek. 'We can't just keep calling you "the baby" until we find out who your mummy is, though, can we?'

'That's what I thought when I was talking to the doctor. The very least the poor little thing should have is a name. Even if it's only temporary.' At least Jess had always had that. And despite her father abandoning her, knowing who she was and where she came from had always been important to her. It was why she'd gone back to her maiden name of Kennedy so soon after splitting from Dom.

'Have either of you got any ideas?' Dexter stood up too, his eyes meeting Jess's and she couldn't help wondering if he could read what she was thinking – that being the one to choose the baby's name would make it even harder to let him go.

'If we knew for sure he was Faith Baxter's baby, then I'd know exactly what to call him.' Jess sighed. 'She's had the name Titus picked out ever since she found out she was expecting a boy. But I don't want to give him that name because of the tiny chance he isn't Faith's baby. And that needs to be her thing anyway, naming her son, when they're back together.'

'If he'd been a girl, we could have called him Agnes.' Madeline grinned. 'Although it's hard to imagine calling a newborn that anyway, especially as it's my great aunt's name!'

'What about Theodore? It means gift of God, or something like that.' Jess was trying to play it cool, but she knew exactly what it meant. She'd decided a long time ago, if she ever had a son she'd call him that, because it would mean she'd found a way around her infertility and that really would have felt like a gift from God. 'And he could be called Theo or Teddy for short.'

'I think that really suits him.' Madeline smiled again and right on cue the baby opened his eyes.

'Me too. Hello little, Teddy.' Dexter stroked the baby's head. 'Welcome to the world.'

'Do you think I could have a photo of him before you take him?' Jess would only be torturing herself, but she still wanted a picture of Teddy in her arms. If this was the closest she ever got to being a mother, then she wanted to remember it. If he was Faith's son and she needed a lot of help to come to terms with everything that had happened, there was no way of knowing when Jess would see Faith or the baby again. If at all.

When she held him in her arms, it felt like he belonged there. If someone had asked her why, she wasn't sure she could have explained it, but there was something so achingly familiar about it, especially when she gazed down at him. Maybe it was because she'd imagined it so often that it felt like she'd held him countless times before – as if she already had thousands of memories of the little boy she'd only just met.

'Actually, I've been talking to Dex and I wanted to run something by you.' Madeline furrowed her brow. 'This is a big thing to ask, and I know you were only planning to do respite so you can keep on working. But I've spoken to my manager and we both think you'd be the best person to keep Teddy until we find his mum. But it would mean you being off work full-time in the short term.'

'You really want *me* to have him?' Suddenly Jess was struggling to speak and breathe at the same time. Her head was telling her to stop this now and let Teddy go before she got even more attached to him than she was already at risk of becoming, but her heart wanted her to throw her arms around Madeline and agree to keep Teddy forever, if that's how long it took to find his mum. This was dangerous, she knew that, but when she looked at Dexter he was already nodding.

'His mother chose to leave him with you and we don't think that's a coincidence.' He put his hand on her arm. 'The likelihood is that she'll be more willing to come forward if Teddy is with you and it's our best chance of reuniting him with his mum. Not to mention that you're a midwife and that makes you better qualified than anyone to look after a newborn. But like Maddie said, it's a lot to ask of you and I didn't know if you'd be able to get the time off? That's if you even want to?'

'I do, I definitely do.' Jess already loved the solid feeling of Teddy's body in her arms and even if she was setting herself up for agony further down the line, there was no way she was going to miss out on her chance to be a 'mum', just for a little while. Her heart had already won the battle over her head the moment she'd picked up the little boy from her doorstep.

'Do you think you'll be able to get the time off work?' Madeline pulled her mobile phone out of her bag as she spoke.

'My manager and deputy manager are both really good friends of mine, so I know they'll do everything possible to make it work for me. I'm almost certain I can swing it.'

'Fantastic!' Madeline scrolled through her contacts. 'I'm just going to go outside and ring my boss so we can arrange an initial payment to cover the cost of some of the things Teddy's going to need. Then we can get the ball rolling.'

'Thank you.' Jess turned to face Dexter as Madeline headed off down the corridor. She hadn't missed the look the two social workers had exchanged and it meant the world to Jess that he thought she'd do right by Teddy. She might even be able to start believing it too.

'Thank you for what?'

'I know you put a good word in for me to look after Teddy.'

'Maddie didn't need any persuasion. I don't think she could believe her luck when she found out you're a midwife and that you'd just been approved as a foster carer.' Dexter stroked the baby's head again. 'I'm really glad I didn't put you in an awkward position, but watching you with Teddy I was pretty sure you'd want the chance to look after him.'

'I just don't want to do anything wrong. Faith must have been in pieces when she walked away and left him on my doorstep, so I can't let her down. You will be there to help me if I need any advice, won't you?'

'Any time, but you won't need me. I've got a hundred per cent confidence in you.'

'I wish I could be as sure. I know you've got a lot on, but I really think I might need your help.' Looking after the baby was one thing, but letting him go again was when she felt she might really need Dexter.

'Hey, I'm just getting used to being a part-time stay-at-home dad and it might surprise you to know that things don't seem to have moved on all that much. A lot of the mums at the kids' clubs and soft play places still seem to think there's something weird about a dad who goes to all of these things. I certainly get stared at a lot.' He shrugged. 'So how about we make a pact? I'll be around for you whenever you need me, as long as you and Teddy promise to keep me company on some of my days out with Riley. Having a friend to talk to might make the hell of a soft play a bit more bearable!'

'It's a deal; a good friend is the one thing I need in my life right now.' Jess wasn't going to explain to Dexter that the looks he was getting almost certainly had nothing to do with him being a stay-at-home dad and everything to do with the yummy mummies liking what they saw and brightening up the apparent hell of soft play for them too. She wasn't going to tell him that if things were different she'd have liked the idea of being a lot more than friends with him either. Neither of them needed that sort of complication right now, even if he felt the same. But the idea of spending time with Dexter and Riley was one she could happily get on board with, and not just because of the reassurance he could give her about how she was doing with Teddy – although that was a huge added bonus and it made her so much more confident she could give the baby everything he needed for the best start in life, even if it was only for a little while. Her dream of becoming a mother could finally come true too – at least until they found Faith.

3

Izzy screeched to a halt in the car park outside the Port Agnes midwifery unit, feeling like one of the policemen in the horribly dated 1970s cop shows that her granddad loved to watch. She'd only been working in the unit for a few months, and she didn't want to be late again. Anna, Ella and the other midwives had all been really understanding when she'd explained her situation at home, but that wasn't the point. Midwifery wasn't the sort of job where people could hang around waiting for you to turn up when you felt like it and she hated letting anyone down.

'A whole two minutes to spare before this morning's meeting then, Izzy?' Toni, one of the other midwives on the team, raised an eyebrow as she set a cup of coffee down on the desk that Izzy had almost cannoned into in her attempt to get into the staffroom before the team meeting started. When she'd first started at the unit, she hadn't been sure of Toni – she'd seemed so much more standoffish than the rest of the team – and it had taken Izzy a while to get used to her dry sense of humour. But beneath the slightly gruff exterior, she was really kind and she was only teasing Izzy about being late. Toni had been through a hell of a lot too. She'd told Izzy during a recent shift about losing her fiancé to a brain haemorrhage five years beforehand. But things finally seemed to be coming right for her now and she was expecting a baby with her partner, Bobby, the only male midwife on the team. Between Toni's pregnancy and Anna expecting twins, the midwifery unit was in danger of creating a Port Agnes's baby boom all of its own.

'I know, I was really worried I was going to be late again. You're an angel for having a coffee waiting though, it's been one of those mornings already!'

'How's your grandma doing?' Toni held her gaze and Izzy had to swallow hard as tears stung her eyes.

'They're saying six months.'

'I'm so sorry.' Toni wasn't the hugging type, so when she reached out and squeezed Izzy's shoulder it was almost enough to send her over the edge. Why was it that you could hold it all together until someone asked if you were okay? She shook her head, trying to brush off the feeling of impending doom that was in danger of settling there.

'The worst part is that my granddad just won't seem to accept it. My nan has all these things she wants to tick off her bucket list and he won't even listen to what she's got to say. He just keeps saying she isn't going anywhere.' Izzy wrapped her hands around the coffee cup. Nonna wasn't asking for much. It wasn't like she wanted to visit Machu Picchu or walk the Great Wall of China. She wanted to go to Lands' End again before she died, to have lunch in her favourite beachside café on Tresco in the Scilly Isles, and go to the Trebah Garden to see the spring flowers in bloom one last time. Nonna was Cornish born and bred, and she'd never seen the appeal of leaving her beloved home county even before she'd fallen ill.

'Sometimes it takes a while to come to terms with the reality of a situation like this, just give him a bit longer.' For a moment, Toni looked like she was about to say something else, but then the rest of the team started coming into the staffroom for the morning briefing.

'Sorry!' Anna, whose baby bump seemed to have almost doubled in size over the last month, came in first. 'We were just trying out the new ultrasound machine.'

'Is it easy to use?' Izzy was grateful for the chance to change the subject. Her long black hair was tied up in a high ponytail, the way it always was, but today it felt too tight, almost as if every hair follicle had a lead weight attached to it.

'It's exactly the same model they showed us in training, thankfully, so I think we should be able to use it okay. Although I'm still a bit apprehensive about how much responsibility it's going to be for us.' Anna shrugged. The rural nature of the Port Agnes's Midwifery Unit meant that there were women under their care who had to travel miles for emergency scans which could determine whether everything was okay with their pregnancies. The decision to have an ultrasound machine at the unit wasn't an easy one for Anna and Ella, because midwives could never take the place of qualified sonographers. They'd debated the pros and cons with the team and in the end they'd decided to go for it.

'Once you're at home with the twins you'll be too busy trying to find the time to go to the loo to worry about all of that.' Gwen, the oldest of the midwives on the team, dropped one of her trademark winks. 'And you'll have to book in an appointment if you ever want to have time to shave your legs again.'

'I bet you'll all be glad when I finally go off on maternity leave full-time, instead of cutting my hours down to the point of uselessness. I feel like I've been slowing you all down for ages, but you'll be free of me soon and Ella will do a great job of running things.' Anna took the cup of tea that Toni had passed her, sitting down at the desk with a thud that made her office chair squeal in protest.

'Don't be ridiculous, you haven't slowed us down. We're all going to miss you so much while you're off!' Ella turned to Bobby, who was nodding.

'But with Jess's news, by the time Toni goes on maternity leave too, we'll be down to half a team.'

'What's happening with Jess?' Izzy had been to the drinks party to celebrate the fact Jess had been approved by the foster panel, but as far as she knew there was no date for her to start taking respite placements yet and she'd only be doing it on a part-time basis anyway.

'Someone left a baby on her doorstep.' Gwen made it sound like someone had unexpectedly dropped off half a dozen eggs they couldn't use before their best before date. 'Social Services think it might be Faith Baxter's baby, the woman who's gone AWOL.'

'And Jess has been asked to look after the baby?'

'For now.' Ella let go of a long breath. 'Everyone's just hoping that his mother can be found and that it isn't already too late. Who knows what state she must have been in to leave her baby on a doorstep like that?'

'How awful. I can't imagine anyone wanting to leave a child of any age, let alone a baby.' Izzy tried not to picture her mother's face as she spoke, or the words her mother had repeated to her time and time again in the months leading up to her leaving. *You're nearly sixteen, Isabella, almost an adult and you can't expect me to put my dreams on hold for you forever. If you don't want to come to Australia, that's up to you.*

'Do you really think it's Faith?' Toni's eyebrows disappeared behind her fringe as Ella nodded.

'I think it must be. Why else would anyone else choose Puffin's Rest to leave their baby? It's hardly the first place you'd think of and I hate to think about what would have happened if Jess had been out?'

'It doesn't bear thinking about that it could be one of our ladies who was feeling that desperate.' There was a note of something in Toni's voice, as if she could almost recognise that level of desperation herself.

'At least that shows how much trust Faith has got in Jess. The social workers seem to think there's a good chance she'll come back for the baby sooner rather than later, if she knows that Jess is looking after him.' Ella glanced at her watch. 'Which means we've got to get cover in the meantime. I'm interviewing some extra agency staff this morning who can hopefully start in a few days, but it's going to be all hands on deck until then, if anyone wants to pick up any extra shifts?'

'My Barry's been getting himself all lined up to watch a three-day golf tournament on Sky Sports and there'll be the perfect imprint of his bum indented into the sofa by the end of it. So I'm more than happy to take on some extra shifts.' Gwen grinned. 'Personally, I'd rather have mad passionate sex with Donald Trump than watch three days' worth of golf. Although I'd probably have to do it right in front of the TV screen for Barry to even notice when the sport is on.'

'There's an image I can't get out of my head.' Bobby laughed. 'I can do some extra shifts too, Ella, if you need me to.'

'Thank you, you're both stars.' Any minute now, Ella was going to look in Izzy's direction with a hopeful expression on her face, so she might as well get in there first. She hated letting her new colleagues down, but there was no way she could be away from home any more than she had to.

'I'd love to help out, but with things the way they've been with my grandmother...'

'It's okay, Izzy, don't worry, I wouldn't expect you to work any extra shifts with all you've got going on.' Ella's smile was so warm it made Izzy even more desperate to help out. It would be easier than being at home anyway, but she just couldn't do it. She owed a huge debt to her grandparents; one that could never be repaid, no matter what she did.

4

Jess had another go at collapsing the pram. It had looked so easy when Madeline had dropped it off and told her she just needed to push down on a lever on the left-hand side and it would all fold up. The reality was she'd pressed every bit of plastic and metal on the pram that seemed to have the capacity to move, but it was still completely upright. This parenting lark was harder than it looked.

She was supposed to be meeting Dexter and Riley for a walk in fifteen minutes, but if she didn't manage to fold the pram up to carry it downstairs, she was just going to have to bump it down and then come back for Teddy. She was using the inside staircase that led down to the ticket office now anyway, as it was part of the health and safety requirements for fostering that she didn't use the outside staircase whilst she had any children in placement. Hopefully one of the staff down there would have some idea how she was supposed to get the flipping thing to fold down.

Taking care of Teddy for the past three days had been fairly straightforward. He was a really good baby and after she'd fed him at around midnight, he only woke once more in the night between then and about six a.m. when he was up and alert, his blue eyes still seeming to search hers as they had from the moment she'd found him on the doorstep. What she hadn't appreciated was that it was a military operation just to get him out of the house. She'd had no idea just how much stuff you needed for a baby as young as Teddy. Just because she was a midwife, it didn't mean all of that came naturally to her. So aside from a couple of quick trips to the mini-market and Mehenicks' Bakery, it had seemed far easier to stay at home with him.

It was strange how easily she slipped into the role she'd never allowed herself to imagine fulfilling. Even as she'd tried to make taking care of Teddy all about him, every time she looked at him it was like an emotional chain reaction was somehow set off. Echoes of songs that her mother had sung to her when she was little had started to play in her head. A week ago, if someone had asked her what those songs were, she wasn't sure she'd have been able to tell them. Yet, suddenly, with the little boy cradled in her arms in the dead of night, all the words had come back and she'd almost been able to hear her mother's sweet voice feeding her each line before she sang them softly to Teddy. He was like a connection to the past and a dream of the future, all rolled into one.

All of that meant she'd wanted to keep him to herself. Teddy might have only been with her for three days, but she already knew she'd do anything for him and there was no telling when his mother might turn up and take him away again. Jess had never expected to foster a baby, to be able to hold one close as he nuzzled into the crook of her neck. She had to keep reminding herself that he wasn't hers – that he would never be hers – otherwise she might not ever get over letting him go. If she allowed herself to think about how that was going to feel it was terrifying. Having Teddy had brought her mother back to her in a way that nothing else had, so she wouldn't just be losing him when they said goodbye. She didn't let herself think about that. Instead she wanted to savour every moment of having Teddy with her and if it had been anyone but Dexter asking her to go out and meet him, she'd have turned them down flat.

Dexter had been over every day while Riley was at school, and she'd been grateful for his reassurance that she was doing okay. Madeline, Teddy's social worker, had called her daily too, but thanks to Dexter popping in, she'd obviously felt okay about leaving Jess to get on with it. Having a social worker breathing down her neck would have terrified her in case she did something that meant they took Teddy away. Dexter might still be a social worker too, but he'd had the knack of making her feel comfortable instead of judged almost from the first time they'd met. Madeline, on the other hand, immediately made Jess feel defensive. Jess was the one who Faith had chosen to leave her son with and she was determined not to part with him until his mother came back. But if she didn't get her behind in gear and go out to meet Dexter soon, he'd think she'd stood him and Riley up. So she was going to have to go with plan B if they were ever going to make it out of Puffin's Rest.

Teddy was in his cot, happily watching the mobile above him spinning slowly around. Blowing him a kiss and reassuring him that she'd be back in two ticks, she grabbed the pram, bumped it down the internal staircase and ran back up, two stairs at a time, to get Teddy and the nappy bag, which was almost the size of a carry-on suitcase. Surely it had to contain everything they could possibly need.

'There you go, sweetheart.' Strapping Teddy into the pram, his face contorted with what could only be a gripey belly. But it looked so much like a smile that Jess couldn't help smiling back and Teddy took ownership of another piece of her heart. The rate he was going, he was going to have it all long before his mother came back for him. 'You're such a gorgeous boy, Teddy Bear.'

'How are you two getting on?' Gloria Baker, who ran the ticket office at weekends, bent over the pram to look at the baby.

'He's been brilliant. I can't believe how good he is at night, he only gets up once for a feed and then goes straight back down again.' If Jess sounded every inch the proud parent, she couldn't help it. She'd seen hundreds of babies in her job and she knew a special baby when she saw one. However hard she might be trying to hold back, Teddy had already captured her heart more than any other baby; even the very first baby she'd delivered, when she'd been so elated it had felt as if her feet were barely touching the ground afterwards.

'My son was like that, he lulled me into a false sense of security and when I had my second I thought she'd be exactly the same.' Gloria laughed. 'She turned out to be a total nightmare, up every two hours with colic and screaming the place down. We had the neighbours banging on the walls and I think half the street were sleep-deprived for the first two years of Joanne's life!'

'I bet it was all still worth it in the end, though?'

'It was. Joanne's not just my daughter, she's my best friend. I got my payback in the end anyway, when her two boys were both colicky babies who kept her up all night too. Not that I'd have wished that on anyone really, especially not Joanne. But at least it meant I was able to help her out with them and understand what she was going through. No one knew the tricks that worked better than me, so I got loads of grandma time.' Gloria smiled again. 'Even with the hard parts, it all goes too fast, so you just make the most of him while you can.'

'I will, even if it's only for the rest of this week.' Jess forced herself to smile in response. She wouldn't have a lifetime with Teddy the way Gloria had done with her son and daughter. Teddy could be taken away from her at any moment, with almost no notice. She just had to enjoy having him around while she could and keep trying not to think about how much it was going to hurt when it was all over. As scared as she was of just how hard her emotions were going to hit her and as much as she might not want to let him go, she'd said enough goodbyes during her lifetime to know she could survive it and at least she'd have the comfort of knowing Teddy would be with someone who loved him. She'd have given anything to have that chance as a child.

* * *

Despite the debacle with the pram, Jess was still five minutes early to meet Dexter – having realised pretty early on that everything took much longer with a baby and planning accordingly. They'd agreed to meet on the opposite side of the harbour to Puffin's Rest and then decide whether it was complete madness to try and spend a couple of hours on the beach at this time of year. Teddy had fallen asleep almost as soon as she'd lain him back down in the pram, so she grabbed the opportunity to scroll through her phone.

Toni had booked a private scan and had promised to upload photos to the WhatsApp group the Port Agnes midwives shared. There was nothing on there yet, but one of her old uni friends, Jasmine, had set up a new group on the Messenger app to discuss the plans for her hen night. There was no way Jess would be able to go to that if she still had Teddy with her. Even if she didn't have him, she still wasn't sure she'd want to go. Her life had moved in such a different direction to some of her old friends, despite the fact that they all worked as midwives too. They probably wouldn't understand why she wanted to foster and she found it hard to explain to people who didn't really understand what she'd been through over the past couple of years.

The truth was she didn't always want to explain. When she'd been at school, she'd done everything she could to pretend that she was just like her classmates. She'd hated it when one of the teachers had mentioned her being fostered, or when there'd been a visit to the school from her social worker, clearly marking her out as 'different' from everyone else. No adolescent wanted that and the feeling had somehow stuck with her. She didn't want to have to tell the whole world about the series of rejections in her childhood, or the infertility that had ended her marriage. When she and Dom had discovered she'd never have children naturally, she'd stupidly thought he'd be there for her to lean on. Instead, he'd started the blame game, interrogating her about just how many people she'd slept with in her teens and telling her it was her own fault that her fallopian tubes had ended up so badly scarred because of an infection one of those boys had passed on. He'd called her all sorts of names, adding to the shame she'd carried anyway. It wasn't like there had been that many, but she'd been so desperate for love and there were some she wished she hadn't spent time with. It shouldn't have mattered to Dom anyway, even if there'd been a hundred. If he really loved Jess, he wouldn't have cared, he'd have just tried to make things better somehow. So having to explain to old friends, who hadn't been witness to her marriage imploding, held little attraction for her. She had all the friends she needed in Port Agnes and, just for now, the appeal of keeping her world small was definitely winning.

Closing the message, she shook herself. She didn't have to

decide yet. She could put off contacting Jasmine until later, just like she could put off thinking about Teddy not being around until she had to. Scanning the app again, her eyes were drawn to the alert for a message request which had already been sitting on her phone for three weeks. It was something else she'd put off dealing with, but there was no rule to say she *ever* had to deal with that particular request. She could just continue to ignore the notification from her father and pretend to him, and herself, that it had never arrived. Part of her was still that little girl longing for her dad to turn up and tell her how much he loved and missed her. But it was too little, too late and he'd only end up letting her down as he had before. She couldn't let him hurt her again, the scars already ran too deep and her breathing started to get quicker at the thought of seeing him. She should just delete the message without reading it, she knew that, but for a second or two her fingers hovered over it. If someone had asked her later why she'd decided to finally open it, she couldn't have told them, but she did it anyway.

Message request from Guy Kennedy
Baby girl. I used to call you that, do you remember? I've been agonising over sending this message for months. I don't know if you'll ever see it and I wouldn't blame you for deleting it as soon as you saw my name, but I hope you do at least read it. I don't want to make excuses for what happened, but I was so messed up when your mum died and I honestly thought you'd be better off with me out of the picture. I kept letting you down and with the spiral I was in, I knew it was only going to get worse. I hope it was the right decision and that you had a good childhood. When I googled your name it took a while, but I found out you were a midwife. I recognised you straight away, you look so like your mum. I don't expect you to want to meet up with me, but I had to tell you how proud I am of you, not

that any of your achievements are down to me. It's all you J-J. Your mum would be so proud too. If you want to talk, any time, just message me back. I'll be waiting, even if it takes a month, a year, or the rest of my life. It might not feel like it J-J, but I've always loved you. All my love, Dad (or Guy if you prefer, this is all on your terms whatever you decide) X

Jess had already read the message three times over by the time Dexter arrived with Riley holding on tightly to his hand, but she still had no idea how to feel about it.

'Are you okay?' Dexter furrowed his brow. Was it that obvious that something was up? She hadn't given in to the expected tears, but her face felt frozen in place instead.

'I'm fine, it's lovely to see you. How are you doing, sweetheart?' Bending down to Riley's level she smiled at the little boy, at least that was the expression she was going for.

'Why has your face gone all funny. My auntie says if you pull faces, you stay like it!'

'That's only if the wind changes.' Dexter laughed. 'He's got a point though. Are you sure you're okay? You looked so engrossed in your phone. It's not bad news, is it?'

'I got a message from my dad.' Jess had told Dexter about everything that had happened in her childhood during the fostering assessment, and he knew more about her than her closest friends did. So she felt comfortable telling him about her father getting in touch; he was probably the only person she could tell.

'So you've had contact with him?' There was no judgement in Dexter's tone, even though she'd promised to let him know if they did get back in touch, given the impact that his disappearance had had on her. Dexter might not be her social worker any more, but he'd still have expected her to notify Madeline if something significant like this had changed.

'No, he just sent me a message request on Facebook and like an idiot, I opened it.' Jess didn't admit she'd been weighing up the decision whether or not to open the message for three weeks and that for some unknown reason, she'd chosen the last five minutes to do it.

'Does he want to see you?'

'He's left that decision up to me.' Jess looked at Dexter again. He knew the whole story; how her parents had met when Guy was at university in Bristol and her mother had left home after falling out with her stepfather. Jess hadn't found out until years later – from a box of stuff her foster carers had given her when she left their house at eighteen – that her mother had been working in what was euphemistically called *a gentleman's club*. Jess had tracked down one of her mum's old friends on Facebook, who'd explained that her mother had got into the party scene and that's where the addiction had started. Guy's background couldn't have been more different; he seemed to be from a wealthy family from everything Jess had been able to discover, but somewhere along the line he too had been drawn into drugs and alcohol and eventually his family had cut him off.

When her mother had found out she was expecting Jess, they'd finally managed to turn their lives around and the first ten years of Jess's life had been perfect in their mundanity. Jess's maternal grandmother had become a part of their lives again, until she'd died when Jess was six. Even then her parents had stayed clean. But when her mother had been killed in a car accident just after Jess's tenth birthday, it had only taken days for Guy to be drawn back into the world of drugs. At least that's what Jess had overheard her social worker telling her foster carers when she'd begged to go back to him. He'd tried at first to make things work, with the support of social services, but in the end he'd asked for Jess to be taken into care. When she'd been with her first foster carers, he'd visited her a couple of times and promised it wouldn't be long before she could come home, but then he'd disappeared completely. There'd been nothing since then, no phone calls, not even a letter. And now suddenly he wanted to make contact. Dexter was the only person in the world who knew all the details of her early life and there was such kindness in his eyes as he looked at her that she was suddenly really glad that she'd been forced to open up about it all during the assessment, despite how hard it had been at the time.

'That's a lot to think about, but if you want to talk anything through, you know I'm always here for you?'

'Do you think agreeing to see Guy would affect my chances of keeping Teddy? You know, if he ends up needing longer-term fostering for some reason and Faith isn't able to take him back?' It was the first time that Jess had admitted out loud that she'd like to be given the opportunity to keep Teddy for as long as possible, even if the chances were slim. As soon as Faith came back, the baby would be returned to her. But if there was even the tiniest chance that Teddy might continue to need Jess, she wasn't going to let him down for a man who'd let her down time and time again. If Guy hadn't been willing to make any sacrifices for her over the years, she certainly wasn't willing to sacrifice this opportunity for him.

'Whether you're fostering Teddy or anyone else, the important thing is your ability to manage your feelings around all of it. If you're taking care of a young person who's been through a similar experience, it might trigger some difficult feelings in you which might affect your ability to support them. There are no easy answers though, so just take this a step at a time, do what feels right for you and keep Madeline in the loop.' Dexter's voice was gentle, but he was talking about a child who wasn't Teddy. He obviously didn't think Jess had any chance of keeping the baby long-term and she dug her fingernails into the palm of her hand in the way she'd learned to as a child to help manage her emotions.

'I don't think I need someone like Guy Kennedy in my life complicating things. I've done all right without him for twenty years.' Jess shoved her phone in her pocket and straightened the blankets in Teddy's pram. Dexter might not think that seeing her father would change her chances of looking after the baby for longer, but it wasn't a risk she was prepared to take.

Riley was attempting to build castles to house the selection of toys he'd brought down to the beach, but the upturned sand kept collapsing almost as soon as the buckets were tipped over. Dexter had tried to help, bringing buckets of water up from the sea and risking getting soaked as the freezing waves swept in and forced him to dart out of the way as soon as his bucket was full. Unsurprisingly, the beach was deserted, despite being an unseasonably mild day for February, because it still wasn't what anyone in their right mind would call beach weather. They'd decided to go for it anyway and both Teddy and Riley were bundled up in extra layers. Riley was wearing a blue duffle coat and red wellingtons that made him look like Paddington Bear come to life.

'Jess, have you got any idea what we're doing wrong?' Despite Dexter's efforts, the sandcastles weren't getting any better. While they weren't collapsing, the wet sand was now clinging to the upturned buckets and no amount of hitting them on the top with a spade would bring them out in one piece.

'You need to give the water somewhere to drain away. If you take Teddy for a minute, I can show Riley how I used to do it.'

'It's a deal.' Dexter came over to take the baby and lowered his voice. 'I know it's only making a few sandcastles, but I can't stand seeing the disappointment on Riley's face about anything. The poor kid has been through so much and I just want every day to be a good one for him.'

'That's what parents should want for their kids, but they have to be there to pick up the pieces when some days turn out to be bad ones too. You can't make everything go well for Riley, you know that, but you've picked the right person to show him how to make the perfect sandcastle!' Jess headed over to where the little boy was still kneeling on the floor next to a row of four buckets lined up on the sand.

'Okay, sweetheart, I can show you how to make the perfect sandcastle, but we're going to have to make a hole in a couple of the buckets.' Jess reached out to squeeze Riley's hand, as a look of alarm crossed his face. 'Don't worry, we'll get some new ones from Neptune's Cave to replace them, but I promise this is really going to help.'

'Won't all the sand come out of the hole?' Riley gave her a serious look.

'The hole is just to let the water drain away a bit and I've got the perfect thing to make the holes, you just need to choose which two buckets we're going to use.' Jess grabbed her keys from her bag while Riley carefully selected which of the buckets he wanted. The small red penknife attached to her keyring was something she'd had for as long as she could remember, even if she didn't want to acknowledge why. Her father had always had a Swiss Army knife attached to his keyring too. It had seemed capable of solving any problem when she was a kid, from cutting a very ungrateful seagull out of some plastic it had got wrapped around its legs, to digging out a stone that had been wedged into the sole of her wellies when she'd been about six and had made it feel like she was walking with the stone inside her boot. When she'd bought a much smaller version of the penknife, she'd tried to tell herself it had nothing to do with her dad; it was just a useful thing to carry, that was all. But try as she might, she couldn't wipe out all of the memories of her father before he'd disappeared from her life and sometimes that was the hardest part. Thinking about him risking life and limb to untangle that seagull could still make her laugh, or cry, depending on how the mood took her.

'This one and this one.' Riley pushed two buckets forward, his eyes widening as she flicked out the corkscrew from the penknife.

'They look perfect. Now we've just got to drill a few holes in them and we can start filling them up again.'

'I'll get the sand all nice and sticky.' Riley picked up one of the other buckets and headed down towards the water's edge. By the time he got back, it looked like he had sloshed most of the water down himself, but there was still enough to make the first two sandcastles. Although Riley clearly hadn't bargained on the fact that there was some waiting involved.

'Can we tip them out now, pleeeaaasse?' he had already asked three times in the space of about ten seconds and it was hard not to get caught up in his enthusiasm when he was so excited about the prospect of finally having the perfect sandcastle.

'How about we go up to Neptune's Cave while we're waiting and get you some new buckets and some flags for the top of the sandcastles?' Jess grinned, as Riley let out a cheer in response.

'And if it's okay with Dexter, maybe we could even get some sweets.'

'I love sweets!' Riley danced what could only be described as a little jig at the prospect of a visit to the souvenir shop on the harbour, just a few doors down from Mehenicks' Bakery. With Dexter okaying the plan, they'd left him and Teddy on the beach to hunt out the perfect replacement for Riley's old buckets, bought the promised sweets and by the time they got back, Jess had taught him a song that her grandmother had sung to her when she was his age – and he'd mastered a couple of lines of it, at least.

'There's a hole in my bucket dear Liza, dear Liza!' Riley merrily belted the words out again, as they walked back down to the sand and Jess had a sudden urge to scoop him up and hug him tightly. He was such a happy little boy and spending time with him had allowed her to remember bits of her own childhood that she usually pushed down. What she hadn't realised all this time was that she'd been blocking out the good bits just as hard as the bad bits. It had taken this little boy, whose hand snaked into hers at every opportunity, to make her see what she was missing by not letting herself focus on the good memories as often as she could. And, like Dexter, the only thing she wanted in that moment was to make Riley smile.

'Do you want to try turning one of the sandcastles over now?'

'Yes!' Riley didn't hesitate and as he upended the bucket, Jess held her breath. 'One, two, three...'

'It's perfect, sweetheart, well done!' Almost before she'd got the words out, Riley was hurtling towards her and hugging her legs.

'Now that looks impressive.' Dexter came over to join them, a sleeping Teddy cradled in his arms. 'Jess did promise she knew what she was doing and she was right.'

'It's all down to Riley's skill as a sandcastle builder. I just passed on a few tips that my...' She caught herself just before the words were out; she wasn't quite ready to relive some memories just yet. 'That someone taught me.'

'Jess knows everything!' Riley sounded like he was stating an indisputable fact. 'Can she come out with us every day?'

'I think she might have other things to do, buddy, sorry!' Dexter smiled. 'But we'll see her and Teddy as often as they can.'

'Oh, I think Teddy and I could squeeze my other two favourite boys in.' The words were out of Jess's mouth before she could filter them, but the truth was she meant it. Building sand-castles on the beach like this was a perfect snapshot of how she'd pictured family life. The links to the best bits of her past were back again, meshing with the dreams she'd had for her future. But this time it wasn't just Teddy who'd taken up space in her heart because of that. Riley had too, and she was fighting hard not to let Dexter take up even more space there than he already had. None of them belonged to her and they never could, but telling yourself something and feeling it were two entirely different things.

* * *

'It was a genius idea to bring camping chairs, blankets and a flask.' Jess laughed as she turned towards Dexter. 'We might look like a couple of pensioners on a Sunday afternoon out, but at least we're comfortable!'

'Would it put you off being friends with me if I told you I was thinking of getting a special pair of gloves, just for driving?' She could tell from the look on his face that he was joking, but she was hard pushed to imagine anything that Dexter could do that would put her off him. Seeing him interact with Riley had just convinced her all the more what a good man Dexter was. The little boy, whose dark curly hair made it look like he'd stepped off the pages of a Boden catalogue and straight onto the sand in front of them, was busy using his new sandcastle-making technique to put the finishing touches to a row of about twenty, which he'd insisted on putting all in one long line like terraced houses.

'I think I can learn to live with the gloves thing for the sake of our friendship. After all, I've got a pair of jelly shoes, not often seen on someone over the age of four. I have to wear them whenever I go into the sea because I don't like the idea of stepping on anything but sand – even if it's only seaweed.'

'We all have our quirks and I'm looking forward to the day I get to see you wearing those jelly shoes!' Dexter grinned.

'Some of us have more quirks than others.' Jess tried for a casual shrug, but she didn't quite manage it. If Dexter discovered all of hers, he'd get more than he bargained for and Dom had found them less and less charming over the years they'd been together. She could still picture the look on her ex's face when she'd refused to book a holiday that would mean leaving on a Friday, even though it would cost them three hundred pounds more to leave on the Saturday. She'd tried to explain that it was a superstition her mother had always held and the one time her mum had decided to ignore it, to go and visit a friend who'd desperately needed her support, she'd been involved in a car accident and killed outright. All these years later, Jess still wouldn't start a long journey on a Friday and even the memory of Dom calling her ridiculous couldn't change her mind.

'Those things just make you more interesting and Maddie thinks you're brilliant too.' Dexter's voice broke into her thoughts. 'She said you've taken to caring for Teddy like you've been doing it all your life.'

'He's such an easy baby.' It had surprised Jess to hear that Madeline had complimented her, but it was good to know that everyone thought she was doing okay by Teddy.

'The uncertainty that comes with looking after him isn't easy, not to mention having him arrive in your life out of nowhere.' Dexter had done it again and picked up on what she was struggling with without her even having to say a word. She'd been just about to confide in him, tell him that he was right, when his phone started to ring.

'Sorry, I better get this. The number's not in my contacts, but I'm expecting a call from the clinic where Riley's dad is staying, to give me an update.'

'No problem at all. I'll keep an eye on Riley so you can concentrate on the call.'

'Thanks.' Dexter answered the phone. 'Hello, Dexter Rowe speaking.'

Jess could hear the muffled sound of another voice on the other end of the line, but she couldn't even tell if it belonged to a male or a female, let alone what they were saying.

'Hi, Maddie, I didn't recognise the number... oh I see, new offices, that's how things roll after I've quit then!' He laughed and Maddie said something else in response that Jess didn't catch. But the longer Maddie was talking, the more serious Dexter's face seemed to grow. 'But she's all right, she's not hurt in any way?'

Dexter turned to Jess, furrowing his brow, and there was more muffled conversation from Maddie's side. Then he spoke again. 'Okay, I'll let her know and just give me a call if there are any more updates... Thanks, Maddie, speak to you later.'

Jess was already holding her breath before Dexter ended the call. This had to be about Teddy – she was going to lose him already, after only three days. That same urge she'd had at the hospital, to pick him up and run away as fast as she could, hit her again. It was only Dexter putting his hand on her arm that stopped her from jumping to her feet and actually doing it.

'You probably heard that was Maddie?' He paused as she nodded. 'They've found Faith Baxter.'

'Where was she?' The words sounded strangely subdued, even to her own ears. She wanted to be overjoyed that Faith had been found and she felt like the worst person in the world for not being able to feel that way, but her heart was already aching for Teddy.

'She'd been staying in a hotel in Bideford. She said she needed some headspace and to be on her own for a bit.'

'Is that where she had Teddy, in the hotel?' It seemed crazy that Faith had gone over the border into Devon and then driven back to Port Agnes again, straight after the birth, so that she could drop Teddy on Jess's doorstep.

'Jess.' Dexter took hold of her hand. 'Faith hasn't had her baby yet, she's still pregnant.'

'But Teddy—' The fact that he wasn't Faith's had blindsided her and it felt as if the sand was shifting beneath her feet. She'd been so certain that he was and that he'd be going back to Faith as soon as she was found. Now nothing was certain and she was already imagining what that might mean. Someone, who wasn't Faith, had chosen to leave their baby with Jess and suddenly the possibility that he might be allowed to stay with her was flooding her body with warmth. At the same time, her heart was racing because the one thing that had made the prospect of handing Teddy over easier was the fact she'd be giving him back to Faith, a woman who deserved to have her baby in her arms more than anyone Jess had ever met. All of that meant she had no idea how to finish the sentence, so Dexter did it for her.

'Teddy's not Faith's baby, he belongs to someone else. And

now the police and social services have got to start all over again, but this time they don't even know where to begin.'

All Jess could do was nod. Teddy wasn't Faith's baby and at least for now that meant he was no one's baby – no one's except hers. And she already knew she wouldn't give him up without a fight.

* * *

Jess got the phone call from Faith's husband just as she was finishing Teddy's lunchtime feed. According to Michael, Faith had already been in labour for eight hours and the contractions were now only three minutes apart, but she was refusing to go into the hospital unless Jess was there. Given that she'd run off as a result of the anxiety she felt about giving birth, neither Jess nor Michael were prepared to take any chances.

Dexter had told her to phone him if she needed help with Teddy at any point and thankfully his sister had agreed to pick Riley up from school, so he was meeting Jess at the hospital and taking Teddy from there.

'Thanks so much for doing this.' She'd checked Teddy's nappy bag three times to make sure Dexter would have everything he needed to take care of him for as long as it took Faith's baby to arrive. Teddy was all ready to go, having slept through her lifting his car seat out and slotting it into the chassis of his pushchair. The technology involved in designing some of these travel systems must have rivalled NASA, but at least she'd learned how to operate this one. She'd never managed to get to grips with the pram Madeline had dropped off for Teddy, so the easiest solution had to been to borrow one from a friend that came with a fool-proof tutorial.

'It's no problem and don't worry about us, we'll be fine. I'm going to take him for a walk first and then I'll take him home with me.' Dexter hooked the nappy bag over his shoulder. 'I've become a bit of an expert over the years at fitting car seats and I could probably give Halfords a run for their money. So it's no problem, and Riley would love to see Teddy again when he gets back from school.'

'You're amazing.' Jess went up onto her tiptoes and brushed her lips against Dexter's cheek, trying to ignore the way her body reacted when her lips made contact with his skin. It was just because he always smelt so lovely and his kindness shone through in everything he did. She liked him – a lot – but that was all. 'I'll text you as soon as I know how long it's likely to be. Her contractions are quite close together from what her husband has said, but it could still be hours before the baby puts in an appearance.'

'Good luck, I really hope everything goes okay for Faith.'

'Me too. I'll see you later.' Jess dropped a kiss on Teddy's head too. He and Dexter had both come into her life unexpectedly and she didn't have a claim on either of them, but she was already struggling to imagine her life without both of them in it. For now, though, she had a job to do that was still incredibly important to her, especially when it came to someone like Faith. Thankfully the team at the hospital had agreed to Jess leading the delivery and it had all been set out in the birth plan that she'd finally persuaded Faith to put together before she'd disappeared. Just like they'd discussed, it was more a list of all the things she didn't want, than a list of what she did, so that it would feel as different as possible to when she'd delivered her first son, but Jess was determined to make sure she followed the plan as closely as she could.

Ten minutes later, Jess had examined Faith and established, to everyone's surprise and relief, that she was fully dilated.

Snatching twenty seconds to send a text, she'd told Dexter that it might only be a couple of hours after all, but then she'd turned her full attention back to her patient. There was an obstetrician on standby because of her previous stillbirth, but with Faith having run off once already, the hospital was doing whatever it could to accommodate her wishes.

'How are you doing, Faith?' Jess squeezed the other woman's hand. 'Just let me know if this is all getting too much at any point.'

'I'm okay, I just want this to be over and to have Titus in my arms.'

'I know you do.' Jess was trying to find the words to say what she needed to, but sometimes you just had to come out with it. 'This is probably really scary for you on so many levels, but you can do this. I don't want you keeping it to yourself if you get overwhelmed again. Even after Titus is here, you need to tell me if you start to panic about anything.'

'I'm not going anywhere, I promise. I don't think I could get up and walk out now if my life depended on it anyway.' Faith managed a half-smile. 'I know I scared everyone half to death, Jess, and I'm really sorry, but I just couldn't face things turning out like they did last time and it seemed easier just to disappear and pretend none of it was happening. But there's no pretending that now, is there?'

'There really isn't and there's absolutely no need to apologise for anything, as long as you're okay that's all that matters.' Jess returned her smile and checked the monitor again.

'Is the baby's heart rate okay?' It was already the third time Faith had asked the question in the ten minutes since Jess had arrived.

'It's all looking good, but I'm keeping a really close eye on it and so is Michael.' Jess exchanged a look with Faith's husband.

This was never going to be easy, but they'd get through it together. This baby was longed-for and already so loved by his parents – something every child deserved, but Jess knew only too well that they didn't all get. 'You should feel the urge to start pushing any time soon.'

'There was a lot of pressure down below with the last contraction, but I'm scared to push too hard in case it hurts the baby.' Faith's face was pale except for two deep red spots of colour on her cheekbones, giving some indication of the workout that labour was putting her body through.

'I know you are, darling, but you're doing brilliantly.' Michael stroked his wife's hair as he spoke.

'You really are, both of you.' Jess smiled at them. 'You've been through the toughest thing possible losing Archie, but I want you to remember that you didn't lose him during labour, so the fact that the baby is looking this strong is an excellent sign and when you feel the urge to push you just need to go with it.'

'We're never going to feel like a family until we've got him here. There's been an empty space since we lost his brother and there's only one thing that can fill it.' Faith gripped Michael's hand and a lump formed in Jess's throat. She understood exactly why Faith would feel that way, but it didn't stop her hoping it wasn't true. She had to believe she'd finally find a way to create the family she hadn't had since losing her mum, even if she never gave birth. But after losing Archie, Faith was always going to feel like she had empty arms until she held a baby in them. She couldn't ever replace Archie, but Titus really did represent hope. Jess had briefed the other midwife, Karen, who'd come into the room to join them as soon as Jess had realised it was almost time. To Karen's credit, she was doing her absolute best to blend into the background and they'd agreed she'd only spring into action if Jess asked for her help, or if it looked like Faith or the baby were at risk at any point.

'There's only one way of getting Titus into your arms and that's to give it everything you've got with the next contraction. You can do it, Faith, just listen to your body.' Jess looked up at the other woman, who was already clenching the muscles in her jaw. There was another contraction coming and she needed to use it. 'If you get the urge to push, just make sure you go with it.'

Faith dug her toes into the mattress, pushing against it, her hand still gripping Michael's. She'd chosen to lie on the bed to give birth so she could see what was going on and hold on to her husband's hand throughout. Going onto all fours often allowed gravity to give nature a helping hand, but lying on her back didn't seem to be slowing Faith's delivery down.

There were another six contractions like that before the baby started to crown, with Faith staying more or less silent in between, and using all of her energy to push.

'I can see the head.' Jess was smiling almost as widely as Michael. 'Do you want to reach down and touch the baby's head, Faith?'

'Not until he's out, I'm still scared I might hurt him.' She shook her head from side to side to emphasise her answer. 'You can have a look if you want to, Michael.'

'No, I'm staying right here with you, Titus will be here soon enough.'

'There's another contraction coming!' Faith's voice was raspy now and it was obvious she was getting tired.

'This could be the big one, just keep listening to your body.' Jess was ready and waiting at the end of the bed, willing it not to be much longer. If Faith ended up needing help delivering the baby, it was almost certain to make her panic and there would be no choice but to involve Karen too. At least for now the baby's heart rate was still in the safe zone, so they could stick with Plan A for a bit longer.

'It feels like I'm on fire!' At the exact moment Faith screamed the words, Titus arrived into the world, without even the usual pause or extra contractions between the appearance of his head and the rest of his body. He was clearly as keen to meet his parents as they were to meet him.

'Congratulations, you've got a very bonny-looking son!' Jess grinned and Karen couldn't help but call out a congratulations too, despite all her efforts to remain unobtrusive.

'Is he breathing?' Faith hadn't even got the words out before Titus gave an almighty wail and Jess lifted him onto his mother's chest to give them skin-to-skin contact. It was considered an essential part of the bonding process, but she had a feeling Faith and her new son weren't going to need any help.

'There's nothing wrong with his lungs, that's for sure.' Michael looked down at his newborn son. 'And he looks okay in the other important department too. His balls are absolutely massive!'

'He's perfect.' Jess grinned, deciding not to break it to Michael that it was really common for baby boys' testicles to be swollen at birth and not to read too much into it. Some men were so funny, but there was a good proportion of them who took considerable pride in the size of their newborn son's appendages.

'He is perfect, isn't he?' Faith was staring at the baby lying on her chest as if she couldn't believe he was actually there. Jess might not have been confident about the likelihood of Faith bonding with her son, but there was still a chance that her fear of losing a second baby could interfere with that process and the shell-shocked look on Faith's face was a reminder not to take anything for granted. 'And there definitely aren't any problems with him?'

'I'll give him a proper check in a minute and the paediatrician wants to check him over too. But he looks great and he's already rooting for a feed.'

'Thank you, Jess.' Faith looked up at her, tears filling her eyes. 'I couldn't have done this without you and I really am sorry for putting everyone through such a scare by disappearing the way I did.'

'Like I said before, you've got nothing to apologise for and you'd have been fine with or without me. Titus's arrival into the world is all down to you.' Jess breathed out. She loved her job and sharing the intimacy of a new family's first moments was such a privilege. But even as she stood watching the Baxters, her own arms were aching, the longing to get back to Teddy almost unbearable. She really was trying her hardest not to let herself love him like he was hers to love, but it was a battle she had to admit she was losing. And fast.

5

Izzy was driving a lot faster than she should; she didn't need the flashing *Please Slow Down Driving Through Our Village* sign to tell her that. She'd already narrowly avoided being run off the road by a tractor that was taking up at least half of the lane she was in as well as its own, and she'd only been saved from ending up in a ditch by the good fortune of being able to squeeze into a passing place. Even then the tractor had clipped her wing mirror so hard it had cracked the glass. She was supposed to have been at her grandparents' house half an hour ago, but she couldn't just leave the tearful new mum who'd been the last person on her rounds for the day, not until she was sure the woman was going to be okay. Telling people *'Sorry, but it's the end of my shift'* just wasn't an option in midwifery.

'I can't get Jasper to take a feed.' Martha Edwards had burst into tears the moment she'd opened the door to Izzy. It was less than seventy-two hours since she'd given birth to her first child and the poor woman already felt like a complete and utter fail-ure. 'He doesn't want me to feed him and my partner, Jonny, just keeps telling me to give him a bottle if that's what he wants. But I want to do what's best for him.'

'What's best for Jasper is to have a mum who isn't exhausted, in pain or terrified that her baby isn't getting enough to eat.' Izzy had given Martha what she hoped was a reassuring smile. 'Let's see if we can't persuade Jasper to latch on if we try a few different things together. But if he really isn't taking to it, or it's causing you too much discomfort, then I'm with Jonny on this one. There's absolutely nothing wrong with formula and you might find there are some benefits, like Jasper's dad being able to do some of the night feeds for one.'

'And you really don't think it'll be worse for him? I just feel like the most awful mum in the world, especially when both my sisters keep telling me how brilliant breastfeeding was and how much it helped them bond with their kids.'

'Ah, well-meaning advice...' Izzy gave Martha a conspiratorial grin. 'You'll soon discover that you need to ignore at least ninety per cent of that if you want to make it through the first year without running yourself ragged.'

'My sisters are full of advice on anything I do. They both keep telling me how they did it all so perfectly, even though the two of them disagree on almost everything.' Martha smiled for the first time, her shoulders visibly relaxing as she did.

'Well, there you go then. Shall we try out a few feeding techniques with Jasper then and see how we get on?'

'Thank you, I feel better already. Even if none of the techniques work, at least I can say I tried my best.'

'That's all any parent can do and all any child can ask for.' Izzy had followed Martha through into the lounge, silently praying that the other woman hadn't only heard what she'd said, but had believed her too. There were definitely things every new parent should avoid doing, but there wasn't one perfect way to do the rest and it was obvious Martha was trying as hard as she could to give her son the best chance in life. But Izzy wasn't going anywhere until she was sure that Martha trusted herself enough to make the right decisions for herself and her son, whatever her sisters had to say on the subject. It meant that the next hour had somehow disappeared in what felt like half the time. Jasper was feeding like a pro by the time Izzy realised how late she was, and the journey back to her grandparents' house in Redruth had turned into her personal Grand Prix as a result.

She couldn't be late, not when her grandfather asked for so little. His almost slavish devotion to his wife of over fifty years, Eileen, hit Izzy like a thunderbolt every time she witnessed the little acts of kindness he provided throughout the day just to make her grandmother's illness just that little bit more bearable. None of them really talked about Eileen's prognosis, but Izzy had been there, holding her grandmother's hand with her grandfather on the other side, when the doctors had said there was nothing they could do to treat the cancer, except make her comfortable.

There'd been talk of finding her a place in a hospice, but Izzy's grandfather, George, wouldn't hear of it. Instead the palliative care nurses came to the smart semi-detached home her grandparents had always been so proud of. Every plant in the well-stocked garden had been planted and cared for by Eileen, after they'd bought the house as a new build in the early seventies, before Izzy's mother was even born. Her grandfather had kept the grass in immaculate condition – good enough to host a bowls tournament as Eileen had often said – and every year he'd put a fresh layer of paint on the cherry-red front door and matching garden gate. Despite all the hours he'd spent caring for his wife, her grandfather had made sure the painting was done as usual, but when Izzy had gone out to take him a cup of tea while he worked, she'd seen the tears rolling down his cheeks.

'The garden's already going to pot without her, Izz – and she hasn't even gone yet.' He'd shaken his head so hard that his glasses had slid down his nose. 'I know I should be doing it, taking over all of that, but I can't bear it. Every time I try, I just have to go back inside and sit with her. I don't want to miss a minute more than I have to.'

'I'll sort out the garden, Pops, don't worry.' When she'd made the promise, George had almost managed a smile. He knew as well as she did that she didn't have the first clue about gardening and she had a reputation as a serial killer of house plants. When her grandparents had been on their last annual holiday to Benidorm, before Eileen had started to feel unwell, Izzy had somehow managed to kill more than half the plants in the house in a single fortnight. To say she was no Monty Don was the least of it. She'd done her best to keep her promise to her granddad, though, and had stopped the garden getting completely out of control. Thank God for Google and those apps that told her the difference between bindweed and a prize begonia. Otherwise, she'd probably have ripped up all the wrong things in her attempt to keep the garden tidy. She might not have her grand-mother's passion for gardening, but she'd grown up in the neat little semi and she didn't even want to imagine where she'd have ended up if they hadn't always had a place waiting for her when-ever she'd needed it. So learning how to prune a rose bush, without losing a pint of blood in the process, was the very least she could do.

Her granddad would never have actually asked for her help

with the garden if she hadn't stepped in and offered. So for him to actually reach out and ask her to do something was a real rarity and she had to make sure she got there on time. It was the skittles League Cup at The Red Lion and he needed to be there for eight o'clock sharp. For years he'd been the team's star player and this year's final was a home match. Even though he'd only played a handful of times over the last six months, the team had still begged him to be there for the big final and Izzy knew only too well how desperately he needed a break and the chance to think about something other than what was happening to his beloved Eileen – a tiny bit of normality in his life when everything else was falling apart. Izzy had her job and her own little flat, but her lovely grandfather had to virtually be prised from his wife's side. So even if it meant she got a speeding fine, it was a price she was more than willing to pay.

Izzy pulled up outside the house where her grandparents had lived all their married lives. They'd just started talking about finally moving – to somewhere without a steep staircase – when her grandmother's diagnosis had hit them all like a ton of bricks. She hadn't been able to manage the stairs for more than a month, so the nursing team had arranged loan of a hospital bed which they'd put into what had been the dining room. Now the highlight of her day was when Izzy's grandfather wheeled her bed to the window and she could look out. It was another reason why Izzy was so determined to get on top of the garden and keep it looking at least a tiny bit like the one that Nonna had loved so much.

'I'm so sorry, Pops.' Izzy breathed the words out as she finally drew level with her grandfather, who was waiting at the door, already wearing a sweatshirt with 'The Red Lion Raiders' printed across the front.

'Don't panic, Baby Belle.' Her grandfather squeezed her waist, using the pet name that both her grandparents had given her when she was tiny. Most people called her Izzy, or occasionally Izz, but hardly anyone used her full name of Isabella. The nickname Baby Belle had come into being when Izzy had got chicken pox, at the age of four. Her skin had been itchy and as red as the wax skins on the Babybel mini cheeses, and her grandparents had apparently taken the inspiration for her nickname from that. Even almost twenty-five years later, it was still what her granddad called her most of the time. 'Worst case scenario I'll miss the first leg, but I'll be there for the rest.'

'Will they let you substitute if someone else plays in the first leg?'

'Frank Higgleston has said he'll fake an aneurism if the other team even think about trying to stop me playing. He's been cast as the lead in enough am dram productions to convince the paramedics if it comes to it!' Her grandfather had a twinkle in his eye that she hadn't seen for a very long time.

'Please don't let him do that, he could be tempting fate.' Izzy planted a kiss on her grandfather's cheek, which was warm and soft and always clean-shaven, no matter what else he might be going through. He had a collar and tie on under his sweatshirt too; there were some standards that George Redford never let slip no matter what. The world was a better place for having people like her grandparents in it and Izzy couldn't bear to think of the huge gap her grandmother's death was going to leave behind. For once she was going to channel her mother's philosophy and live in the moment. Kirsten Redford had never given too much thought to the future, even when she'd found herself pregnant with Izzy at the age of eighteen, but then she'd always had George and Eileen as a safety net too. Things were going to change for all of them soon and there was nothing Izzy could do about it. So for now she was going to sit with the woman she loved most in the world and ask her advice about when to plant the sack of summer bulbs she'd bought for the garden – and try not to think about the fact that her grandmother might not even live to see them flower.

6

Hanging out with Dexter and Riley had become the norm for Jess and Teddy, the four of them slipping into an easy routine as if they'd been a part of one another's lives for years. The reality was that Jess didn't have any friends who were parents of young children, at least not yet. The big day for Anna and Brae was just around the corner, and Toni would be just behind her, but for now the only parents of young children who Jess knew were her former patients. Maybe it was because Madeline had asked Dexter to keep an eye on her, or perhaps it was because he'd suddenly found himself as a part-time stay-at-home dad to his stepson, but either way Jess was glad that Dexter seemed willing to spend so much time with her.

Riley was a lovely little boy and remarkably easy-going despite the tough start he'd had in life. He didn't cling to Dexter the way Jess remembered clinging to everyone who'd shown her the slightest bit of affection in her life after her mother's death. But then Dexter had been in Riley's life since before he could even remember, and he'd been the one stable factor that every child needed – which Jess had never had. Riley was sitting on a play mat in front of the windows in Puffin's Rest, concentrating very hard on colouring in a picture of Fireman Sam with the set of crayons Jess had bought for him, his tongue sticking out as he focused all his attention on trying to keep the colours inside the lines.

'How's Connor doing?' Jess kept her tone low enough to be certain the little boy couldn't overhear their conversation. Riley's father was halfway through a rehab programme and she couldn't help wondering if Dexter was as torn as she was about the outcome. Dexter was such a decent man, he'd definitely be rooting for Connor to make a complete recovery, but Jess would have felt strangely reassured if there was part of him that didn't want Connor to step back into the role of full-time parent again, even if he made a full recovery. She'd been caring for Teddy for two weeks now and sooner or later social services would make a decision about his future – which almost certainly wouldn't include her, even if they didn't manage to track down his mother. Jess had started having pointless fantasies about her coming forward and saying she'd only hand custody over to Jess, that she was the only person who could be Teddy's adoptive mother, like something out of a cheesy daytime movie on the Hallmark Channel. Real life never turned out like that and deep down, she knew Teddy deserved to know his birth mum, and that his mother deserved to get the help she must have so badly needed for her to abandon him on Jess's doorstep.

'He seems to be doing okay so far, but the real test is always when the programme ends and Connor's given the opportunity of freedom. That can bring a lot of challenges with it.' Dexter frowned. 'Chloe had just finished rehab when I met her and she was incredibly vulnerable. If she hadn't had the right support when she came out, I don't think she'd have made it.'

'How did the two of you meet?' It was weird that they'd never discussed that, but then she'd tried to avoid talking too much about her ex now that the fostering assessment was over, or telling Dexter just how often her estranged husband messaged her suggesting they meet up for dinner or just to chat about giving things another try. He still wasn't taking no for an answer, but Jess wanted to keep the past in the past and discussing it with Dexter would just make it feel even more like Dom still had some kind of hold over her new life. All of that meant she hadn't wanted to push Dexter for more information about Chloe, and they didn't have the kind of relationship where exchanging that sort of information was a necessity. Except now she really wanted to know.

'I was just finishing a contract with social services in Barnet and I actually met her on my last day, when I took her and Riley to look at a flat that her social worker had sorted out for her.' Dexter glanced at the little boy and lowered his voice even further. 'She'd already split with Connor by then and he wasn't ready to face up to his addiction.'

'And the two of you got involved?'

'At first we were just friends and I wanted to make sure she was doing okay after I'd left the job in Barnet, but after a while I could tell she was struggling. She kept saying she couldn't do it, that she couldn't raise Riley by herself and I'd already grown really fond of him by then. And of Chloe, of course.'

'So the two of you got together after you left the job in Barnet?' There were some unsettling parallels between the start of Dexter's relationship with Chloe and his friendship with Jess. He'd been a knight in shining armour for both of them and it was another reason why she couldn't even let herself imagine this turning into something more. Getting into a relationship with someone who might be only attracted to her because he thought she needed rescuing was uncomfortable to say the least.

'It was a gradual thing, but I fell in love with her and Riley and in the end I couldn't bear the thought of not being with them, or of letting them down the way everyone else in their lives seemed to have done. Within a year we were married.' Dexter shrugged. 'Eventually Connor got into rehab for the first time too and he started seeing Riley again.'

'Was he always okay with the fact that you'd married Chloe and that the two of you were raising his son?'

'His priority has always been his music, so I think he was glad not to have the physical or financial responsibility. He was in a band and even now he's convinced that a record deal is just around the corner.' Dexter rolled his eyes. 'That might be okay at twenty, or even twenty-five, but at thirty-five it's starting to get a little bit sad, especially when it's at the expense of his little boy.'

'It was a good job you came along when you did.' Jess glanced over at Riley, who was still concentrating on his colouring in. His hair ruffled where Dexter had run a hand through it as he'd walked past the boy a couple of moments beforehand, the affection between the two of them obvious. Whatever happened with Connor, Riley had a father who'd always be there for him. 'I've got no idea why my dad walked away, aside from the fact that he didn't seem to be able to cope with me or conquer his addictions. Losing out to max strength cider and whatever drugs he could score might be even sadder than losing out to a rock star fantasy.'

'It's amazing you've turned out the way you have.'

'And how is that exactly?' Jess raised an eyebrow.

'I don't know, what's the word...' He looked up towards the ceiling.

'Umm, I'm not sure I want to guess! But I'm hoping at least for something like... stable? Productive? Functioning?'

'No, you're all of those things and loads more.' He paused again and then he smiled. 'Most of all you're kind.'

'Is that one of those things you say, like nice, when there's nothing that really stands out about a person?' Despite what she'd said she smiled, because kind was one of the first words she'd have used to describe Dexter too and it wasn't because nothing else stood out about him. It was just that she'd realised that kindness was more important to her than anything else. If it had been Dexter she'd been married to when she discovered her infertility, she knew that his first reaction wouldn't have been to start playing the blame game. He'd have looked for solutions, but most of all he'd have wanted to know she was okay and he'd have done whatever it took to make sure she didn't feel like it was her fault. If having men in her life like Dom and her own father hadn't made her certain she was better off alone, then she could imagine falling for someone like Dexter. The trouble was there was no such thing as 'someone like Dexter', he was a one-off. It made her wish she'd been completely honest with him about her infertility during her assessment, instead of just telling him she and Dom hadn't been ready for kids. Back then, before she'd really known him, she'd been terrified that he'd judge her too – for the same reasons Dom had – and now it was too late to blurt out the truth.

'There are hundreds of things that stand out about you, Jess, but I've got to stay on safe ground. I know you're not looking for anything more than friendship and as much as I might like that to be different, even if you were, it's not the right time for me either. Your friendship is really important to me and I don't want to do anything that would risk you ending that. So for now, kindness has got to come top of the list of things I like about you.'

'You're doing okay so far on the friendship front, so I'm definitely willing to extend your trial.'

'That's all I can ask for and Riley will be pleased too, because that picture of Fireman Sam he's working so hard on is especially for you.'

'Now that really is a compliment.' Jess smiled again, pushing her worries about how she was going to cope when Teddy was gone, and whether that meant Riley and Dexter would drop out of her life just as quickly, to one side. In that moment life was good and that's all anyone could really ask for. But if she'd known what was around the corner, she'd have wanted to hold on to that moment forever.

The rain had been falling relentlessly since about an hour after Dexter and Riley had arrived, beating against the windows and scuppering their plans to head down to the harbour to go crabbing. Instead they'd watched *Finding Nemo* and then Dexter had taught Jess how to whip up some play dough, that Riley had used to create some brightly coloured blobs, which were apparently the stars of his favourite movie. Teddy had lain contentedly against Jess's chest, as she and Dexter sat either side of Riley watching the film and for a moment she'd let herself picture this being her life. It was something most people took for granted, but she would have swapped the promise of this for the biggest win the EuroMillions had to offer, ten times over. It felt like this was where she was meant to be, but they were all just on loan – Teddy, Riley and even Dexter – none of them belonged to her and no amount of wishing or bargaining for it to be true would change that.

'Here we go then!' The smell of fish, chips and vinegar filled the air as Dexter set down the paper bag emblazoned with the logo of Penrose Plaice, the restaurant Anna's husband, Brae, owned. Dexter had suggested going out to get them all dinner after hearing Jess's stomach rumbling when Riley was remodelling his fish for the tenth time, and she'd had to admit that even the home-made play dough was starting to look appetising.

'That smells delicious.' Jess's stomach offered up another growl as if to echo her statement and even Riley looked up from the play mat.

'Have I got a sausage?' The little boy widened his eyes, as Dexter nodded.

'Yes, and I got some extra ketchup.' He grinned at Jess as their eyes met. 'I swear this kid would ask for sausages and tomato sauce even if I took him to a Michelin-starred restaurant!'

'You can't argue with that and there's nowhere that can rival Brae's fish and chips as far as I'm concerned.' Jess put out the plates and opened the bag. She could feel the chips' warmth even through the paper they were wrapped in. She was officially ravenous now, but as she peeled back the first layer of paper her phone started to ring. With Anna's babies having the potential to put in an early appearance and worries about how Faith Baxter was settling into motherhood still on her mind, Jess was never going to be able to resist answering the call, no matter how hungry she was.

'I'm sorry, I really need to answer this, just in case...'

'It's okay, get the call.' It was just one more reason why she liked Dexter. He understood from his own work that what she did for a living wasn't just something you could clock off from when your time on duty was over. It really was amazing to have a friend like him right now, one who understood both sides of her life. But when she saw whose number had flashed up on her phone, her stomach was gripped by a panic that not even Dexter's presence could still.

'Hi, Madeline. I wasn't expecting you to call today.' Teddy's social worker had been great, despite Jess's early misgivings. She'd been there whenever Jess needed something, but she'd also let her get on with things without it feeling like she was constantly being checked up on. So an unexpected call from her after hours didn't feel like a reason to expect good news.

'I know and I'm sorry for calling you when you're probably busy with Teddy, but there's been a development in his case.' The word *development* was so innocuous, but Jess knew what was coming before Madeline said it. 'A woman claiming to be his mother has come forward.'

'Who is she?' Jess's mouth had gone dry, the words coming out as barely more than a whisper.

'I can't give you those details yet. She's being examined by one of the police doctors and some information she's given us is being verified. Until then, I can't really say any more.'

'Will you take Teddy straight away?' The now familiar urge to run was building up inside of Jess, but she couldn't let Teddy go through the things she had. If he had the chance to be with his mum she had to let him go, although she could hardly bear to think about it. Even if she'd been clever enough to hide him from all the people who'd be searching for him, a lifetime of looking over her shoulder was never really going to be an option. But none of that made the thought of giving him up any easier.

'We won't be taking him anywhere until we know if she's definitely who she says she is and even then, not until we're sure she's capable of looking after him, if she even wants to.' Madeline cleared her throat. 'Are you happy to carry on fostering him in the meantime?'

'Of course I am.' Jess could barely think straight, but that was the one thing she was certain of. 'Did she... his mother, I mean, say anything about why she left him with me?'

'Well, yes, that's something else we're still trying to verify and I wasn't really planning on going into that now, but I think I should tell you what she's saying, just in case it changes your mind about whether you're happy to keep looking after him.'

'I can't imagine anything changing my mind on that, but go on.' Jess's heartbeat was thudding in her ears, filling the silence as the social worker hesitated.

'The thing is, she says she chose you because you know the baby's father.' Madeline's voice had tailed off and for a second Jess thought they'd lost the connection, but she could still hear Madeline breathing.

'Who is it?' Biting her lip, Jess was certain she knew for a second time what Madeline was going to say. The social worker was going to tell her that Teddy was her half-brother and that her father had done the same thing to him as he'd done to her, but this time his child's mother had abandoned the baby too.

'She's saying that the father of her baby is... is...' As Madeline struggled to get the words out, Jess gripped the kitchen counter.

'Just say it please!'

'I'm really sorry, Jess, but she's saying that Teddy is your husband's son.'

7

The three days after Madeline's earth-shattering phone call had passed in a blur. If Dexter hadn't been there to help Jess hold it all together, she wasn't sure she'd have made it through. Within a few hours of the call, the police doctor had confirmed that Miss B, as she was still only known to Jess, had recently given birth. Even then Jess had tried to hold on to the fact that it might just be a coincidence. But when Madeline told her that Miss B knew details only the person who'd left Teddy would know, and that a DNA sample was being checked against the blood they'd taken from Teddy when he was first abandoned, she'd had to start accepting it was true.

As for Dom being the father, he seemed to have disappeared off the face of the earth considering that up until the last few days, he'd been calling or texting Jess as often as ten times a day. Now he wasn't taking her calls or answering her texts, and when she'd phoned Diane, his mother, she'd insisted she didn't know where he was either. She'd told Jess that the police had been in touch with her too and that she was just as desperate to get hold of him to find out if the little boy that Jess had been raising for the first weeks of his life was really her and Bill's grandson. Jess didn't need to wait for any DNA tests; she was already certain that Teddy was Dom's. Looking at him with fresh eyes, the resemblance was suddenly obvious. The shape of his brow line and even his mouth were all Dom. She couldn't believe she'd never noticed before and it explained why holding him in her arms had felt so familiar. He was Dom's child, the baby she'd imagined when they'd first decided to start a family.

She'd worried at first that it would change the way she felt about Teddy and that she wouldn't even be able to bear being around him any more – this living, breathing reminder that all Dom had needed to do to create the family Jess had longed for was to sleep with someone else. But it hadn't changed her feelings for the baby at all, at least not in terms of making her love him any less. If anything, she was more possessive of him than ever. When she'd thought he was going back to the loving family that Faith and Michael Baxter could provide, she'd been able to accept that was the best for him. Now she knew that Dom was the father, the desire to scoop Teddy up, jump in her car and get as far away from Port Agnes as possible almost overpowered her. She'd even got as far as packing up some of his stuff, and hers, and she'd been just about to force a very reluctant Luna into a cat box, when Madeline had turned up on her doorstep. She'd explained she was there to do an assessment and check that there was no risk to Teddy, given Jess's relationship with his alleged birth father. They must have thought there was potential that Jess would hurt Teddy to get back at Dom for what he'd done, or to punish the baby himself for being the result of Dom's latest affair. But she'd do anything it took to protect that little boy.

Somehow she'd managed to get through the interview which Madeline, to her credit, seemed embarrassed about carrying out.

Her social worker had confirmed with Jess before she left that she had no concerns and that, as far as she was concerned, keeping Teddy in the placement until longer-term decisions were made was still in his best interests. It was those last words Madeline had said – *Teddy's best interests* – that had brought Jess to her senses too. She couldn't go on the run, with Teddy and Luna dragged along for the ride, because there was nowhere they could run to that would keep them safe from discovery, and a life like that could never be in his best interests. So Jess had unpacked the bags and started jumping every time her phone rang or pinged with a text, wondering if the latest call or message would be when she'd be told that Teddy was going back to his birth parents, or when Dom finally decided to get in touch. Living in limbo was hell, but she still didn't want it to end because she knew that would mean losing Teddy.

The fact that everyone was suddenly laying claim to the little boy was probably what hurt the most. All of the people who'd either abandoned him – or been oblivious to his existence – got to have a label that showed he belonged to them; his mother and father, even his grandparents. One of them had dumped him as soon as he was born and the other three had never held him close or soothed him to sleep the way Jess had. But now they all had a stake in what happened to him, when all Jess could do was wait for the social workers to knock on her door and take the baby she loved away from her.

Her friendship with Dexter had stepped up a level. He'd held her when she cried, never once judging her for all the uncharitable thoughts that had seemed to pour out of her like a river that had broken its banks. Now she knew who Teddy's father was, she seemed to have lost the ability to show any empathy for his mother. The one thing Jess hadn't said in front of Dexter was how unfair it all seemed and how somehow that was much worse than the betrayal itself. She was the one who couldn't have a child of her own and desperately wanted one, when Dom and this Miss B – whoever the hell she was – appeared to have had Teddy completely by accident and had then abandoned him like he was a piece of trash. Dexter might have been able to help if she'd told him and found some way of helping her feel less bitter, but she'd only gone as far as confessing that she was terrified she'd never have a child of her own, not the reasons why. Maybe he'd read between the lines, because he didn't try to promise her she would, but what he'd said had helped more than he'd ever know.

'You don't have to have a biological link to a child to be a parent, I know that better than anyone and every time I see you with Teddy or Riley, I can see what a great mum you'd be. You'll find a way and when you do, that child will be the luckiest kid in the world.'

So when the call finally came from Madeline asking Jess to bring Teddy to a contact centre to meet with his mother, she'd known she could only do it with Dexter by her side. She might have fought since she was ten years old never to allow herself to completely rely on another person again, but she was losing the battle with Dexter. Whatever she might try to tell herself, she needed him, and that took what they had beyond friendship, even if nothing physical had ever happened between them, or ever would. The level of vulnerability that came with physical intimacy was something she could control, but she'd lost the battle with being emotionally vulnerable with Dexter a long time ago.

'Are you sure you want to do this?' He pulled into the car park outside the contact centre and brought the car to a stop. 'If you'd rather not face Teddy's mother, I can take him in for you. Maddie will completely understand. She thinks you're amazing

for even considering agreeing to this, let alone actually doing it.
We both do.'

'I bet I'm the main talking point in your old office.' Jess
grimaced. 'It must be quite the story, a foster carer who's discovered that the baby she's looking after is actually her husband's.
It's like something out of an *EastEnders* script.'

'No one finds this entertaining, Jess. I promise you that.'

'Just for God's sake don't say you feel sorry for me. I'd rather
people were laughing at me than that.'

'I won't say it then.' He squeezed her shoulder, but she could
just about cope with that, as long as he didn't say the words.

'Let's get this over and done with then.' Jess's stomach was
churning, although there was a part of her that was desperate to
see the woman who'd left Teddy on her doorstep and who'd
been in a relationship with her husband for God knows how
long. Jess already knew Teddy's mother wasn't the girl from
Dom's office who he'd been having an affair with, though. A few
clicks on Instagram and Facebook had soon revealed there was
no way she'd been heavily pregnant over the summer. She was
working as a holiday rep out in Tenerife now and no one could
wear a bikini that skimpy and hide a baby bump.

'I'm here for you every step of the way if you want me to be,
but just say the word if you want me to back off at any point too.'

Dexter got Teddy's bag out of the car as she lifted the baby
out of his car seat. It was probably only thirty metres across the
tarmac from where her car was parked to the door of the contact
centre, but Jess's legs suddenly felt as if they didn't belong to her
any more. Her brain was telling her to go in one direction, but
the rest of her wanted to go anywhere else.

She lifted Teddy up onto her shoulder and he nuzzled into
her neck as she pushed open the door of the contact centre with
her free hand. If she'd stood back, Dexter would have done it for

her, but she knew that if she hesitated even for a second she might not be able to go in at all.

'Hi, I'm Jess Kennedy and I'm here to bring Teddy for contact with his mother. His social worker, Madeline Kane, has arranged it.' Jess's voice sounded weirdly normal and the receptionist smiled and nodded, as if it was all just routine. But for her it probably was.

'Ah yes. Madeline called, she's on her way, but she's been held up in the office because of a bit of a crisis with another carer. But Teddy's father is already in the waiting room, so I'm not sure whether you'd feel comfortable going in there before Madeline arrives?' The receptionist was still smiling, so at least there was one person who didn't seem to know that Dom was Jess's husband.

'Teddy's father?' Her legs definitely felt like they were going to give way as she repeated the words that still didn't seem to make sense. Dom wasn't supposed to be there, she'd never have agreed to come otherwise.

'His mother's decided she's not ready to see Teddy yet and his father asked Madeline if he could come instead. She said she'd called you?'

'I haven't checked my phone since we left Port Agnes.'

'You don't have to do this, Jess.' Dexter put his hand on her arm. 'Let's wait out in the car until Maddie gets here and she can deal with Dom.'

'So, you've already met the baby's father? That might make things easier.' If the receptionist thought that, then she *definitely* didn't know the full story. But to her own surprise, Jess found herself nodding.

'I just want to go in and get this over and done with. We've got no idea how long Madeline might take to get here and I don't want Teddy to have to sit in the car and wait.'

'Whatever you think is best.' Dexter touched her arm. 'Do you want me to come in with you?'

'I think I need to do this by myself, but I'll call you if I need you.' She turned towards him. 'Is that okay?'

'Of course, I'll be just outside if you want me.' Dexter headed back out of the centre without even trying to persuade her round to his point of view, even though he'd clearly thought it would be better for them to wait. It was knowing that he'd be back within a minute or two if she needed him that just about made it possible for her to go through with seeing Dom, though. Whatever her estranged husband had to say, she wanted to hear it and get some answers, but she didn't want Teddy to be caught in the crossfire. If she couldn't hold it together when she saw him, she'd have to call Dexter. Because screaming at Dom in front of the baby definitely wasn't an option.

'Shall I just go through to the waiting room?' Jess turned back to the receptionist, who still seemed completely oblivious to the amount of tension hanging in the air.

'That would be great and I'll send Madeline straight through when she gets here.'

'Okay, thanks.' Despite her best attempts, there was a definite shaky note in Jess's voice. But if she just pushed on, it would all be over in the next half an hour or so.

'Thanks so much for agreeing to this, J-J.' Dom was on his feet the moment she came into the room. He looked exactly the same as he had the last time she'd seen him. She didn't know what she'd expected; that he might suddenly have grown two heads or had '*cheating pig*' branded onto his forehead, but from the outside nothing had changed. Sickness was churning in her stomach, but she had to pretend she was okay with this too, because if the mask she was wearing slipped even a tiny bit, then Dom would know just how badly he'd broken her heart by so casually creating the one thing she could never have. He didn't deserve anything from her, least of all her pain.

'I'm not doing this for you, I'm doing it for Ted... the baby.'

'I'm so sorry, I never meant for this to happen.'

'Oh what, so you were just walking along and accidentally fell into this Miss B, penis first, when all this time you've been telling me how desperately you wanted to give things another go between us?' Jess could feel the hysteria bubbling up inside her, but she still wasn't sure whether she wanted to laugh or cry.

'No, of course not, it's just that we were going through a rough patch and I—' Jess cut him off.

'I don't want to hear your excuses, Dom, but I do want to know who she is.'

'His mother's name is Natalia Barreto. She was working in the Jolly Sailor, helping out while they were busy during the Easter holidays and all through the summer. It was just a fling, one or two nights. Three at the most.'

'Oh, well that's okay then. As long as it was just a fling.' Watching Dom squirm didn't give Jess the pleasure it might have done and the fact he thought he could talk his way out of this would have been laughable if losing Teddy wasn't part of the equation.

'I know there aren't any excuses, but I was hurting so much over what had happened between us and I was looking for a bit of comfort, that's all. When Natalia contacted me a couple of months after we'd last got together and said she was pregnant, I didn't even think it was true. Because it didn't mean anything to me, I promise you that.'

'I don't care what you did or who you did it with, Dom, because you showed me who you were the moment I found out I couldn't get pregnant. But surely this baby means something to you? Especially since the reason we split up in the first place was supposedly because you couldn't cope with the idea of not being able to father a child?'

'I've been an idiot and losing you was the biggest mistake of my life. I just want to put it right.' Dom was still wheedling, trying to worm out of taking responsibility, like he had so many times before. It was suddenly blatantly obvious to Jess now that this was who he was and that he didn't deserve Teddy, he didn't deserve to be a father at all. But if the social workers decided otherwise, Jess would do everything she could to make sure that Dom didn't let his beautiful baby boy down, even if the idea of handing him over made her blood run cold.

'This little boy is the best mistake you're ever likely to make. You might not be worthy of him, but you're his father and you better be a good one, or I won't be responsible for my actions.' Jess's arms ached from holding them like a ring of steel around Teddy, but sooner or later she'd have to hand him over to his father, as much as she might not want to. There were tears stinging her eyes and she had to keep blinking them back in a desperate attempt not to let Dom see her cry. The tears would be for Teddy, not for him. 'Do you want to hold him?'

'I've got no idea what I'm supposed to do.' For a moment there was a hint of vulnerability about Dom that almost made her feel sorry for him, but she couldn't let herself see even a glimpse of the person she'd fallen in love with. He'd never really existed, after all.

'You just need to support his head properly.'

'I don't mean about holding him. I mean I've got no idea how to go on from here. I want to be in Teddy's life, but only if you're in it too. We could do this together, it could be exactly what we've wanted for so long.'

'You are joking, aren't you?' Jess shook her head. Dom seemed to have forgotten that Teddy already had a mother and that you couldn't just slot a baby into the gap and think it would fix everything else between you. 'And where exactly do you see Natalia fitting into this?'

'She wants to go back to Portugal and her parents don't even know about the baby.' Dom shuffled from one foot to the other. 'They're quite religious and she's a little bit younger than us.'

'Exactly how young is she?' The sick feeling in the pit of Jess's stomach was suddenly churning like it was on a spin cycle.

'She's eighteen.'

'*Eighteen!* Dom, for Christ's sake. What the hell were you thinking?'

'I wasn't, clearly. I was gutted about us. I talked to Natalia a bit when she was behind the bar about how bad things had got between us. We met up a few times and then she headed to London. When she told me she was pregnant, I didn't believe her. It was only when I heard she'd left the baby on your doorstep that I knew it must be true.'

'I hope to God you offered to help her, Dom. Or the last shred of anything good I might think about you will have disappeared.' Jess held the baby to her chest. How could anyone treat Teddy like he was an inconvenience? Even if Dom hadn't believed he was his, anyone with an ounce of decency would have reached out to help a young girl like Natalia, who was so far away from home, and offered to help. Dexter would have done it in a heartbeat and so would Jess, and suddenly it was much easier for her to feel empathy towards Teddy's mother again.

'It was too late for me to do anything much by then. I rang her and she told me she'd come back down a week before the baby was due and had him on her own in an Airbnb in Port Agnes. She knew you wanted a baby and that we couldn't have one together. In her head, I suppose she thought this was the best solution for all of us.' Dom tried to put his arm around her, but she flinched away from him. He might have dismissed Natalia's solution for the situation initially, but he seemed to think it really could be that easy and that somehow she'd forgive everything that had gone before in order to keep Teddy in her life. If she let her heart rule her head, there was a good chance that Dom might be right, but she wouldn't go back to her ex, not even for his son's sake. She was almost sure of it, but Dom wasn't giving up yet. 'Seeing you with the baby now, I think maybe she was right. Maybe this was meant to be, to give you – us – the baby we've always wanted.'

'You seriously think it's going to be that easy?' Jess was shaking, emotional strain manifesting itself in physical symptoms. Could she really have been married to someone so incredibly thick-skinned? But glancing down at Teddy, her heart contracted. Dom was giving her a chance to stay in the little boy's life and suddenly she really wasn't sure she was strong enough to walk away, even though she knew deep down it was the craziest idea anyone had ever suggested.

'That's the thing, Jess. It *can* be that easy, if we want it to be. Natalia's going to give the baby up for adoption anyway, if we don't take him.' This time, when he reached out for her, she stayed rooted to the spot, feeling like she was made of concrete as he draped his arm around her. She'd never been more certain that her feelings for Dom were dead and buried, but he was right. He held the key to everything she'd always wanted – a family of her own – and if she rejected him, she might be throwing away her final chance. This wasn't even just any baby, this was Teddy, the little boy who'd crept into her heart despite her best attempts to remind herself that his place in her life was only ever going to be temporary. The idea of giving him up had always been incredibly painful, but how the hell was she supposed to do it if she didn't have to?

'Dom, I—' She couldn't even work out what she was going to say, because neither of the answers worked for her. Even the idea of telling Dom she was willing to give it a go made her flesh crawl and when she looked at him all she could think about was how wrong he was for her on so many levels. If it had been Dexter... but thinking like that was the road to hell. Rejecting Dom, and Teddy along with him, wasn't something she couldn't find the words for either. She needed more time to think, but Dom was relentless.

'Just tell me you'll think about giving the two of us a fresh start.'

'I love Teddy so much.'

'I know you do and we could have such a good life together. I promise I've learned from my mistakes with Natalia, and that stupid fling I had with Serena from work. I'll never be such an idiot again.' For the first time, he reached out and touched the baby, running a finger down Teddy's cheek. 'Having a baby's what we always wanted, Jess. Don't throw this chance away.'

'I don't know what you want me to say.' Her heart felt like it was about to burst out of her chest. Maybe that was the answer; if she collapsed on the floor, no one would expect her to give them any definite answers about anything. She wanted Teddy more than anything, but he only came in a package with his father. No wonder her body was reacting the way it was.

'Just say you'll think about it.' Jess opened her mouth again to respond, but nothing came out. She just couldn't say no, despite knowing it was the right thing to do. Taking a deep breath, she was about to try again when the door to the waiting room was almost thrown off its hinges.

'I'm so sorry I'm late, Jess.' Madeline burst through the door, panting as if she'd just completed a 10k run. 'You should never have had to face this on your own, I can't apologise enough.'

'It's fine. We needed to talk anyway and it was probably easier without anyone else around.' Jess gave Dom a pointed look. It was a relief to be part of a conversation she could handle, but the last thing she wanted was for Dom to tell the social worker the solution he'd put to Jess. Not only would it probably mean both of them losing Teddy if Madeline thought they were capable of making such crazy decisions within the space of ten minutes, but it would also get back to Dexter and for some reason Jess couldn't fathom, she really didn't want it to.

'I can imagine it was.' Something flitted across Madeline's eyes as she looked at Jess. Maybe she was a mind reader; Jess had always worried that her new social worker saw far more than she wanted her to.

'So what now? Do I just leave Teddy here with you?' They might have to prise Jess's arms open to make it happen, but Madeline was nodding. The thought of leaving the baby with Dom was almost enough to make her agree to his suggestion. In that moment she'd probably have agreed to anything if she'd thought Madeline wouldn't overrule them anyway.

'I can take over now, if you want to come back at two o'clock? Assuming that you and Dominic are done, that is?' Madeline looked at Jess again, her eyebrows raised. She was definitely fishing for some idea of how things stood between them, but Jess had no more idea than she did, not when Teddy was at stake. All she knew was that she couldn't just tell Dom to get stuffed, no matter how much she might know that was the only logical decision.

'We're done for now.' It was a bald little sentence, but it didn't close the door on anything and everyone in the room knew it. Whatever Madeline might think of her, Jess couldn't worry about that at the moment. It was going to take everything she had to hand Teddy over to the other woman and step away, rather than snatching him back when her inner voice was telling her to do exactly that. Teddy could be hers, something she hadn't even allowed herself to believe could ever happen, but the caveat that came with that was huge. Dom would have carte blanche to do whatever he liked, knowing he had the power to take Teddy away from her at any point. He'd already shown he was capable of being cruel, but he'd never had this much power over her before. Taking another deep breath, she squared her shoulders and handed the baby to the social worker, because if she didn't go now, she wasn't sure she'd ever be able to.

Madeline would probably pass the baby straight to Dom as soon as Jess walked out of the room. He had God-given rights after all. Dexter had explained that the point of contact visits like this was to give social workers the opportunity to assess how the parents interacted with the child and if they had what it took to be 'good enough' parents. The concept of good enough was a difficult one for Jess to swallow, even before she'd known it would be down to Dom to provide that level of care. Teddy deserved far more than just *good enough*.

'I'll see you later, Jess.' Dom's words were more of a statement than a question, but she found herself nodding, despite hating his assumption that all he had to do was click his fingers and back she'd run. She was going to have to make the biggest decision of her life, much bigger even than deciding to marry Dom in the first place and whatever option she chose, it was going to involve making the biggest sacrifice of her life too.

Closing the door to the waiting room, she stood for second, an awareness that she could hear Dom and Madeline's conversation on the other side making the back of her neck prickle, as the social worker explained her role to Dom. The bottom half of the door was wooden, but it had a large glass panel above, presumably so that whoever was in reception could see whether anything was kicking off in the waiting room. Only the two contact rooms beyond the waiting area offered any kind of privacy. If she could hear Madeline and Dom's conversation on the other side of the glass, then there was a good chance that the social worker had heard some of what she and Dom had said too, before she'd burst in. The thought that Madeline might report back anything she'd heard to Dexter made Jess's heart start to race all over again. There wasn't much that Madeline could say, though, not when even Jess had no idea what she was going to do. She hadn't made Dom any promises, at least not yet. When she stepped out of the contact centre and saw Dexter waiting for her outside, his concern for her written all over his face, she wasn't able to stop herself from bursting into tears. He held her in his arms again, just like he had when she'd first discovered Dom's betrayal, and he'd promised her that it would all be okay. But not even Dexter could fix this, no one could, and whatever decision Jess made she was going to lose at least one person who meant the world to her.

* * *

Jess had half expected to return to the contact centre at two p.m. to be told she wasn't needed any more and that she wouldn't be taking Teddy home. She'd almost sagged with relief when Madeline had handed him back and said she'd be in touch about next steps when she'd found out a bit more about what was going on with the baby's mother and what Dom's intentions were. Maybe Jess was imagining it, but she could have sworn Madeline had given her another funny look when she'd said that last bit.

She'd cancelled a planned get-together with Dexter and Riley for dinner and another Disney movie marathon the day after the first contact. She'd had no idea what to say to him when he'd asked what it was like seeing Dom again while they were driving home from the contact centre. The reality was she'd felt nothing but disgust for her ex when he'd given her that little-boy-lost look and tried to excuse all the things he'd done to hurt her. But when he was the one person who had the power to keep Teddy in her life, it wasn't as easy to write him off as it should have been and she still had absolutely no idea what she was going to do.

Dom must have sent her at least twenty texts in the day and a half after their meet up, but she didn't feel ready to talk to him either. It was far easier just to spend the time with Teddy and pretend that the rest of the world didn't even exist. She only very briefly responded to messages from Ella and Anna; despite being grateful for how much they cared, she just didn't have the headspace for it. So when Dexter turned up on her doorstep, she was in two minds about whether to even let him in, but she owed him an explanation. He'd been a good friend to her and she couldn't just drop him out of her life because she had a feeling she knew exactly what he'd have to say about Dom's suggestion and it wasn't something she was ready to hear. The thought that it might make him think less of her still bothered her too, but she was going to have to deal with that from everyone – including herself – if she decided to take Dom up on his offer.

'I thought I'd bring you some lunch as we didn't manage to have dinner last night.' Dexter held up two bags as she opened the front door; one from Mehenicks' Bakery and the other one from the delicatessen in Church Street. 'But if you're busy, I can just leave the bags and disappear.'

'I'm not busy, come in.' Teddy was having a nap and there was no reason not to let Dexter in, except for the guilt that gnawed at her stomach from keeping a secret from someone who'd done so much to support her. 'I'll make us both up a plate, if you've got time to stop?'

'I've always got time for you, Jess. You know that.' If he was deliberately trying to make her feel bad, he couldn't have done a better job. But that was the thing about Dexter, she couldn't imagine him ever wanting to make someone feel bad. If he'd been the one who held the key to giving her the family she so badly wanted, she wouldn't have hesitated for a second – even if she'd told herself a thousand times that she didn't want another relationship every time she'd felt that now-familiar frisson of attraction towards him.

'This is lovely.' Opening the bags, she found fresh bread from the bakery which was still warm to the touch, as well as a couple of split cream buns that made her stomach rumble. She'd barely been able to face eating since the contact centre visit and she hadn't realised how hungry she was. In the other bag there was St Agnes brie, roasted peppers, hummus and a delicious-looking couscous salad, as well as some cloudy apple juice. Dexter was a class act in every sense of the word, which just served to remind her all over again that Dom wasn't.

'I thought you deserved a treat after everything that's gone on in the last few days, but I didn't want to put any pressure on you yesterday when you cancelled.' Dexter gave her a long look. 'That's why I wanted to come over while Riley was at school, because I didn't want him to be disappointed if you didn't feel up to seeing us. I really wanted to see you, though.'

'I'm sorry about last night. I just don't seem to be able to think straight at the moment.'

'You know you can talk to me about anything, Jess.'

'I know.' She wanted to, she really did, but how the hell was she supposed to sit down and tell him she was seriously considering going back to Dom, just so she could hold on to Teddy? It was ridiculous, completely insane, but she still couldn't tell Dom to stick his suggestion where the sun didn't shine, even though that was exactly what she should have done.

'We don't have to discuss anything if you don't want to, we can just sit and eat and talk about the weather, or Luna, or whether I should let Riley persuade me to paint his room with orange and white stripes like Nemo.' Dexter's tone was as warm as the smile, but then a much more serious look crossed his face. 'You must be so torn at the moment and Maddie's really worried Dom's going to take advantage of that, but if you want to tell me to mind my own bloody business, I'm not going to take offence.'

'Maddie?' Jess clenched her teeth together at the sound of her social worker's name; it was exactly what she'd been dreading. She hated the idea of Dexter and his ex-colleague talking about her, especially when she had no idea how much of her conversation with Dom Madeline had overheard. She was bound to have told him straight away if she'd overheard Dom's suggestion about them getting back together. Some of that frightened little girl Jess had been when she'd first gone into care must have stayed with her, because attack still felt like the best form of defence when she was backed into a corner and her scalp prickled as she fired the words at Dexter. 'What the hell gives Madeline the right to comment on how I might be feeling, or on my relationship with Dom come to that?'

'So there is still a relationship with Dom?' Dexter kept his tone even, but his eyes never left her face. She should have just gone with her gut and not even let him into the flat. This was all such a mess and knowing how crazy it looked on the outside didn't help.

'He's my husband.'

'Technically, yes, but I thought that was something you wanted to change?'

'I did, I do...' The words were catching in her throat. 'But he's Teddy's father too.'

'And he's using that to control you and get you to do what he wants.' There was sympathy in Dexter's eyes now and the tendons in Jess's neck seemed to tighten in response. He knew she loved Teddy, but he didn't know how big the stakes were and that Dom held her only chance of having a baby. But that didn't matter. Whatever she decided would be because of Teddy. Nothing else. She'd be the one using Dom, not the other way round, and she didn't want anyone making her out to be a victim. That was one place she definitely wouldn't be going back to, whatever she decided.

'I suppose you and Madeline have been talking about that too, have you? Poor little Jess, Dexter's latest project. I'm just like Chloe to you, aren't I? A fragile little thing who can't possibly take care of herself or make her own decisions.' Jess couldn't stop herself, even as Dexter tried to protest. 'I bet your eyes lit up when I told you about what happened with my parents and then with Dom, and what a whole messed-up ball of crap my life was until you walked into it. Do you get off on that, Dexter? The whole knight in shining armour thing? Because if you do, you've lucked out this time. You'll have to find someone else to save, if that's what you're looking for.'

'I never once said you needed saving. I could reel off a whole list of reasons why I liked you, Jess. But, believe me, you being some kind of victim was never one of them, because I never thought that about you.' Dexter frowned but he still didn't raise his voice, which somehow made it worse.

When he'd spoken about liking her, he'd used the past tense. That had stung more than it should, because she still wasn't sure he didn't see her as a victim and that was a deal-breaker for her. She didn't need anyone who saw her as some kind of pity project and he wouldn't be the first person to act as a saviour to boost his own ego. Making a clean break would give her one less thing to worry about too and in the heat of the moment, it felt like by far the easiest solution.

'I think you should go.' She was already shoving the food he'd bought back into the bags, but he shook his head. For a moment she thought he was refusing to leave and she had no idea how to react, mainly because she'd already realised she didn't want him to. Saying that out loud was never going to be an option for her, though. Deep down she was the same girl she'd been when her foster carers had told her they wanted her to move on, pushing everyone new she met away as soon as there was the slightest inclination that they might reject her. It wasn't until Dom that she'd let anyone back into her heart and look how badly that had ended.

'I'm not taking the food back, Jess. I bought that for you, because I wanted to make sure you actually ate something.' Dexter sighed. 'I'm sorry if that makes it look like I think you can't fend for yourself, because that's not what I think at all. Just because someone does something nice for you, because they care about you, it doesn't always mean they have a hidden agenda.'

'I can look after myself, thank you very much.' The words that came out of Jess's mouth weren't what she'd been intending to say, even as she'd started to speak. She'd wanted to tell him he was right and that she was sorry for overreacting, but it was that knee-jerk reaction again, a desperation to reject before she could be rejected.

'I'll leave you to it now that I've said what I came to say. Whatever you decide, I hope it works out for you. I really do.'

Turning away from her, he walked out without a backward glance.

He might not have actually said '*it's been nice knowing you*', but the sentiment was there all the same. Dexter wouldn't be coming back and Jess didn't blame him, because she hated herself more than he ever could for the way she was treating him.

8

Jess had lost count of the number of times she reached for her phone to text Dexter in the days that followed them falling out. She knew she should have contacted him to apologise, but he'd stayed true to his word and left her to it. She'd almost given in to the urge to call him when Madeline had contacted her to set out a schedule of contact visits that Dom would be having with Teddy. There were a couple of half-day sessions when Teddy would get to meet his grandparents too, and if the supervised visits went okay, Dom would start being able to look after Teddy without a social worker watching over him for whole days and even overnight. Jess had never known jealousy like it. When she'd discovered Dom's affair there'd been a twinge of it, but mostly she'd been glad not to have wasted any more time with a man who didn't really love her. But the thought of someone else spending so much time with Teddy was a bitter pill and her jaw clenched every time she imagined handing him over. She couldn't even start to think about when she might have to do that for good or she wouldn't be able to get through the day. It was all happening so fast, too. Dom had rung her and asked her to be at the sessions with him, employing his usual technique of not taking no for an answer.

In the end, Jess had lied and told him she'd agreed to help out at the midwifery unit whilst Teddy was at the contact centre with him. When she'd mentioned the possibility to Madeline, the social worker had seemed to think it was a good idea and had even said it would probably help Jess handle the goodbyes better when Teddy left the placement. The words had been like a punch in the stomach – an acknowledgement that the inevitable was about to happen and there was nothing she could do about it. When Anna had called to check on Jess, she hadn't been able to keep up the pretence that she was doing okay.

'I just wanted to see how you were doing. I got your message about Dom and the baby, but if you don't want to talk about it just say.' Anna's tone had been gentle and a sob had escaped from Jess before she'd even been able to get a word out in response.

'Oh, sweetheart, do you want me to come over?'

'Thank you, but I don't think I can face seeing anyone yet.' It had hurt her throat just to speak and tears were rolling down her face. 'I just don't know what to do. Dom keeps saying that we should give it another try and it might be my only chance of being a mum, but more than that it means I wouldn't lose Teddy. I don't know if I could stand going back to him, but I'm terrified I'm going to do it anyway.'

'Oh, Jess, I wish I could give you the biggest hug.'

'You'll all hate me if I take Dom back.'

'No we won't, whatever you decide we're all here for you because we all love you.' Somehow Anna's kindness made it harder, just like Dexter's had. There were so many good people in Jess's life – at least there had been – and no one would hate Jess more than she hated herself if she ended up pushing all of them away because of Dom.

'I've been an idiot with Dexter too. Throwing him out of the house because I can't trust it when someone's nice to me.' Jess had let out another shuddering sob, as she'd caught sight of the blank space on the fridge door where the picture Riley had done for her had been. 'I miss Dexter and Riley so much, I even had to take down a picture Riley did for me because I kept bursting into tears every time I looked at it.'

'Oh, sweetheart, I want to cry for you too. But whatever you decide about Dom, I think you should call Dexter. He's been there for you through all of this and if you open up to him, he might be able to help you more than any of us can. But if you want to talk, or if you need anything, you know where I am.'

'My social worker thinks it would be a good thing if I can come back to work for a bit on the days Dom has got Teddy.' However much Jess might hate Madeline's reminder that Teddy was almost certainly going to leave her soon, her social worker was right about her needing to fill her time with something else. And if she couldn't spend her days taking care of Teddy, there was nowhere she'd rather be than at the unit with her closest friends.

'Just let me know what shifts you want and I'll sort it, but if anything changes we can get agency staff back in. It'll be great to have you back, even part-time, but the rest of us will do whatever it takes to make that work for you.'

'Thank you.' The words hadn't seemed enough, because she knew that having her job to go back to – whatever happened with Teddy – would give her a reason to keep going.

Within a week of Dom's first contact visit with Teddy, he was allowed to have him home for a whole day, as the social worker had been satisfied that there was no risk to the little boy being in his father's care. Jess would be spending the time working her first shift since Teddy had been left on her doorstep. It had barely been a month, but it already felt like a lifetime ago when all she'd had to worry about were her patients. Being with Teddy full-time had been an intense experience and she'd allowed herself to think about her own mother more than she had in years, picturing what she might have been like as a grandmother if she'd lived long enough. Caring for Teddy and knowing how much she loved him had reminded her of how loved she'd been before her mother's accident. She'd even dug out a book her mother used to read her from the memory box of stuff she kept safely tucked away and started reading it to Teddy, despite the fact he was far too young to understand. It had done more for her than all the abandoned attempts at counselling she'd tried over the years and it was like she'd found the person she was meant to be. Jess had even thought about contacting her father, opening the message again and trying to remember what his voice sounded like as she read his words. But her life was already far too complicated to think about letting Guy Kennedy back in.

Until Dom had turned up, sometimes it had felt like Teddy was actually hers. She needed to get back to work to get some perspective, it was the only hope she had. Anna had all but finished work now, but there were a handful of patients she was still taking care of because of her existing relationship with them, or problems they'd had with past pregnancies. It almost certainly wasn't with the blessing of Anna's consultant, given that her twins could arrive at any time and a lot of twin pregnancies would already have delivered by this stage, so anything Jess could do to lessen the load felt good.

'It's so lovely to have you back, Jess!' Ella wrapped her in an embrace as soon as she walked into the staffroom. Even if Jess had wanted to break free, she'd probably have found herself in an inadvertent headlock, wedged under Ella's armpit. It was one of the perils of being so small. That and having to ask random tall people in the supermarket if they could help her reach the Crunchy Nut Cornflakes when they'd been positioned too high.

'If I ever go on extended leave, in fact, even when I come back after my maternity leave, do *not* hug me like that!' Toni winked as she looked in Jess's direction. 'A pat on the shoulder, preferably even a hovering hand that doesn't actually make contact, will more than suffice.'

'You know you're going to want to hug me like this and don't pretend otherwise.' Ella laughed. 'Anyway, Anna made me promise that I'd give Jess a hug from both of us, so it was always going to be a bit full-on. She really wanted to be here for your first day back, but she's got another scan and appointment with her consultant to see if they need to induce her, or if they can leave the babies to decide when they're ready all by themselves.'

'I can't wait to see her either and she'll be getting a huge hug in return. I need to see for myself just how big she's got now that the twins are almost due.'

'The best hug I've ever had was from a topless waiter at my niece's hen night.' Gwen's tone was deadpan. 'I told him it was my sixtieth birthday, even though that was long-gone, and he offered me a birthday kiss. There was so much baby oil on his torso that I nearly slid in a direction that he definitely wasn't anticipating, but those biceps certainly made me feel like I was wrapped in two strong arms. My Barry's got office arms, they're like overcooked spaghetti in comparison!'

'Poor Barry.' For the first time since discovering who Teddy's father was, Jess felt a genuine smile tugging at the corners of her mouth. It was so nice to be back at the unit with her friends and to be reminded that she'd had a life she loved long before she'd even thought of fostering. She hadn't intended to give up midwifery before Teddy had been left on her doorstep and she already knew it was going to be her survival mechanism and safety net if he was taken away from her.

'*Poor Barry?*' Gwen pulled a face. 'He laughed his head off when I told him what the waiter said to me in the midst of the best embrace of my life!'

'Do I need to sit down for this?' Toni rested a hand on the baby bump which was just starting to put her clothes under a bit more strain. 'After all, you're the one who warned me that sudden shocks can be deadly for a pregnant woman's bladder control.'

'I was leaning in close to him and trying not to slide straight off, and do you know what he said to me?' Gwen paused for dramatic effect, before shaking her head. 'He said you smell absolutely lovely... just like my nan!'

'Oh, I'm sorry, Gwen, but I'm definitely with Barry on this one. That's too funny!' Ella grinned and Jess couldn't help laughing too. This was like coming home and she had to remember just how much she still had, even if she lost the one thing she wanted the most.

'Apparently we wore the same perfume. I said to my Barry when he finally stopped laughing that there was no way I was wearing old lady perfume again, I'm only sixty-three! So I threw it straight in the bin and that's when I started wearing the Ann Summers one. The other perfume was nearly full and it cost him forty quid for my anniversary present, that soon wiped the smile off his face.'

'Do you see what you've been missing all this time?' Toni gave Jess an affectionate nudge. 'It's really good to have you back,

I'm just sorry I've got to rush off to run the infertility group meeting.'

'Give everyone my love, won't you?' Anna had set the group up before she'd started fertility treatment and got pregnant with the twins. With nothing else local to Port Agnes, the group had already doubled in size and would soon outgrow its regular meet-up spot at The Cookie Jar café. Jess had offered to help out and share her own story, as well as her journey to becoming a foster carer, to help any other group members who might be thinking of taking an alternative route to parenthood. Toni had started supporting the group too, not long after Anna had discovered she was pregnant, and both of them had worried that the other group members might resent the fact that they were now expecting children of their own. It hadn't turned out that way, though, and some of the women had even joined in the hope that Anna and Toni's luck might rub off on them too. Jess had every intention of going back to the group at some point, but things with Teddy were just too raw at the moment and the uncertainty didn't help. The last thing she wanted to do was to put anyone else off pursuing adoption or fostering, so it was best if she stayed away for the group for now.

'Of course, I will. I know they're all really looking forward to seeing you again when you can face it and you know where I am in the meantime if you need me, don't you? I mean it, any time, day or night, me and Bobby will be there for you.' Toni fixed her with a level look to show that she meant every word, not that Jess needed any convincing. She might have come to the wrong conclusion about Toni when they'd first met and her friend had determinedly held everyone at arm's length, but the more she'd got to know her, the more she'd realised that was just a façade. Even before Toni had finally told the other midwives about losing her former fiancé to a brain haemorrhage – and the fall out that had left her desperately trying to fill his place in his parents' lives – Jess had known that Toni was one of the good ones. It's just a shame her radar had apparently been so faulty when she'd met Dom.

'Thanks and I'll see you soon. I need to get you and Bobby signed up for more antenatal classes too, I don't want you thinking you know it all, just because you're both midwives!'

'Don't worry, I'm already anticipating it being very different at the sharp end and any torture I can put Bobby through between now and then, to make up for me doing all the work at the birth, is good for me. Brae told Bobby that he was traumatised by some of the things he heard when he came to the classes with Anna.'

'I like to make the men face up to the realities of it all!' Jess laughed again and turned to Ella. 'Although I'd better get on the road for home visits if I'm going to get through them all by the end of my shift. Can you tell Izzy and Emily that I'm sorry I missed them too? Hopefully I'll have caught up with everyone by the end of the week.'

'I will. They're in with a lady who's been in labour for quite a long time already and there's still not a lot of progress, so I think we're going to have to make the call to transfer her to hospital soon. I said I'd go in and talk it through with them as soon as I'd seen you.'

'I won't hold you up any longer then, but it's really great to be back. I'd forgotten how much I missed Gwen's stories, but it's going to take me a while to get the image of that baby-oiled topless waiter pressed up against her out of my head!'

'I just want to know what perfume she was wearing. After all, it doesn't matter how old we get, none of us want to smell like someone else's nan!' Toni waved a hand as she left the staffroom and Jess felt her shoulders relax for the first time in days. She was going to be rushed off her feet fitting in all the home visits she needed to cover and with any luck she might not have time to think about how much she was missing Teddy. If she could get through this shift, then maybe she could find a way to get through the rest of her life without him too, if she had to. She just had to take it an hour at a time.

* * *

The main road that led out of Port Agnes to the surrounding countryside was flanked by steep banks, already dotted with primroses, making the promise of spring suddenly feel like a possibility. One of the things Jess loved most about her job was that no two days were the same. One day she'd be at the midwifery unit running clinics and patient check-ups, the next she might be at a home delivery, or even accompanying one of her patients to hospital when things at home hadn't gone according to plan and the stakes couldn't be higher as a result. Home visits were mostly reserved for postnatal checks in the first two weeks after women had had their babies, or for any patients who were unable to attend clinics or check-ups at the unit for some reason. Daisy Williams was one of those people and she was Jess's fifth appointment of the shift. Daisy was eight months pregnant and already had three little girls under the age of five. She didn't drive and the prospect of her having to catch two different buses with her children in tow had been enough for the midwifery team to decide she should have home visits for the remainder of her pregnancy.

Selston was a tiny hamlet about six miles out of Port Agnes, with less than twenty houses strung along a single road on either side of a fifteenth century church. The house where Daisy and her family lived was a single storey wooden-framed building that looked as though a strong breeze might blow it off its foundations. It was probably why the plot was surrounded by eight-foot-high conifers, shielding it from the road and offering protection from any strong winds that might blow across the fields from Port Agnes, or Port Kara on the other side.

Daisy was a year younger than Jess, at twenty-eight, but she'd be a mother of four within a month and Jess didn't feel anywhere near grown-up enough to take on that much responsibility. Four little people dependent on you, not just to keep them alive, but to make them happy and turn them into well-rounded, resilient adults, felt overwhelming. Jess would happily have settled for one little person, but she shook herself as she pulled up outside Daisy's house. Thinking like that wouldn't help her hold it together for the rest of the shift, because suddenly there was only one little person she wanted to take care of. Focusing her mind back on Daisy and the challenges of juggling the needs of her three daughters, Jess wasn't surprised to see her looking as exhausted as she did when she opened the front door. It was hell of a lot to deal with even without the added demands of being heavily pregnant.

'How are you doing?' Jess smiled as Daisy stood back for her to come in.

'I've got to admit I'm much more tired with this one. It must be because I'm having a boy this time.' Daisy gave a hollow-sounding laugh as they went through to the lounge on the left-hand side of the hallway. 'If I'm totally honest, I'd forgotten you were even coming today.'

'Don't worry, I know you've got a lot on your plate.' One glance around the room made that obvious. Daisy's youngest daughter was strapped into a baby bouncer in front of an episode of *In the Night Garden*. Her middle daughter was smearing what looked like porridge into the armchair, and her eldest daughter was painting a picture at the table, most of the paint going onto the wood instead of the paper. Daisy looked like she was almost entirely made up of baby bump. Even though she was wearing a long-sleeved T-shirt, Jess could see that her arms were painfully thin. She'd had one pregnancy after the other, barely giving her body a chance to recover and it looked like it was starting to take its toll.

'I just keep thanking God that this one's a boy. I always said I only wanted two, and then when Ava was a girl too, Geraint wanted to try again. I swore number three would be the last, but Lily came along and Geraint just couldn't seem to let the idea of having a boy go. I almost kissed the woman doing the ultrasound when she said this one was a boy.'

'I bet you did!' Jess put her bag at the opposite end of the table to where Daisy's eldest daughter had now abandoned using paper altogether and was just painting straight onto the wood. 'How are you managing having all the girls at home for half term?'

'It's called damage limitation. If we all make it through the day in one piece, I consider that to be a win. And when the nursery and school open again I might be tempted to kiss the teachers too. I won't know myself when I've only got Lily at home.' Daisy sounded as exhausted as she looked.

'I think you should definitely consider making it through the day a victory, but I'm worried about you not getting enough time to rest. Is there anyone who could help you out with the girls a bit?' Jess had read through Daisy's notes before heading over. Toni was her primary midwife, but the unit had a policy of trying to make sure all the midwives had met each mum-to-be at least once before the birth so that no matter who was on call, when she went into labour they wouldn't be a stranger to the woman. It was the third time Jess had met Daisy and aside from the baby bump, she looked like she'd lost a lot of weight since the last time.

'My mum and sister would probably give me a hand, in fact I know they would, but Geraint wants to be able to relax when he gets in from work and having my family about doesn't exactly help with that.'

'I can't imagine that having three under-fives is conducive to a relaxing life either.' Jess's stomach muscles contracted. She'd never met Geraint Williams, but she already knew she didn't like him. There was a name for fathers who said they wanted children and then devolved all responsibility when it came down to the hard work, but she'd probably get struck off the midwifery register if she said it out loud.

Daisy sighed. 'It's just easier sometimes to go along with what he wants.'

'Not if it ends up making you ill.' Jess bit her lip to stop herself from blurting out what she'd been about to say next. There was a line she couldn't cross as a midwife, no matter how much she wanted to. 'Shall we get you and baby checked over, then? Just to make sure everything's okay.'

'I'll get on the sofa, it'll be a good excuse to have a lie-down!' Daisy pulled up her shirt once she was lying flat so that Jess could measure the fundal height. She was clearly an old hand at this.

'Good news, you look spot on for your dates.' Jess checked for a heartbeat next, the reassuring *dee-dum, dee-dum, dee-dum* sounding out loud and clear. The baby was doing fine, but it was Daisy Jess was really worried about. 'Okay let's have a check of your blood pressure next. Which arm do you usually use?'

'The left.' Daisy sat bolt upright and rolled up her sleeve so that Jess could put the blood pressure cuff on.

'It's not too bad, just a little on the low side at ninety over sixty. It's probably nothing to worry about, but I think we're going to need to run a blood test just to make sure it's not anaemia or anything else.' Looking at her bare arm, it was even more obvious to Jess that Daisy was underweight and low blood pressure could be a side-effect of malnutrition. She was going to need to rule that out. 'I can take some blood before I give you your Anti-D shot.'

'We might as well get it over and done with in one go, I suppose. Can you do that on the left-hand side too please? I'm left-handed, but I just seem to be able to cope better with the whole needle thing on that side. You'd think I'd be over my fear of needles after having this many kids, wouldn't you?'

'You'd be amazed at how many people are like that about needles, even my ladies who've had lots of tattoos. I suppose it's like most phobias, there's not always much logic to it.' Jess took the blood pressure cuff off and replaced it with a tourniquet to help make Daisy's veins more prominent, so that taking the blood would be as straightforward as possible. 'Can you make a fist? Your veins don't look like they want to give up any blood today.'

'They're always a bit like that. Sometimes they have to take it from my hand.'

'We can give that a go if you like.' After a couple of minutes of trying, it was obvious that they weren't going to have any luck with her hand either. 'Maybe we should try the right-hand side instead?'

'I dunno, maybe it's just better if I make an appointment to get my blood taken at the doctor's next time I'm there?' Daisy was holding on to the end of her right sleeve from the inside, like a makeshift glove puppet. It may well be the needle phobia kicking in after too many attempts to get blood, but Jess was going to have to find a way of making sure there wasn't anything else going on.

'No problem, I'll ring your GP surgery and make sure they fit you in ASAP. If you can't make it in there, I'll ask if they can send the district nurse out instead. The best thing you can do is try to drink a lot of fluids before your appointment, that'll make it easier for them to take your blood.' Jess did her best to give Daisy a reassuring smile. 'But I'm still going to give you your Anti-D shot if that's okay?'

'No problem, I'm better with needles that put stuff in, rather than the ones that try to take it out.' Daisy grinned and for a moment she looked like a woman in her twenties should, before the smile seemed to slide off her face. 'I'd never forgive myself if I delayed having it and the baby got sick.'

'He'll be fine once you've had your injection.' Jess was glad Daisy didn't want to delay it either. Being rhesus-negative, and expecting a baby that had rhesus-positive blood meant there was a danger of Daisy developing antibodies that could destroy the baby's blood cells. 'But I think we should use your right arm for the injection, since the left-hand side seems to have had enough for one day.'

'Can you just try?'

'I'd just end up bruising you. Why don't we try the right? You're left-handed anyway, aren't you? So it's best if we use the other side. Unless there's a problem?'

'I...' Daisy was still scrunching up the end of the sleeve in her right hand, but she slowly released her fingers as Jess met her gaze. 'It's just that I had a fall and my arm got a bit banged up.'

'Don't worry, I can work around that and I promise I'll do my absolute best not to cause you any more pain. A sharp scratch is a bad as it should get.' The smile froze on Jess's face as Daisy finally rolled up her sleeve. The bruising was obvious, but so was something else and there was no way it was the result of a fall. There were clearly finger-shaped bruises on her upper arm, as if she'd been grabbed with enough force to burst the blood vessels under the skin. 'Let's see what we can do here, I'll try not to put the tourniquet anywhere near your bruises.'

'Okay.' Daisy's eyes filled with tears as she turned her head away and Jess would have bet her last pound that it had nothing to do with fear of needles.

'Well done, that's it.' The injection had been straightforward, but the question Jess had to ask next was anything but. 'So you got the bruises from a fall?'

'Uh-huh, luckily Geraint reached out to try and grab me, but he couldn't quite stop me falling. It slowed things down or it might have been a lot worse.'

'When did it happen?'

'Er, Saturday I think.'

'And did your bump make contact with the floor or any other hard surface when you fell?' Jess was trying to read Daisy's face, but it was mask-like as she shook her head. 'Well baby sounds fine, but I'm going to give you some leaflets to have a look through in case you have any more *accidents* and you need to know what to do.'

'Thank you, but I'll be fine.' Daisy's face was closing down by the second.

'If you ever need to talk to any of the midwives about anything, at any time, you know you can, don't you?'

'Uh-huh, but I'm okay, honestly.' Daisy had rolled her sleeve down again and she was back to clutching the screwed-up end of it in her hand.

'Just have a read through all of the leaflets and give me or Toni a call if you want to talk.' Jess took an information pack out of her bag. They were intended for first-time consultations with mums-to-be, and Daisy had almost certainly been given a pack in the past. If she was like a lot of their patients, it had probably ended up in the bin first time round, but it was really important she had access to the information now and the details of all the helplines she might need – especially the domestic violence one. There was a leaflet on first aid in pregnancy too, for genuine accidents, but Jess was certain now that wasn't what had happened to Daisy.

'Okay, thanks, but I need to get back to the girls now.'

'Of course and don't worry about trying to go to the GP for the blood test. I'll get straight on to the district nurse, like I said before you've got enough on your plate. I can see myself out, but remember, just call if you need us.'

'I will.' Even as Daisy said the words, Jess knew she wouldn't and by the time she'd got to the car, she'd made up her mind to do something about it herself.

'Everything okay?' Toni answered the phone on the second ring. She'd finished for the day, after running the infertility group, and Jess felt bad for having disturbed her, but she was certain Toni wouldn't mind when she found out why.

'Yes, sorry for calling. I'm not interrupting anything, am I?'

'No, I'm just hanging out at home, putting my swollen ankles as high up as I can so that no one mistakes me for an elephant next time I go out.'

'I've just been to see Daisy Williams.'

'And you're worried?' There was a weary note in Toni's voice. She'd been a midwife for almost fifteen years and she'd probably seen and done it all before, but Jess knew that didn't make it any easier to deal with.

'She looks exhausted, but she said she can't let her mum and sister help because Geraint doesn't like them hanging around the house. She looks really underweight too and she's got finger-shaped bruises right across her upper arm. She said it was from Geraint reaching out to grab her and trying to stop her falling, but I don't buy it.'

'Have you met Geraint?'

'No, have you?'

'Only once, and he was charming on the face of it, but there were just little things he said that were controlling. Like commenting on what pregnant women should and shouldn't wear and the sort of pain relief Daisy should have.' Toni sighed. 'They only moved to Selston six months ago and Daisy said she felt a bit isolated. All her family are in Truro and even though it's not that far, she didn't want to move. But apparently Geraint insisted.'

'So you think there's a good chance something's going on, too?'

'I think so, but unless she's willing to open up to us it's going to be hard to get her the help she needs. I take it she had all three girls with her?'

'Yes and that obviously makes it more difficult for her to talk, even if she wanted to. They all looked okay, just a bit scruffy.'

'I think the best thing for us to do is to get the health visitors involved and see if they've got any concerns about Daisy or the girls. If we work with their team so they're assessing the girls at the same time as I'm next there to see Daisy, it might actually give me a chance to have some quiet time with her and see if I can persuade her to open up to me.' Toni didn't sound convinced.

'Do you think she'll go for that?'

'The health visitors can do the pre-school tests with her middle daughter and the youngest will be due a progress check soon anyway. I'll have to get at least two health visitors to be there at the same time, but I'm sure they'll be willing to help. All we can do is hope she'll confide in me, but sadly not everyone wants to be helped.' Toni might have sounded matter-of-fact, but there was a kind heart beating behind her somewhat gruff exterior. It made her the perfect person to tackle this too. Unlike Jess, there wasn't much danger of Toni getting overly emotional and muddying the waters with her own issues. She had exactly the right sort of tough outer shell for the job.

'That sounds like a good plan. I didn't want to disturb your afternoon, but I wouldn't have slept tonight if I hadn't called.'

'I'm glad you did and don't worry. We'll give Daisy all the help we can, but in the end it's up to her. If she's going to break away from Geraint and make a fresh start, she's going to have to want to do it for herself and her kids. We can't fix everyone's problems for them.'

'I know and I used to be all right with that, but just lately I can't help wishing we could. At least she's got a chance now.' Jess sighed. 'Thanks again for everything and I'll see you soon.'

'That you will.' Disconnecting the call, Jess let go of a long breath. Toni was right, all they could do was their best. It must have been so hard for Daisy, isolated from her family by her husband's actions and terrified to talk to anyone about what was going on. How she was coping with all of that and bringing up her children was beyond comprehension. Jess was surrounded by good friends and Dexter had been there every step of the way when she'd first started caring for Teddy, and when she'd been forced to come to terms with the fact that he was Dom's. She couldn't have done it without him and unlike poor Daisy, she'd had the best of people there to support her, but she'd still ended up pushing Dexter away.

What terrified Jess now was that her best might never be good enough for Teddy. Whatever decision she made it was going to affect him in ways that could influence his whole life, but she still had no idea what to do for the best. The worst part was that she couldn't talk to the one person who might have been able to help her make sense of it all and she'd started to realise that whatever losses she might be about to face up to, she'd already lost a friend she'd never be able to replace.

9

The first time Dom was due to have Teddy overnight, Jess had been pacing the floor for at least forty-five minutes before he arrived, wondering how on earth she was ever going to get any sleep, knowing that she couldn't just reach out to where Teddy's cot was and check that he was okay. Even after Dom had arrived and she'd given him a long list of instructions, Jess still wasn't feeling any more at ease.

'Why don't you just come back with me, then you can be sure I've got all of your instructions straight in my head and it would be great for the three of us to spend some time together. Maybe then you'll finally feel ready to give things another try between us?' Dom said it so casually, as if the decision was as easy as choosing between white and brown toast for breakfast. She'd loaded up Teddy's bag with everything he could possibly need and reeled off the instructions that Dom didn't even seem to have listened to.

Maybe she should have just gone with them, at least that way she could make sure Teddy was okay, but she didn't want to give Dom the wrong idea. More than that, she didn't want to risk thinking that a life with him could be a possibility. Deep down she knew it would be a horrible mistake and that one way or another, it would end badly. After everything he'd put her through, she couldn't imagine spending the rest of her life with Dom. But there was a part of her that was still plotting for another scenario, one where she stayed with him for just long enough to officially adopt Teddy, before she broke free. She couldn't knowingly put the little boy she loved through all of that, though. Dom wasn't the sort of person who could co-parent in a civilised way, especially if the breakdown of the relationship was instigated by her.

He was struggling to accept the end of their marriage as it was, but he'd only really started wanting her again after he'd realised she was moving on. Putting Teddy in the middle of that and making him a pawn in whatever game Dom decided to play just wasn't an option. There was still no sign of Natalia wanting to be reunited with her son, either, and with Teddy's future hanging in the balance, Jess couldn't afford to alienate Dom just yet. If she didn't fall in line with his plans, there was every possibility he might decide single fatherhood wasn't for him and then maybe, just maybe, there was a chance that Teddy could stay with Jess for longer.

One of the foster carers she'd met at a support group meeting had told Jess that she'd ended up adopting a little girl after her birth mother had absconded from a parent and child placement. The courts had taken far too long to reach a decision about putting the little girl forward for adoption, so she was almost three and calling her foster carers mummy and daddy by the time they agreed that she could never return to her birth family. In the end, the social workers had decided that someone on the waiting list adopting the child would introduce more trauma into her life and when her carers offered to adopt her themselves, usual protocol was bypassed and they were able to become her forever family. It was the grain of hope Jess was holding on to and she'd continue to cling on to it until someone prised Teddy out of her arms for the last time. If that meant keeping Dom on side for the time being too, then it was a sacrifice she was more than willing to make.

'We don't want to risk anything going against you in the assessment and if Madeline finds out, she may take Teddy away from us.' Even the word *us* was hard to swallow, but Jess painted on a smile. 'You'll be absolutely fine with him and if you need me, just call. I'm not working tomorrow, but I'm planning to go over and see Anna when she finishes at lunchtime. We haven't managed to catch up for more than about ten minutes at a time since I started back at work, and the twins are really starting to outgrow their space. So it could be any day now.'

'With Anna and Toni both expecting, you'll have a ready-made group of mummy friends when we get ourselves sorted.' Dom returned her smile, seeming to have forgotten all the things he'd said when she'd first discovered she couldn't have a baby and how quickly he'd found comfort with at least two other women, probably a whole lot more. But now wasn't the time to bring any of that up.

'I'll see you both tomorrow.' Leaning down to where Teddy was sleeping in the car seat, she planted a kiss on his warm forehead. He smelt of baby lotion and his eyelids flickered for a second or two before he settled down again. 'Bye-bye, gorgeous.'

'Do I get a kiss too?' The thought of kissing Dom made her flesh crawl, but she just smiled again.

'Not just yet. Have a good time together and remember, just call if you need me.'

'I thought I'd already made the fact that I need you crystal clear. You've only got to say the word. Think about it some more while I've got the baby and we can talk when I drop him off tomorrow, before I go to rugby practice.' Dom gripped the handle of the car seat and it swung forward, waking Teddy, who immediately started to protest about the rude interruption to his slumber.

'Do you want me to try and get him settled again before you go?'

'I've got Mum and Dad coming over and they'll start to panic if we're not back by the time they get there.' Dom shrugged. 'Like you said, we'll be fine and Mum will be able to settle him if I need some help. If you want to come over too, you know you can, but it's going to have to be all or nothing for me, J-J.'

'I'll think about it.' Jess bit her lip, trying not to flinch at Dom's continued use of the pet name he'd had for her, the same one her father had put in his message, as Teddy's cries continued to get more indignant. It took all she had not to run straight after Dom. She had a horrible feeling that even if she stuck to her plans and held out for him to get bored of fatherhood, her ex would make sure the last person Teddy would end up with was Jess. Her only hope might be building some kind of relationship with the little boy's birth mother, but she had no idea where to start and she'd never wanted Dexter's advice more.

Jess must have woken up at least six times during the night, torturing herself about whether she'd done the right thing in turning down Dom's offer to go with him and Teddy. It was a bright day for the first day of March and sunlight coming through a tiny gap at the bottom of the blackout blind had woken her up again, much earlier than she'd planned after she'd finally got back to sleep. She might even have managed to drift off again after that had it not been for Luna deciding to jump onto the bed and lick her with a tongue that would have made high-grade sandpaper feel like silk.

In the end she'd given in and got up. Her only must-do for the day was to buy Luna some fish, straight from the harbour-side, to reward her for being the world's best alarm clock and to pick up something delicious from Mehenicks' Bakery to take over to Anna for a treat. She loved living where she did, where freshly baked croissants could be picked up just across the harbour from Puffin's Rest and where there'd always be a friendly face to greet her, even on days like this, when her head and her heart were both hurting from trying to work out her next move.

'Morning, Jess!' Ruth Mehenick came out from behind the counter as soon as she spotted her, folding her into a hug the way she always did. Ella's mother was like a surrogate mum to all the midwives from the unit. It was just lucky there weren't any more of them than there were, or the bakery and café would never have turned a profit. Ruth absolutely refused to take full price for anything she served the midwives and she'd always slip a little extra treat or two into their bags. Ella was so lucky to have her parents living in the same village as her. For a second, Jess's mind drifted back to the message her father had sent her, which she still hadn't deleted, but even if he'd lived right next door, it wouldn't be anything like what Ella had.

'You give the best hugs, Ruth.'

'Tell that to Jago, he reckons you girls secretly try to work out when I'll be on a break so you can come into the bakery and get in and out again without having to suffer one of my hugs!'

'He's only saying that because he wants to keep all your hugs for himself.' Jago and Ruth bickered all the time, but the love between them was obvious all the same. Surely that was what everyone wanted; a sparring partner, but someone who was still on your side when push came to shove.

'You're probably right, my love, I mean who could resist this?' Ruth ran her hands down the sides of her body. 'I've eaten so many pasties over the years, I'm starting to take on their shape!'

'You look amazing.' Ruth might be what clothes shops termed plus-sized, but it made her hugs all the more comforting.

'You're such a sweetheart, Jess, but believe it or not I used to be quite skinny before I met Jago. Ella's upstairs with her dad now, actually, dragging my size ten wedding dress down from the loft. She's thinking about wearing it for the wedding, although God know why when we've offered to get her any dress she wants.'

'She probably hopes it'll bring her the same sort of luck you and Jago have had.'

'That's such a lovely thing to say.' Ruth gave her another squeeze. 'And it's about time some lucky guy snapped you up too. You deserve some happiness after what Dom put you through, I bet he's kicking himself now.'

'I'm not—' She'd barely started speaking before Ella burst into the bakery and cut off her response.

'Oh, Jess, perfect timing! Anna's with Molly Trelawney. It was supposed to be a routine check-up, but Molly's in labour and everything's happening really quickly. She asked if I could come down, but with Anna as far along as she is, it might be a good idea if you came too, if you're free? Just in case Anna needs to stand down. I know she's only been seeing a couple of patients, but I kept telling her she should have finished altogether by now. She's almost thirty-seven weeks pregnant with twins and she'd have told any of her patients to be at home with their feet up weeks ago. I'm worried that something could happen with Anna too and I definitely don't want to be delivering three babies all at once!'

'Don't worry, I'm right behind you.' Jess didn't even need to think about it – she could never do enough to thank Ella and Anna for their friendship and it meant her head would be occupied with something other than the situation with Dom and Teddy.

* * *

Molly Trelawney lived at Wagtail Farm, a boarding kennels and cattery set a couple of hundred metres back from the cliff edge about two miles outside the centre of Port Agnes. It took less than ten minutes to get there from Mehenicks' Bakery, but Anna had already called again to say that she'd rung for an ambulance because Molly was struggling with labour and there was limited pain relief the midwives could administer at home.

It wasn't uncommon for mums-to-be to find the reality of childbirth meant they were unable to stick with a planned home delivery, but there was a tension in Anna's voice that suggested it might be more than that. Whatever the problem, Jess and Ella were more anxious than ever to get there and offer whatever support they could until the ambulance arrived.

'I love you both for coming, now get yourselves inside!' Turning to the side, Anna almost filled the narrow corridor that led from the front door into the old farmhouse, as she rattled off an update barely pausing for breath. 'Molly's in the sitting room, her waters broke while I was taking her blood pressure and she went into labour straight away. She's thirty-eight weeks, but she hadn't even had Braxton Hicks up until now. She's had some pethidine because she wasn't really tolerating the Entonox very well. I've phoned her husband, Giles, but he's off collecting some bulldog semen from a breeder in Poole. He was already on his way back, but he'll be at least an hour and a half.'

'Bulldog semen?' Ella pulled a face.

'Don't ask!' Anna was already hurrying along the corridor and all Jess and Ella could do was follow.

'Hi, Molly, how are you doing?' Jess hardly needed to ask, given the very unnatural expression Molly's face was twisted into.

'Bloody awful!' Molly had a cut-glass accent and the sort of velvet Alice band that even Princess Anne might think was a bit old-fashioned. 'This can't be natural, can it? It's like trying to drive a Range Rover through a polo neck!'

'That's a good way of putting it.' Jess exchanged a smile with the others. 'Why don't you try a bit more of the gas and air?'

'Bloody stuff makes me feel as sick as a dog!' Molly flung the mouthpiece away from her, as if to emphasise her point. 'None of the dogs seem to have this much bother, though. Maybe we should have six all at once, like they do with puppies. At least they'd be more likely to fit through the exit door then.'

'Tell me you still want six when you've got one.' Anna patted Molly's arm. 'I know it's really painful, but I think one of us is going to have to take another look at you because the baby's heart rate is dropping a bit. I'm sure it's nothing to worry about, but we just need to check what's going on.'

'I couldn't give a flying fig who looks up my noo-noo, as long as it means I can get the bloody thing out.' Molly grimaced as another contraction took hold of her body. 'I'm going to get Giles's testicles and squeeze them with a nutcracker when this is all over. "It'll be easy," he said, "the dogs do it all the time." Well I'd like to see him squeeze a melon out of his bum. Then we can talk.'

Jess tried to swallow the laughter that was bubbling up in

her throat but when she caught Anna's eye, she had to turn away and stuff her fist into her mouth. Poor Molly was in agony, but that didn't make what she was saying any less funny. Thank God Ella was managing to remain professional.

'Right, let's take a look and see what this baby's up to.' Ella waited until the contraction seemed to have passed and Molly had finally stopped threatening to castrate her husband. 'I'm not sure if you'll consider this good news or not, Molly, but I can see the head.'

'I just want it over!'

'The head's retracted.' Jess whispered the words as she stood at Ella's shoulder, while Molly gripped Anna's hand. 'You don't think it could be shoulder dystocia, do you?'

'God, I hope not.' Ella turned to look at her. Shoulder dystocia was one of the things midwives dreaded most at a home delivery. It meant the baby's shoulder was trapped, preventing it from being delivered, and the retraction of the baby's head was a classic sign. If it was shoulder dystocia, Molly would need to be transferred to hospital urgently, but there were no guarantees the ambulance would arrive in time. Even if it did, there was a chance they still wouldn't be able to get Molly to the hospital before it was too late to save the baby.

'Let's just see if it happens again.' Jess automatically crossed her fingers when the baby's head appeared again, willing it not to disappear, but a few seconds later it was gone again.

'I've got a horrible feeling you're right about this.' Ella's words were barely audible.

'OH MY GOD!' Molly screamed so loud that some of the dogs who'd been shut in the kitchen started to howl. 'My noo-noo's on fire! Giles Trelawney, you're a total bastard!'

'It's just the baby crowning.' Ella's voice was steady, but when she turned to Jess she was shaking her head, lowering her voice again as Molly writhed in pain. 'With the baby's head coming out as far as it did, it should only have taken one more good push to be delivered.'

'The baby's cheeks looked puffed out too.' Jess had been desperately hoping that she was wrong, but she was almost certain now it was shoulder dystocia. She'd been involved in a handful of these types of deliveries in the hospital, but never one at home. The turtle sign was the best clue to diagnosing it for sure; when the baby appeared and disappeared like a turtle going in and out of its shell, its face taking on a red and puffy appearance. Molly's baby was almost a textbook example. Now they just had to decide what on earth they were going to do.

'Did the operator give any idea of how long the ambulance might be?' Ella looked towards where Anna was standing, still at the head of the bed.

'They just said they'd get here as soon as they could. They know Molly's in labour.'

'I don't think we can risk waiting, we'll have to perform a McRoberts manoeuvre.' Jess was already taking hold of one of Molly's legs. 'We're going to have to bend your knees and raise your legs up towards your belly to help the baby out, Molly, because it looks like it's coming out shoulder first.'

'No wonder it's so bloody painful! Just do whatever you need to do to, I can't stand it!'

'I'll take Molly's right leg.' Anna moved opposite Jess. 'Ella, if you can just let us know it's having any effect.'

Jess and Anna flexed Molly's legs up towards her abdomen, widening her pelvis to give the baby a better chance of delivery. Every muscle in Jess's body tensed as she looked at Ella.

'Any luck?'

'Not yet, but it might make a difference when the next contraction comes.'

'There's another one coming. Argh!' Molly gave another ear-splitting scream. Giles would only need to be halfway home from Poole before he heard her at this rate.

'Okay, Molly, go with it and we'll see if your little one is ready to put in an appearance.' Anna's voice was almost melodic; if she was even half as worried as Jess she was doing a good job of hiding it.

'How can this be natural?' Molly was still yelling as the contraction started to ease, and Ella shook her head.

'Do you think I should put some pressure on her abdomen?' Jess looked from Ella to Anna and back again. There were still a few things left that they could try to get the baby out safely, but with each one that didn't work, the danger was starting to ramp up. Anna was nodding though.

'We've got to try everything we can until the ambulance gets here. It'll be at least half an hour from here to the hospital and if she needs a C-section, the baby will have been stuck for over an hour.' The colour seemed to drain from Anna's face, but she must have been exhausted. This late in her pregnancy, Anna had to be feeling the pressure even more than Jess and Ella were.

'Okay, Ella, if you can take Molly's left leg, I'll start applying the pressure.' Jess turned back to Molly, whose hair was sticking to her forehead. 'I'm going to push down on your lower abdomen, and Ella and Anna will keep your legs raised to try and help baby out.'

'What if it doesn't work?' All the fire that had been coursing through Molly's veins earlier, making her protest so loudly against the pain, seemed to have drained out of her and her face had taken on a greyish sheen.

'Don't worry, there are lots of other things we can try, but this stands a good chance.' Jess just hoped she hadn't just done the one thing she usually tried her best to avoid, and lied to a patient. There *were* other things they could try, but if something didn't work soon the best chance the baby had was to be delivered by caesarean section and that was one thing they definitely couldn't try at home.

'On the count of three we'll flex Molly's legs as much as we can and you push down.' Anna looked across at Jess. 'One, two, three.'

Jess held her breath as she pressed down on Molly's abdomen, just above the pubic bone. If this didn't work, they'd have to try rotating the baby's shoulder or delivering it shoulder first. Neither of those options were particular appealing, but both were a damn sight better than having to resort to fracturing the baby's collarbone. All Jess could do was keep praying that it worked this time.

'The baby's head is crowning again, just keep pushing down, Jess, and we might have this.' Anna didn't need to ask twice.

'JESUS CHRIST!' Molly found another burst of energy from somewhere, screaming out the words, just as the baby's shoulders finally emerged.

'That's it, Molly, you've done brilliantly.' The relief on Anna's face said it all. 'One more push and we'll have baby here, just let your body go with the next contraction.'

'I'm never doing this again! If you even hear me say I'm thinking about it, I want you to have me committed.' Molly had barely got the words out before she started to grimace again. 'Oh God, here we go.'

Tucking her chin into her chest, Molly made a throaty growl as she pushed her baby into the world. Jess couldn't stop smiling as the little boy who'd caused so much trouble finally emerged.

'Baby's here!' It didn't matter how many deliveries she attended, it never ceased to move her when a whole new life began. That moment when a new mother held her baby in her arms was the best bit of all. Although Jess had to admit Molly had a very different take on it.

'It's a boy then?' Pulling back the blanket as Jess took the baby from Anna and lifted him onto Molly's chest, his mother wrinkled her nose. 'I've always preferred puppies to babies if I'm honest, but it's different when it's your own. I suppose he's quite cute, in a squashed tomato sort of way, almost like one of the bulldog pups.'

'He's lovely.' Jess couldn't help laughing. 'But because the delivery was a bit more traumatic, it might be an idea for the paramedics to take you both in and get you checked over.'

'I was never planning on a home birth anyway. When Giles gets to the hospital I'll be telling him that he better have a bloody big bouquet of flowers and a crate of champagne waiting for me when I get back here. Trust him to miss the whole thing.' Despite her words Molly's eyes were shining as she looked down at her newborn son, although Jess had a feeling she was never going to let poor old Giles forget he'd missed the baby's arrival.

'Have you got a name for him yet?' Anna rubbed the small of her back with both hands as she straightened up. 'We've got two names to come up for each gender with and we're still nowhere near even settling on one.'

'Monty, well Montgomery really, but I don't suppose we'll call him that very often.' Molly stroked the baby's head. 'Although looking at him now, I'm wondering if he's not more of a Winston. He's definitely got the look of Churchill about him, but then in my experience most babies have.'

'I think Monty's a great name.' Ella's reply was almost drowned out as someone rang the doorbell and all the dogs in the kitchen started another chorus of howling. 'That'll be the paramedics with any luck.'

By the time Molly and Monty were being wheeled out to the

ambulance, her husband, Giles, had finally turned up. He was so red in the face he looked as though he had run all the way back from Poole rather than driven.

'Congratulations.' Jess smiled as Giles was handed his newborn son and cradled him in his arms.

'Thanks and thank you ladies for doing such a wonderful job. I'd like to have been here, I suppose, but I've seen enough puppies and kittens born over the years to know I didn't miss anything camera-worthy! I can get all the good shots for the family album now he's actually here.'

'It was our absolute pleasure and Molly was a star.' Ella returned Giles's smile. 'I'm going to come with you in the ambulance, though. The birth was quite hard going for Molly and the baby, so I just want to make sure they're okay until we hand over to the hospital.'

Jess started to protest, wanting to offer instead, but Ella shook her head. 'I was going there later anyway, to meet a friend of mine who works there. So this way I get a free ride there and Dan can come and pick me up afterwards.'

'Are you sure?' Jess couldn't help feeling guilty, even though it was her day off. It was Ella's day off too and Dan was probably waiting on her to go home. Luna wouldn't even realise that Jess wasn't there until she got hungry.

'Absolutely and I'm hoping I'll get an extra cuddle or two with Monty as well.' Ella followed Giles as Molly was loaded into the ambulance, leaving Anna and Jess standing and waving until the doors were closed and the new family was driven away.

'Well that was quite a delivery.' Jess was about to suggest that they went to Mehenicks' for some cake to celebrate Monty's safe arrival, when the last of the colour drained out of Anna's face. 'Are you okay, you don't look very well?'

'I don't feel great.' Anna suddenly slumped sideways and Jess just managed to slide an arm around her before Anna's legs seemed to almost give way.

'You need to sit down before you fall down, sweetheart, and then we're going to get you checked over as soon as we can. You've been doing too much when you should have been resting and you look exhausted. But perhaps you're anaemic too.'

'I just hope that's all it is.' Anna looked up at Jess as she helped her sit down on the low wall in front of the Trelawney's house, her eyes like dark pools in the pallor of her face. 'Because I can't remember the last time I felt the babies move.'

10

Anna had insisted she didn't want to go to the hospital to get checked out, so Jess had driven her back to the midwifery unit. Maybe it was because going to the hospital would have meant facing the fact that there was something really wrong; Jess was almost as terrified as her friend that it would turn out to be the worst possible news. Guilt was gnawing at her stomach too. If she hadn't been off work, Anna would probably have taken Ella's advice and stopped seeing patients altogether and gone on full-time maternity leave weeks ago. If she had any part in something bad happening to the twins, she wasn't going to be able to live with herself and she was silently praying all the way back to the unit, wishing the car would go three times as fast as it did. There still wasn't much colour in Anna's face by the time they arrived but she didn't seem to be panicking. At least not yet. Jess, on the other hand, felt as if her heart was beating out of her chest.

'Let's get you into the examination room and put your mind at rest.' The words stuck in Jess's throat and she couldn't bear to think about what she was going to do if there really was something wrong. Anna was the lynchpin that held the whole midwifery unit together and her pregnancy was incredibly important to every single member of the team. If anyone deserved a happy ever after it was Anna and Brae, and the idea of being the one to break bad news to them made Jess's stomach feel like it had hit the floor. When Anna had been told that she was unlikely to ever have children of her own, she and Jess had set up the infertility support group together. So when Anna had discovered she was expecting twins, Jess had been delighted for her. Now she was terrified.

Anna had made revealing the most painful parts of her childhood much easier for Jess by sharing her own story. She'd told Jess about losing both her parents at a relatively young age and they'd found a lot of common ground as a result; not least an understanding of the sanctuary that work could offer and the importance of the friendships they'd found there. When Anna had married Brae the summer before, Jess had never felt more like she belonged to part of a family than she did at their wedding reception, surrounded by the friends who had to have absolute trust in one other when they were faced with the highest of stakes on a day-to-day basis.

'Let's go round the back way, I don't want to have to say anything to the others unless there's something to tell.' Anna screwed her eyes shut. If she was secretly fighting back tears, she wasn't the only one.

Jess was desperate to find the right words, but the sort of platitudes she might have rolled out – about being sure every-thing would be okay – dried up as soon as she looked at her friend. Anna knew better than anyone that not every pregnancy went smoothly and that twins presented a higher risk, especially with Anna having the unflattering label of being a geriatric mother.

'There aren't any clinics using the examination room four on

Fridays from what I can remember, so we should be able to get in there. I'll check the babies' heartbeats, do your blood pressure and then we can give you a scan.' Jess had no idea why she was running through the process when Anna had almost two decades of experience, but it was something to fill the silence – with all the possibilities of what could be wrong still hanging in the air.

'I keep thinking maybe I can feel something, but I don't know if it's my imagination playing tricks on me. I just want to feel a massive kick, or one of them stomping across my bladder, so I know for sure they're okay.' Anna cradled her bump with both hands as they walked down the corridor from the doors at the back of the unit, which were usually used to accept delivery of supplies and Anna was the only midwife who had a key to open them from the outside. Treatment room four was second on the left and Jess just hoped Anna couldn't see her hand shaking as she reached for the door handle.

'The twins are running out of space to stretch out and give you a really good kick, and your placentas are in the anterior position, so that's cushioning the kicks too.' Jess opened the door to the consulting room, keeping her tone deliberately upbeat despite the rising sense of panic she was struggling to push down. 'Good, there's no one here.'

'I know it's probably nothing, but I daren't even mention the possibility of something going wrong to Brae. He's been so protective and kept saying that I should have finished work completely by now, but I insisted I'd be fine because I was only seeing five patients.' A tear rolled down Anna's cheek as Jess helped her up onto the examination table. 'What if I've blown it by being so stubborn and lost my one and only chance of being a mum?'

'Whatever's going on, Anna, it's not your fault.' Jess's hand was still shaking as she picked up the Doppler to try and find the babies' heartbeats, neither of them saying a word as she moved it around Anna's abdomen. Thank God, there was the first heartbeat – Jess finally letting go of the breath she'd been holding. 'Okay, there's twin one. Sounding strong and steady, I've just got to find the other one now, so try not to worry if takes a while.'

'Last time I had a scan they were both head down, but back-to-back with each other, which would mean Twinkle's over to the right-hand side.'

'Twinkle?' Jess smiled for the first time in the twenty minutes or so since Anna had told her about not feeling the babies move.

'When we found out I was pregnant, we talked about whether or not we wanted to find out the gender. Brae wanted it to be a surprise and at first I wasn't sure. But then I realised this was going to be our only experience of pregnancy and I wanted it to be as exciting as possible. I knew there was always a risk that I'd see something at one of the scans that gave the game away, but I wanted to try.' Anna adjusted her position on the bed. 'When we found out that we were having twins, I knew there'd be even more scans than normal and that at some point, I'd probably work out what we were having. So I decided to give the twins pet names, so I could refer to them like that and not spoil things for Brae by saying him or her. Hence Twinkle and Twinkie. It's silly, I know.'

'It's not silly at all, it's lovely, and you might find those pet names stick.' As a youngster Jess had always been J-J – Jessica Jade – something her Mum and Dad had called her from when she was tiny. The nickname had disappeared when she'd gone into care and she'd only ever been called Jessica or Jess. She'd never shared the term of endearment with anyone, until she'd met Dom. When he'd first started calling her J-J, she'd almost wished she hadn't told him either. Part of her had loved hearing it again, but part of her wanted to keep it locked away with the other memories she had of her mother that were just for her.

'I'm not sure about the names sticking! If I've got a couple of boys in here who grow up to be like their dad, then I don't think they'll appreciate being called Twinkle and Twinkie.' Anna managed to laugh, her bump moving up and down as she did, and Jess was almost certain she saw a knee or a foot pressing outwards in response. Whatever it was – if it wasn't just wishful thinking – it had disappeared as quickly as it had appeared.

'Let's track Twinkie down then, shall we?' Jess moved the Doppler around, down towards the left and then up again towards the centre of Anna's sternum. There it was, the sound they'd been waiting for – a second heartbeat thumping away. It was a bit slower than the first baby's heartbeat, but it was there. And that was all that mattered.

'Oh, Jess, thank God and thank you so much.' Anna struggled to a sitting position, hugging Jess close to her bump; it was like trying to do a sit-up with a medicine ball up her jumper.

'I didn't do anything, but I'm so happy they're okay.' Jess smiled, but they weren't out of the woods yet. The babies were okay – at least for now – but there were a few potential reasons for decreased foetal movements and just because they could hear the babies' heartbeats, it didn't mean there was nothing to worry about. Checking Anna's blood pressure and scanning the babies would give them much more of an idea whether it was just the position the twins were in. 'Do you want to give Brae a call?'

'Let's do the other checks first, so we know exactly what we're dealing with.' Anna finally had a bit of colour back in her cheeks, but there was still a deep crease between her eyebrows as she looked at Jess. They both knew what could go wrong. It was one of the downsides of being a pregnant midwife, but that was one thing Jess would probably never have to worry about.

'I'll do my best not to reveal all about Twinkle and Twinkie's true identities on the scan.' Jess smiled again. The likelihood was that they'd be pretty safe; Jess couldn't perform the sort of expert scan a sonographer could and the last thing she wanted to do was reveal the twins' secret, if Anna didn't already know for sure.

'Unless I'm very much mistaken there's definitely at least one boy in here. There was a bit of a dead giveaway dangling between his legs at the last scan.' Anna grinned. 'Brae would be thrilled if I told him, but having come this far I want to keep it a surprise.'

'There's always a chance you were mistaken, even the sonographers get it wrong sometimes and I've lost count of the mums-to-be who are convinced they are having little boys, but what they've actually seen is the umbilical cord.'

'I'm handing in my notice if that's the case.' Anna smiled as Jess took her blood pressure.

'It probably wouldn't be your best day!'

'That's why I haven't told the others. Can you imagine what Toni would say if it turned out I'd got it wrong?' Anna pulled a face. 'She'd have a field day with that!'

'I'm very honoured to be in on the secret and I promise to guard it with my life. Right, your blood pressure looks good, so we just need to see how things look on the scan.' Jess squeezed some gel onto Anna's belly, running the scanning device from side to side. There were definitely two very strong heartbeats and the babies looked to be about the same size. Twinkle, the twin nearest the top of Anna's bump, had its legs curled up tightly towards its belly, so there was no way of telling its sex, but Twinkie was definitely a boy – if he wasn't, Jess would have to hand her notice in too. Either way he looked completely perfect, with one of his little hands raised up towards his face like he was sucking his thumb.

'Is everything okay?' Anna turned her head towards the screen.

'I think so, but the amniotic fluid looks as if it might be a little bit on the low side.' Jess peered at the screen again. A sonographer would be able to take detailed measurements and know for sure if there was anything to worry about. All Jess could do was make an educated guess and she didn't want to cause Anna any more worry than she had to.

'They told me my fluid was a bit low when I had a scare earlier on, but we know that's a risk with twins.' Anna seemed determined that everything was okay and the admiration Jess had for her grew again. In her position she'd probably be falling apart, even though it looked like Anna was right. Jess wasn't going to let her friend just brush it off, though, until they were both certain there was definitely nothing to worry about.

'It's probably fine, but I think it might be worth you going to the hospital and getting another scan. You must be due an appointment with your consultant soon. Are they letting you see if you can get to full-term?' Anna's babies were due in less than three weeks and it was quite unusual for twin pregnancies to go beyond thirty-eight weeks, either naturally or by induction.

'Because the twins have got separate placentas, my consultant has said she'd be happy to let me go to thirty-nine weeks if I'm still feeling okay and the babies don't decide to put in an appearance by themselves. I've got to admit it is starting to feel like I've been pregnant forever. That's what comes of discovering I was pregnant so early on, because the symptoms with the twins were so strong from the outset. But I think it might be time to take Brae's advice and to stop work completely. Even seeing five patients – well four since Molly delivered – seems like an unnecessary risk.'

'I think Brae's right too and it does look like you've just lost a bit more of the fluid. Have you noticed any water,' Jess hesitated, it was always a delicate question to ask, especially when it was to one of her best friends, '*leaking out*?'

'What, you mean apart from every time I cough, laugh or go over a speed bump?' Anna grinned again. 'When you're in your forties and having twins, I think it comes with the territory.'

'I'm sure it'll only be that, but let me ring the hospital to set up another scan and you can phone Brae. Just to put all of our minds at rest.'

It took Jess less than ten minutes to set up Anna's appointment with the hospital and brief the team there about the pregnancy, the details of Anna's consultant, and the checks she'd done so far. Somehow she'd done it all without being seen by any of the team on duty, but it was a busy day. According to the whiteboard in the staffroom, there were two deliveries in progress in the unit's birthing centre and an antenatal clinic on the go. Izzy, Toni and Gwen were all on shift, and they'd been joined by agency staff who they were still relying on whilst Ella tried to recruit a temporary replacement to cover Anna's midwifery hours. Jess felt another pang of guilt about the impact that her absence was having on the team. But as much as she wanted to pull her weight at the unit, she couldn't bear to think about coming back full-time, because it would mean that Teddy was gone for good.

By the time she got back to the examination room, after contacting the hospital, Brae was already in there, his arm around Anna.

'Superman's got nothing on you.' Jess smiled at Anna's husband, who looked over when she came into the room.

'You're the superhero as far as I'm concerned. These three are my whole world and I don't care if that's a soppy thing to say.' Brae must have been at least six-foot-four and had a big ginger beard, which made him look a bit intimidating if you didn't know him. But he was a total teddy bear of a man and so obviously devoted to Anna, even when he wasn't saying the sort of thing he just had.

'I haven't done anything. Anna's the superhero, growing two new people.'

'Tell me about it. I keep trying to suggest she takes it a bit easier, but you know Anna.'

'Indeed I do.' Jess raised her eyebrows.

'You can both stop talking about me like I'm not here.' Anna was laughing, despite her words. 'What was the verdict? Do the hospital want to see me?'

'Yes, to check on what's happening with the amniotic fluid and to discuss your options for inducing delivery again, if you all agree it's time.' Jess turned to Brae. 'If Anna's lost some of her waters, it could explain why the babies' movements are getting a bit less obvious.'

'I better get my bum in gear and finish the last bits of the nursery tonight then, even if the babies are going to be in our room at first, I still want it to be finished.' Brae took Anna's face in his hands. 'And you've got to promise me you'll tell me next time you're worried about anything and not try to take it all on yourself.'

'I promise.'

'You know Jess is here to witness that promise, don't you?' Brae turned back towards Jess and winked. 'My wife still thinks she needs to take the weight of the world on her shoulders all by herself. But that's what she's got me for.'

'The babies are going to be really lucky to have parents like you two.' Jess had to look away as Brae wrapped his arms around Anna again. Whatever life threw at them, they'd always have each other. She might never have a relationship like that, but at least it meant she could pour all her love into a child. The only problem was that she had already done that, and any day now he could be taken away from her forever – unless she decided to sacrifice everything else and be with Dom for Teddy's sake.

11

The back of Izzy's car was filled with bags. She was pretty sure she had everything she needed, including six brand-new sleeping bags, which looked like the Very Hungry Caterpillar was nestled on Izzy's back seat. There were bags of popcorn, chocolate and crisps in all varieties, ice cream in three flavours, magazines, face packs, and nail varnishes. The pizzas would be ordered later and they could stream almost any movie they chose, but Izzy had still ordered DVDs of a few of her grandmother's favourite old movies, just in case they weren't on Netflix or Prime. That had to cover everything needed for Nonna's first ever sleepover, and she didn't even know about the secret purchase that Izzy would only reveal when the time was right.

The whole idea of having a sleepover with her grandmother's three closest friends and her sister, Izzy's great aunt Glo, had come about when they'd been having a conversation the week before about finally completing some of the things on the very modest bucket list her grandmother had come up with. The doctors had put Eileen on a new regime of medication, which included a steroid that they could be forgiven for thinking was working some kind of miracle. Eileen had been so much better for the past two weeks, but the doctor had been frank with them about the dangers of believing she really was getting better. The medication was lessening the side effects of the cancer, but it wouldn't stop its progress. Her grandmother had nodded and smiled, saying that she just wanted the chance to do some of her favourite things one last time, and maybe even a few things for the first time ever before she *had to go*, as she always put it. Izzy's granddad, George, had finally agreed that it was safe for her to go to Lands' End and the Trebah Garden, and they were even planning a trip over to Tresco – the simple things that had been on Eileen's bucket list ever since she first got her prognosis. But then she'd started to talk about some of the things she'd never done, things she still wanted to try – before it was too late.

'Do you know what, Izz?' Eileen had leant her head against her granddaughter's as they'd sat side-by-side on the sofa watching a rerun of *Grease*. 'I've never once had a sleepover, not as a teenager and not even when I was little. It was different back then, I suppose, but I watch all these American films and the young girls are always over at a friend's house, or having friends over to them. This film is set in the fifties and I had a dress just like Olivia Newton-John's, but I never had a moment like that, all girls together, gossiping and doing each other's make-up.'

'I have to say that once me and my friends got into our late teens, it was less about the gossip and more about who could sneak in what alcohol! When I had friends over here, you and Pops were so good about giving us our space that it was pretty much a free for all on the alcopops front. Luckily we are all light-weights!'

'Isabelle Redford, I'm shocked!' Eileen had laughed, not even managing to keep up the act for thirty seconds. 'Well, alcohol or otherwise, I'd like to have tried it once with my best friends and your Auntie Glo. She'd never have forgiven me if I didn't include her.'

'Who would you invite if you had a sleepover now?' The thought had popped into Izzy's head and straight out of her mouth without her having time to even process it properly. But there was no real reason why Nonna couldn't have a sleepover. Pops might go into a bit of a panic about the idea, in case it made her tired or exposed her to too many germs. The sad truth was that she was dying anyway and Izzy just wanted to make as many of her dreams come true as she could, even if it meant bumping heads with her grandfather, something she'd normally do whatever she could to avoid.

'It would have to be Glenda, Maggie and Linda, they've all been friends of mine for at least thirty years – Maggie since we were kids ourselves – and they've not treated me any differently or left me out of any of their plans since all this started.'

'Well, why don't we do it then? Have the sleepover and I'll stay here with you too to fetch you all snacks and drinks, and order the pizzas in like they do at all the best sleepovers!'

'And can you paint our nails and do those face mask thingies that are made of cucumber gloop? Maybe you can make me look like I did in my twenties, just for one night!' Eileen's eyes had sparkled at the prospect and Izzy had found herself nodding, despite not knowing much at all about makeover parties. From the photos of her in her twenties, Nonna had looked like a carbon copy of Izzy now, at twenty-eight; the same blue eyes and long black hair. She'd always loved that she looked so much like her grandmother and even if she couldn't make Nonna look like she was in her twenties again, she really hoped she could make her feel like it – if only for a little while. It had all happened pretty quickly after that. Eileen had texted the guests and Izzy had ordered six airbeds from Amazon, after her grandmother had insisted she wanted to do it all properly and have the sort of camping experience she'd never had either.

After that, Izzy had been tasked with persuading her grandfather that it was a good idea and getting him to agree to stay in her flat, just around the corner, in their shared hometown of Redruth. That way, in Eileen's own words, he wouldn't cramp his wife's style. The whole thing had been set up in less than a week – seizing the day had become a necessity rather than just a mantra to live by. Now here she was, about to channel her inner Frenchie to her grandmother's Sandy, but even a beauty school dropout would have had ten times Izzy's knowledge when it came to hosting a makeover party. She just hoped the home-made sloe gin, which Maggie said she was bringing by the litre-load, would mean any varnish that didn't manage to stay on their fingernails would go completely unnoticed. As long as her grandmother had a good time, that was all that mattered.

'You can go now, George, Izzy's here.' Eileen all but shoved her husband out of the door the moment Izzy arrived. Izzy might even have felt sorry for Pops if it hadn't been so brilliant to see some of her grandmother's old spark coming back. Her grandfather had invited a few of his buddies from the skittles team over to Izzy's flat anyway, and they'd be having some beers and a fish and chip supper. So there was every chance her grandfather might end up with an inadvertent sleepover of his own – if one of his mates had a pint or two too many and crashed out on Izzy's sofa. She was half hoping they did. Pops deserved to have a good time too and he was so used to having someone to take care of that tending to a worse-for-wear friend might take his mind off missing Eileen quite so much. She was so glad she'd decided to put her plans on hold to try and move to Port Agnes. Putting her name down with the agents there had come to nothing, as there wasn't anything suitable on their books, but in the end she'd turned down the offer Bobby had made her to take over his old flat when he'd moved in with Toni. She needed to be around for her grandparents and she'd have commuted any distance to work to be there for them when they needed her, just like they'd always been there for her.

'All right, love, I'm going, you don't have to be quite so keen to get rid of me.' Pops lowered his voice as he turned to Izzy. 'You will be okay, won't you, Izz?'

'It's going to be fine, just go and enjoy yourself. I'm off work tomorrow, so there's no rush to come straight back in the morning if you want to go out for breakfast with your friends.'

'Just text me and let me know you're all okay before you go to sleep, please.' Pops dropped a kiss on her forehead. 'You're a good kid, Baby Belle, the best in fact.'

'It's nothing and I'm really looking forward to a girls' night in!' She caught her grandmother's eye and smiled. She really was looking forward to it. Life just lately had been all about work and worrying about her grandparents. She'd had a Christmas party at her flat and some of her new friends from the midwifery unit had come along, but she'd had to turn down a few of their other get-togethers, or leave so early it had seemed quite rude – like when they'd gone out for drinks to celebrate Jess being approved as a foster carer. Whatever Pops might think, she wasn't the best, her grandparents were, and spending quality time with her grandmother was priceless. So, as much as she loved her grandfather, if she had to help Nonna shove him out of the door to make him go, then that's what she'd do.

* * *

Aunt Glo was lying back on her airbed as if it was a chaise longue, and dangling a piece of pizza above her mouth despite the fact that she had a full face mask on and two slices of cucumber resting on her eyes.

'I think this might be my ninth slice.'

'I'm all for us having a big blowout tonight, sis.' Izzy's grandmother, who'd already had her face mask removed, winked in her direction. 'But if you carry on like this, I'm going to outlive you because your heart will be seventy-five per cent mozzarella and processed meat.'

'It's fine, I'll just have a bit of this.' Aunt Glo whipped one of the pieces of cucumber off her eyes and dropped it straight into her mouth. 'There you are, my diet's all back in balance now!'

'God, if only it was that easy!' Maggie, Eileen's oldest friend, patted her tummy. 'I weigh more these days than I did when I was pregnant and look, my airbed's already deflating!'

'You've only got yourself to blame. It's all those Paul Hollywood videos you keep watching on YouTube, they make you eat more and then you try cooking the recipes and make us all fatter too!' Linda shook her head.

'You can't blame her, those blue eyes are the perfect distraction.' Izzy's grandmother shrugged. 'I know he's a ladies' man and we shouldn't like him, but there's something about a man who bakes that you just can't beat.'

'Oh, Nonna, now I know why you make me watch all those *Bake Off* reruns!'

'The calendar Maggie got me for Christmas should have given you a clue too.'

'It did actually and that's why I got you girls a little treat.' Izzy stood up and Aunt Glo whipped the cucumber off her other eye.

'Ooh, is it a naked Paul Hollywood lookalike, or one of those butlers in the buff?'

'Sorry to disappoint you, Auntie Glo, but it is something else that Nonna has never done before and I thought the rest of you might want to give it a go too. Although, who knows, it might not be the first time for some of you…'

'What is it?' Maggie sat up on her fast-deflating airbed, as she spoke, causing another whoosh of air to escape.

'Tattoos.'

'Oh, I'm not sure I'm up for that.' Glenda was already shaking her head. 'It's not even so much the fact that I'll have something drawn on me for the rest of my life, or how much it'll annoy my husband, because he hates tattoos – that bit might even be fun! I just hate needles.'

'No needles involved with these tattoos and they'll only last about two to four weeks before they start to fade away, but there's no need to tell Ian that straight away, is there?' Izzy smiled. 'I found this place online that makes bespoke temporary tattoos. So I got us all one, of Paul Hollywood!'

'I know exactly where I'm having mine.' Auntie Glo pulled herself up and pointed towards her bum cheek. 'One benefit of it being twice the size it used to be is that it's the smoothest part of my body these days and nine slices of pizza must have done something to help plump it out even more.'

'What about you, Nonna, where do you want yours? Assuming you do, of course?'

'Definitely! You know I want to squeeze in all the firsts I can. I was thinking the back of my hand, so I can look down and see Paul's lovely face every time I need a pick-me-up. It'll give the nurses something to think about too, if they need to take a blood sample or put a cannula in over the next few weeks.'

'And you don't think Pops will mind?'

'No, we can just order him one of Angela Merkel from that website of yours.'

'Angela Merkel?' Izzy had had her share of weird celebrity crushes in her time, but the news that her grandfather had a thing for Angela Merkel was still a bit of a shock.

'Apparently she reminds him of me.' Eileen shook her head. 'Let's just say after that particular revelation, I moved the calendar Maggie got me so that George would have to look at Paul Hollywood smiling back at him every time he makes a cup of tea.'

Eileen dropped another perfect wink and Izzy wanted to soak in the moment and remember it; her grandmother's head thrown back as her throaty laugh competed with those of her friends. This was what bucket lists were for, making memories that they could all come back to and relive every time they needed to. Even when the person who'd made the bucket list was no longer around.

* * *

After the hospital scan, Anna's consultant had agreed to let her go into labour naturally, if she gave up work completely and took it very easy. Jess and the rest of the team were really relieved that their boss was finally putting her health first, but it meant that the shortage in permanent staff was felt all the more keenly. Ella would hopefully be making two more full-time appointments to the team soon, but in the meantime they were still relying on agency staff to plug the gaps.

They'd also started to have some midwifery students join them on rotation at the unit, to see whether they enjoyed working in the community and to broaden the experience they got in hospital. For the last two weeks, a girl called Lara had been working with the team, although Jess hadn't had the opportunity to get involved with her until now. It was Jess's long day at work, when Dom had Teddy overnight and the social worker seemed to be pleased with how it was going. Jess was glad she had an antenatal class to distract her from missing the little boy and Lara would be joining her to help run it. She was determined to show the younger woman just how rewarding community midwifery could be.

'Are you all ready to go?' Jess met Lara in the staffroom, where she was putting together the boxes for the antenatal class using the list Jess had given her. The session would cover what to expect during labour and delivery and there were several props that Jess used to explain the process, including a model of a baby that looked like it had seen better days.

'I've put in everything on the list and I even managed to get some of the marks off the baby's head.' Lara smiled. 'He looked a bit like my little's sister's dolls after she tried to give them all a makeover with a marker pen she found.'

'The poor thing gets dropped by at least one expectant father in each lesson and quite often the mums too.' Jess returned her smile. 'It's definitely best to get those sort of accidents out of the way when the babies are only plastic though!'

'I'm always terrified of dropping the babies, which is a bit worrying when it's going to be my job. It's such a big responsibility and I just don't want to get anything wrong.'

'From what I hear, you're doing great so far and I'd be more concerned if you weren't worried about doing a good job. Let's get stuck in, shall we?' Jess picked up the larger of the two boxes. 'We're in the training room at the end of the corridor and we should have six couples, if no one has dropped out since last week.'

'Does that happen often?' Lara picked up the other box and followed Jess down the corridor.

'Not usually after week one, because we just cover staying

healthy in pregnancy in the first session. It's this session that sometimes causes dropouts; the reality of labour and delivery is a bit much for some of them. Although it's a bit late by this point to back out either way!'

'It might be better for me if there aren't many people here and I just hope no one asks me any questions I can't answer.'

'You'll know much more than them, don't worry. You'd be surprised by how little most people know about the realities of labour and delivery before they get pregnant.' Jess laughed. 'It's probably a good thing or we might die out as a species otherwise.'

'I'm just glad I've got you there and hopefully I won't freeze up in front of a classroom full of people.'

'You'll be fine, I promise.'

Whatever her doubts about her abilities, Lara was certainly efficient at helping get everything set up and she had a really easy way with the expectant parents-to-be when they started to arrive for the class. She just needed a little push and Jess was certain she'd rise to the occasion and prove to herself she could do it.

'Do you want to run through what to expect from the first signs of labour?' Jess gave Lara a nod of encouragement, but she didn't miss the look of doubt that crossed the younger woman's face. 'You'll be absolutely fine and I'm right here if you get stuck.'

'Right, everyone.' Lara launched straight in, clapping her hands together to still the chatter in the room. 'I know you all know Jess already, but my name's Lara and I'm going to run through the first signs of labour with you, so you all know what to expect. Can anyone tell us what those first signs are?'

'Your waters breaking?' One of the women near the front of the room shouted out the first answer.

'Brilliant, you're right, that's often a sign, but sometimes waters can break without it being the start of labour and some-times the midwife will need to break your waters during labour, if they don't break naturally.' Lara was already getting into her stride. 'Can anyone name another sign that labour might be starting?'

'Lots of pain in the lower back?' Another woman on the other side of the room called out the answer, and she was quickly joined by a third at the back of the room.

'Contractions or a show?'

'Great, thank you. The start of contractions is probably the most common and women often feel them in the lower back, as well as in the abdomen and down into the pelvis.' Lara wrote the answers on the whiteboard as she spoke.

'How will we know if Jenny's really in labour, or if it's just more of those Braxton Hicks things?' The partner of the woman on the left of the room raised his hand. 'She's been having those for weeks and we've already been into the labour ward twice and got sent away!'

'Contractions are usually much more intense, although they can start off similar to Braxton Hicks or period type pains and then get stronger.' Lara turned back towards the group.

'How would you know what they feel like, I bet you've never had a baby, have you?' The partner of the woman at the back of the room, who'd already complained about the lighting being too bright and the chairs being too hard, called out the question. When he'd listed his complaints to Jess before the session even started, she'd been tempted to ask him if he had a sister called Goldilocks. *This chair's too hard, this lighting's too bright.* Instead she'd smiled and told him as politely as she could that both the lighting and the chairs were standard NHS issue for centres like theirs. When he'd pulled a face, it had taken all she had not to tell him there were plenty of private antenatal classes he could pay for if he wanted a more luxurious experience, but she'd bitten her lip, determined to set the best example possible to Lara. If he was intending to pick on the trainee midwife, though, he'd be in real danger of Jess telling him exactly where to go.

'No, I've never had a baby, but—' Lara didn't even manage to finish the sentence before he cut in again.

'So how can *you* possibly know what contractions feel like? I don't think they should allow women to train as midwives before they've had babies of their own.'

'I, er...' Lara looked to Jess for reassurance and she nodded, before turning towards the idiot at the back of the room.

'And what about male midwives? What would you suggest they do before training?' Jess crossed her arms over her chest, digging her hands into her sides to stop herself from wagging a finger at him.

'It's ridiculous a man even wanting to be a midwife. There's got to be a dodgy reason for that as far as I'm concerned and I wouldn't let them near my Angie.'

'Jason, don't be silly.' His partner tried to cut him off, but Jess was more than ready for him.

'And what about women who want to be midwives, but can't have children of their own?' Her scalp was bristling, but somehow she was managing to keep her voice steady and she didn't dare let her thoughts drift to Teddy or there was every chance she'd burst into tears that she wouldn't be able to control. She couldn't let this get personal, no matter how much it already felt like it was.

'They need to choose another career then.' He was so smug and Jess swallowed hard. She wasn't going to let him have the satisfaction of seeing how much this was affecting her.

'Would you say the same thing to a nurse or doctor treating cancer patients? Or a heart surgeon? That they couldn't possibly understand, or treat their patients, because they haven't had cancer or heart disease themselves?'

'That's not the same thing.'

'Why not?' This time Jess didn't need to speak, another man in front of Jason turned around to him instead.

'It just isn't.'

'Well, when you put it that way, who could argue with such a compelling case!' The other man laughed, a few snorts of derision coming from elsewhere in the room before he turned back to the front. 'I know I'm going to regret asking this, Lara, and you've done a grand job of explaining it all so far, but what exactly is a show?'

At that point almost all the women in the room gave in to laughter and, to her absolute credit, Lara handled it all without missing a beat. Jason might have given her a hard time, but it didn't seem to have put her off and she was still buzzing with enthusiasm by the end of the session.

'That was great. I was so nervous, but once I got into my stride, I really enjoyed it.'

'You did brilliantly, especially after what Jason said. Not that I had any doubt that you would.' Jess held the door open for her as they made their way out to the car park. She didn't like the idea of Lara having to get the bus back home after such a long day at work. 'Do you want me to drop you off somewhere, or have you got your car?'

'I haven't passed my test yet. Although I better keep my voice down or that will be another mark against me being a midwife, as far as Jason's concerned.' Lara grinned. 'Thanks for the offer of a lift, but my uncle's picking me up. Actually, that's his car over there.'

'That's lovely of him.' Jess had never had any extended family around who could step in when she needed them, but

Lara was a lovely girl and it was nice to know she had that sort of support.

'Yes, he's brilliant. That's Uncle Dex though, always running around after everyone else.'

'Dex?' Jess had barely said his name before he stepped out of the car, waving and walking towards them. She went hot and cold all at the same time, not knowing whether she should dart back inside the centre and pretend she hadn't seen him, or act like a grown-up and apologise for what she'd said the last time they'd been together. She regretted her words so much and she really missed Dexter and Riley, but there was a strong possibility he was relieved not to have a loose cannon like her in his life. She could hardly blame him after the way she'd acted. It would definitely have been easier to duck and run, but she wanted to talk to Dexter more than she wanted to save face.

'I wondered if you two would get a chance to work together before Lara's placement ended.' Dexter smiled at Jess when he reached them and her stomach flipped. She told herself it was just nerves at how he would react to seeing her again, that was all – even if he was giving her absolutely no cause to worry. He was smiling as if they'd only seen each other the day before and had a nice chat, instead of her all but throwing him out on his ear.

'Why didn't you say she was your niece?'

'I haven't exactly had the chance lately.' Dexter held her gaze and the stomach flipping went into overdrive.

'Do the two of you know each other then?' Lara furrowed her brow and Jess tried not to be bothered by the fact that Dexter clearly hadn't said anything about her. There was no reason why he'd mention one of the foster carers he'd assessed to his niece, especially when she'd blown any chance they'd have of becoming close friends, despite it feeling like it had already happened. He'd probably just been helping Madeline out by keeping an eye on her, after all. She might have thought it was more than that but, after what Dom had done, she couldn't help thinking that there was an agenda behind everything.

'I'm a foster carer and Dexter did my Form F assessment.'

'Oh, I bet you're a brilliant foster carer!' Lara clapped her hands together for the second time that evening. 'She's been so great tonight, giving me the push I needed to give a talk to the antenatal class and backing me up when one of the expectant dads got a bit stroppy.'

'It was all Lara, she handled it like a pro.' Jess shook off the compliment. It was true anyway, Lara would have handled it just as well on her own if she'd needed to.

'Sounds like you've got a mutual appreciation society in the making here.' Dexter smiled again. 'Although it's not surprising, I already know you're both great.'

Jess opened her mouth to respond, but the words wouldn't come out. He was still being so nice and he was acting as if the row they'd had had never happened. Luckily Lara stepped in to fill the silence.

'Don't tell anyone, but Jess is my favourite of the midwives I've shadowed.' The younger woman lowered her voice as if she really was imparting a deep, dark secret instead of just saying what she'd probably have said to all the other midwives she'd worked with so far. At least it meant that Jess could put her flustered state down to Lara's compliment, instead of trying to work out why Dexter was being so nice.

She didn't know if he'd meant what he said any more than Lara had, but the truth was she cared a lot more than she should whether he really thought she was great. She thought he was great, too, but she'd rather the ground opened up and swallowed her than admit that out loud, even to herself, not when she had no idea where their friendship stood any more. It was much easier to pay his niece a compliment.

'Lara's going to be an asset in whatever area of midwifery she goes into, but I can't help hoping she'll choose community midwifery in the end and maybe even join the unit. I'll be keeping everything crossed.'

'I'm definitely going to ask for another placement here and I've got to say that working in the community does appeal to me. Will you still be working at the unit, or are you going to be fostering full-time?'

'I'm part-time at the moment, because I'm looking after a baby boy who's just started having contact with one of his parents. That's where the baby is tonight, on an overnight contact visit.' Jess tried to keep her tone casual, but then she caught Dexter's eye and her throat started to burn, the rest of the sentence in danger of getting stuck there as she fought not to give in to tears. 'So until social services and the courts work out a plan, I'm hoping he can stay with me and I can carry on working part-time. Whatever happens, I don't want to give up the midwifery altogether. Unless it comes down to a straight choice between leaving and keeping the baby.'

'Not many people do one job that does so much good for the world, let alone two.' Dexter reached out and touched her arm as she did her best to swallow down the lump in her throat. It wasn't easy when there were a million questions bubbling up inside her. She desperately wanted to ask Dexter if he thought there was any chance of social services letting her keep Teddy if Dom decided fatherhood was too much like hard work, but she wasn't sure she wanted to hear the answer. Seeing Dexter again was bittersweet, too. She missed him and Riley so much, but she had no idea whether he was just being his usual lovely self, or whether the fact he'd reached out to her meant something more.

She'd couldn't have come out and asked him if he'd missed her too, even if her life depended on it, let alone with his niece there to witness every word they said.

'You do two jobs that really matter, Uncle Dex, the lifeboat and your social work stuff, not to mention looking after Riley.' Lara linked her arm through her uncle's. 'Are we picking him up on the way home?'

'No, he's staying at your Auntie Amanda's tonight. So it's just you and me for a catch-up and a takeaway pizza tonight, kid.'

'Perfect.' Lara turned back to Jess. 'You could always come and join us for pizza if you're free, seeing as you haven't got the baby tonight?'

'I'm meeting a friend for a late dinner, otherwise I'd love to.' Jess crossed the fingers of her right hand. Okay so maybe rushing home to give Luna some food didn't exactly count as *dinner with a friend*, but it wasn't technically a lie.

'No problem, thanks again for tonight. I really enjoyed the challenge, even dealing with Jason! See you soon, hopefully.'

'Definitely.' Jess's voice was muffled as Lara gave her an enthusiastic hug.

'Here, take the keys.' Dexter handed his car keys to Lara as she let go of Jess. 'I won't be a sec, I just need to talk to Jess about something.'

Lara grabbed the keys and sprinted across the car park, whilst Jess's heart broke into a gallop all of its own, wondering if Dexter had decided that having a conversation in the midwifery unit's car park was a good place to tell her what he really thought of her after the way she'd treated him. But he was still smiling.

'It's so nice to see you, Jess.'

'I thought you were done with me, given that you haven't been in touch.' She sounded like a truculent teenager, but she couldn't seem to help herself. She'd known where she was with Dom and how to act around him, but it was harder with Dexter. Jess had more experience of being treated badly when she didn't deserve it, than she did of someone being so nice to her when she didn't deserve that either and it had made her defensive.

'I just wanted to give you some space and I hoped that would give you time to think about what you said and realise that I wasn't spending time with you because I thought you somehow needed me. I was spending time with you because I like you, Jess, and because I wanted to.'

'Oh.' Jess seemed to have lost the ability to string even two words together now.

'Look, I understand if you've got enough on your plate with everything that's going on with Teddy and work on top of that, but if you want to get together, we'd love to see you. Any time. Riley keeps asking me when we'll be coming over to yours again, but I don't want you to feel under any pressure. We've just really missed you.'

'I missed you both too. I'm sorry for the things I said, I didn't mean any of them. It was just the shock of the whole thing with Dom being Teddy's dad... I wanted to lash out at him, but you got it instead because you were the one who was actually there for me.'

'I'll always be there for you, Jess.' For a split second Jess wondered if he was going to kiss her as his eyes never left hers. She was still trying to work out whether she wanted him to or not, when he stepped back. It would have complicated an already messy situation, so the sensible response would have been to experience relief that he'd moved away, but something inside her slumped. 'I'd better get going otherwise Lara's going to be starving, it's been a long day for both of you. Just give me a call when you're free and I'll bring Riley over.'

'That would be lovely and thank you.'

'What for?'

'For understanding why I acted the way I did. I'll call you when I've looked at my rota and the days Dom is having Teddy.' Jess stepped towards him, going up on her tiptoes to kiss his cheek and fighting the urge to brush her lips against his instead. Kissing Dexter in front of his niece would have been really awkward, even if it hadn't been a totally crazy idea. The last thing she needed was more complications and uncertainty. It would be much easier to stay friends and know where they both stood, but more than anything she was just glad she hadn't lost his friendship altogether.

12

There was a cove at the end of Port Agnes beach that could only be reached when the tide was out. It was just beyond the lifeboat station, which was handy because it had caught out more than its fair share of stranded people when the tide had come in faster than they'd expected. Luckily, most holidaymakers didn't even seem to realise it was there and over the years the locals had learned enough from its reputation to play it safe. Jess might have grown up in Bristol and technically been an incomer to Port Agnes, but being a West Country girl didn't seem to be much of an issue for the *real* locals. To be a real local, you had to be a third-generation Port Agnes family at the very least and unlike a lot of the resorts dotted along Cornwall's rugged North Atlantic coast, there were still a good number of qualifying families – Ella's definitely being one of them.

It was Ella who'd introduced Jess to Ocean Cove, and it had quickly become one of her favourite places. The sheltered beach flanked by jagged cliff faces on all sides, which were almost impossible to climb up or down, meant the water was clear and calm until the tide came in and covered the beach up altogether.

Jess had never really been the sunbathing sort, though. A few girls' holidays away with some of the other midwives at the first hospital she'd worked in had reinforced the fact that spending a fortnight lying on the beach wasn't her idea of fun. But spending half an hour sitting on the beach at Ocean Cove, looking out to sea, was like a mini holiday in itself. It was where she did her best thinking, and right now there was so much on her mind that she needed all the help she could get to make sense of it all.

The biggest thing was Teddy. Madeline had commented on how well Dom seemed to be doing and the fact that Teddy's mother had returned to Portugal without even seeing him meant that she was now very unlikely to change her mind before a decision had to be made. Every time Jess held the baby in her arms, she tried to remind herself that he was only on loan to her and that there wasn't any solution to the situation that would mean she'd be allowed to keep him. Madeline had squashed any hope she might have had that he could stay with Jess if the court took a long time to decide what should happen. If Dom followed Natalia's lead and surrendered his parental rights, there were plenty of prospective adoptive parents on the waiting list and she couldn't foresee any lengthy delay. The only chance of that would be if Dom decided he did want to keep the baby, but the social workers didn't think it was a good idea. Then it could end up in a protracted court case and Teddy would probably stay in foster care in the meantime.

The message from her father was still on Jess's mind too. She still hadn't responded to him, and it was something she wanted to talk to Dexter about – but that was another problem in itself. Jess was already having to come to terms with the fact that she was going to end up losing Teddy and she had no idea how she was going to cope with the reality of that when it came. It was hard enough on the nights his cot was empty when he was staying with Dom, and Madeline had told her that if her ex wanted to take over full parental responsibility for Teddy, she doubted there'd be anything to stand in his way. So it could happen any day. Getting close to Dexter would be all too easy, but she hardly had a great track record with relationships and so she couldn't risk losing him – either if she'd misread the signals, or when things went wrong. It wasn't just Dexter either, she felt a pang every time she opened the drawer where she'd put the colouring stuff she'd bought for Riley. Dexter didn't have much more control over how long Riley stayed with him than she did with Teddy. His father could come out of rehab and decide to take Riley away somewhere for a fresh start. She couldn't lose another little boy, not when she was already waking up with a racing heart and tears running down her face, after dreaming that Teddy had gone for good.

Dom had taken Teddy to visit his parents and he'd asked Jess to go with him, but she'd lied and told him she'd be working. Every time she was with Dom, a life as a family, with Teddy at the centre of it, seemed so tantalisingly close and she couldn't think straight. She didn't trust herself not to agree to anything just to keep Teddy in her life, so she'd needed to be at Ocean Cove where she had the chance to really think. The trouble was it didn't matter what scenario she imagined with Teddy, Dom, her father, Dexter or Riley, there wasn't a single one that could solve all her problems and what she needed now was a miracle.

Her head was actually aching with the effort of trying to work out what to do as she spotted the lifeboat racing across the water, bouncing on the waves that were breaking in white peaks a hundred metres or so offshore. Someone out there needed rescuing and when the lifeboat suddenly appeared, answering all their prayers, their body would no doubt sag with relief, knowing they were safe at last. It was so easy to underestimate the feeling of safety until you didn't have it. People tended to crave happiness or excitement instead. But Jess had understood the need to feel safe, above everything else, for a very long time.

When her phone started to ring, for a few seconds she couldn't bring herself to look at it. If it was Dom, she wouldn't be able to resist picking it up in case it was an emergency, but the likelihood was he'd just be pressurising her to join him and Teddy again – grinding her down until she came around to his way of thinking, just like he always had done.

But there was a chance it could be Anna calling and something was happening with the babies and she'd never forgive herself if she didn't answer. Looking down at the screen, she sighed and the temptation to hurl the phone into the sea almost took over. It was Dom, but she couldn't risk ignoring it, not when Teddy was with him.

'This better be important.'

'It's Mum, she's in Truro hospital.' Dom's voice caught on the words. 'I've still got Teddy with me but I'm there with her now, they think it's a heart attack. Please, J-J, can you come?'

'I'll be there as soon as I can.' Disconnecting the call, Jess ran across the beach as fast as the shifting sand beneath her feet would let her. Diane had been the closest thing she'd had to a mum in almost twenty years and whatever had happened between her and Dom, Jess had to get to her, and to Teddy. Before it was too late.

* * *

Screeching to a halt in the hospital car park, Jess checked her mobile phone. *Please, please don't let it be too late.*

✉ From Dom

Mum's been admitted 2 the cardiac ward, I'll be there waiting. Love U
xxxxx

Ignoring Dom's inappropriate terms of endearment until
later, she let the good news sink in. If Diane's life had been
hanging by a thread, then they'd have admitted her to intensive
care. None of that stopped Jess breaking into a run again as she
headed across the hospital grounds to the cardiac unit, especially as Teddy had been dragged into all of the drama.

'Hi, my mother-in-law, Diane Rossiter, has been admitted to
the unit.' Jess was struggling to catch her breath as she spoke to
the nurse on the desk at the entrance to the cardiac ward. Diane
had gone through a whole series of tests before and they'd never
seemed to quite get to the bottom of things, but at least now
she'd get the help she needed.

'Ah yes, your husband said you were on the way.' The young
nurse smiled, but it felt weird for someone to call Dom her
husband. Technically he still was, but she hadn't really thought
of him that way in months. Even saying the name Rossiter made
her mouth feel like it was full of marbles. She'd gone back to
being Kennedy the day after she'd caught Dom with Serena, the
girl from his office, and it had been part of the new start she'd so
desperately needed. Not that she had any particular allegiance
to the name Kennedy either. It was hard to have that when the
man who'd given it to her had turned out not to have any allegiance to her either. 'Just go through the double doors and she's
in bay three, on the right-hand side.'

Jess pushed opened the doors, starting to wonder if she'd
made a mistake coming up to the ward instead of just meeting
Dom by the main entrance to take Teddy home. Diane obviously
wasn't seriously ill, the nurse had been far too smiley and casual
for that. Jess wasn't even sure if her mother-in-law would want to

see her. Dom's mum and stepdad had been devastated when the two of them had split up and not just because they'd just shelled out thousands of pounds on their only son's wedding. Diane had called Jess, begging her to reconsider and give Dom another chance. He'd just been seeking comfort with Serena, according to his mother. It was Jess he loved, they all did. That was the bit that had nearly broken her, because she knew it was true. Diane and Bill had welcomed her into the Rossiter family with open arms, and she'd loved them every bit as much as they loved her. She still did.

'Thank God you're here.' Dom was in the corridor outside the bay and he pulled her into his arms before she could even answer, but there was no sign of Teddy. Despite the fact that at six feet tall, Dom was just shy of a foot taller than her, they'd always fitted together in a weird sort of way. At five feet and half an inch – the half being very important to Jess – her head rested on his chest between the muscles on either side. When they'd first started getting serious, he joked that his body had been designed that way, with just the right amount of space for Jess to fit up against him. It might have been just one more of the corny lines he'd come up with, but she'd loved them back then – latching on to that sense of belonging she'd been searching for. And she'd fallen for Dom, hook, line and sinker.

'How she's doing?' Jess let him hug her – this wasn't the time to be petty – and tried not to think about the fact that she still fitted perfectly up against him, like a piece of a jigsaw slotting into place. 'And where's Teddy?'

'It was definitely a heart attack and she's had a scan to see if they can work out what caused it.' Dom shook his head. 'It scared the hell out of me, and Dad was beside himself. He's taken Teddy for a walk in his pram, just to take five minutes out so he didn't start crying in front of Mum.'

'But she's stable now?' Jess pulled away and Dom nodded. Bill would be taking good care of Teddy, she had no fear of that, and the tension in her spine started to ease now that she knew both Teddy and Diane were okay. 'Can I see her?'

'Absolutely, she knows you're coming and she's really pleased you still want to, now that we're...' When Dom didn't finish the sentence, Jess shrugged.

'Of course I was going to come. Your mum and dad have always been so lovely to me. Is Bill coming back?' Dom had always referred to his stepfather, Bill, as 'Dad'. He'd been part of his life since he was just over a year old. Dom saw his biological father occasionally, but he'd never got on with his stepmother who had three children of her own and, according to Dom, had always favoured them over him. Diane had never been married to his biological father either. So, when she'd married Bill, Dom had been given his name too.

'Yes, but he said he'd only come back when he got himself straight. Dad was in such a state by the time he got here. He was in Pembrokeshire picking up a bull when it happened. He headed straight back when Mum first called to say she was feeling rough. He was almost home when we decided she needed an ambulance, but he got stuck in traffic and didn't make it until half an hour after she'd been admitted. He was terrified he was going to lose her before he got here.' Dom's parents ran a cattle farm on the road into Port Agnes from neighbouring Port Kara. Not long after Jess had met Dom, they'd headed up there for the first time. She'd never realised until then just how big cows were up close.

It was winter and Dom had taken her for a walk across the farm, with fields and fields of these huge beasts whose breath billowed out of their nostrils, creating vapour as it hit the cold air and making them look like dragons. When some of the cows had started following Dom and Jess across the field, he'd held her close and told her the worst thing they could do was break into a run. They just had to stay calm and stand their ground. She'd trusted him totally, even as the cows' hooves thundering across the ground had made her want to run for her life. As soon as they got back to the farm, she'd told him for the first time that she loved him. He'd done enough to convince her that he was the protector she looked for in every relationship, without even knowing it. Until he'd turned out not to be and he'd let her down like every other man before him, including her own father.

'Oh, poor Bill. I can imagine how stressed he is, but hopefully a bit of time with Teddy will help, it always makes me feel better.' Jess saw the look that had crossed Dom's face; if he'd been in any doubt that he had the upper hand he knew it now. 'Maybe, when I've seen your mum, I could go and find Bill and check that he's doing okay. Hopefully I'll be able to reassure him a bit about her condition too?'

'He'd like that and he'd believe you over me, seeing as you're the only medic in the family.' Dom smiled, but she shook her head. She wasn't part of his family any more, but he knew her Achilles heel better than anyone and he was trying every trick in the book. Either way, she was a midwife not an expert in cardiac medicine.

'I don't think my job qualifies me to make a diagnosis, but I might be able to translate what the doctors say into plain English.' Jess moved to get past Dom. 'Is it okay if I go in and see her now?'

'She's in the bed by the window on the right-hand side. I'll just go and get us some drinks, although God knows what hospital coffee's going to taste like. Certainly nothing like the stuff from our Melitta.'

'A coffee would be great, thanks. See you in a bit.' She wasn't going to acknowledge his comment about the coffee machine the other midwives had bought them for their wedding present, which was one of the few things Jess had taken when she'd moved into Puffin's Rest. Dom couldn't accuse her of being greedy about what she took and thankfully they'd never got into a slanging match over possessions – whose books were whose or who should get custody of the John Lewis sofa, where not so long ago they'd sat holding hands watching TV. Nearly all the wedding gifts had been from family members on Dom's side anyway. Splitting up so soon after the wedding had been mortifying; it felt like the guests were barely home from the reception by the time she and Dom were thinking of dividing up their possessions. She'd wanted to return all the gifts, or sell them all and give the money to charity to make her feel less of a fraud. But now Dom had the one thing that Jess would have traded everything for and she had no rights at all to Teddy.

'Oh, sweetheart, look at you! Pretty as a picture, like you always were.' Diane held out her arms, drawing Jess towards her as she walked towards her mother-in-law's bed, like a moth to a flame.

'I'm not going to hurt you if I give you a cuddle, am I?'

'I'm fine. They said it was a very mild heart attack, thank goodness. I'm still attached to all these blessed wires but apart from that I'm not in any pain now.'

'I'll try not to dislodge anything, but I really am going to have to give you a hug.' Jess put her arms around her mother-in-law and squeezed as tightly as she dared. 'You scared us half to death.'

'Now don't you go fussing too, sweetheart.' Diane lay back against the pillows as Jess pulled away. 'It was just a warning sign that's all, one of my arteries has got a bit bunged up or something. They'll sort me out, don't you worry.'

'You've got to start taking better care of yourself. Working fourteen-hour days on the farm is not going to give you your best chance of recuperating.' Jess gave her a level look.

'I know, I know. The doctors have already told me that, you medics are all the same. I don't plan on going anywhere anytime soon, especially not now I've got a grandson.' Diane laughed. 'Now tell me, little Jess, are you okay? I worry about you a lot and we all miss you, you know.'

'I miss you and Bill too, but I'm fine, really.'

'Dom was an idiot and he knows that better than anyone now. I know he doesn't deserve it, but I can't help wishing you'd give him another chance. He told me how much you love Teddy and how well you've been looking after him since... well since you started fostering him.'

'Dom told you about all of that?'

'He's told us everything. He hasn't stop talking about you and he even showed us the reference he had to write when you first applied to start fostering.' Diane pulled a face. 'All the lovely things he should have said to you when you were together; how you'd make such a lovely mum and how you understood better than anyone that making a baby isn't what makes you a parent. You both know that, what with Dom being raised by Bill like he was his own. It was why I could never understand Dom not wanting to consider adoption. But now Teddy's here and you don't even have to worry about going through all of that. The two of you could finally have the family you deserve, Jess, and I'm sure Dom will do whatever it takes to make you happy.'

'Teddy's a wonderful baby and I really do love him, but it's not that simple.' Diane had made it sound so easy and if Jess could just go back to feeling even a hundredth as much for Dom as she once had, then maybe it could have been enough. But every time she looked at him, she heard the words he'd said when they'd discovered she was infertile. He'd seemed to rejoice in the fact that it was 'her fault' and even if some of that had been borne out of fear and relief that his own fertility was intact, it had been incredibly cruel.

Jess had never felt more like she was being pulled into two directions. It didn't matter how many times she told herself she couldn't settle for Dom, every time she looked at Teddy she doubted herself. What if she never got over letting him go, because she knew she could have kept him if she'd been prepared to make that sacrifice?

'It could be that simple if you let it be, Jess. Dom might have a funny way of showing it, but he still loves you and he always has. That woman, the one who gave birth to Teddy, doesn't deserve the title of mother, but you do and he couldn't ask for a better mum.' Diane's tone was getting more and more insistent and the monitor tracking her heart rate was starting to react too.

'Let's not talk about any of this now, you just need to concentrate on getting yourself better. Like you said, you've got a lot to look forward to.' If Jess was using Diane's fluctuating heart rate as an excuse to change the subject, then she wasn't going to feel guilty about it. She didn't want to talk about this to Dom's mother and even if she did, now really wasn't the time or the place. But Diane clearly had other ideas.

'Me and Bill would love to be grandparents and I don't know what will happen with Teddy if you don't want to be with Dom. You and Bill are cut from the same cloth, those special sorts of people who can love other people's children every bit as much as you would do if they were your own flesh and blood, and I just love having kids around. I always wanted more of my own and I can't bear the thought of Teddy not being a part of our lives.'

Diane wasn't giving up easily and it broke Jess's heart to see the pleading look in her eyes, partly because it looked so much like her own reflection every time Dom took Teddy for a contact visit.

'You're going to be such wonderful grandparents. I'm sure Teddy's just the start for you and that Dom will give you a houseful of grandchildren who are going to love having a farm to visit for all their adventures. But, like I said, for now the important thing is to focus on getting you well.' Jess squeezed the older woman's hand, trying to get the picture she'd just painted for Diane out of her head. They were supposed to be her children – hers and Dom's – tearing around the farm and climbing trees, the sort of childhood she'd never had and now all she could envisage was Teddy right at the centre of that picture. But she couldn't be a part of that, even if the image did come to life, and wishing that she could wouldn't do her any good either. She'd learned that wishes were futile a long time ago.

13

There were three other midwives working part-time at the unit who Jess didn't often work with, as they covered the majority of the on-call night shifts. It had always suited the unit to have two teams, even though Anna oversaw them both, and everyone on the other team had their own reasons for wanting to work nights, mostly to fit in around their partners' shifts and manage childcare. It meant that the day team had been able to get even closer to one another, because they generally had evenings free and could get together outside of work more easily. But they also ran all of the clinics and home visits, and with Anna now finally on maternity leave and Jess only working very part-time, they were so busy that they rarely saw each other these days. So when the opportunity to get together with some of the team after they'd finished work finally came along, Jess wasn't going to turn it down.

She'd had to miss the last shift she'd been scheduled to cover as Dom had wanted to be at the hospital with his mother and so Jess had needed to take care of Teddy. As awful as she felt for not being at work, which meant Ella had to arrange extra agency cover, she couldn't pretend she wasn't glad of the extra time with Teddy. He was getting more alert all the time and it didn't seem possible that she wouldn't get to witness the next stage of his development. When he looked at her now, he really seemed like he was trying to focus. He'd just started to develop a social smile too, responding to Jess's cues, and he seemed more fractious every time she handed him over to Dom, almost like he wanted to be with Jess as much as she did with him.

That didn't stop parts of her job being on Jess's mind a lot too though, and when Toni had phoned her to make plans for the get-together with the other midwives, she was already crossing her fingers that her friend would be able to give her the news she wanted to hear.

'How's Daisy Williams getting on?'

'She went to stay with her mum after one of the health visitors managed to get her to admit what was going on, but it looks like it'll only be a temporary thing. It's massively overcrowded at her mum's place and, of course, her husband is making all the promises under the sun that he's changed and it'll never happen again. Daisy was already talking about going back the last time I saw her.' Toni sighed. 'I just hope the council offer to rehouse her quickly, close to her mum and sister, because she's going to need their support more than ever with four young children. Otherwise she'll almost certainly go back to him. I've seen it too many times before, I only wish I hadn't. But at least there are a lot of support services keeping an eye on her too.'

'Going back to him would be the worst thing she could do, even if she thinks it's for the children's sake. Growing up in a household where the parents are at each other's throats is so much worse than growing up with parents who live separately. Lots of the other foster children I was placed with as a kid came from homes where domestic abuse was an issue, or even just where there were toxic rows every day.' Jess shivered, hearing the irony in her own words. That's what she'd be condemning Teddy to if she went back to Dom, just so that she could stay in the baby's life. Dom wasn't the violent sort, but the atmosphere was bound to turn toxic when he started messing around again, which he would without any shadow of a doubt.

'I couldn't agree more, but we've done all we can for now and it's thanks to you that she's taken the first step. It's up to Daisy what happens next. It really is great to have you back, even just part-time, and I can't wait for us all to meet up outside of work. It'll be like old times, except Bobby and I won't have to pretend we don't like each other any more!'

Toni had run through the evening's plans before ending the call and Jess hadn't needed to be asked twice; she couldn't wait to spend time with her friends again either. All the midwives would be heading over to Anna's place for a last get-together before the twins arrived, and Jess would be bringing Teddy with her. Toni and Bobby had said they'd cook dinner and bring it over, Ella and Gwen were making desserts and Izzy and Emily were sorting the drinks, so all Jess had to do was bring the nibbles. She had a bag of treats ready by the door and she was just packing up Teddy's things, when her phone started to ring.

'Jess, it's Ella. There's been a bit of a change of plan! Anna's in labour and I'm with her in the maternity unit at Truro. We've got them to agree for you to be the second midwife, if you can get here in time?'

'I wouldn't miss it for the world! I just need to get Teddy sorted and I'll be right there.' Jess ended the call, her mind already racing. If Teddy had been her child, it would have been easy. She could have rung any of her friends and asked them to take care of him while she was with Anna. Toni and Bobby would have happily stepped in and the practice would have done them good for when their own baby was due in the summer. But as a foster carer, she had to make sure anyone taking care of Teddy had already been approved by her social worker and that left her two choices – Dexter or Dom.

'Hey, J-J, I've been waiting for you to call.' Dom answered the phone just before Jess was about to give up on him.

'Can you come over?' Her first instinct had been to call Dexter, but Dom was Teddy's father and the social work team seemed to think that the best thing for the baby would be to be raised by a biological parent, even if Jess had her doubts.

'I thought you'd never ask! Want me to stop off for dinner and a bottle of something on the way? Should I bring my toothbrush?'

'There's plenty of food in the fridge here and it might be worth you packing an overnight bag, because I've got no idea how long I'm going to be. Anna's in labour and I need to get to Truro as soon as possible, but you could always take Teddy home with you, or I could bring him over if that's easier? I just need to get on the road as quickly as I can.'

'You're not going to be there?' Dom sucked in a breath. 'In that case, I don't think I can. I mean if it was me and you, then it would have been worth giving up watching the footie with the boys, but I did have plans to do that before you called.'

'You do remember Teddy, don't you? Your son?' Jess might actually have given in to the urge to scream if she hadn't thought it would scare the baby. Dom was a selfish pig and he hadn't changed one bit. It was all just an act and barely a couple of weeks in, the mask was already slipping.

'I know, but it's not my day to have him, is it? And like I said, I've made plans.' Dom really was a piece of work and if he'd been there, Jess would have given him a hand gesture to let him know exactly what she thought of his response. How could she even think about getting into a relationship with him again, let alone parenting Teddy with Dom? He wasn't capable of making the sort of sacrifices a good parent would, or even of putting his son's needs over an evening with his friends. There was no way Jess or Teddy would ever be able to rely on him. The little boy deserved so much better than that and so did she.

'Okay, thanks for nothing then.' Ending the phone call by jabbing the red button so hard that it hurt her finger, Jess gritted her teeth. If she called Dexter, he'd drop everything to help her out, but even after their chat when he'd picked Lara up from work, it still felt a bit awkward to ask. If it had been anything other than the delivery of Anna's twins, she probably wouldn't have done it.

'Hi, Jess, it's great to hear from you.' The warmth of Dexter's tone as he answered her call on the second ring was a stark contrast to Dom's; he'd sounded borderline sleazy when he'd hinted that they should spend the night together.

'I'm so sorry to spring this on you, but Anna's gone into labour and I really want to be there, but obviously I can't take Teddy. I've already tried Dom, but he's... busy.'

'No problem. Riley's just flaked out for the night after a busy day at school and he was almost falling asleep over his dinner. But if you can drop Teddy on your way over, I'll put the travel cot up for him here, or I can call one of my sisters, or Lara, to come here and sit with Riley while I come over to yours.'

'That's great, I'll drop him off, I don't want you have to go to even more trouble. Thanks so much, Dexter, I'd be lost without you.'

'I think that might be the nicest thing you've ever said to me!' He laughed and if Jess hadn't been so desperate to get over to Truro, she might even have paused to think about what she'd said, and whether or not it had revealed more than she'd wanted it to. But for once she didn't have time to overthink it.

'I'll be about ten minutes at the most.'

'I'll get everything set up and don't worry about anything. I'm not working tomorrow and I've got Riley, so if you need to catch up on your sleep, just let me know when you're ready and I'll bring him home.'

'Thanks again, you're the best.' It didn't matter if she was revealing too much, sometimes you just had to say what you felt and the comparison between Dom and Dexter couldn't have been more stark. Whatever happened with Teddy, she wanted Dexter to be a part of her life. Good friendships like that didn't come along every day. What she had with him was different to what she had with her friends from the unit, but it was just as valuable. Right now, though, she needed to get to Anna and Ella and prove she was every bit as good a friend to them as Dexter was to her. This was one delivery she definitely didn't want to miss.

* * *

By the time Jess arrived at the hospital, breathless from having run all the way from the car park for the second time in the space of a week, Anna was almost ready to deliver the first twin.

'Talk about perfect timing!' Ella gave her a quick hug and even Anna managed to blow her a kiss, her husband, Brae, clinging on to her hand for dear life. 'The first baby's crowning.'

'I'll leave you guys to it then.' The hospital midwife smiled at Jess, having already got gowned-up ready for the delivery. 'The on-call obstetrician is on her way, but would you believe we've got another twin delivery down the corridor just ahead of you and premature triplets in theatre for a C-section? So all the on-duty doctors are tied up already. There must be something in the water! Just push the emergency button if anything changes though, as one of the doctors is only a few rooms down with the other twins. But fingers crossed that things will carry on going really well for you.'

'We'll be fine. Jess and I have got it covered.' Ella smiled at Jess as the other midwife disappeared. 'I think that's why they were willing for us to take over, it's chaos in here today and two of their midwives have already gone home sick with a bug that's been doing the rounds, so they're waiting for on-call staff to come in. I'm just glad you could make it.'

'Not as glad as I am! Oh, here comes another contraction!' Anna gritted her teeth, giving it all she had, and seconds later the first baby's head was out.

'I really did cut it fine!' Tears were already choking Jess's throat, but Brae was openly crying as his first child emerged into the world. Somehow she managed to get her next sentence out, sounding much calmer than she felt. 'You know the score, Anna, a big push with the next contraction and the rest of baby should follow.'

'Okay, it's coming.' Anna made a guttural sound as the next contraction took hold, Brae stroking his wife's hair away from her forehead.

'Come on, darling, you're doing amazingly.'

'Number one is here.' Ella literally caught hold of the baby and an almighty cry filled the room as she lifted the first twin straight onto Anna's chest.

'It's a boy and he's got my hair!' Brae was laughing and crying all at the same time, his baby son's red hair an obvious hand-me-down from his father.

'Do you want to cut the cord?' Jess looked up at Brae who

was vigorously shaking his head and Anna managed to laugh, despite the extra effort it took.

'We talked about all of this when I said I didn't want deferred cord clamping if I was going to try and deliver the twins naturally.' Anna grinned and she collapsed back against the pillows, adrenaline obviously keeping the total exhaustion, which would inevitably follow a twin delivery, at bay for now. 'And let's just say Brae didn't need to think for long about the offer of cutting the cord before he declined it!'

'I just thought Ella or Jess should have the honour, that's all.' Brae winked and Ella stepped up to do the job in question.

'I'll just check him over quickly and then you can have skin-to-skin contact while we wait for the third stage of labour to complete and for his sibling to arrive. When you start labouring with number two, we'll wrap him up and his daddy can take over for a bit.' Ella picked up the baby. 'Hello, little one, I'm your Auntie Ella.'

'Let's have a look at what's going on with his brother or sister then, shall we?' Jess examined Anna, feeling her abdomen to check the second twin's position. 'The good news is he or she is still head down too, so it doesn't look like we're going to have to turn the baby.'

'Let's just hope number two doesn't decide to start turning somersaults now that it's got more room!' Anna barely had time to get the words out before another contraction took hold. 'Thank God I'm only going to have to do this once, twins don't give you a break!'

'I think that's something you might have to get used to.' Ella grinned at Jess as she came over and placed Anna's newborn son on her chest. 'Everything looks perfect with this little one and he's a great weight for a twin, at six pounds bang on. He's just waiting for his other half.'

'He's not the only one.' Jess hadn't meant to say the words out loud, but watching Brae's total devotion to Anna forced her to admit that that's what she wanted one day. Okay, so she might never give birth herself, but there were other ways of having a family. She deserved to have that unit as a grown-up, having missed out on a family as a child. She couldn't help wondering what Dexter was doing now, whether Teddy was still awake and being soothed to sleep or if Dexter had already managed to get him down and was finally having a few minutes to himself. It didn't matter how a family came about, that was what it was supposed to look like. But today wasn't about Jess or how much she longed for all of that, and thankfully the others didn't seem to realise what she'd meant. All eyes were on Anna, exactly as they should be.

It took almost another fifteen minutes of strong contractions before baby number two started to crown. By that the time one of the doctors had made a flying visit to check on twin one and support Ella's view that he had a clean bill of health, before rushing back down the corridor to another of the multiple births that was underway. It had definitely been a day the hospital staff would never forget.

'Okay, Anna, here we go, the head should be out with your next contraction.' Jess looked up at her friend, who had her eyes shut.

'I'm so knackered, I don't think I can do it.'

'Yes you can, my angel, you can do anything, and I love you so much.' Brae dropped a kiss on her forehead and Anna's eyes opened, fresh determination taking over as she gripped his hand.

'I love you too, but I've got about three more pushes in me and that's it.'

'Let's make them count then.' Jess looked at Anna, who nodded in response.

'I've got another contraction coming.' Putting her chin to her chest, Anna gave it everything she had for a second time, as baby number two's head finally emerged.

'Well done, sweetheart.' Ella was on Anna's other side, holding the opposite hand to Brae, who had the first twin nestled in the crook of his other arm, already handling fatherhood like a pro. Everyone in the room was willing the second twin to make its safe arrival and complete Anna and Brae's brand-new family.

'One thing's for sure, we've got another redhead.' Jess grinned. Brae certainly had strong genes and there'd be no doubting who the babies belonged to, even if twin number two needed a bit more help than its brother and ended up having to spend some time in special care, as almost half of twin deliveries did.

'I'm going to be the odd one out, seeing as my red comes out of a bottle these days!' Anna's smile slid off her face as another contraction took hold and there was an echo of the sound she'd made with twin one as she pushed his sibling into the world and into Jess's arms.

'That's twin number two!' Jess held her breath for a second as the baby stayed silent, rubbing its body to stimulate the first breath. Thankfully it only took seconds to come and when it did, it filled the room, meaning Jess could finally breathe out too. Lifting the baby onto Anna's chest, she was dying to see her friend's reaction. 'Have you seen what you've got?'

'It's a girl!' Brae was crying so hard now he could hardly get the words out. 'I've got everything I ever wanted because of you.'

'Me too, I love you so much.' Anna sank back into the pillows again and this time not even adrenaline could mask the exhaustion. 'And I'm not going to be completely outnumbered by boys, like I thought I might be!'

'You've got the perfect family.' Jess had given up even trying to hold the tears back now. They were tears of pure joy for Anna and Brae. They were both so lovely and the twins were going to be the luckiest children in the world to have them as their mum and dad. 'Let's just get your gorgeous girl checked over, shall we? And give her some skin-to-skin contact, then you can start family life properly.'

Ten minutes later, the third stage of labour for twin number two had been completed. All of the little girl's checks had been done too and she'd been weighed, coming in at just over five and half pounds with neither of the twins looking like they'd need any time in special care. With one twin in the crook of each arm, Anna's face was shining and Brae couldn't stop smiling and snapping away with his mobile phone. He must have taken more than a hundred photos of his new family already.

'Let's get a picture of the babies with the wonderful midwives who delivered them, then they'll always know who helped bring them into the world.' Brae looked at Anna, who nodded. 'So, Ella, that's you with Kit, and Jess with Merryn.'

'Proper Cornish names, I love it and Dad is really going to approve!' Ella grinned as she scooped baby Kit up from Anna's arms. Jess knew all about Ella's father, Jago, trying to fix her up with Brae when she'd first returned to Port Agnes from London, but she'd fallen for an incomer instead – even if Dan and her father had ended up being really close. Jago was clearly still very fond of Brae, though, and he'd no doubt go up even higher in his estimation as a result of choosing the names he had. Ella's full name was Ysella, equally traditionally Cornish, although her parents seemed to be the only people who called her that.

'Merryn is such a pretty name.' Jess looked down at the baby girl she'd lifted into her arms, her long eyelashes as red as her hair. 'What does it mean?'

'It's a saint's name.' Brae smiled. 'I just hope that's going to be an omen for good behaviour!'

'Either way, I think Jess and I will always be willing to help out with babysitting our special deliveries, won't we?' Ella rocked Kit gently in her arms as she spoke.

'Absolutely.' Jess was already worried that Brae might have to pry his daughter out of her arms; she couldn't stop looking at how perfect the little girl was, just like Teddy. It was crazy when she'd delivered so many babies over the years, but Merryn and Kit were always going to be special, and there was no denying the place Teddy already had in her heart.

'It's just as well you've offered.' Anna raised her eyebrows, a slow smile spreading across her face. 'Because I'd expect nothing less from their godmothers!'

'Really?' Jess's eyes filled with tears again as Anna and Brae both nodded.

'That's if you're willing to? Ella already knew about it, because we've asked Dan to be godfather too, but I wanted to wait until the twins were here to ask you. You've had so much to deal with lately and I didn't want you to feel pressured.' Anna must have known what her answer would be, even before Jess responded with the sort of enthusiasm that couldn't leave her friend in any doubt about how thrilled she was.

'Just try stopping me! These two are going to smothered in love by their godparents and they'll probably be fed up with the sight of me by the time they turn eighteen, but I promise to be there for them whenever they need me.'

'We knew what we were doing when we picked their godparents and you're officially part of our family now.' Anna smiled and Jess had to blink back the tears that had filled her eyes again.

Looking down at her new goddaughter, she wanted to hold on to the moment forever. When Anna married Brae, she'd made a speech about finding a whole new family in Port Agnes. In that moment, staring down at Merryn, Jess understood every word she'd said. Even if social services decided to remove Teddy from her life forever, no one was going to stop her being a part of the twins' lives and for the first time since discovering Teddy was Dom's son, she felt genuinely hopeful that things could be okay again, whatever the future held. It still hurt like hell to imagine her life without Teddy in it and she'd do almost anything to stop that from happening, but she knew now that it didn't include going back to Dom. That was one sacrifice she just couldn't make, even for Teddy.

14

Jess was still so angry with Dom that, for once, she'd decided to take Madeline up on her offer to drop Teddy over to his house for contact. She didn't want him coming to Puffin's Rest and she didn't want to have to see him at his own place either. After the way he'd disregarded Teddy on the night Anna's twins were born, she'd become more and more determined that, whatever it meant for her, she needed to make sure that social services saw what sort of man her ex really was.

'When will you make a decision about what's happening with Teddy?' Jess had been psyching herself up to ask the question ever since Madeline had arrived.

'The assessments with his father have all gone well from our point of view and if Dominic feels ready to take on parental responsibility, we don't have any grounds to block that.'

'Huh!' Jess couldn't hold back her response and Madeline gave her a quizzical look.

'Do you think we should have concerns, then?'

'He doesn't prioritise Teddy, not the way he should.'

'What do you mean?'

'I asked him to take Teddy the other night, when one of my best friends went into labour and I was assisting with the delivery, but he told me he already had plans to watch football with his mates.' Jess stared at Madeline's face, waiting for the reaction she was sure was coming – when the social worker would finally see the truth about Dom too – except it didn't.

'Ah yes, he told me about that. Apparently, it was the anniversary of one of his friends losing his father and the whole group of them had decided to get together to support his friend through that. He said that any other time he'd have dropped everything to have Teddy, but he was worried what effect it might have on his friend if he let him down.'

'Funny that, because he was perfectly willing to drop his plans to be with his friend when he thought I was inviting him over to spend the night here.' Jess sounded every bit as bitter as she felt, but it was such a disappointment that Dom had managed to fool Madeline into believing he was this great guy. But then the social worker's job was just to assess if Dom could be a 'good enough' parent; it was Jess who couldn't stand the idea of that being all Teddy ended up with.

'Are you sure that all of this – how you feel about Dominic – isn't because of the history you two share? Don't get me wrong, Jess, you've been brilliant to be as open to these arrangements as you have been, especially after the way you discovered that Dom had fathered a child with someone else, but you're only human.'

'It's got nothing to do with that!' Jess was annoyed at herself for snapping, because it fitted Madeline's view that she was overly emotional when it came to Dom and that she couldn't see the truth of the situation, but she couldn't help reacting. Time was running out and she had to make sure she did all she could to do the best for Teddy. 'What if Dom decides he doesn't want to take responsibility for his son, what happens then?'

'If Dominic and Natalia both decide not to take parental responsibility for Teddy, then he'll be put up for adoption.' For the first time Madeline's face softened. 'But I'm really sorry, Jess, like I said before, even if that's the case, there's absolutely no chance of Teddy staying with you.'

'What about if Natalia agreed to it?' Jess knew she was clutching at straws, but the social worker was already shaking her head.

'Even on the off-chance that both she and Dominic agreed they wanted you to take Teddy, it's not just their decision to make. It's the job of social services and the courts to make sure we're acting in Teddy's best interests and your relationship with Dominic is just too complicated for you to raise Teddy. There'd be a risk that Dominic wouldn't be able to step back and allow you to make parental decisions, even after he'd given up his rights, or that Dominic would be in and out of Teddy's life. What children need is stability and clear boundaries and I don't think any court would see you being able to provide those things for him, not when your relationship with Dominic is the way it is.'

'I haven't even got a relationship with Dom!' Her voice had become high-pitched and whiney, like a child begging for something they really wanted, but no amount of pleading was going to change Madeline's mind. She was probably right, too, but that didn't make it any easier to accept.

'I'm going to have to take Teddy now, Jess, or I'll be late to drop him off, but I really think it would be a good idea for you to make an appointment with one of the therapy team to talk about how you're feeling. This must be really tough for you and anyone can see how much you care for Teddy, but I know Dexter will have gone through all of this with you during your assessment. Sometimes placement endings can be the hardest part of fostering.'

'Thanks, but I'll be fine. I've been through enough endings in my life to know I can survive them.' Jess screwed up her eyes to stop the tears that were threatening to escape. She'd survive this, like she'd survived everything else, but she couldn't help wondering whether just surviving was enough when she wanted so much more.

* * *

Bobby still hadn't quite broken the habit of leaping away from Toni every time one of the other midwives came into the staffroom. They'd tried to keep their relationship a secret, but in reality they'd always been pretty terrible at keeping things quiet, though the other midwives had played along with it because they'd known it was what Toni wanted. When Jess arrived in the staffroom, Bobby had his hand resting on Toni's growing bump and it had cheered her up no end to see the look on her friends' faces as they shared a moment together. She was only sorry that her turning up had spoiled it.

'I didn't mean to interrupt.'

'You didn't.' Bobby smiled. 'It's just that Toni's feeling the baby moving now and I wanted to see if I could feel it from the outside too. For a moment I was almost sure I could, but with an anterior placenta I think it might be wishful thinking.'

'It'll just be gas.' Gwen, who'd arrived seconds after Jess with Izzy right behind her, was as pragmatic as ever. 'I doubt very much you could feel anything this early from the outside, not even with hands as soft as yours, Bobby.'

'Are you implying that these aren't the hands of someone who does *real men's work*?' Bobby laughed, having no doubt heard those kind of digs hundreds of times before.

'Not at all, soft hands are definitely a plus for a midwife of any gender.' Gwen dropped her bag on one of the desks. 'After all, no one wants someone with rough hands covered in calluses rummaging around in their cervix.'

'To be fair she's got a point.' Toni shot a look in Jess's direction. 'And I vote that Gwen inducts all of the new midwives who join us from now on, to make sure they've all got a very thorough skincare regime!'

'Is there any news on whether Ella's managed to recruit anyone?' Izzy raised her eyebrows. 'It would be lovely not to be the new girl! I know Emily's hoping there'll be a couple more midwifery care assistants appointed too.'

'The really good news is that Frankie is coming home!' Bobby delivered the announcement with the relish it deserved. Frankie was a midwifery care assistant, who'd been one of the original team at the unit, but had spent most of the past year in New Zealand. She'd gone over to visit her daughter after the breakdown of her marriage, but when her daughter's marriage had followed suit, the visit had kept getting extended, until the rest of the team had started to worry that she'd never come home.

'That's brilliant news!' Being at the unit was working its magic with Jess all over again and she was already feeling so much better. Frankie had been another mother figure to some of the midwives, including Jess, and it would be brilliant to have her home again, especially after all she'd been through over the past year or so. It was also a reminder that everyone went through tough times, no matter how settled their lives might look from the outside. Frankie's divorce had seemed to come out of the blue and what had happened to her daughter over in New Zealand had been even more of a shock.

'I can't wait to see her, so much has happened since she left.' Toni shook her head, as if she couldn't believe it herself. 'She'll be desperate to see Anna's twins and she might even be able to get involved in the delivery of this one.'

'I thought you might want it to just be you and Bobby, in a birthing pool, in your lounge, with candlelight and whale music.' Jess was trying not to smile, knowing what Toni's reaction would be before she even started to speak.

'You've got to be joking! I want to have complete access to *all* the drugs on offer, if I need them!'

'At least you're realistic about your pain threshold.' Bobby slipped an arm around the point where Toni's waist used to be. 'I mean you did scream like a banshee for about ten minutes last night, after you stubbed your toe!'

'Oh very funny, well let's see if you're laughing when you've tried out the labour simulator I've ordered from Amazon. We'll see who's screaming then.'

'Can we all come and watch?' Jess couldn't help laughing this time.

'Only if Gwen makes one of her cakes.' Toni looked at the oldest member of their team, who was happily nodding.

'I'll make a whole buffet to keep us going. After all, a labour simulator's only really going to work if Bobby's hooked up to it for the full eight hours of an average first labour.'

'I feel like I'm seriously being ganged up on here.' Bobby rolled his eyes. 'I'm just going to have to hope that one of Ella's new midwifery recruits is a man.'

'Did I hear someone taking my name in vain?' Ella came into the staffroom, looking like she'd pulled an all-nighter. It must have been tough managing the unit by herself now that Anna was on maternity leave and trying to plug the gaps in the team too. Especially since the area they provided maternity services to had been extended by another twenty square miles.

'We were just talking about whether you'd managed to fill the vacant posts?' Jess could potentially be available to come back to work full-time very soon, if Dom decided he was ready to take care of Teddy on a permanent basis. If that happened, she wasn't sure about continuing to foster at all any more. She'd thought she'd known what the difficult parts of fostering would be, the challenging behaviours she might experience from the children or their birth families, and the rejection she might face from children who didn't want a foster carer to be a part of their lives at all. But she hadn't really thought about how the endings were going to affect her, because she'd only ever really imagined being a respite carer. She just wasn't sure she wanted to keep putting herself through that, especially when she hadn't even had to say goodbye to Teddy yet and it was already breaking her heart.

'I think I've made two new appointments, one temporary full-time role to cover my job, while I'm doing Anna's, and one part-time, but with enough flexibility to cover full-time if needs be, depending on how many hours Jess is doing around her fostering. We've also got a new MCA starting and we'll have midwifery students on a more regular basis, so we might even be able to get a few more tea breaks!'

'That sounds like a great idea and I think we should start as we mean to go on.' Bobby looked at Ella. 'Can I get you a tea or coffee to celebrate?'

'I could murder a coffee. Mum's already sent me through the wedding planning itinerary for the next week. We've got the florist tomorrow night, a tasting menu on Friday and we're going to see three different bands at the weekend. There's still ages to go before we get married and it's already taking over my life.' Ella looked exhausted at the thought of it. 'Unbelievably we've got to rock up at two pubs and a strangers' wedding at the hotel on St Agnes Island just to watch the bands performing. It's getting more out of hand every day.'

'Why don't you just tell your mum that it's not what you want?' Toni handed her cup to Bobby as she spoke, and he started loading up a tray with other stray cups, ready to make the round of drinks.

'The problem is this is low-key in Mum's book. She'd have a flotilla coming into the harbour at Port Agnes if she had her way, with me on the boat at the front like a carnival queen. I've already cut the numbers down from two hundred to eighty, so I've got to pick my battles where I can.'

'And how does Dan feel about all of this?' Jess couldn't see Dan as the sort who'd want a big fuss on his wedding day either, but he'd also be the kind of person who'd do anything to make Ella happy, even if that meant going along with whatever his new in-laws wanted.

'He doesn't mind, he's just—' Ella held up a hand as the phone on her desk started to ring. 'Sorry, I better get this.'

Jess was straining to hear what she was saying, given the way her mouth had turned down at the corners just seconds into the call. Even piecing it together from one side of the conversation, it was obvious it wasn't good news.

'At Ocean Cove? Okay and how long have they been stranded?' Ella paused as whoever was on the other end of the line relayed the information. 'And do you know when the baby's due? Any injuries as far as you know? Right, okay, I'll send a team down to the lifeboat station and we'll get an ambulance en route too.'

'What's wrong?' Jess had picked up enough of the conversation to know that whatever had happened, it was definitely an emergency.

'There's a couple trapped on the rocks at Ocean Cove. The

woman's mother rang the coastguard to report that her daughter, who's eight months pregnant, had called her and that the daughter and her husband were stranded. They got caught out after going on an early dog walk and not realising what happens when the tide comes in there. Apparently they were planning to try and walk around the headland before the tide cut them off completely, but they haven't answered any calls since and the coastguard is sending the lifeboat out.'

'Oh God, that doesn't sound good.' Toni widened her eyes.

'I know and here I am moaning about getting too much help for my wedding.' Ella glanced at the whiteboard. 'I said I'd send a couple of midwives down to the lifeboat station, to see if we can do anything when they bring the woman in. I don't think it's a good idea for you to go, Toni. Izzy and Bobby have got clinics this morning, and Gwen's supposed to be covering any deliveries, which you can support her with Toni, so it's probably best if I do it. If I need help, I'll just have to call and take Bobby or Izzy out of clinic.'

'I can come.' Jess was already starting to pack a bag as she spoke.

'Are you sure? You're only supposed to be doing a half-day shift today and there's no way of knowing what this might turn into.'

'Dom has got Teddy all day and the flat feels completely empty when he's not there, so I'm in no hurry to go home.'

'You're a total star, Jess.' Ella gave her a quick hug before following suit and starting to pack a bag with all the stuff they might need. 'I don't know what we'd do without you.'

'I'm not intending to let you find out!' Jess could feel the adrenaline running through her veins already. Being a midwife was sometimes the toughest job in the world, but it was also the best and whatever else happened, she was determined to keep reminding herself how lucky she was and how far she'd come from the days of couch surfing on friends' sofas because she didn't have a home to call her own.

* * *

There was a big crowd on the south end of the beach where the Port Agnes lifeboat station was situated. One woman was sobbing hysterically and being supported by a group of others who Jess could only assume were the family and friends of the missing couple. Miles Denvers was also on the beach. He was the new editor of the *Three Ports News* and Jess had met him when he'd come in to interview all of the midwives for an article on community heroes. Right now he had a camera with a tele-scopic lens slung around his neck, clearly keen to capture the drama of the rescue however it might turn out.

Andy Jenson, a long-standing member of the lifeboat crew, was also on the beach. If anyone knew what was going on, it would be Andy.

'Any update on whether they've found them?' Jess kept her voice at a low register; the last thing she wanted was to make the missing couple's friends and family panic any more than they already were.

'They're doing the first sweep now and if they don't find them this time, they'll go out again. Mandy, the woman whose daughter's missing, is absolutely convinced they're at Ocean Cove. They're here on a family holiday, they have the same week in March every year before it starts to get really busy from Easter onwards. There are twenty of them all told apparently, and they rent out the same row of cottages on Church Street every time they're here too.'

'So they know the area pretty well, then?' Ella asked the

question that had been on the tip of Jess's tongue. If they knew anything about Ocean Cove, they'd know it got cut off scarily fast at high tide.

'They only discovered the cove this time around, so Mandy said. And they've been taking their dog there every day, but she didn't seem to know anything about the tide cutting the cove off, so I don't suppose they did either. I guess they just struck lucky the rest of the time. I've lost count of the amount of people we've rescued from there over the years and we must have asked the council twenty or thirty times to put some warning signs up.' Andy sighed. 'They said it would spoil the look of the cove! Never mind the lives that will be lost, sooner or later, if they don't do something about it. I just hope it's not too late.'

'Do you know the couple's names?' Jess shivered, despite the appearance of the sun from behind the early-morning cloud. They must be terrified stranded on the rocks, with no way to protect themselves or their unborn baby. The sky was getting bluer by the second and, given that the Easter holidays had started already, the beach would soon get much busier with holidaymakers and locals alike, making the most of the spring sunshine. Then Mandy and her family would have an even bigger crowd of onlookers watching the drama unfold.

'They're called Tasha and Adam. They're pretty young, too, only in their early twenties apparently, but youth might stand them in good stead if it comes to having to wait in the water at this time of year.' Even a battle-hardened lifeboat crewman like Andy shuddered at the prospect. 'But with her being eight months pregnant, the lads were desperate to find her on the first sweep.'

'Please God they do.' Jess had barely said the words before a roar came up from the crowd as the lifeboat appeared from behind the rocks that hid Ocean Cove from view. The cheering was getting louder and Miles moved along the beach with his camera, ready to capture the moment when the drama reached its conclusion. But as Jess and Ella followed Andy, running along the beach to the launch ramp at the lifeboat station, the coxswain was standing on deck waving his arms across one another, making it obvious they hadn't found the stranded couple, even before he called out.

'No sign on sweep one, so we're going out again.' He shouted over to Andy. 'Are the midwives here yet? We'd like one on board for sweep two, just in case.'

'This is them.' Andy gestured towards Jess and Ella. 'I'll get the dinghy and bring one of them out to you, if that's okay with you girls?'

'I'll do it.' Jess volunteered as Andy turned towards them, before Ella even had the chance. The sea wasn't rough and the risk to whoever volunteered was low. But even if it had been dangerous, Jess would have wanted to be the one to go. Ella had a lot more to lose than she did and a lot more people who'd miss her if anything happened. She couldn't let Ella know that was the reason, though, or she'd never agree to it. 'I did a couple of emergency medicine training courses last year when I was thinking about volunteering for the search and rescue team, which might help if they've got injuries. And Ella will be far better at managing the family's anxieties than me, I'd probably just make them panic more.'

'No you wouldn't, but you're right that you've got more experience with emergency medicine than me. It's more likely they'll need that sort of help, than for Tasha to actually have gone into labour.' Ella looked at Andy. 'They might make out in films that women go into labour from shock all the time, but it's really not that common.'

'That's settled then.' Andy waded into the water as he

spoke, untying the motorised dinghy from the side of the ramp. 'Let's get you out there, Jess, and get this second sweep underway.'

'I'm right behind you.'

'Better make sure Miles gets your best side, because if this doesn't make the front page of the *Three Ports News* I'll eat my mother-in-law's Sunday roast.' Andy laughed, despite the tenseness of the situation. 'And with beef as dried up as she makes it, that's no mean feat. I could resole my shoes with it.'

'Good luck!' Ella's voice drifted on the breeze and Jess raised a hand in response as she waded into the water. As soon as she climbed in and Andy started up the dinghy, she could barely even hear the crowd gathered on the shoreline, which seemed to be getting bigger with every passing moment.

'I'll take you up to the fixed ladder and keep the dinghy as steady as I can,' Andy shouted as they approached the lifeboat and he cut the engine, 'but the lads on board will give you a hand up if you need it.'

'I'll be fine.' Jess silently prayed that her optimism wouldn't prove misplaced. Never mind that a midwife falling into the sea mid-rescue would definitely give Miles his front page, she definitely didn't want to delay the lifeboat making its second sweep any longer than she had to.

'Right, up you go then.' Andy held on to the bottom of the ladder, keeping the dinghy from drifting away as Jess stepped out and grabbed the metal poles with both hands. If she'd known she was going to be getting on board a lifeboat she'd probably have rethought her footwear and worn shoes with a lot more grip on the sole, especially as they were already soaking wet. Maybe she could even have asked Andy for some of his mother-in-law's roast beef. If she slipped and it came down to upper body strength, she was going to be in trouble, seeing as the average seven-year-old could probably beat her in an arm wrestle.

'I'm just going to grab hold of your arm to steady you when you climb over.' The voice was familiar and as she looked up, Jess found herself staring straight into Dexter's face. She'd briefly wondered if he might be on duty, but the odds had seemed pretty long, seeing as he was doing even fewer shifts with the lifeboat at the moment than she was doing at the midwifery unit, what with fitting in his freelance work and looking after Riley. He was obviously just as surprised to come face to face with her. 'Well, I certainly wasn't expecting to see you today.'

'Me neither.' Jess caught her foot as she lifted it over the top rail of the boat and she'd have gone sprawling onto the deck if Dexter hadn't been there to catch her. Lying in his arms she couldn't help thinking it would have been less embarrassing if he'd let her hit the ground. Their faces were only inches apart and she couldn't help wondering what it would have been like to kiss him, now that his mouth was so tantalisingly close to hers. Thank God he couldn't read her mind.

'If you're going to throw yourself at me like that, people will talk!' He grinned, looking strangely even more at home on board the boat than he did in his day job. Being completely windswept really suited him, whereas Jess probably already looked like she'd been plugged into an electric socket.

'It won't be the first time I've been the subject of gossip in Port Agnes.' Jess tried not to notice how many different colours Dexter's irises were made up of as the boat started to move out for the second sweep – the greys and blues that seemed to mirror the sea he appeared to be so at home on. She was still having to hold on to him to steady herself, but it was only because she was having trouble finding her sea legs, despite the calmness of the water, and because she was so worried about the missing couple. It couldn't possibly be anything else.

'It's good you're here, either way.' Dexter smiled again, as the coxswain turned the boat back out to sea. 'I don't think any of us fancied getting involved in a delivery.'

'I just hope we find them.' Jess lost her footing again, accidentally leaning into him even harder as the boat bounced against the waves. Grabbing hold of the side rail to stop it happening a third time, she had to shout to be heard. 'How high was the water when you first went past Ocean Cove?'

'There was no sign of the beach at all and we couldn't see them on the rocks above it either. Not that there were many places to climb, even if we weren't talking about a heavily pregnant woman.' Dexter moved closer to her so he didn't have to work quite so hard to shout to be heard, suddenly looking much more serious. 'We're just hoping that somehow they got out on the Port Kara side of the cove, even though it's a much longer walk, before the tide closed in completely. The beach is a bit wider on that side and you could probably scramble over the rocks if you had to.'

'Are the Port Kara crew out looking too?'

'Whoever finds them has got to stand the other crew a round of drinks.' He shook his head. 'Sorry, you probably think having a wager like that is really bad, but a dark sense of humour is the only thing that gets us through sometimes.'

'When I worked at the hospital we were all like that, especially the paramedics. So I get it.' They locked eyes as she spoke and her stomach dipped. This wasn't good and suddenly she found herself wishing she'd been paired with anyone but Dexter. Her head was already full of the situation with Teddy and Dom and the terror that when she got home, there'd be a message waiting from Madeline to tell her that the arrangements had already been made for Dom to keep the baby full-time. Deep down, she knew that was not how it would be handled, but she was still terrified of getting the news that meant the same thing – the decision had been made. So worrying about how much she liked Dexter too was a complete waste of energy. She couldn't control either situation and Dexter hadn't once made a move to suggest he wanted to be more than friends, even if he had hinted at it. It was probably just her brain's way of distracting her from the gravity of the situation, like Dexter's wager with the other lifeboat crew, because Teddy wasn't the only baby she was at risk of losing if they didn't find the missing couple soon.

'Either way, let's just hope one of the crews will have to buy a round of drinks, the alternative doesn't bear thinking about.' Dexter turned away as they rounded the rocks and Ocean Cove came into view. Jess held her breath – thoughts about anything other than finding the stranded couple carried away on the breeze.

'Everyone, eyes on the cliffs, they've got to be here some-where.' The coxswain shouted the instruction as the boat moved closer to the rocky cliff face; the beach where Tasha and Adam had been walking their dog, less than an hour earlier, completely hidden beneath the waves.

'Did you hear that?' It was Dexter who called out first, making Jess jump because she'd been staring so intently at the cliff face. 'I'm sure that was a dog, up on the left-hand side of the cliffs.'

'I'll check it out.' The coxswain manoeuvred the boat closer to the jagged edge, where shards of rock looked as though they were just waiting to impale anyone stupid or desperate enough to try and clamber up the side of the cliff.

'There, look! About forty feet above sea level.' Dexter called out again and Jess looked in the direction he was pointing. At first she didn't see anything, but then there it was, a small brown and white dog, almost disappearing against the cliffs and scaling the rock face with almost as much skill as a mountain goat. 'That's got to be Adam and Tasha's dog.'

'Hello! Tasha and Adam, can you hear us?' The coxswain spoke into the sound system that projected from a megaphone on the front of the boat. 'We can see your dog but we can't see you. If it's safe to do so, without risk of you falling, you need to try and signal to let us know where you are.'

For a moment the only sound was the waves breaking against the rocks and the little dog yapping. Jess hadn't even realised she was holding her breath again until she heard a male voice call out.

'We're up here, but Tasha's hurt.'

'We can help you, but we need to know exactly where you are.' The coxswain's voice echoed as it amplified and bounced against the rocks.

'We're here!' Finally Adam stood up, so he could be seen from his position in between two enormous jagged rocks about thirty feet above sea level. He was shouting something else, but the lifeboat was too far away for Jess to be able to hear what it was.

'I'm sending two of the crew over to get you. They'll climb up and bring you both back to safety.' The coxswain sounded so certain that, for a moment, even Jess felt her shoulders relax. It was going to be all right, the coxswain had said so, which meant it must be true.

'Right, Dex and Johnny, you've got the most climbing experience, up you go.' The coxswain didn't wait for their agreement, turning towards the only female crew member instead. 'Gemma, if you can check everything in the first aid kit please, I'll radio back to the station and make sure they've got the ambulance on standby and they can update the family on what's going on.'

'I should go over with Dexter and Johnny.' For the second time in less than twenty minutes the words were out of Jess's mouth before she'd even had a chance to work out if she should be saying them.

'I don't think that's a good idea. For a start you'd have to be able to scale the rock face without all of the proper equipment.'

'I've got climbing experience, I've done loads of climbs with Dorton's Adventure Centre in Port Kara, and I'm trained in emergency medicine. If Tasha has got a serious injury she might need me to stabilise it before you can move her. Plus I'll be able to secure the harness so that it doesn't put the baby at any more risk than necessary.'

'What's your swimming like?' The coxswain narrowed his eyes. 'It might not look all that rough today, but you'd be surprised how tough it can be with the current against you and it's still freezing cold at this time of year.'

'I'll be fine.' Jess wasn't sure she would be, but if the coxswain – or anyone else – even tried to stop her, then she'd jump over the side. Maybe it was foolhardy, but she'd never been able to refuse if someone needed her help, and she wasn't going to start today.

'Just make sure you get a life jacket on and go as carefully as you can.' The coxswain nodded and turned to Dexter. 'Take the abseiling gear and harness for the descent back down, but if you don't think you can do it when you get up there, we're just going to have to wait for the helicopter.'

'The air-sea rescue were called out to another job near Holly Bay.' Dexter filled Jess in as he helped her with her life jacket. 'Some kids went out too far in a dinghy and they've been scouring the area, trying to find them. It's not been a good day on this stretch of coast so far. But hopefully we won't need them because there's no way of knowing how long they'll take.'

'I really hope we don't.' Jess looked over the edge of the boat as the coxswain manoeuvred it slightly away from the cliffs, so they could launch the on-board dinghy over the edge. The water in the cove looked much darker than on the main beach back at Port Agnes and if they went in at any point, Jess had no doubt it was going to be every bit as cold as the coxswain had warned her it would be.

Dexter and his colleague, Johnny, went down the ladder first, helping Jess steady herself after she reached the lowest visible rung of the ladder and get seated in the dinghy.

'You okay?' Dexter shouted over his shoulder to Jess, who nodded in response as Johnny steered the small boat towards the edge of the cliff. Seconds later they were as close as they were going to get. The rocks directly below the ledge where Adam had stood were too jagged to tie the boat onto, even Jess could see that. There was a good chance it could be ripped to shreds if they tried it and the sea suddenly got a lot rougher.

'I think this is the best we can do.' Johnny cut the engines about twenty feet away from where they needed to be.

'Me too.' Dexter stood up. 'I'll tie the dinghy on here, there's a decent shard of rock I can secure the rope around which should hold it until we get back, but we're going to have to jump in and swim from here to the climbing point.'

'Maybe you should go first?' Johnny looked at Jess, as he spoke. 'That way, we can tie the rope around you and one of us can spot you until you can get a foothold on the cliff and pull you back in if you get into trouble.'

'Sounds like a good idea.' Jess was still determined to do her best for Tasha and Adam, but she had to admit that the closer to the cliff face they got, the rougher the water seemed to be. She might have been trying to convince herself and the coxswain that she'd be fine when it came to the swimming part, but now she wasn't so sure. The fact that she'd only learnt to swim as an adult, and then only in preparation for her honeymoon with Dom in Cuba, wasn't something she openly admitted. It was another legacy of being a foster kid; she'd never had the swimming lessons that kids from birth families seemed to get as a rite of passage, in much the same way as learning to ride a bike. By the time she'd joined her '*permanent*' foster family at the age of eleven, they'd assumed that she already knew how to swim. And when they'd eventually discovered she couldn't, it had just seemed to give them one more reason to leave her in a respite placement when they spent their annual family holiday in Spain without her. So yes, she could swim, but she was hardly Michael Phelps. Climbing, on the other hand, was something she'd embraced as an adult, especially since living in Port Agnes. Scaling a difficult ridge gave her a massive sense of achievement every time.

'I think I've got a better idea.' Dexter already had one leg over the side of the boat. 'I'll get in first, just in case the current is stronger than we think. It'll be better to have one of us on either side of Jess anyway. That way I can check if it's even possible to get a foothold on the cliff before either of you come over.'

'Go for it.' As Johnny replied, Dexter leapt into the water carrying a climbing pulley, the harnesses, and two spare life jackets. He reached the edge of the cliff in a matter of seconds and scrambled up the rock onto a ledge just above the surface of the water, where he'd already thrown the life jackets.

'There's quite a decent-sized flat section here, so just head for where I am.' Dexter shouted across and Jess looked over the edge of the boat as Johnny fastened the rope around her waist, her stomach churning almost as fast as the black stretch of water between the boat and the section of the cliff where Dexter was waiting.

'You okay?' Johnny gave her the thumbs up sign, which she mirrored, hoping he couldn't see how much her hands were shaking.

'I'm going in.' Counting to three in her head, she slipped over the side of the dinghy and into the water, which despite the early spring sunshine overhead was cold enough to make her struggle for breath. Pushing against the waves, she was level with Dexter in just a few strokes and he held out his hand to her.

'Right, I've got her Johnny. You can let go of the rope your end as soon as she's up on the ledge.' Dexter pulled Jess out of the water with one arm, as if it was nothing at all. She couldn't help wondering what the other carers who'd been on her pre-approval fostering training with her would think if they could see their social worker now. Still waters ran deep, so they said, and there was certainly a lot more to Dexter Rowe than met the eye.

'Thanks.' She was trying and failing to stop her teeth chattering as she joined him on the cliff, her life jacket acting as a buffer as they stood facing one another on the narrow ledge.

'You're doing great, but I think we need to try and get up to Adam and Tasha before Johnny comes over. There's a lot less room here than I thought.'

'Are you calling me fat?' She couldn't help laughing at the look of mortification that crossed his face.

'No! Of course I wasn't, it's just—'

'Don't worry, I was just proving that midwives can joke at the darkest of times too.' She looked up at the cliff above them. 'If you tell Johnny to stay put for a bit, I can climb up and see if we need him. It might be safer if he stays with the dinghy otherwise, because you're right, there really isn't much room to manoeuvre.'

'Are you sure you still want to do it? I could try lassoing the rope around one of the peaks on the cliff face.'

'There's no way of knowing whether that will be stable enough until we get up there. It'll be safer if I free climb and we secure the ropes when we're at the top and we know it's safe enough to get Adam and Tasha down.'

'What if you fall?'

'It's less than thirty feet up to where we saw Adam. I'll be fine.' Jess pulled in the remainder of the rope that Johnny had released at his end and looped it over her shoulder, securing the end so it wouldn't come loose as she started to climb. 'Just let Johnny know what we're doing and I'll throw the rope down when I'm ready for you to follow me up with the rest of the gear.'

'Okay, be careful. And if it looks too risky, just come back down and we'll wait for the helicopter.'

Jess didn't answer him, already focusing on climbing the cliff face in front of her. She just had to take it foothold to foothold, finding a safe space before she pushed on to the next level. It was down to her and like Dexter had said, there was no safety net if she fell. But then she was used to that, she hadn't had a safety net she could rely on since she was ten years old.

Dexter was shouting instructions to Johnny below her and at first, she couldn't hear anything from above, but then she heard someone sobbing. Whatever was going on with Tasha and the baby, Jess didn't want them to have to wait for a helicopter. Otherwise it might be too late.

Pulling herself up on a piece of rock that jutted skyward, like a broken tooth in the mouth of a giant, Jess finally made it to the ledge where Adam and Tasha were sheltered, pressed into a narrow gulley in the rock face. It had obviously protected them from the incoming tide, but it had also hidden them from view when the lifeboat made its first sweep. They'd done really well to get up this high and make it this far, but there was nowhere left to go from here but back down into the water again. Their little dog, who'd needed less of a foothold, was still about ten feet above them on the cliff face, barking for all he was worth.

'Oh, thank God!' Adam looked up as Jess got onto the ledge, his face almost colourless. 'Tasha called her mum, but she dropped her phone on the way up here and we didn't know if anyone was coming.'

'I hit my belly against the rocks and I think the baby might be hurt.' Tasha was sobbing much harder now that Jess had arrived and she barely seemed able to get the words out.

'It's going to be okay. I'm Jess, one of the midwives, and the lifeboat crew are all down below. They're going to get you back to the beach.' Jess said the words with no way of knowing if they'd turn out to be true, but she needed Adam to be calm enough to give her the full story. 'What happened? Are either of you injured?'

'I went up first, trying to find footholds and telling Tasha to follow me and use the same footholds as I did, but she slipped about three feet from the ledge. I managed to turn and grab the shoulder of her jacket, but she swung out and back again, smashing into the rock face.'

'You did amazingly well to hold on.' Jess had seen it before, superhuman strength in people when it came to the seemingly impossible. Women who had to go through labour and give birth to babies they already knew wouldn't take a breath, and the fathers who kept families together in the wake of crippling post-natal depression. But for Adam to manage to hold on to Tasha like that and cling to the rock face himself, was nothing short of miraculous.

'I think I've done something to my shoulder, but I managed to hold on just long enough for Tasha to get a foothold again.

When we got to the ledge, I knew that was it, there was no way we could go any further.'

'You're safe now and we're going to get you down, I promise.' Jess kept her voice steady, needing to believe it as much as Tasha and Adam did. 'I'm going to tie up this rope and then Dexter, one of the lifeboat crew, will come up and use the winch so you can abseil down and we can get you on the lifeboat. Once he's on his way up here, I can take a look at you both.'

'Thank you.' Adam wrapped his arms around Tasha, who still couldn't seem to stop crying, as Jess tied the rope off and threw the other end to Dexter, shouting down to give him an update.

'That should get you up here, but there are pretty decent footholds in the cliff anyway and there's just about enough room for the four of us on the ledge.'

'On my way.' Dexter grabbed hold of the other end of the rope and Jess turned her attention back to Adam and Tasha.

'I need to take a look at you first, Adam, to see how badly you've injured your shoulder, because that's going to affect how we get you down the cliff.'

'Whatever you need to do, but I want Tasha to go down first. I'm not leaving her here.'

'Okay, I'm just going to lift your top up at the back, so I can see what you've done. I'll try not to cause you any more pain.' Jess lifted the back of Adam's jumper as gently as she could, but he wasn't the only one wincing when she saw the obvious injury. He couldn't hide the pain in the end, no matter how desperately he might want to protect Tasha.

'Jesus Christ that's killing me.'

'I'm really sorry, but you've definitely dislocated your shoulder.'

'Can you put it back in?' Adam looked paler than ever and it was no wonder given the agony he must have been in, but Jess shook her head.

'The space is too tight and, if I get it wrong, I'm going to cause you even more pain. We need to get you down and onto the boat and there'll be an ambulance waiting on the other side. I know you're in agony now, but I can give you some pain relief when we're on the boat and it should be a relatively easy fix once they get you to hospital.' Now wasn't the time to tell him that he might need an operation if he'd torn the ligaments or tendons around the joint. All of that was still relatively easy to fix compared with what could have happened.

'How are we doing?' Dexter had pulled himself onto the ledge, to a frenzy of barking from the little dog still perched above them on the cliff face.

'Adam's dislocated his shoulder and I'm just going to check Tasha out.' Jess positioned herself as close to Tasha as possible. The younger woman's back was flat against the cliff, her arms wrapped around her bump. 'It's okay, sweetheart, you're going to be okay.'

'I got knocked really hard against the rock.' Tasha turned her face towards Jess, her eyes red and swollen from crying so hard, pulling up her jacket and the T-shirt underneath it. 'I've lost the baby, haven't I? It can't possibly be okay when my belly looks like this!'

There was a huge bruise across Tasha's abdomen, already turning a deep shade of purple, with nasty grazes that lacerated the skin all around it. Her bump had obviously taken the full force of the impact when she'd swung out and back against the rock.

'You've got some nasty cuts and bruises there, but it doesn't mean you've lost the baby.' Jess hoped to God she was right. 'I've had mums-to-be who've been in nasty car accidents and fallen down whole flights of stairs, and their babies have still made it out okay. You'd be amazed by how much protection the baby's got in there.'

'I just want to feel him move.' Tasha ran her hands over her bump, which must have hurt even more but she was clearly desperate for some sign that everything was going to be okay. Jess was almost as desperate herself, but there were more reliable ways of checking than hoping to feel the baby kick in the midst of all this chaos.

'When we get you safely on the boat, I might be able to hear baby's heartbeat through a stethoscope, but you won't be able to hear it like you can with a Doppler at your check-ups. There's a chance I won't be able to hear it either, because of the noise of the lifeboat, but that doesn't mean it isn't there. Like I said to Adam, the best thing we can do is get you both back to Port Agnes and into the ambulance, where they can start to run all of the proper checks.'

'What about Ralph?' Tasha bit her lip as she looked at Jess.

'Ralph?' For a second Jess thought she was talking about the baby, but then Tasha pointed up above her head.

'He's our Jack Russell. Adam's been calling him to come back down, but he won't. We can't leave him here, he was our baby before this one.' Tasha cradled her bump again. 'And I'm not losing him either.'

'We can sort that out too, don't worry.' Dexter made it sound so straightforward. 'Let's just get the two of you down and into the dinghy first. If I need to come back up for Ralph after that, then I will, I promise.'

'Adam wants Tasha to go first.' Jess exchanged a look with Dexter that didn't need words. 'I'll winch the two of you down first so you can get her back to the boat, and then I'll lower

Adam down and come down last. Depending on what Ralph decides to do.'

'Are you sure you can take that much weight? We must be at least three times heavier than you between us.'

'At least.' Jess gave him a brief smile. 'It's all down to the equipment and the belay device will let me lower down up to three hundred kilos, so it'll be fine.'

'I would ask if you wanted me to come down last with the equipment, but it didn't take me long to work out you're a much better free climber than me.' Dexter gave a brief nod and turned towards Tasha. 'Okay, let's get you down to the boat and back to your family. They're all waiting on the beach for you and they're going to be so happy to see you all back in one piece.'

'Mum must be having kittens. She fusses over me like mad since I got pregnant and it was as much as Adam and I could do to get a twenty-minute walk out by ourselves each day on this holiday.' For the first time Tasha's face seemed to relax a tiny bit. 'I wish we'd stayed in the cottage with her clucking around us now and telling me to put my feet up every five minutes to make sure I don't get varicose veins like she did with me!'

'Mums always like hearing they were right, so I'm sure if you tell her that when you get back, she'll be delighted to hear it.' Dexter helped Tasha step into one of the harnesses and Jess could see how much trust the younger woman already had in him. He just had this way of making it sound like everything was going to be okay. Exactly like he'd done every time he'd had an assessment visit with Jess.

'You don't appreciate what you've got until you almost lose it.' Tasha looked at Adam, as Dexter checked her harness. 'The tide just came in so quickly today and when I thought I might not see the rest of my family again, I was just glad I had Adam with me, because I can't imagine being without him.'

'You'll never have to be without me.' The words seemed to catch in Adam's throat and Jess had to swallow hard too. There was still so much that could go wrong.

'I really love you, Adam, and me and the baby will be waiting when you come down.' Tasha put her hand on her bump again as she took a step towards him.

'I'll be right behind you.' Adam's face twisted in pain as the young couple exchanged a brief kiss and Tasha accidentally brushed against his injured shoulder. Neither of them had assigned any blame to the other for getting stranded in the cove. If Jess had been stuck on the ledge with Dom, there was no way he'd have let it lie like that. It would have been her fault for wanting to walk the dog in the first place, or for not knowing that the tide came in as fast and as high as it did at this time of year. Looking back, whenever something went wrong, Dom's first instinct was to look around and decide who to blame. More often than not, he'd apologise for that later, but it was just one more thing that had chipped away at Jess over time. Dom wasn't a bad person, not really. But selfishness and pride had always been his downfall. Being the adored only child of Diane and Bill had given him a confidence he couldn't allow to take a knock. He'd never have done what Dexter did either, and admitted in front of people that Jess was a better free climber than him. It was no wonder he hadn't been capable of showing her an ounce of empathy when they'd discovered she was infertile; all he'd cared about was the proof that it wasn't him.

'Are you ready?' Jess attached the ropes so that Dexter could take Tasha safely down the cliff, positioning the harness so it minimised the impact on her bump and then feeding the rope slowly through the pulley. The last thing Tasha needed was another sharp drop that might result in her bump hitting a hard surface.

'All good to go.' Dexter leant back with Tasha facing towards him, her back parallel with the cliff face and his legs bracing her from any contact, as he walked slowly downwards. It probably took less than two minutes, but Jess only felt like she could breathe again once they were safely on the bottom ledge; pulling the harnesses back up as soon as they'd stepped out of them.

'I'll start lowering Adam down when you're back in the dinghy.' Jess shouted down, as Dexter put a life jacket on Tasha and seconds later he'd lowered her into the water, jumping in after her and swimming the short distance to where Johnny could pull Tasha into the dinghy. Turning round, Dexter headed back towards the lower ledge, pulling himself up and calling out to Jess.

'Send Adam down when you're ready and I'll get him into the boat, in case we can't get the life jacket over his injured shoulder.'

'He's coming now.' Jess turned towards Adam, who she'd already helped into a harness. 'You can hold on to this part of the rope with your good arm, if you want to, but you just need to lean back, keeping your feet flat against the rock face and walk down slowly as I feed the rope through.'

'I must weigh at least twice as much as you. Are you sure this is going to work?'

'I've just lowered Dexter and Tasha down, and their combined weight is far more than yours. It'll be fine, I promise.' That was one promise Jess felt confident to make and Adam got down to the lower ledge without even a single slip. As Dexter lowered Adam into the water, the barking from Ralph on the cliff face above reached a crescendo. By the time Jess looked up, he was scrabbling down the rock, dropping onto the ledge next to her and carrying on down before she had a chance to stop him. The little dog had played a big part in Adam and Tasha's rescue and he clearly had no more intention of being left behind than they did of leaving him.

'Just me now then.' Jess untied the abseiling ropes and dropped them onto the ledge below her, leaving just the original climbing rope she could grab on to if anything went wrong. She might not want to leave any more of the rescue equipment behind than she had to, but there were some chances that weren't worth taking, even if it would only be Luna who relied on her coming home in one piece, once Teddy was gone. Although even the crafty little cat had enough of the fishermen under her spell to never need to worry about starving to death if Jess didn't make it back home. Looking down, she saw Dexter was already lowering Adam into the water, holding on to the end of an unsecured rope so that Adam could do a mini abseil down the jagged rocks they'd climbed up and into the water. There was nowhere to secure a rope on the bottom ledge and it was that or take a giant leap over the rocks. Adam was in no fit state to do that and Tasha certainly wouldn't have been either.

Dropping down onto the lowest ledge, Jess scooped up the little dog who was still barking furiously a few feet from the edge. There was no way Johnny or Dexter could move the boat any closer. It was even more obvious now that she was looking down on them, that the rocks just below the ledge would have torn the dinghy to shreds. So she'd have to climb down to get back into the water and take Ralph with her.

'Just drop the dog in, he'll swim over.' Johnny shouted the instruction, but the little dog was already shivering in her arms.

'Come on, Ralph, let's do it.' Walking to the edge of the ledge, Jess was going to have to push off hard to make it past the rocks, but it was the only way if she didn't want to put the dog down.

'Wait, I'll come back and get you.' Dexter called out, but there was no way Jess was letting him do that. He'd already had to lower Adam and Tasha into the water on an unsecured rope. They were only twenty feet or so away. She could do this, even if the wind had suddenly picked up and Ralph felt like a lead weight in her arms.

'It's fine, I'm just going to jump.' Jess put her right foot on the edge of the rock, leant back and pushed off hard, hitting the water with more force than she'd anticipated, Ralph immediately leaping out of her arms and into the water to their left. 'Come back, boy, *please*.'

But he was already swimming in the opposite direction to the dinghy, and away from the lifeboat itself. She had to follow him, but the sky was getting darker, grey clouds closing out the promised sunshine, and the water seemed to be getting colder and choppier by the moment. 'Ralph, come on, this way, pleeeaaase!'

She couldn't just leave him. Tasha and Adam were calling out from the dinghy now too, the desperation in their voices obvious. There were people who'd say Ralph was just a dog and she should leave him, but the family dog at her last foster carers' house had soaked up more tears in her fur than Jess could bear to think about. But even as she tried swimming towards Ralph, the waves seemed to be pushing her back towards the dinghy.

'Ralph!' She was still barely any closer to the dog. Then suddenly there was a huge splash behind her. Turning her head, she saw Dexter moving through the water towards them as if he was in a race.

'Swim back to the dinghy. I'll get the dog.' She didn't even have a chance to respond before he swam past her and seconds later he'd caught hold of Ralph. It was only then that Jess finally turned back towards the dinghy and let the force of the waves move her in that direction, only just making it to the edge of the dinghy before Dexter. Johnny hauled her over the side, swiftly followed by Ralph and Dexter. There was hardly any room in the tiny boat, but Ralph was already in Tasha's arms.

'Are you all right?' Dexter turned towards Jess as he spoke.

'I'm fine. I'm just glad all of us made it back okay.' She was breathing hard as she answered, leaning against him again to try and get some air into her lungs. Thank God they hadn't needed to swim any further, because she wasn't sure she'd have made it.

'You're quite a woman, Jess, and anyone who thinks they've got the measure of you probably needs to think again.' Dexter brushed a hand against her cheek making her shiver again, but her teeth were chattering so badly, she was struggling to even answer.

'You're not too bad yourself, but if I don't concentrate on breathing I'm not sure I'll remember how.' When he pulled her even closer to him, she didn't try to fight it. She desperately needed the warmth he was offering and she was in no position to deny herself that. At least not until they made it back to the lifeboat.

* * *

Jess was still struggling to get her breathing into a normal rhythm by the time they got back onto the lifeboat. It was only when the coxswain turned the boat straight back towards the beach at Port Agnes that the burning in her chest finally started to ease. Steadying herself against the railing, Jess edged towards where Tasha was leaning up against Adam, on his good side, Ralph wedged in between them.

'How are you doing, Adam? Do you want some pain relief, or can you hold out until we get to the ambulance? They can probably give you something much stronger than I can and I don't want to give you anything that might stop them doing that, unless you really can't wait.'

'I can hold on, it's the baby we're really worried about.'

'Let me have a listen and see if I can hear the heartbeat, but don't worry if I can't. Like I said before, it'll probably be because of the background noise or the position of the baby.' Jess pulled her bag out from underneath the bench and grabbed the stethoscope which would give her the best chance of hearing the heartbeat. Moving the end gently across Tasha bruised skin, Jess felt as if every muscle in her body had contracted as she waited to hear something. Finally it came, the best sound in the world and proof that Tasha and Adam's baby boy had made it through.

Passing the earpieces of the stethoscope to Tasha, Jess smiled. 'Have a listen.'

'Oh, thank God!' Tasha was sobbing again, even harder than she had when Jess had first made it to the ledge.

'They'll give you a scan and check you over completely at the hospital, but it's a really good sign.' Jess squeezed her hand. 'You're going to have quite the story to tell him when he arrives.'

'Thank you all so much.' Adam had tears streaming down his face too by the time Dexter came over to join them, just in time to hear that things looked okay with the baby.

'We'll be back at the lifeboat station in a couple of minutes and Gemma has just told me there's already an ambulance waiting, so they'll get you both sorted out and give Adam some pain relief straight away.' Dexter ruffled the top of the dog's head. 'And what about Ralph, do you want me to take him to the vet in town and get him checked over too?'

'Thanks, but I think he'll be fine. We can give him to Tasha's mum when we get back and I'll ask her to take him to the vet if she's worried about anything.' Adam grimaced as the boat hit a wave. 'I might be in agony, but thank goodness you heard him barking, otherwise I don't think I'd have made it.'

'He's definitely a hero and I think he deserves a steak when you're all back at home.' Dexter patted the dog's head again and Jess's stomach did another flip. She desperately wanted to put it down to the boat bumping over another wave, which would have been far more convenient than the truth.

'He's not the only hero.' Tasha had finally got control of her tears. 'Adam stopped me from falling, and the two of you got us off the cliff and back to the boat. Then I thought we were going to lose Ralph and you both went in after him. We really can't thank you enough.'

'You make a pretty good team.' Adam looked from Dexter to Jess, and the familiar sensation of heat creeping up her neck was only disguised by the wind whipping her hair across her face. It was an innocent enough comment, but the relief that flooded Jess's body as the lifeboat was winched up the ramp wasn't just because the paramedics were about to take over. She had to put some distance between herself and Dexter before she did something that would really embarrass them both. She'd only just got his friendship back and the last thing she wanted to do was risk losing it again.

'Jess!' Ella ran over as soon as Jess stepped into the lifeboat station, throwing her arms around her. 'Are you okay? Andy has been relaying updates to us and I couldn't believe it when they said you'd climbed up the cliff! You're like Superwoman.'

'She really is.' Dexter came up behind her. 'I've done a bit of climbing, but I wouldn't have free climbed up the cliff face like Jess did. If she hadn't been there, we'd have had to wait for the helicopter and they could have been in real trouble by then.'

'She's amazing, isn't she?' Ella finally released Jess and

turned towards him. 'Anyone who underestimates her is an idiot.'

'That's exactly what I said!' Dexter looked at Jess, a smile playing around his mouth that made her wonder what it would be like to kiss him. 'Do you fancy getting together with the kids tomorrow? They've set up a wooden play park at Thunderhill Farm and they've opened part of it up as a petting farm. There are some new lambs up there and I've told Riley that I'll take him up to feed them. He's desperate to go, but he's desperate to see you again too, so I thought maybe you could join us. If you're not busy?'

'I'd love that.' Jess had to look down at the floor when she answered, because it sounded like a date. It was stupid, when they'd been meeting up with the kids almost every day at one point. But Ella was still grinning like an idiot as Dexter moved off to join the rest of the lifeboat crew.

'Sooo...' She drew out the single syllable for an amazingly long time. 'Did you pick up more than a stranded couple while you were out there today?'

'What? Dexter? No! I told you about him, he's the social worker who did my assessment and we just got more friendly once I started looking after Teddy. That's all. To be honest, I think my new social worker, Madeline, asked him to keep an eye on me to make sure I was managing okay.' Why wouldn't Jess's face stop burning? She was telling the truth, so there was no reason to turn as red as she had. But Ella couldn't seem to wipe the smile off her face, however much she protested.

'Hmm, maybe that's all he is for now, but I recognise the look he gave you. He likes you. A lot.'

'Don't be daft, he's just a nice guy that's all, he's like that with everyone. And he was surprised I'm not just the bubbly blonde everyone has me pegged for, because I could climb up the cliff face.'

'If he did your fostering assessment and has seen you with Teddy, then he already knows you're far from being just a bubbly blonde. You're amazing, we all know it and he does too, trust me.'

'All that matters is that he thought I was good enough to be a foster carer and now all I care about is whether he thinks I've done a good job with Teddy.' Jess gritted her teeth, willing it to be true even if a little voice inside her head was calling her a liar.

15

When Madeline had dropped Teddy back from his visit with Dom, she'd delivered the hammer blow that Jess had known was coming. If Dom decided to go ahead with taking on parental responsibility for Teddy, he'd be expected to make a firm commitment to a date for the baby to move in with him permanently. If he wasn't ready for the commitment, and it was deemed appropriate to give him more time, or if he decided to waive his parental rights as Natalia had and put Teddy up for adoption, the likelihood was that he'd move to carers who were specialists in offering bridging placements between fostering and adoption.

It made every moment with him all the more bittersweet and the only way Jess could handle it was to pretend that the end wasn't hurtling towards her like an out-of-control train. She found herself thinking about her father's message again and wondering if he'd felt even a tenth of what she was feeling about letting Teddy go. If Teddy ever found out about his start in life when he was grown up, he might wonder why the woman who'd cared for him in his first few weeks had given him up so will-

ingly, especially if he discovered she'd been married to his
father. What he'd never understand was that even if giving him
up broke her completely, she was doing it for him. She couldn't
give him the childhood he deserved if she stayed with Dom and
she had to do what was best for him. She couldn't help
wondering whether, just maybe, there'd been something like
that behind her father's decision to opt out of her life. If there
had, she was starting to think he might deserve the chance to
explain. She still wasn't ready, though, not with Teddy likely to
leave any day; that was all the heartache she could deal with
for now.

Meeting up with Dexter and Riley to go and see the lambs at
Thunderhill Farm had been a welcome distraction. Dexter had
also been able to pass on the great news, via an update to the
lifeboat crew, that Tasha, Adam and their unborn baby had all
come through the drama at Ocean Cove relatively unscathed. It
was difficult to wallow in self-pity after hearing that Adam's
shoulder had been the only injury, and when you were in the
company of a little boy who was having the greatest day of his
life. Riley was absolutely obsessed with Shaun the Sheep,
second only to Fireman Sam in his affections, so watching him
running from field to field at the farm was the best tonic Jess
could have hoped for.

When they stopped at the play area, Dexter went off to get
them some drinks and she kept an eye on Riley. At first he
hurtled round like the other children, but then he sat down on a
giant wooden mushroom, watching some of the other children
crossing a rope bridge that led to some monkey bars and a slide
at the end. Most of them were being assisted by their parents so
that they didn't just drop straight down as they tried to swing
from bar to bar. Dragging Teddy's buggy across the woodchips
on the floor of the play area, Jess crouched next to Riley.

'Are you okay, sweetheart? Do you want me to give you a push on the swings when Dexter gets back?' She knew Dexter would be more than willing to keep an eye on the baby while she helped Riley navigate some of the trickier parts of the play park.

'I want my daddy.' Riley stuck out a bottom lip and Jess's heart felt as if it was about to lurch out of her chest. It was almost an echo of the words she'd said hundreds of times in her fostering placements, mostly when no one else would hear. After the first few times of saying how much she wanted her dad – and being told that she couldn't see him – she'd taken to whispering it into her pillow at night, like a sort of prayer that might make him finally come back for her. She'd stopped eventually, but looking at Riley now her heart was breaking for him and she just wanted to make everything okay. But no one could do that, not even Dexter. She just had to hope that anything she said wouldn't make Riley feel even worse.

'I know you do, darling, and I bet your daddy is missing you like crazy. But you've got me and Dexter here now and we can help you with anything you need.'

'Daddy helps me at the park, when the slide is too fast.' Riley widened his eyes at the memory and Jess hugged him into her side.

'When I was little, I used to be too scared to go on the slide by myself because of how fast it was too, so I'd sit on my mum or dad's lap and we'd go down together.'

'Can I sit on your lap?' Riley looked up at her, his dark eyes searching her face and she felt her heart contract again, this time for a very different reason. All the time she'd worried about falling too deeply in love with Teddy, or letting herself do something really stupid like fall for Dexter, and she hadn't been on her guard about falling in love with Riley too.

'I'd love to go down the slide with you, I just hope my bottom's not too big and we don't get stuck!' As Riley started giggling at the mention of the word bottom, Jess had to accept the facts. She'd developed feelings for Dexter and Riley that had never been part of the plan.

* * *

Half an hour after they'd finished at the play park and Jess had been down the slide with Riley a total of twelve times – thankfully without getting her bum wedged even once – it was finally time for the best part of their day out.

'Look how much he likes his milk, Jess!' Riley was feeding one of the lambs with a bottle of milk about four times the size of the ones Jess fed Teddy with, and he was having to use both hands to keep hold of it because of how enthusiastically the lamb was sucking, its tail wagging from side to side like a dog.

'You're really good at that Riley and you're making him so happy. His tail's wagging like crazy.' As she spoke, Riley looked up at her, his dark eyes locking with hers as they shared a moment of pure magic.

'This is the best day ever, this is the best lamb and you're the best Jess!' Riley was so excited by the revelation that he let the teat fall out of the lamb's mouth and earned himself a headbutt for his troubles, but he didn't even seem to notice and the lamb soon latched back on.

'I think you're the best too, Riley, and so does your lamb.' Jess caught Dexter's eye and he smiled, sharing a moment of undiluted affection as they watched the little boy, like thousands of parents did every day. Falling in love with Riley had probably been inevitable all along. There was something about herself she recognised in him, except he was so much better than her.

He'd been through what she had at an even younger age, but it didn't stop him having the biggest heart in the world. He was always launching himself at Dexter for a hug and not in the sort of desperate way Jess might have done as a kid, in the hope that someone would give her a hint they cared about her, but because love oozed out of Riley. Jess could see it in how gently he handled the lambs and the way he stroked Teddy's cheeks and spoke to him in whispered snippets of nursery rhymes and songs he'd learned at school. She'd fooled herself into thinking that Teddy was the only little boy who'd stolen her heart, but Riley had too, when she hadn't even been looking.

'What's it to be?' Dexter topped up Jess's glass. 'Shall I whip us up one of my world-famous omelettes now that the boys have both flaked out, or shall we get a takeaway?'

'I don't want you to have to go to any trouble.' Jess was feeling almost too relaxed to move, so she couldn't imagine why Dexter would want to start cooking. Teddy had fallen asleep in his car seat on the way back from the farm and he hadn't even stirred when she'd put him down in the travel cot at Dexter's house. He'd be a due another feed before he went down for the night, so when he woke up again she'd take him home and settle him in his own cot then. She was trying not to count down the number of sleeps they might have before his cot at Puffin's Rest was empty forever – like the reverse of the thrill in the build-up to Christmas – but it was getting harder and harder to block that out. After the excitement of the farm, Riley had just about managed his dinner before he'd lost the battle to keep his eyes open and Dexter seemed confident he would sleep through until morning.

'It's hardly Michelin-starred stuff, but it'll only take me about ten minutes to knock up a couple of omelettes.'

'I can't understand why you're single, you've got what every woman is looking for.' Jess hadn't meant to say what she was thinking out loud, but it seemed to be happening to her more and more whenever Dexter was around.

'Oh and what's that? The ability to crack a few eggs and whisk them up with cheese and mushrooms?'

'That's useful, but it wasn't what I meant.' It was too late to backtrack now, so she might as well just say it. 'You're kind and patient, you want to help everyone and nothing is ever too much trouble for you. Oh, and you're not too shabby in the looks department either.'

'You do know you're describing yourself, don't you? Except that you're far better looking than that.' Dexter sat down next to her on the sofa and suddenly she wished she'd kept quiet, because laying out all her feelings like that meant they were far too close to the surface to push them down again. If he so much as leant towards her, she was going to be powerless to stop herself leaping on him.

'I'm damaged goods, that's what Dom said and he's right. I was so desperate to be loved and to be part of something that I latched on to him and his family, even though I knew from the beginning that he wasn't right for me.' Biting her lip, she couldn't risk looking up at Dexter. 'And now I'm so scared of getting hurt again that I don't even want to risk starting something new, in case it ends. I was even thinking of giving up fostering after Teddy, because I wasn't sure I could ever let myself love another child enough to be a good foster carer, but then today I realised I already had. I haven't been able to help falling in love with Riley too, but I'm so scared that every time I lose one of these children and they go back to other foster carers, or their birth parents, that I'm going to lose another bit of myself too. And I just don't know how many more parts of me I can lose before I break apart altogether.'

'You aren't damaged goods, Jess.' Dexter touched her hand and she forced herself to look up at him. 'But you've been through some really tough times and I think it's made you who you are. You know that quote? Some things are more beautiful when they've been broken? Every time someone has tried to break you a little bit more, you've put yourself back together again. You're the strongest person I know and you don't need anyone, but I'm hoping that maybe you might want someone.'

'I do.' Jess had known she wasn't going to be able to stop herself responding if Dexter gave even the slightest inkling that he felt the same way about her as she had about him from almost the first moment they'd met. She hadn't allowed herself to admit it until after they'd rescued Tasha and Adam, but she had too many regrets in life to let this moment pass her by. It might just be that – a moment – but she was going to take it anyway. She didn't even have time to worry about whether the kiss she'd been anticipating for far longer than she'd admit to anyone, even herself, would live up to expectation. Sliding one leg across his lap, she was suddenly face to face with Dexter, his back against the sofa and every nerve ending in her body standing to attention. It was Jess who leant in first, but when she kissed him, he responded in a way that left her in no doubt that he'd been anticipating this for just as long as she had. And a moment later she was lost. Whatever happened next there was no pretending that Dexter was just a friend, or that she hadn't just had the best kiss of her entire life.

* * *

Dom still hadn't accepted that Jess wasn't going to come back to him and she'd agreed to let him pick Teddy up from her place for his next overnight contact visit. It had already gone past the date when Madeline had said he was supposed to make a decision about taking over the baby's care full-time. According to the social worker, Dom had said he couldn't do it yet because his mother was still continuing to recover from her illness. Jess didn't buy it, though. Dom was still hedging his bets and when he was around Teddy, he never seemed to focus his whole attention on the little boy. Despite using his mum's illness as a reason for not making a final decision, Dom seemed to spend a lot of time round at his parents' place, or with his best friend and his wife. And he was proud of the fact that he still hadn't changed a nappy, apart from when he was being watched by a social worker.

'You look good, Jess, motherhood suits you. I always knew it would.' Dom tried to catch hold of her hand as she moved past him, packing up Teddy's bag for his overnight stay with his father.

'I'm not Teddy's mother.' It was the mantra Jess had forced herself to adopt, ever since Madeline had told her that there was no chance of her being allowed to keep the baby, no matter what Dom decided.

'You could be. When things were right between us, we were great together and we can be again. All you've got to do is let go of your pride and you could have what you've always wanted, then nothing would stand in our way.'

'Do you really believe that?' Jess shook her head. 'We were *never* great together, not really. I was just desperate to be loved, and my desperation flattered your ego. It wouldn't work between us, and you just need to concentrate on being the best dad you can to Teddy if you really are going to step up. But it needs to be a hundred per cent, Dom. Please don't mess him around, he's had a tough enough start already and he deserves the best from here on out.'

'There's someone else, isn't there?' She might as well have saved her breath for all the notice Dom had taken of what she'd said. He was determined to find an explanation for her turning him down and it couldn't possible just be that she didn't love him any more. 'That's why you don't want to give things a go with me and Teddy. All that talk about how much you love him, but there's obviously someone else you'd rather spend your time with.'

'The reason I don't want to give things a go with you and Teddy is because we'd end up dragging him through another messy break-up somewhere down the line. The only *someone else* in all of this is him. As easy as it would have been to convince myself we could make a go of things so that I could keep Teddy, I owe it to him not to take the easy route. And so do you.'

'Come on, Jess, I wasn't born yesterday! I hope you think it was worth it when this is all over. This can't go on forever, they're going to force me to give them a decision before much longer.' Dom snatched up Teddy's bag. 'Get it out of your system and choose me and Teddy before it's too late. Otherwise you're going to regret it for the rest of your life.'

Whether Dom had meant his words to sound like a threat or not, that was the effect they'd had, and Jess couldn't bring herself to respond because there was every chance it was true. She'd never regret finally admitting that her relationship with Dom was over, despite her one-time desperation to make it work so she could be a part of his family. What she might regret forever – especially if she had to watch Dom do a half-hearted job of parenting the little boy – was letting Teddy go. But Dom was right about something else too, this couldn't go on forever and sooner or later he'd have to make his decision. She might not be allowed to keep Teddy, but she could pray, as hard as she'd ever prayed for anything, that Dom would decide he didn't want to keep Teddy either. She didn't care what the social workers said, staying with his birth father wasn't the best option for the little boy she adored. Jess knew exactly what sort of damage could be done when your father, the one man in the world you should be able to rely on, let you down. She was terrified that if things ended up like that for Teddy, Dom would be proved right again and she'd regret the decisions she'd made for the rest of her life. But she couldn't see what other choice she possibly had.

Jess padded barefoot around the kitchen feeling gloriously indulgent to still be wearing just her underwear and Dexter's shirt from the night before, which admittedly reached almost down to her knees because she was so much shorter than him. Riley had asked if he could stay over at one of Dexter's sisters' houses which had given Dexter and Jess a chance to have the whole evening alone, as Teddy was with Dom.

There'd been nothing to stop them. Other than the fear that the slowly, slowly approach that Jess had told herself was for the best – especially while things were still so tense with Dom and Teddy's future was hanging in the balance – might now have gathered a pace that neither of them could control. Asking Dexter if he wanted to stay over was the first time Jess had let herself be truly vulnerable since discovering Dom had cheated on her. When Dexter had said yes and they'd spent the night together, it had changed things but this wasn't a casual fling for him either, he'd made that obvious. She tried not to think about the fact that she was still keeping something from him. Instead she convinced herself that, in any other circumstances, it would have been way too early in the relationship to bring up the fact that she couldn't have children and talk like that would probably have sent any sane man running for the hills. For once she'd let herself live in the moment and, when she was alone with Dexter, she hadn't been capable of thinking about anything else.

'I've thought about this moment for longer than I should probably own up to.' He'd pushed a stray strand of hair behind her ear as they stood opposite one another, after she'd suggested in her best seductive voice that they move things to the bedroom. For one horrible moment she'd thought he'd been going to turn her down, but he'd just wanted her to be sure. 'I don't want you to do anything you're going to regret and I don't want to do this if you're not looking for something more. As much as I've wanted this, I like you way too much to throw away our friendship, unless there's a chance of us being even more than that.'

'Has anyone ever told you that sometimes you talk too much?' Jess had laughed, teasing him, as the subtle scent of his aftershave filled the space between them. Reaching up, she wrapped her arms around his neck. 'I don't want to lose our friendship either, but I'm hoping this could really be something. Otherwise I wouldn't take the risk.'

'I guess sometimes you just have to...' Dexter had barely got the words out before he started kissing her again and there'd been no more attempt to stop things while they still could. It would have been like trying to stop a tsunami anyway and they'd both wanted it every bit as much. They'd taken the next step now and sooner or later she was going to have to let her social worker know she was in a relationship, so that a risk assessment could be carried out; something that all foster carers had to do. Although given that Dexter was a social worker himself, and already had a DBS check and more knowledge of safeguarding than any normal person could be expected to have, she didn't anticipate it being too much of a problem. But making their relationship *official* would change things again. There was a good chance it could end up being another failure for Jess to tack on to all the others.

Making it official would also mean that other people would know if it turned out to be just one more break-up and it put the sort of pressure on that she wouldn't have chosen so early on, if she'd had the option. They had to do it, though, otherwise there definitely wouldn't be a future for them and she had to admit she wanted there to be. Spending the night with him had shown for the hundredth time what a good guy he was – making sure it was definitely what she wanted and proving he was as generous in the bedroom as he was in every other way.

When she'd woken up at six, the time when Teddy usually had his first feed of the day, she'd slid out from beside a sleeping Dexter and snuck into the lounge. She sat watching the fishing boats heading out to sea from the window and trying not to think about who was feeding Teddy and whether they'd settled him back down okay. An hour later, she was making some coffee and planning to go back into the bedroom to wake Dexter, when he suddenly emerged, wearing the jeans that had lain in a crumpled heap on her bedroom floor the night before. The broadness of his naked chest had taken her by surprise and lying in his arms had felt weirdly like she'd found the place she was always meant to be. It was as if they'd slept next to one another a thousand times before, but she couldn't work out how it was possible to feel so safe and yet still have that thrill of a new relationship all at the same time. She'd have to be dragged over hot coals before she admitted any of those things out loud, but she still wanted him to know that it had meant something to her.

'Thanks for a great night last night.' She smiled, handing him a coffee. 'I'm guessing you'll be needing this shirt back soon, though.'

'It looks far better on you than me, but I might get some funny looks on the way home if I stroll around the harbour topless!' He grinned in response. 'I'd let you keep it in exchange for the toothbrush you gave me last night, but I just don't think it's big enough to protect my dignity.'

'Did it make me look brazen, buying you a toothbrush on the assumption that you'd want to stay?' She did up another button at the top of the shirt, suddenly feeling far more exposed.

'Not at all. I just can't believe someone like you is interested in someone like me.'

'A lot of people would look at my past and say you're way too good for me, me included. I've made so many mistakes.'

'So has everyone else and if they say they haven't, they're either liars or really boring. Possibly both.' He smiled again, setting his coffee cup down on the kitchen counter and putting a hand under her chin so she had to look up at him. 'Jess Kennedy, you are the most beautiful person I've ever met, inside and out.'

'I don't always think good thoughts.' She laughed as he raised his eyebrows. She tried not to remember how often she'd hoped Dom would show the social workers who he really was, so that there was no chance of him keeping Teddy. Wanting someone to fail that badly was hardly charitable.

'For my sake, I should hope you don't always think good thoughts!' Closing the gap between them, he kissed her, wiping all thoughts of Dom out of her head. She might not believe she was good enough for Dexter, but surely she deserved a bit of good luck. And being with him made her feel luckier than she had in a very long time.

* * *

Dexter left half an hour before Dom was due to arrive with Teddy. So when there was a knock on the door of Puffin's Rest just five minutes later, Jess was half-expecting it to be him. The idea that he might be sneaking back for one more kiss made her smile. Luna shot out of the gap as Jess opened the door, heading for her morning raid on the harbour to see which trawlermen might spare her a fish, but it was Dom standing outside, not Dexter, and there was no sign of Teddy.

'You're early.' There was a muscle going in his cheek as she looked at him.

'I bet you're thinking it's a good job that I wasn't here a few minutes earlier, aren't you? Because then I might have seen your boyfriend creeping out of the house, wearing the same clothes he was wearing last night.'

'It's none of your business who I have over to my house.' Despite knowing she was right, nausea was swirling in Jess's stomach, because she had no idea where Teddy was. She'd suspected that Dom might be capable of mediocre parenting, maybe even borderline neglect if he didn't have enough willing hands to take the load off of him. But she'd never thought he might deliberately hurt Teddy. At least not until now. 'Where's the baby, Dom?'

'None of your business.' The way Dom smiled made Jess shiver, his eyes completely dead. 'You've made your choice and now I've made mine. So you'll never get to see Teddy again. I hope shagging your social worker was worth it, because I've reported him too. He probably does it all the time, getting off on persuading lonely women with backgrounds like yours to drop their knickers for him. The pair of you deserve each other.'

'Just tell me where Teddy is please, all I want to know is that he's safe! Dom!' Even as she screamed his name he was turning away, shaking off her attempts to grab hold of his jacket like he was swatting away a fly. She was powerless to stop him leaving, but Teddy was even more helpless and if her actions had caused the little boy to come to any harm, she was never going to forgive herself.

16

'You're going to have to slow down, Jess. I can't understand a word you're saying.' Dexter had picked up her call almost immediately, but the words had still rushed out of Jess's mouth and tumbled over one another in her attempt to explain what had happened and get help to find out where the hell Teddy was. Her whole body seemed to be pulsating to the beat of her racing heart and she could only ever remember being that scared once before – on the day her father had abandoned her and she'd realised she had no one left. The thought that Teddy might be on his own somewhere and terrified too was making her retch. She had to get Dexter to understand, so they could make sure the little boy was safe.

'Dom was here. He must have seen you come over last night and he definitely watched you leave this morning.' She was talking as slowly as she could, over-pronouncing every word in a way that made her mouth feel strange, like her teeth didn't even fit. 'He's always been like this when he doesn't get his way and he was so bitter when he turned up here. Teddy wasn't with him and he wouldn't tell me where he was. He just said I'd never get to see him again.'

She was crying now, noisy body-wracking sobs that she couldn't hold back any longer once she'd reiterated Dom's threat – she was never going to see Teddy again – and Dexter had to repeat himself twice before she could take in what he'd said.

'I'll call Madeline now and let her know what's happened. If Dominic won't tell her where Teddy is either, we can get the police involved. Try not to panic, Jess, the chances are that he's just trying to scare you.'

'But what if he isn't? What if he's hurt Teddy and it's all my fault?'

'Whatever's happened, Jess, none of it is your fault. I'm going to call Maddie now and I'll phone you back as soon as I know anything. Just try and hold it together, is there someone you can call to be with you?'

'All the girls are at work and I can't ask Anna, she's got enough on her plate with the twins.' It had been on the tip of Jess's tongue to say that she just wanted her mum, to be folded in those arms that had somehow had the power to make everything okay. But she hadn't had that since she was ten years old and she didn't have a single family member she could rely on when she needed them most. All she could do was hope that Teddy did have some family he could count on, and that Dom had left him in Diane and Bill's care, with the threat he'd made nothing more than a way to punish Jess. The alternative was too awful to even contemplate.

'We've found him, Jess. He's okay.' Dexter hadn't bothered with any niceties, knowing that she'd need to hear the bottom line before he explained any of the rest. It had been three hours since she'd last spoken to him and she hadn't managed to stop pacing the floor at Puffin's Rest the whole time.

'Where was he? With Dom's parents?' Her heart was still thudding in her ears and she wasn't even sure she could believe that the little boy was okay until she saw him with her own eyes, but she had no idea if she was going to get the chance.

'No. Dom left Teddy at his friend's house last night and when he didn't turn up to pick him up this morning, they tried to call but there was no answer. Then they got a message from him to say he was getting on a flight to Tenerife to see an old friend and that this was all too much for him. "*Doing his head in*" was the phrase he used apparently.'

'Serena's out in Tenerife, the girl from his office who he had the affair with.' If there'd been any doubt in Jess's mind about whether she harboured even a shred of feeling for Dom, this was the proof that she didn't. It was like a wave of relief had washed right over her. If he stayed in Tenerife, it would mean he was out of her life and it looked like he was out of Teddy's too, thank God. It was just as well for Dom's sake too, because she'd never been as angry with anyone in her life and if he'd suddenly been standing in front of her, she wouldn't be responsible for her actions. She felt sick every time she thought about the fact that she'd considered going back to him; the idea made her flesh crawl and she hated that she'd let him think she would, even for a second.

'That'll be who he's gone to see then. He still wouldn't answer his friend's calls and they had no way of finding out what he wanted them to do about Teddy, so they called social services to report that a baby had been abandoned and someone made the connection and got hold of Maddie. We're going to wait until the doctor has examined Teddy, just to make sure everything's as okay as it seems to be, and then we'll come over.'

'You're bringing him home?' Jess knew that Puffin's Rest could never be Teddy's actual home. Not really. But for one last time she wanted to pretend that it was. She almost lost him once already, in the worst way possible, and there was no doubt she was going to have to face up to losing him all over again. But just for today she was going to pretend he really was coming back to her.

* * *

Jess had all but snatched Teddy out of Madeline's arms when she'd arrived at Puffin's Rest with Dexter and they'd been ushered inside.

'Hello, sweetheart, I've missed you so much.' She'd almost had to bite her tongue to stop herself from promising Teddy that she was never going to let him go again. If it had been in her power to keep that promise, she'd have done it in a heartbeat and there was still a battle raging inside her that insisted there had to be a way of keeping Teddy.

'I've spoken to Dominic.' Madeline looked from Jess to Dexter and back again. 'He told me about the two of you and that's none of my business, except from a safeguarding point of view... but it might have made things easier if you'd told me what was going on.'

'There was nothing to tell until recently.' Jess's cheeks were burning and she didn't dare look in Dexter's direction. 'But you're right, I should have known that Dom would default to type when he realised he wasn't going to get what he wanted. He couldn't stand the thought that I'd finally decided to walk away from him after the affairs. Then Teddy arrived and he could see how much I love him, so suddenly he had the perfect bargaining chip, but he still couldn't win. I don't know if he ever felt anything for Teddy, or if he just wanted to be able to get me to dance to his tune again, but either way I'm glad of one thing, that Dom isn't going to be able to do what my dad did to me and abandon him when he's old enough to know what it feels like to be rejected by a parent. Please tell me you're not going to let him do that?'

'Dominic is saying he wants to follow Natalia's lead and give up his parental rights, which would mean Teddy could have an uncontested adoption.' Madeline shook her head. 'But it won't be quick and they'll both get the right to change their minds before the adoption can be finalised, as will Dominic's family. He claims he's planning on staying in Tenerife indefinitely, but we both know he's capable of doing an about-turn. So it will have to go through the court process.'

'Could Teddy stay with me while that's happening?' Jess's heart was racing again, but this time it was hope instead of fear making the blood pump as fast as it was.

'There's a family we'll be moving him to. They're foster carers already, but they've been on the list for adoption for a while. The plan is for Teddy to go there and if Natalia and Dom don't change their minds, his new carers will adopt him.'

'I know they've been on the waiting list, but no one could love Teddy more than I do.' Jess's eyes had filled with tears, despite knowing that this news was coming.

'I'm sorry.' It was Dexter who slid an arm around her waist and did his best to comfort her as she desperately tried to stop the tears falling onto Teddy's head.

'I'm really sorry too, Jess, but it doesn't work that way, you've always known that.' To her credit, Madeline looked pretty close to tears herself. 'No one doubts you'd be a great mother to Teddy, but I think maybe it was wrong to let you get this attached to your first placement, especially given Dominic's involvement... If I could go back and change things, I would.'

'I wouldn't!' Jess's response had been so emphatic that the baby's eyes had shot open in surprise, but instead of bursting into tears, he'd just watched her as if he was trying to take in every feature on her face and remember them, the way she did with him. 'How long until he goes?'

'His new carers are on holiday until the day after tomorrow, but they want to move forward as soon as they get back. So we'll arrange a first contact visit and then, if all goes to plan, Teddy will move in with them.' Madeline sighed. 'Look, I think it might be best if he goes to another respite carer until then, you've been to hell and back already and I'm really worried this might be too much for you.'

'Please let me keep him until they come back from their holiday. All his stuff is here and he's got his routine. Surely he needs that more than ever after what Dom did?' Jess couldn't keep the pleading note out of her voice, but she'd drop to her knees if she had to.

'Let me just run it past my supervisor, but if you really think you can cope with it, then you might be right that Teddy will feel more settled here, rather than moving twice in such a short space of time.'

'Thank you.' Jess whispered the words, pulling Teddy towards her as she spoke. She was going to have him for a tiny bit longer. It wasn't anything like enough, but it was better than nothing and right now she'd take whatever she could get.

* * *

Jess had gone through to the kitchen to sort out a bottle for Teddy while Madeline called her supervisor, and Dexter came out to give her a hand.

'How are you doing?' His tone was gentle as Jess held Teddy in one arm and tried to scoop powdered milk into the bottle with her other hand, spilling it all over the worktop as she did so. 'Let me do that for you, Jess.'

'Do you think Madeline is right that I should never have looked after Teddy?'

'No one could have looked after him better than you have.'

'That's not what I was asking.' She waited for him to turn towards her and finally he shook his head.

'I don't think Maddie was talking about you not having Teddy for his sake, she was talking about what it's done to *you*.' Dexter reached out and stroked her arm, resulting in a fresh crop of tears filling her eyes. 'I know what it feels like to love a child and then discover you've got no say in his life or where he lives. When Riley's mother died, I went from being almost a full-time dad, to taking whatever crumbs of his life Connor let me have. Even now there's no guarantee that he won't do that again one day. But I wouldn't change being a part of Riley's life for anything, even if that means I have to let him go in the future. And I don't think you feel any differently about Teddy, do you?'

'No, but I don't think I really understood how much it was going to hurt.' She couldn't help picturing Riley, even as she held Teddy closer to her body. One of the things that had been helping her hold it all together was the thought that even when Teddy was gone, she'd have Dexter and Riley. But she was real-ising just how precarious Dexter's role in Riley's life was too. A second little boy could be taken away from her and if that happened, it was Dexter who was going to need all her support. There was no way she could promise to give him that, though, not when the thought of losing Riley as well was making it feel like the world was spinning. The fact that Dexter still didn't know she'd never be able to have a baby of her own was like a shadow looming over her too. If he knew that, however sympathetic she was certain he'd be, it might still be a deal-breaker. Maybe Madeline was right, maybe she needed to protect herself from any further hurt by walking away from Dexter and Riley before her feelings for them got any deeper. The trouble was, it was already far too late to stop the thought of losing them from breaking her heart.

Despite being rushed off her feet with newborn twins, Anna had insisted on hosting a get-together for the midwives at her house to welcome Frankie back home from New Zealand, although it was made easier by the fact that they'd be ordering a takeaway.

When Jess had phoned to explain the situation with Teddy, Anna had insisted that she bring him with her. She'd been in two minds about whether to go at all, but she needed to think about something other than the fact that the hands of the clock were ticking past and every hour that went by was an hour closer to Teddy leaving. It also meant that she'd have an excuse not to meet up with Dexter, who'd suggested that he bring Riley round for an early dinner. She hadn't been able to shake off the thought that she was bound to lose them both too eventually, and out of a sense of protection, she was already pulling away. She didn't want to think about what Dom had said either, how it was only her desperation Dexter was attracted to, but the trouble was it had played on Jess's own fears about what he saw in her. What else was there after all, except a string of failures?

The midwives' meet-ups were definitely getting earlier and

the days of karaoke parties until closing time at Casa Cantare were long gone. Jess was due at Anna's for dinner at half-past six, along with Frankie, Gwen, Toni, Bobby, Izzy, Ella and Emily. Ella and Toni would be on call, so they'd have to leave if someone with a planned home delivery went into labour, but the chance of seeing the whole team all in one place was just too good to miss and everyone wanted to welcome Frankie home, including Jess.

Setting off from Puffin's Rest an hour early, she strapped Teddy into a papoose on her chest and headed out to make the most of a mild spring evening. It was the last week in March and the days were really starting to draw out, but the clocks still hadn't moved forward for the summer. Walking with Teddy strapped against her in his papoose had quickly become one of her favourite ways to spend the time and it was just one more thing she wanted to make the most of whilst she still could.

The tide was a long way out, which meant Jess was absolutely certain there was no risk of getting caught out at Ocean Cove. Heading there had always been a comfort, somewhere she could go to think and make sense of whatever was happening in her life. It had got her through the break-up with Dom, well that and the other midwives rallying around her, but getting over Teddy was going to be so much harder and she didn't even want to think about how she'd do that without Dexter's support. But how could she let herself lean on him, when that would mean getting closer to both him and Riley and storing up a whole other avalanche of pain? Even if she managed not to drive Dexter away eventually, Connor could still take Riley from them at any point and Jess couldn't give Dexter another chance to be a dad. Dom was right, and whatever Dexter might say to try and reassure her, she was broken in more ways than one and not even he could fix that.

At least Teddy hadn't chosen to leave her. Looking down at him, she wanted to stop time; his long eyelashes sweeping down towards his chubby cheeks as he peacefully slept in the papoose, the picture of contentment.

'Shall we make a run for it, Teddy Bear?' She whispered the words to him and he grimaced in his sleep. 'I know, I know. It's a crazy idea, but look at the boat out there. In a minute it'll disappear over the horizon and then who knows where it will have gone? We could do that, Teddy Bear – run away where no one will ever find us.'

Turning towards the water, as Teddy slept on, she watched the boat travelling out to sea. It was gleaming white and heading directly for the horizon, where the sun was already beginning to sink lower, the sky changing to shades of burnt orange and pink. It made it look as though the boat was sailing too close to the sun and might be reduced to ashes any minute. And the people on board weren't the only ones who'd sailed too close to the sun. She'd been stupid to think she could take care of Teddy and not fall hopelessly in love with him, but now it was too late.

* * *

'Thanks so much for letting me bring Teddy.' Jess hugged Anna as her friend opened the door, standing at a weird angle so that they didn't squash the baby in between them, now that she'd taken him out of the papoose.

'Teddy's always welcome and so are you. It's really great to see you both.' Anna smiled. 'I love being a mum, but I've got to admit I really miss not being with you guys at work every day.'

'I did too.' Jess swallowed hard. Her feelings might have mirrored Anna's, but she wasn't a mum. There'd be no one for

Jess to come back to after a long day at work and no one to hug to make it all seem worthwhile.

'The others are here already, so we can decide what everyone fancies to eat and order.' Anna linked her arm through Jess's as they headed towards the living room. 'It's just so rare that we actually all get the opportunity to get together any more. We'll have to keep our fingers crossed that Ella and Toni don't have to disappear to a delivery at any point.'

'Jess! Ooh and Teddy, now that's an extra bonus I wasn't expecting. I've heard all about him and I'm going to bagsy the first cuddle, as soon as I've given you the biggest hug you've ever had!' Frankie was already holding out her arms and this time Jess was powerless to stop Teddy getting caught in the middle of it and he immediately started to stir.

'I've really missed you, Jess, and from what I hear, you've been through an absolute nightmare since I left.'

'We all really missed you too and it doesn't exactly sound like you've had an easy time of things either.' Jess couldn't face going over everything that had happened, not when it already felt like she was made of glass. 'But Teddy is obviously desperate to get to know you and get some of that famous Frankie cuddle time, given that he's now wide awake. You could give him his bottle too, if you like?' Jess had barely asked the question before Frankie had scooped the baby into her arms, not needing to be asked twice.

'He's so adorable! Although looking at him makes me miss my grandkids in New Zealand even more. I was desperate to come home to see you all and get back to work, but leaving my daughter and her kids behind feels like someone's chopped off one of my arms!'

'That must be so hard, Frankie.' Anna squeezed her shoulder

before taking Teddy's formula from Jess. 'I'll warm up his bottle whilst the twins are asleep and Frankie can make the most of her cuddle time.'

'Teddy really reminds me of my grandson, Mo, at the same age. I missed out on so much of that and after spending most of the last year with them, I'm still not sure if I'll be able to settle back over here.' Frankie rocked Teddy in her arms as they walked through to the front room.

'Do you still think you might go back to New Zealand then, Frankie?' Toni looked up from topping up the wine glasses on the coffee table in front of her, although her own was filled with what looked like orange juice.

'Part of the reason I split up with Advik is because he wouldn't even consider moving over there. He's so stuck in his ways.' Frankie frowned. 'Although my mother still isn't speaking to me. She's eighty-eight and maybe I should have waited until she was no longer around before I left him, but I'd put up with Advik and his narrow-mindedness for over thirty years as it was.'

'You can't live your life for anyone else, even if they are your family. I tried it for years and I nearly missed out on so much because of it.' Toni leant into Bobby who wrapped an arm around her shoulders. Seeing the two of them finally making a go of things together always lifted Jess's spirits, but it was also even more evidence – if she'd ever needed it – that no one had ever loved her the way Bobby loved Toni. He'd been willing to wait as long as it took.

'Are you okay, Jess? You don't look too well.' Bobby was immediately on his feet, steadying her arm as she swayed left and right, wondering if the ground could really be coming up to meet her or whether it was all down to the sleepless nights that seemed to be her norm these days.

'I'm fine, just tired that's all.'

'If my ex had done to me what yours did to you, he'd have been wearing his testicles as earrings.' Emily, the young maternity care assistant who'd joined the team before Christmas, spoke with all the assurance of youth, but she couldn't have understood Jess's situation any less. No amount of revenge on Dom would make her happy when all she wanted was a chance to be Teddy's mum. But she'd rejected that possibility and she didn't think any of them would understand why that had even been a dilemma for her, if she admitted it out loud. How could she possibly have considered settling for a life with Dom? That would seem ludicrous to someone like Emily, but Teddy made the decision so much harder than it should have been.

'Emily's right.' Gwen nodded. 'I think I'd have been in prison if I'd been in your position, because I'd have put an ice pick through Dom's head and I wouldn't have stopped at making his testicles into earrings, I'd have put them through the blender – while they were still attached.'

'I must admit I might have liked to see that when Dom first dumped me.' Jess managed a half-smile at the picture Gwen had painted, and she realised she wanted to tell her friends about the deal Dom had offered her after all. She needed to tell them and hear them back up her decision to reject her ex and the chance of being Teddy's mother with it. 'I got over Dom a long time ago though, but then he suggested we get back together so the two of us could parent Teddy. I love Teddy so much, but I just couldn't do it. Things between me and Dom would never work out in the long term and how much worse would it be for Teddy if I disappeared from his life when he's actually got an attachment to me? When I told Dom I didn't want to try giving things a go, he decided to get on a plane and go out to visit that girl from his office who he had an affair with and he's told Teddy's social worker that he's not coming back.'

'He did *what*? That man has got the morals of an alley cat!' Ella screwed up her face. 'If you want to go through with Gwen's ice pick plan, Jess, I'll happily help you bury the body.'

'Me too.' Izzy looked around the room at the others. 'In fact, I reckon we could pull together a whole hit squad if we needed to.'

'I'll bear it in mind!' Jess's laugh caught in her throat as she looked at the baby again. 'I just wish there was a way I could keep Teddy, but not have to have Dom as part of the deal.'

'It's all just so sad, my love.' Gwen stood up and pulled Jess into her arms. Her perfume was so strong that Jess could almost taste it. 'There's only one word for Dom and that's cockwomble!'

This time Jess had actually managed to laugh for real and Gwen dropped one of her trademark perfect winks. It felt so good to laugh with her friends again and it only started to die down as Anna came into the room.

'Here you go.' She handed the bottle to Frankie. 'Teddy's growing so quickly, he changes every time I see him and I love that he's just a stage or two ahead of the twins, so I know what's coming.'

'We won't get to see the next stage for Teddy, though, will we?' Jess dug her fingernails into the palms of her hands, the surge of happiness she'd felt melting away as the urge to grab the baby and run almost took over again. 'He'll be part of someone else's family by then.'

'Isn't there *any* chance they'll let you adopt him?' Anna furrowed her brow. 'He already loves you, it's obvious when he's upset and you're the only one who can comfort him. Plus you're sort of related in a very modern family kind of way.'

'It doesn't work like that. If I was a blood relation they might consider letting me adopt him, but I'm not and I'm not even on the waiting list to adopt. There are hundreds of couples, probably thousands, who've already been approved and are just waiting for a baby.'

'Have you actually asked his social worker?' There was a note of desperation in Ella's voice that Jess recognised only too well. She wasn't the only one who'd fallen in love with Teddy.

'Yes. He's already been matched with one of the waiting families and if Dom and Natalia definitely decide they want him to be adopted, it could be made permanent before his first birthday. I wouldn't be surprised if Dom's parents wanted to take Teddy, but because Diane has had a lot of health issues lately, that looks like a no go too.' Jess sighed. 'It probably didn't help my case that Teddy's social worker is one of Dexter's closest friends, seeing as Dom told her we were seeing each other and she clearly thinks that's a massive mistake too.'

'I didn't realise that you'd become more than friends?' Toni raised her eyebrows and Jess had almost forgotten that she'd kept things with Dexter so quiet. Ella and Anna were the only ones who knew and she wasn't sure there was even anything to tell any more, not when she was starting to think that Madeline was right. But it was out there now anyway.

'We were getting really close, but he comes as part of a package with his stepson, Riley.'

'I'd have thought that was a bonus for you. A sort of readymade family.' It sounded so straightforward the way Emily put it, and Jess wished she could remember what it felt like to be that confident that things could come together so easily and that life was all just meant to be.

'I love Riley.' Jess swallowed hard again, knowing that the words were only too painfully true. 'But there's no guarantee that his father won't want to take him back again at some point and then Dexter would be left with me, someone who can't make him the father he deserves to be. Riley will never be Dexter's only chance of being a parent but, if I let Riley become my only chance, what happens if I lose him as well as Teddy?'

'Have you spoken to Dexter about any of this?' Ella searched Jess's face and she shook her head. None of what had happened was Dexter's fault and she knew she owed it to him to tell him why she was backing off, and to give him the chance to talk it through. But sometimes it was just easier to run away and be the one to end things, before someone else could do it for you.

'Not yet, but there's nothing he can do to change any of this, even if he really wants to.' Jess looked down at Teddy again as he lay in Frankie's arms, her throat burning with the desire to scream at how unfair it all was. 'Teddy probably won't even be called that any more once he's with his new family. It's stupid to worry about that when I'm going to miss him like mad, but it just makes it feel like any link he had to me will be completely wiped out.'

'He'll always be Teddy Bear to us.' Frankie leant into her. 'The kids at my primary school gave me the name Frankie and now everyone calls me that. They couldn't get their heads around the name Firaki, so a couple of them kept saying Frankie and it just kind of stuck. If you label all of his photos up with the name Teddy, you might find that sticks with his new carers too.'

'It's worth a try, I suppose. I know it's not important really, but at least then I'll feel like I'll always be a tiny part of his life. It's silly but I don't want him to forget me, because I'll never forget him for as long as I live.' Jess bit her lip, not sure whether to confess what had been on her mind when she'd been at Ocean Cove. 'You're going to think I've completely lost the plot when I tell you this, but I've even thought about leaving Port

Agnes, taking Teddy, and getting as far away as possible where no one will ever find us.'

'You can't do that!' Anna's eyes widened.

'I know, I'd be rubbish at being on the run and I'd probably be caught and arrested before I even got the ferry in Portsmouth.'

'No, you can't leave us, Jess. Port Agnes wouldn't be the same without you and the twins are going to need their Auntie Jess to confide in, when everything their mum and dad does annoys them.'

'And you've got bridesmaid duties, too, don't forget.' Ella met her gaze. 'I need you more than ever to help me get through the extravaganza Mum has got planned.'

'Yeah, and no offence to the rest of you, but with Anna off on maternity leave, Jess is my favourite midwife to work with, so I want you back too.' Toni shrugged and Jess couldn't help laughing again. It might be faint praise, but it was about as gushing as Toni was ever likely to get.

'We'll get you through this together, you know that, don't you?' Anna hesitated as Jess nodded. 'Just say the word and we'll be here for you whenever you want.'

'I know. Thank you all so much – and the twins are going to get sick of me hugging them and wanting to be around them all the time.' Maybe if Jess put all her energy into being the best godmother who'd ever lived, she'd find a way to keep going after Teddy moved on. It had to be her best shot.

'I highly doubt they'll ever get sick of their cool Auntie Jess.' Anna laughed too as, right on cue, the sound of one of the twins starting to cry came over the baby monitor. 'It looks like Merryn or Kit needs you already.'

'I'm on it, but I might need Ella if they're both ready to come down.' Jess headed towards the stairs, with Ella following on behind. For the first time in weeks, it felt like there was a ray of hope that she could get somehow get through the pain that was coming, with the help of her friends. But she knew now that she was going to have to let Dexter and Riley go first, because not even the other midwives could get her through losing them too, if she let herself fall any more in love with them than she already had.

17

Madeline had asked Jess if she could take Teddy to his first visit with the people who, in all likelihood, were going to become his forever family. She'd agreed to do it and she'd even managed to make her tone light, as if taking Teddy to meet the couple who'd get to raise him was nothing much at all. Even heading over there, the thought that she could just take a different turn in the road and keep on driving, had crossed her mind. She could get on a train and be at the other end of the country within hours – an anonymous face in a crowded city, hiding Teddy in plain sight. Once she crossed the threshold into the carers' house there'd be no going back, but she had to do the best for Teddy. Whatever kind of mess she'd made of other aspects of her life, she wanted to look back and know she'd helped in some small way to give this little boy the best possible start in life, no matter how much pain it caused her. Maybe then she could claim the title of having been a mother, even for a blink of an eye. After all, mothers were supposed to be selfless, and letting go of Teddy without a fight was the ultimate act of selflessness. Despite all her best intentions, Jess was fully prepared to hate Teddy's new carers on sight. They were the people who were going to take Teddy away from her, so how could she possibly be expected to like them?

'Hi, you must be Jess. We've heard so much about you. I'm Toby.' The man who answered the door gave her a beaming smile and to her surprise, Jess found herself mirroring him. 'Teddy's been really lucky to have you to look after him by the sounds of it. Come on in, Madeline's already inside and my wife, Sadie, is hovering around. She's barely been able to sit still since we got the call to say we might finally have an adoption match.'

'I can understand how she must feel.' Jess stepped into the hallway with Teddy in her arms. Any minute now she was going to have to hand him over and there was no way of knowing if she'd ever get him back. It still wasn't too late to run and the fight or flight sensation was in danger of overriding all logic. She knew she couldn't, but the adrenaline pumping through her veins said otherwise. It was now or never. She might only be small, but she was almost certain she could outrun Toby and Madeline if she needed to, even with Teddy in her arms. Toby was still talking and sounded so nice, but somehow not hating him on sight made it even harder. Digging her fingernails into the palm of her hand, in the way she always did to push down the emotional pain, Jess concentrated hard on fighting the urge to take flight, no matter how much she might want to.

'Sadie can't wait to meet you. She's desperate to know everything there is to know about Teddy.' Toby showed her into the lounge, where Madeline was sitting in one of the armchairs on the right-hand side of the fireplace. It looked exactly like the sort of room that might feature on a Christmas card; she could almost picture a row of stockings pinned along the mantelpiece – one for Toby, one for Sadie and one for whatever they decided to call Teddy after they'd adopted him.

'Thanks for bringing Teddy over, Jess.' Madeline smiled and Jess forced herself to nod, trying not to hate the woman who had matched Teddy with his forever family, because the truth was that she could already tell that the social workers had done a good job.

'Yes, thank you so much!' Sadie shot across the room, taking hold of both of Jess's arms, the baby between them. 'Madeline has told us how amazing you've been with Teddy, but I didn't realise I knew you.'

'I don't... I'm really sorry, so we've met before?' It should have felt horribly awkward being held so close by a strange woman, especially one who claimed to know her. But Sadie was so smiley and warm, just like her husband, and Jess was almost tempted to ask them if they'd adopt her too. At least that way she'd get to stay in Teddy's life.

'My sister, Cleo, lives in Port Agnes and she had a home birth last year. I was her birthing partner and you were one of the midwives.' Sadie squeezed her hands. 'Cleo wanted me to be part of it, because she knows I'll never get to give birth myself, and it was an amazing experience. Not least because you were so brilliant.'

'I doubt I did anything special, it's all down to the amazing mums and the support they get from their birth partners. I'm just so lucky to have a job where I get to be a part of that.' Sooner or later Sadie was going to let go of her arms, but even when she did, Jess was still going to feel connected to her. Neither of them could have children of their own and she knew exactly how Sadie must have felt watching her sister give birth. It was a joy and a privilege to witness the miracle of birth, but there was a uniquely bittersweet pain in knowing it could never be you. And suddenly the urge to take flight had lessened. Even if Sadie wasn't holding on to her arms, she'd no longer have wanted to run.

'You did do something special, trust me, the way you supported Cleo through it all made more difference than you'll ever know.' Sadie finally released Jess's hands. 'And I know you'll have given Teddy an amazing start in life too. Me and Toby just want to keep that going.'

'I can already see that.' Jess pressed her lips together; even when something was the right thing to do, it wasn't always easy. Turning towards Madeline, she forced herself to ask the question she knew she had to face. 'So what happens next?'

'We'll have one or two more meetings, so you can give Toby and Sadie all the information they need to make Teddy's transition as smooth as possible and then he'll move in.' Madeline let out a long breath. 'I know this is going to be hard on you, Jess, but it's a risk for Toby and Sadie too. Teddy's parents could change their mind and halt the adoption process at any time up until it's finalised. The local authority have only agreed to it because Toby and Sadie are experienced foster carers who've managed the transition to adoption for other children. So they know better than anyone what they're getting into.'

'I'll be terrified the whole time that someone's going to take Teddy away, but we've got to take this chance or we might never get it again.' Sadie shook her head. 'It's been hard every time we've had to let one of the children we've looked after go to a new home and we desperately want it to be our turn to give a child a forever home this time. Fostering for three years convinced Toby he could do it, because he wasn't sure at first if he wanted to adopt after we first found out I was never going to be able to get pregnant.'

'I'm ashamed to admit it now. But I wanted to be sure I could love a child that wasn't genetically mine as much as they

262   JO BARTLETT

deserved to be loved. And now I know I can.' Toby gave Jess
another one of his beaming smiles, as she handed Teddy to
Sadie, her arms shaking with the weight of the moment. It was
their turn, however much that might hurt Jess to admit.

'You're such a beautiful baby, aren't you, Teddy?' Sadie's face
glowed as she looked down at him and, as hard as it was to
watch, Jess couldn't deny that he looked like he belonged in her
arms.

'Are you still going to call him Teddy?' The baby's name had
needed to be registered within forty-two days of his birth, but
she'd known even then that it might be a temporary fix which
could be changed later and Teddy's forever name had never
been in her control.

'We love the name and we also hate the idea of giving him
another one and that being taken away too, if his parents change
their minds before the adoption is finalised.' Sadie leant against
Toby and he put his arm around her. They already looked like a
perfect little family and Sadie could give Teddy something Jess
couldn't: a father. His new carers looked about as stable as a
couple could look. Jess, on the other hand, was still part way
through an increasingly messy divorce and she was back to
ignoring Dexter's calls, knowing she was going to have to walk
away from the kindest man she'd ever met because letting
herself love him completely was far too big a risk. There were
plenty of happy families where a dad didn't play a part, but Jess
knew only too well how tough it could sometimes be for a
parent on their own. Teddy needed the sort of father who'd be
there for him, even if something happened to Sadie, and Toby
looked more than capable of stepping up to the plate.

'Sadie's favourite granddad on her mother's side was called
Edward, which was shortened to Ted, so it seems like it was
meant to be. You couldn't have picked a better name.' Toby

beamed at Jess again. 'We're just struggling for a middle name, but I'm sure we'll come up with something suitable. Won't we, love?'

'We will.' Sadie couldn't take her eyes off the baby lying in her arms. 'I just can't wait until we can make it all official. It's going to be a long six months, but everything we've been through up until now will be worth it if we get to keep Teddy.'

'He's worth going through anything for.' Jess blinked back the tears that were burning her eyes, the way she seemed to be doing so often, and desperately hoped that the others hadn't noticed. She had to stay strong and get through this so that Teddy could have the life he deserved. But she already knew that the life he deserved needed to involve Toby and Sadie, and it was very nearly time to say goodbye.

* * *

Dexter was waiting outside Puffin's Rest when Jess got back from Toby and Sadie's house. Luna, who usually treated everyone with equal levels of disdain, was sitting at his feet and gazing up at him adoringly. Even the cat could tell what a good guy Dexter was, but just like Teddy, he deserved more than Jess would ever be able to give him. He needed someone who could let themselves love him wholeheartedly and Jess had already given away too many parts of her heart to be able to do that.

'I can go if you don't want me here, but I needed to check you were okay after taking Teddy to meet his new carers.' Dexter's tone was warm, despite the fact that she'd been fobbing him off for days. She used the meeting with Toby and Sadie as a reason for cancelling their plans to see one another, but she owed it to him to be upfront with him.

'They're lovely.' Jess's throat felt raw from the emotion of the last few hours and it hurt even to speak, but there were things she had to say that couldn't wait any longer. 'Why don't you come in for a bit and we can talk properly.'

'I'd like that.' Dexter swung into action the way he always did, helping her to get Teddy and all of his stuff up the stairs to the apartment. By the time she'd put Teddy down for a nap, he'd sorted all of the bags out and folded up the buggy they'd carried up the stairs between them.

'Do you want some tea?' Jess was vaguely aware that she was trying to put off saying what needed to be said, but Dexter wasn't having any of it.

'I just want to know what's going on.' His dark eyes never left her face as he stood close to her. 'I thought things were going so well between us, but I don't know, maybe it was all too much for you. I know I haven't felt like this for a long time, probably never, but I'm guessing from the way you've backed right off that you don't want something serious.'

'It's too soon after Dom.' The lie had tripped off her tongue almost without her thinking about it, but the truth wasn't an option. If she told Dexter that she wanted to finish things between them because she needed to be the one in control of ending things, he'd just try to convince her that giving up on something because it might end was stupid. But not even Dexter could make her any promises about Riley staying in their lives, he had no more control over that than she did, and pretending she still had feelings for her ex was easier. Dexter would have too much pride to fight his corner, if he believed she really preferred someone like Dom to him. She was doing it for his own good and he'd thank her for it one day, when he had a child of his own who no one could take away from him.

'You can't let Dom stop you moving forward, after everything you've been through.'

'He's the only family I've had since my mum died and his parents have been so good to me. It's not as easy as I thought it would be to walk away from that and if he changes his mind about giving up Teddy, I need to be there to support him with that too.'

'You can't still be hoping all of that will work out, Jess.' Dexter sounded exasperated, but his eyes were filled with sadness. He felt sorry for her and something about the way he was looking at her hardened her resolve. Maybe she'd been right all along, he was looking for another broken soul to fix and Jess had probably seemed like the perfect candidate. But he should know better than anyone that some people were beyond fixing. If she had to persuade him that she was still hung up on Dom to make him see that, then she would.

'I don't need anyone to tell me how to live my life and I've had just about enough of social workers dictating to me since I decided to become a foster carer.' Jess was doing what she always did, attacking as a form of defence. Focusing on feeling angry about the decisions that Madeline had made was much easier than letting herself experience her real emotions, which were bubbling just below the surface. She was losing Teddy and now she was pushing Dexter and Riley away. She loved all of them so much and if she let the defensive shield she'd built around herself slip even a tiny bit, her legs would probably give out from under her.

'I'm not trying to tell you what to do, Jess, but I can't believe you feel as differently about the situation with Dom than you did before. I just don't want you to do anything you might regret.'

'I'm old enough to make my own decisions and if all you've come round here for is to tell me what you think is right for me, then I think you'd better just go.' Jess actually pointed to the door, because if she didn't act like she really meant it, then neither she nor Dexter were going to believe it. He was right, she was in danger of doing something she was going to regret, in fact she had a horrible feeling she'd already done it. But at least she was in control of causing the pain this time and she just had to hope that would make it easier to bear.

18

In the three days between throwing Dexter out of Puffin's Rest and taking Teddy over to Sadie and Toby's place for the final time, Jess had picked up the phone to contact Dexter about an average of twice an hour. She'd resisted up until the night before she was due to drop Teddy off, but just after midnight, she'd finally given in and sent him an email. She had too much to say for a text.

Email to: @socialworkdex

Hi Dexter

I'm trying to be brave, because in a few hours I've got to hand Teddy over to Sadie and Toby, but I've been a coward in other ways and I wanted you to know the truth. I'm not interested in Dom, but I'm scared of getting hurt again. I'm crap at relationships and everyone ends up leaving me in the end. What I should have said to you is that I'd rather have you as a friend than not at all, which is how it would have ended up. Things are so up in the air with Riley, the last thing you need is someone like me complicating things. But I miss talking to you and you're the only person who really understands how I'm

feeling about letting Teddy go. I don't blame you if you're done with me, after I couldn't even be honest, but I wanted to let you know that I'm sorry and that you didn't deserve any of the things I said.
Jess

She thought about how to end the email. Kind regards had seemed crazily formal, but putting love or a kiss would have opened up a whole other can of worms. Especially when friend-ship with Dexter was already a compromise. She wanted much more than that and after the night they'd spent together, she'd almost been able to convince herself that it could be the one relationship that would finally work out. Then all the doubts had crept in, not to mention the fact that she'd kept something as huge as not being able to have a child from him. So she'd pushed him away altogether in an attempt to protect herself, but she'd been hurt anyway. It was lose-lose and she'd probably already blown the chance of salvaging their friendship, but at least the email had got things off her chest, even if Dexter decided to delete it before reading it.

The rest of the night had been largely sleepless again and it had almost been a relief when the morning sunlight started filtering through the windows, despite the fact that it meant the day of Teddy leaving had finally arrived. A few short hours later, Jess was parking her car on Toby and Sadie's driveway. Teddy was in the back, tucked up in his car seat, and all of his posses-sions were packed up in the boot, except the sleepsuits he'd already outgrown. Jess had packed those into a box and slid them onto the same shelf in the top of her wardrobe where her memory box of things from her mother was hidden. Her two most precious possessions side by side.

She'd made a memory book for Teddy too, so that when he was older he could look back and know what happened in his first weeks. She'd made an identical one for herself, even though she wasn't sure if she was ever going to be able to look at it, when Teddy was living fifteen miles away and she could never be a part of his life.

She was still sitting in the car with her hands on the steering wheel five minutes later when a tap on the window made her jump. Toby held up a hand and gave her one of his warm smiles. Social convention dictated that she should reciprocate, but she'd never felt less like smiling in her life. Instead she forced herself to open the door.

'Sorry, Sadie's been watching out of the window for you to arrive for at least half an hour and we were a bit worried when you didn't come in.' Toby stepped back as she got out of the car.

'I just needed a minute.' Jess's unshed tears were making it hard to breathe, even before Toby pulled her into a hug. He was a big bear of a man, perfect for a baby to cuddle up to, and he couldn't have been more different from Dom if he'd tried.

'This must be so hard for you. Sadie was crying her heart out last night and when I asked her why, she said she was thinking of you and what you were going through.' Toby cleared his throat as Jess pulled away from him. 'We're so grateful for what you've done.'

'Having Teddy for the first months of his life has been the best thing that's ever happened to me, but I've got to admit that this is one of the hardest, even though I know you and Sadie are going to give him an amazing life.'

'We really will, I promise.'

'Let's get him inside then, shall we? You take the car seat and I'll get his bags.' If Jess took Teddy in, she wasn't sure she'd have the strength to hand him over. Madeline would be coming to collect his cot and some of the other equipment in a few days' time, because Toby and Sadie had understandably wanted to buy their own. So Teddy's possessions consisted of the memory book, some clothes, the mobile from above his cot that he loved watching so much, a teddy bear, and a half-empty pack of nappies. It didn't seem like much, considering that he'd completely taken over her life and Puffin's Rest from the moment he'd arrived.

'I love this little outfit you've put him in!' By the time Jess got inside, Sadie already had Teddy in her arms. And the hardest part was that she looked like a complete natural; she was going to be better than Jess at all of this.

'It just seemed like the perfect outfit for him to come to his new home in.' It was a fluffy brown bear Babygro, complete with little ears on the hood, and Jess had taken about thirty photographs of him in it before they'd left the flat.

'You will come and see us, won't you?' Sadie had gone from smiling to tears spilling down her cheeks in an instant and it was just one more thing Jess envied. She felt frozen, the unshed tears were still choking her throat, making it completely raw, and her insides felt as if they'd been hollowed out, but somehow she still couldn't cry.

'You don't really want me coming over. You guys are giving Teddy a fresh start, the last thing you want is to have me hanging around all the time.'

'Maybe not all the time!' Toby laughed. 'But we really want you to stay in Teddy's life. It's been obvious since the first time we met that you love him, and kids should be surrounded by as many people who love them as possible.'

'There's something else we need to tell you too.' Sadie paused and Jess's stomach churned again. If they told her that Dom or Natalia had decided to challenge the adoption, she wasn't sure if she'd be able to stop herself from snatching Teddy out of Sadie's arms and jumping on the nearest boat heading out to sea. Knowing that he was going to be raised by people who'd be as devoted to him as Jess was, was the only reason she was still functioning at all.

'We've finally picked a middle name for Teddy, for when we're allowed to officially re-register it.' Toby picked up a piece of paper from the coffee table and handed it to Jess.

'Teddy Kennedy Fitzpatrick.' Reading his name out loud, she looked up at Toby, tears finally filling her eyes.

'We considered Jesse as a middle name, but Kennedy has a bit of gravitas and there've been a few great leaders with that name. We decided on just Teddy as his first name, rather than Edward or Theodore, so having a more formal middle name seemed like a good fit. But either way we want him to know the part you played in his life and just how important that was to us, and to him.'

'I don't know what to say.' Jess was openly sobbing now, but it was a mixture of complete joy and utter sorrow that she couldn't have attempted to separate if her life depended on it.

'Just say you'll still come and see us. Teddy's going to want to have his Auntie Jess to run to when we drive him mad as a teenager. I've got a feeling you'll always be the cool one!' Sadie mirrored the words that Anna had said, sandwiching Teddy between them just like he'd been the very first time they'd met. Except this time, Sadie would be the one left holding him and Jess would be going home alone.

Once the tears had started it had been impossible to stop them and Jess had spent most of the rest of the day and night folded into a soggy heap on the sofa at Puffin's Rest, with even Luna realising that something wasn't right. The cat had lain with her back against Jess's, purring softly and occasionally flicking her rough sandpaper tongue across the back of Jess's neck.

When Jess had been given the date for Teddy's handover to the Fitzpatricks, the first thing she'd done was to ring Ella and arrange to come back to work full-time the day after she'd dropped him off. There was no way she could spend more than one day on her own doing her best to turn the sofa into a water bed. Going back to work was a welcome relief, but that didn't stop it feeling like she was on autopilot. Dexter still hadn't got in touch, but she could hardly blame him and she figured she might as well go through the grieving process for Teddy, Dexter and Riley all at the same time. After all, that had been the whole reason for ending things when she did, so she was only getting what she asked for. The one bright light was being able to return to the job she loved and the friends who made that feel like coming home. If she hadn't had their friendship and support, she wasn't even sure if she'd have managed to keep getting up in the mornings.

'It's good to see your face around here again, where you belong.' Ella threw her arms around Jess as soon as she walked into the staffroom on her first day back. 'And not a moment too soon. Without Gwen's cakes and biscuits, you're almost disappearing.'

'I haven't had much of an appetite lately.'

'Oh, Jess, you've been through so much and yesterday must have been heartbreaking.' Ella swallowed so hard Jess could hear it, but she didn't want the others to think they couldn't mention Teddy's name. Talking about him would mean that none of them forgot him and she couldn't bear the idea that anyone would.

'Toby and Sadie are such a great couple and they're even giving Teddy the middle name of Kennedy. How amazing is that?' Jess managed a wobbly smile. 'He'll never be able to forget me now.'

'Will you be able to see him?' Ella's voice was gentle.

'They've said they want me to, but I think I need to leave it a while. For my own sake.'

'And what about things with Dexter? Have you done anything about that?'

'I sent him an email and said I was sorry for the way I handled things.' Jess sighed. 'But I haven't heard back from him.'

'There'll be a reason, he wouldn't just blank you like that.'

'Why not? I told him that's what I wanted and it's the second time I've pushed him away and thrown him out of my house without even giving him the chance to put his point of view across.'

'Just don't write it off, Jess. You seemed to really like him and, from what I can tell, he really liked you too. If anyone deserves to have someone great in their lives, it's you.'

'Talking of having someone great in your life, how are the wedding plans going?' Jess couldn't talk about Dexter any more. Her heart was already torn in two over Teddy and she wasn't sure if she could take one more rejection and live to tell the tale. She'd tried to reach out to Dexter and he hadn't responded. Whatever Ella might think, there was only one reason for that.

'I'm starting to wish I'd never agreed to a Valentine's Day wedding, let's put it like that. It's opened the door to a potential cheese-fest!' Ella screwed up her face. 'Mum's going to town on the love heart theme. Every time I go over there she's ordered something else off the internet. The latest thing is a heart-shaped fishbowl on a gold stand for the top table. And I'm not even joking!'

'It'll be a great day whatever happens and a little bit of cheesiness never did anyone any harm.' The lead weight in Jess's chest lifted a tiny bit. Brighter days would come eventually and looking forward to the wedding helped remind her of that. Ella had been through more than her fair share of heartbreak too, and she'd found happiness again. Jess just had to take it a day at a time and try not to think about the chance of happiness that she might have already thrown away. Otherwise she would never be able to move on.

* * *

Being back in clinic had proven to be another great distraction. With the expectant mothers she was seeing, she didn't have to be *poor little Jess*, who'd had to give up the baby her husband had fathered with another woman. They weren't interested in the soap opera her life had become, because their focus was on having a healthy baby of their own, and worries about birth and beyond. Within an hour of starting her first clinic, Jess had fallen in love with her job all over again.

As a rule, two weeks after their delivery, the women and babies the team looked after transferred to the care of the health visitors. Even so, Jess would usually have expected to see a few newborns in the clinic but there hadn't been any. That was probably down to Ella, but sooner or later Jess was going to have to deal with babies who reminded her of Teddy when she'd first found him in the basket on her doorstep. She could hardy avoid newborns forever in her job, after all.

Jess had just seen her last mum-to-be before she was due to stop for lunch, when there was a knock on the consulting room door.

'Sorry, I know I haven't got an appointment, but I wondered if you had minute?' Faith Baxter was standing outside the open door with baby Titus in her arms. 'I popped in on the off-chance that you might be here and one of the other midwives told me it would be okay to come down.'

'Of course, come in! It's so lovely to see you both. He's grown so much since I last saw you.' Titus had chubby cheeks and he looked as though he was smiling at Jess as Faith brought him into the room.

'He's such a good boy too. I almost wish he woke up more often, then I wouldn't have to keep going and checking on him every five minutes to make sure he's breathing.' Faith rolled her eyes. 'Although I am getting a bit better with that and starting to trust that I might actually be allowed to keep my baby this time around.'

'He looks really well and strong, which is obviously down to you. You're clearly doing a great job.' Jess caught her breath as Faith placed Titus into her arms without warning. If she closed her eyes, she could imagine it was Teddy lying there – the same solid, reassuring weight that had left her arms feeling emptier than she'd ever believed possible once he was gone.

'I can't believe I considered never having another baby when I lost Archie. I just wasn't sure I could risk it again, but I'd have lost even more if I'd never tried.' Faith smiled, even as her eyes filled with tears. 'He's taught me the importance of grabbing second chances whenever they come along and never taking the good things in life for granted.'

'He really is gorgeous, thanks so much for bringing him in to see me.' Jess couldn't trust herself to say any more. There were at least two big risks she needed to take if she wanted a second chance at happiness, but she still wasn't sure if she had the courage to take either of them.

* * *

Luna weaved in and out of Jess's legs meowing loudly as she dismantled Teddy's cot ready for Madeline to collect it. Jess had felt like wailing too. It was like wiping out the final reminder of the little boy from Puffin's Rest, even if she could still picture him in every room and had woken up in the early hours the night before, convinced she could hear him crying. It had turned out to be a seagull perched on the kitchen windowsill, but even so, it had been pointless trying to get back to sleep after that. Madeline was coming over on her way to work, so Jess had decided she might as well pack the cot up then. And that's how she'd found herself wielding an Allen key and choking back the tears at four o'clock in the morning.

By the time Madeline arrived, Jess had been out for a run along the headland, showered, made some toast she didn't want to eat, and brewed a fresh pot of coffee.

'Come in, I've got it all packed up and ready.' She ushered Madeline into the flat. 'Have you got time for a coffee?'

'It smells great, so I'm not going to refuse an offer like that. Especially not with the day I've got ahead!'

'Grab a seat and I'll get us both a cup. I always find it helps with the start to a tricky day too. Anything you can talk about?' Jess set out two mugs on the kitchen counter. It might not make her the nicest person in the world, but ever since she'd dropped Teddy off she'd taken some comfort from the realisation that she wasn't the only one who was going through a hard time. It dragged her out of her pit of self-pity to admit that things really could be worse.

'I've got to sit in on a foster panel at eleven where the carers are probably going to be deregistered because the realities of fostering have been too much for them.' Madeline sighed. 'Not everyone's got what it takes, even if they look good on paper. But you've already more than proven you have what's needed.'

'That sounds like a tough morning.' Jess couldn't bring herself to acknowledge Madeline's compliment and she wasn't sure how she felt about taking on another placement when she was still missing Teddy so much. It was easier to stick to the mundane. 'How do you take your coffee?'

'Milk, no sugar, thanks. And I mean it, you're a really good foster carer.'

'Having Teddy was easy.' Jess slid the mug across the counter to where Madeline was perched on one of the kitchen stools.

'But giving him up wasn't remotely easy and you handled that so well.'

'From the outside maybe.' Jess took a mouthful of coffee that burned her throat, but at least it gave her an excuse not to talk.

'I know you chose to foster because you want to make a difference, but have you ever thought about getting approved for adoption?' Madeline had finally come out with the question that her friends seemed to have been skirting around since she'd had to give Teddy up. 'You can't replace Teddy, I understand that, but there are other children out there who are going to need someone like you to give them a loving home and there's no doubting you can do that.'

'I don't know. My head's all over the place. At the moment I can't even imagine fostering again, let alone adopting.'

'You need some time, I get that. But it would be a real loss if you decided not to foster again and I'd hate to think of you missing out on the chance to adopt. Just don't rule anything out.'

'Okay, I promise to think about all the options when I feel more like myself again.' Jess wrapped her hands around the coffee mug, steeling herself to ask the next question. 'How's Dexter?'

'You haven't heard? He's been in hospital for the last three days. Connor dropped out of the rehab scheme and tried to snatch Riley whilst he was on something. He pushed Dexter off the pavement and into the path of a car during the scuffle.'

'Oh my God! Is he okay?' For a moment Jess thought she might actually be sick. Dexter had been lying in a hospital bed, but she hadn't even known or been there for him or Riley, all because of her stubborn sense of self-preservation. She was obviously the worst person in the world. Guilt was churning like a whirlpool in her stomach, alongside terror at how badly Dexter had been hurt.

'He's broken his wrist and he needed an op to have it pinned, but he's going to be okay. His phone got completely crushed by the car too, so that might be why he hasn't been in touch to tell you where he is.'

'Do you think it'll be okay for me to go and see him?'

'I'm picking him up tonight. My wife has sorted out a new phone for him and she's getting it all set up with his old numbers and contacts. So I'm sure he'll want to speak to you.' It wasn't a yes, but it wasn't a no either and right now, Jess had to take what she could get.

'Just tell him I'm really sorry… about the accident and everything else.'

'I think you should tell him yourself, Jess. He's going to need his friends more than ever now. Even if that's all the two of you end up being, I can tell you from experience that Dexter's friendship has been one of the biggest blessings in my life.'

'I can imagine, but I just…' Jess shook her head. 'I'm just not very good at dealing with people showing me sympathy and when he tried to support me through everything that was happening with Teddy, I handled it really badly. Sometimes it's hard to deal with someone who's that nice, when it isn't what you've been used to.'

'I do know what you mean.' Madeline looked down at her

coffee. 'And maybe I was wrong to suggest you getting in touch. It might be just as well for both of you if you do leave things, given that he'll be living five-hundred miles away pretty soon.'

'What do you mean?' Jess's mug banged down on the kitchen worktop, almost slipping from her hands.

'Oh shit, I've done it again and put my bloody size seven feet in my mouth.' Madeline pressed her lips together, but it was too late for her to clam up now.

'You might as well just tell me.'

'He rang me this morning to let me know that he got a call from our old boss who's moved up to Edinburgh, to check how he's doing after the accident. She's offered him a job up there, so he can get as far away from Connor as possible. If his application for sole custody of Riley goes through, he's going to move up there to give them both a fresh start. Given the way Connor's been acting, Dex thinks it's the best chance of giving Riley some stability and keeping him away from all the drama. I'm sure he'd have told you when you finally spoke.'

'I'm sure he would, but there's not a lot of point now, is there?' Jess swallowed another mouthful of hot coffee, barely even feeling the pain. She'd left it too late with Dexter and he'd clearly decided she was right and that a fresh start for all of them would be for the best, especially Riley. She wasn't going to mess that up when she loved them both so much, but it had made her realise something else. There was a fresh start of her own she needed to take a chance on, otherwise it might end up being too late for that as well, and it would be just another regret to add to the long list. It was time to be brave again.

19

Jess looked at her watch for what must have been the fifteenth time. He still had five minutes to show up, but she wasn't even sure she'd recognise him if he did. Maybe she should have suggested he wore a yellow rose in his buttonhole, but she wouldn't have been surprised if he didn't turn up at all. It had been twenty years after all.

When she'd finally decided to reply to her father's message, she'd told him she wanted to meet up and they'd agreed on the Beach Hut Café that had just opened up ready for the summer season in Port Agnes. She could have got into a lengthy exchange of messages with him, but there hardly seemed any point. The things she wanted to ask him could only really be done face to face, because she wanted to be able to see his expression – it was the only way she'd know if he was telling the truth.

'Can I get you anything else?' The young waitress smiled at Jess as she came back over to the table. She'd been nursing a cup of tea for more than twenty minutes already, having got to the café half an hour early. She'd wanted to make sure she was the first one there, so her father would have to walk in and face her for the first time in two decades, rather than the other way around.

'Just another cup of tea please.'

'Can you make that two, please?' Guy Kennedy had appeared out of nowhere. His hair was thinner than she remembered and there were a few lines on his face, but a lot less than he deserved to have.

'No problem and just give me a shout if you decide you'd like some cake to go with that.' The waitress smiled again and headed back behind the counter, leaving Jess's father standing in front of her.

'You can sit down, if you want.' She'd rehearsed what she was going to say to him about ten different ways, but when it came down to it, an invitation to sit down was the best she could come up with.

'You've grown into a beautiful young woman, J-J.'

'Growing up is what kids tend to do, even if neither of their parents are around to witness it.' Jess curled her fingers into a ball, silently cursing herself for not being able to hold on to her composure for even the first five minutes. Now he'd know just how much he'd hurt her and it gave him the power all over again.

'I'm so sorry, my darling, and I know nothing I can ever say will ever excuse what I did.' The fact that he hadn't tried to make an excuse knocked the air out of her all over again. She'd been sure she knew what was coming, all the reasons why none of this had been his fault and how hard it had been for him. The last thing she'd expected was for the first words out of his mouth to be an apology. But she wasn't letting him off the hook that easily, talk was cheap after all.

'You're right about that. I think I could have understood you leaving when you were back in the grip of addiction after Mum died.' For a moment Jess's thoughts strayed to Dexter and the way he'd been left to pick up the pieces after Riley's father had succumbed to his own addictions all over again. She couldn't think about the two of them, though, or she'd have absolutely no chance of keeping control of her emotions. 'But that was twenty years ago and I find it very hard to believe it took you that long to get clean.'

'It took me the best part of ten years to stop drinking or taking drugs for good. Every time I thought I'd cracked it, something happened and I was back in the pit of addiction again.' Guy finally took a seat across the table from her. 'I didn't want to bring that back into your life, Jess, when social services kept telling me how settled you were with your foster carers. I didn't want to rock the boat.'

'Every day I hoped that would be the day you'd get back in touch.' Jess's mouth was so dry she could barely get the words out. 'I probably stopped crying myself to sleep after the first three or four months, but I never stopped hoping that when someone knocked on the door or the phone rang, that it would be you.'

'Your foster carers were good to you, though, weren't they?' Guy knitted his eyebrows together, leaning forward as he waited for her to answer.

'They kept me safe and mostly they were kind, but they weren't you and Mum.' Jess shook her head. 'Every year they'd go on holiday for a break from fostering and take their own children with them, whilst I was sent to stay with other foster carers. It was obvious that it was me they needed a break from and every year I prayed they'd ask me to go with them, or even better tell me that I was going to stay with you instead. Couldn't you have even done that? Put up with me for two weeks once every sodding year?'

'Er, excuse me, but I've got your pot of tea for two.' The waitress cleared her throat, clearly not wanting to interrupt what must have seemed like an intense conversation, even to a casual observer. Setting the pot and some cups and saucers on the table in front of them, she disappeared without even trying to persuade them to add two slices of cake to their order again.

Jess stared out of the window, not trusting herself to hold it together if she spoke first. Instead she fixed her gaze on a man who must have been in his mid-thirties, running along the sand and throwing a kite into the air to try and get it to fly, as a young girl held determinedly onto the other end. That's what fathers were supposed to do with their daughters, not just disappear out of their lives.

'Shall I pour?' Guy didn't sound as if any of this was hard for him; keeping up the niceties as if this was just a casual get-together for two old acquaintances. Maybe this had all been rehearsed and the apology he'd started with was all part of the plan to win her over, except she couldn't work out what would be in that for him. She wasn't a cute kid any more and why he'd want a stroppy and resentful thirty-year-old in his life all of a sudden was anyone's guess. Okay, so it had taken him ten years to finally get control of his addictions, but he'd still waited another ten to get in touch. There had to be a reason – maybe he was biding his time, waiting to ask Jess if she was willing to give him one of her kidneys or something – but she wasn't interested in small talk, she needed to know what his motive for all of this really was.

'What do you want, Guy?' She saw him flinch at the use of his name, but you had to earn the title of dad and he'd lost that chance a long time ago.

'I just wanted to see you, that's all.'

'It's been twenty years and you've just said you've been sober for the last ten. It must have been one hell of a hangover if it took you this long to get round to contacting me.'

'Like I said, I didn't want to rock the boat and I thought dropping back into your life after all that time might do more harm than good.' His frowned. 'And the truth was I didn't think I deserved you.'

'So what's changed now? What suddenly makes you think it's okay to drop into my life now?' She held his gaze for a few seconds longer than was comfortable. 'What makes you think for one second that you deserve to be a part of my life *now*?'

'I still don't, but I realised it was worth risking getting hurt by trying, just in case there was a tiny chance you might not slam the door in my face. I've had years of counselling since I got sober to come to terms with what I did, but I understand if you don't want me in your life.' Guy shut his eyes for a moment and took a deep breath. 'And I figured maybe you might even need me, after what you've been through.'

'What do you mean, what I've been through?' There was no way he could know about Teddy, or Dexter, or even the infertility. Unless someone she trusted had betrayed her. It wouldn't be a surprise, it was the story of her life after all.

'When I looked you up on Facebook, I saw some wedding photos and then I found your husband's Facebook page. It didn't take much scrolling through to work out that the two of you had split up pretty quickly after you got married. From what I can make out in more recent pictures, he's in Tenerife now with a girl who isn't you. That must have been so tough on you, J-J, and I just wanted to be there for you. To see if I could help in any way: financially, practically or even just as a shoulder to cry on.'

'I learnt to get by without your help a long time ago.'

'I know you did, darling.' Guy stared down at the table, his fingers tracing an invisible pattern on the wood. 'But I'd like to be a part of your life again. Whatever you want that to look like. You're my only child and whatever you might think, and however badly I might have failed you in the past, I really do love you.'

'How would you being a part of my life even work? When you haven't had a father for twenty years, it's pretty hard to work out how one might slot into your life.'

'It can work however you want it to. We can meet up for a cup of tea or maybe a bit of lunch whenever you can fit me in. Take it slowly and get to know each other again and hopefully, when you do, you'll want me to stick around. It would all be on your terms, J-J.'

'What if you get to know me and decide you're the one who doesn't want to stick around?' Jess scrunched her hand into a fist again. She'd already had more than enough rejection to last a lifetime.

'I'm never going to be that stupid again, I promise.' His eyes searched her face. 'I know you've been hurt really badly in the past, and not just by me. I also know what it's like to lose the love of your life, because I lost that when I lost you and your mum. And now you're going through it losing your husband and it's so unfair when you've already been through so much. Just let me be there for you, J-J.'

'I don't know if I—' She looked across at him again and he leant forward, waiting for her to finish, suddenly looking much more vulnerable than when he'd been standing in front of her table just ten minutes before. 'I'm not making any big promises, but we can meet again for tea next week if you like? Same time, same place?'

'I'd really love that, but whatever you want is fine by me.' He smiled and she nodded, determined to be more honest with him than he'd ever been with her.

'We'll just have to take it week by week and see how it goes. Starting from now.' Jess poured milk into the cups, noticing for the first time the slight tremor in her father's hands as his picked up his tea.

She'd been certain she'd know what to say when she saw him and even though none of it had worked out how she planned, somehow she had. There were still hundreds of questions she wanted answers to, but her father had already managed to reveal something to her that she'd never admitted to anyone before, not even herself. Dom wasn't the love of her life, he'd never even come close. But there was someone out there who might just be able to fill that vacancy, if she had the courage to follow her father's lead and take the risk of asking for a second chance. She just had to work out if she was.

20

Dexter had finally got in touch with Jess. Typically, he hadn't just accepted her apology, but had tried to make it seem as if what had happened between them the last time they'd met up had all been his fault.

'The things I said to you just before Teddy left...' She'd hesitated, wanting to say so much but having no idea how to do it. It had been so much easier by text. 'I'm so sorry, I was just angry at Dom, myself and the whole bloody universe for giving me Teddy and then taking him away again. So as usual I managed to lash out when you were being so kind and make a mess of it all.'

'I got your message, but you don't need to say sorry and you didn't make a mess of anything. I know I probably came on too strong and I should have given you the space to explain how you were feeling, instead of just trying to make things better when nothing could.'

'You're too nice for your own good, you know that, don't you?' He'd laughed off her comment and she'd been able to picture his face, the strong jawline and the smile that made her believe everything really could be okay whenever he directed it at her. She'd been desperate to see him, but she was terrified that when she did, she'd say or do something stupid and blow whatever tiny chance there might be of things still working out. 'How's the wrist doing?'

'Pretty good, I've even perfected making dinner with only one hand. You could come over and check it out some time.'

'I'd like that.'

'Just name the day and I'll whip you up the best one-handed curry you've ever had. I really want to see you, Jess, and Riley does too.'

'I want to see you both too. I'll check my shifts and we can set a date. Talking of Riley, how's my favourite little sheep farmer doing?' Changing the subject to the little boy they both adored had been a deliberate ploy. It was the one thing guaranteed to make Dexter forget all about setting a date for dinner. It wasn't that she didn't want to see them both – she did, more than anything – but she'd defaulted to cowardice again and they'd ended the call without setting up the dinner.

When Jess had met with her father, she'd been all fired up about the power of second chances and determined to tell Dexter how she really felt about him and Riley. But he still didn't know about the infertility or the reasons behind it. She couldn't imagine Dexter judging her the way Dom had, but the fact that she'd lied to him for so long was unforgivable. Even if he could get past it, she wasn't sure she wanted him to. She was in love with him, there was no doubt about that, and she'd have wanted to be with him whether Riley was part of the package or not. But asking him to choose her, if Riley wasn't a part of the package, still seemed like an incredible sacrifice for him to make.

It would also mean asking him to turn down the job offer in Edinburgh and no one had ever made that kind of decision for her before. That wouldn't be fair to Riley either, not if it meant there was still instability in his life and whatever happened between her and Dexter, Riley absolutely had to come first. She could be the one to make a huge sacrifice of her own and leave all her friends behind to follow Dexter to Edinburgh, but where would that leave her if things didn't work out? If she actually lived with Dexter and Riley, her feelings for them were bound to get even stronger and there was still a chance that Dexter wouldn't get sole custody of the little boy. And even if he did, if things ended between them, Jess would lose the right to be a part of Riley's life too. She didn't trust herself to make the right decision any more, so the chance of spending the evening with her friends from the unit, before she agreed to meet up with Dexter, was just what she needed. The fact that they were having a cocktail evening was just a bonus and she'd been elected to be in charge of the drinks, which meant she'd have something other than the decision which could affect the rest of her life to think about.

Jess had come to the conclusion early on in the evening that she should have worn her sports bra to give her some more support. A lot of other women seemed to think she was lucky to have naturally big boobs, but they had no idea how often they got in the way. There she was, trying her best to channel Tom Cruise in *Cocktail*, but she'd ended up looking like a runner-up in a wet T-shirt competition instead, when the lid flew off the cocktail shaker right in the middle of making Frankie's pina colada.

'Oh no! That's far too good to waste. Will anyone judge me if I scoop it off the floor and back into the glass?' Frankie grinned, but Jess wasn't entirely sure she was joking given the fact she was crouching next to the puddle of rum, coconut and pineapple juice on Ella's kitchen tiles.

'Yes, we definitely will! Don't worry, I'll make you another one.' Jess was already mixing up the ingredients as she spoke. When she'd been with Dom, cocktail evenings had been their favourite way to entertain their friends. He'd even built a tiki bar in the garden of the little terraced house his parents had given them the deposit for. The summer before they'd split up had been one of those glorious and seemingly endless ones, which had made her more grateful than ever that she lived in Cornwall. They must have had at least ten cocktail evenings that summer and they'd joked about how they needed to make the most of it, before a baby came along and the tiki hut would have to make way for a sandpit and a playhouse. They'd already been trying for a baby for nearly a year by then and doubts were starting to nag at Jess, but Dom was still convinced it was only a matter of time.

'*We just need to do it more often, babe,*' he'd said, grabbing her around the waist and pulling her towards him. But he'd been wrong. Even *doing it* at every conceivable opportunity hadn't had the desired effect and eventually, she'd persuaded him they should have some tests. They'd said all the right things to each other, that they'd support one another no matter what, and at first, they really had. But when he'd discovered it was because of her that they hadn't conceived, it had all started to go horribly wrong. He'd slept with someone else within weeks and she was on her own again, just like she'd been since her mother had died. Jess Kennedy, the girl no one wanted, not even her own dad, at least not until now. There was a chance Dexter might really be different from all the rest, but it was hard to believe that when history had taught her what to expect time and time again.

'Are you okay, Jess?' Ella's voice made her jump. 'You're like you're on another planet and if you shake that pina colada for much longer there's a chance you might churn it into a really gross kind of butter!'

'Sorry, I was miles away.' Jess shook herself. She *wasn't* on her own any more. She had friends now, who she could rely on, and no one could just turn up and tell her to pack all her stuff because they were taking her to live in a strange house, with a family she didn't know. Even if Dexter did want to make a go of things, she didn't think she could leave that behind, not when it was her only safety net. 'Here you go, Frankie, a fresh pina colada and I'll even stick an umbrella in the top for you.'

'You know that's the classy kind of girl I am, Jess.' Frankie laughed. 'I think Ella should have you running the bar at her wedding, because no one makes cocktails like you.'

'Or as strong as you do.' Emily widened her eyes. 'One more swig of this pink Cadillac and I'll be anyone's!'

'I didn't think it took that many.' Gwen winked and stuck out her tongue to prove she was only joking, but given that she was drinking Baileys out of a pint glass the near-the-knuckle remarks were probably just going to keep coming.

'I wish I could try some of them, I always seem to be driving home and acting like the team party pooper.' Izzy looked down at the virgin mojito Jess had made her. 'At least I can pretend I'm joining in with this.'

'I told you that you could have stayed at mine.' Emily who'd drained her cocktail despite protesting about how strong it was, nudged her friend. 'We could have got a cab to Port Kara after this and checked out whether the rumours are true about all the celebs moving into the beach houses over there. I quite fancy being papped.'

'What was the plan, to just go and knock on random doors and hope a celebrity answers, lets you in and invites you to be a part of their inner circle?' Toni, who was also on the virgin mojitos, pulled a face.

'I've got to admit I hadn't got that far.' Emily laughed. 'Maybe

I should draw up the plan of attack before I start on the cocktails next time!'

'I can't stay over anyway. I'm taking my grandparents over to Tresco for the weekend, so we've got an early start tomorrow.' Izzy let go of a long breath. 'We're just trying to pack as much as we can in while my grandmother is feeling as well as she is. Especially since my mother has finally decided she's going to fly over from Australia to see her. I was starting to think she might not even bother.'

'I'm so glad that you're getting to do all these things with your nan, sweetie.' Frankie put a hand on Izzy's shoulder. 'Did you never think of going out to Australia with your mum?'

'She decided to move three months before my GCSEs and apparently there was no way she could wait.' Jess recognised the look that crossed Izzy's face, because she'd seen it in the mirror so many times. 'She had me at eighteen and she just wasn't ready for motherhood. She was in and out of my life when I was a kid, so I stayed with my grandparents who were brilliant. Then, when I was fifteen, she begged me to move in with her. But within a couple of months, she'd got a new boyfriend and she decided she wanted to move to Australia with him and I think the decision to go so close to my exams was because she didn't really want me tagging along. She thought I was old enough to stand on my own two feet, but I just went back to my grandparents' house and I was glad she'd gone, because it was always the place I felt happiest. It still is, despite Nonna being so ill. Mum's not a bad person and I'm grateful that she realised early on that she wasn't up to raising me when I was little, other-wise things might have turned out very differently.'

'I'm sure your grandparents have loved having you around too.' Jess smiled, hoping that it somehow conveyed to Izzy that she understood. She hadn't had a chance to get to know the newest midwife on the team all that well yet, but hopefully now she was back at work full-time, they'd have the opportunity. There'd be three others joining the team soon, too, and so much seemed to be changing.

'I wouldn't change things for the world and they've given me everything I could have wished for and more. Nonna kept saying she wanted to see me settled before she goes and she was worried that commuting here from Redruth, where we all live, was getting too much for me. So she used money she'd been saving since I was born to put down a big deposit on a cottage in Port Agnes. She wouldn't take no for an answer and said it was the biggest thing on her bucket list and the thing she most wants to tick off.' Izzy shook her head, as if she couldn't quite believe it herself.

'That's so nice.' Frankie sighed. 'And I'd be exactly the same in your grandma's position, but I hope you have lots more time with her yet.'

'Me too.' Izzy took a sip of her drink, looking like she needed to gather herself together before she could say much more and Jess recognised that feeling too. She still wasn't sure if she was going to ask her friends' advice about Dexter, because if she did, she needed to be strong enough to act on it, even if it turned out to be not what she wanted to hear.

'I've put the order in for the fish and chips so that the drinkers can line their stomachs before Jess's measures have you all on your backs!' Anna came into the room, clutching her phone. It was the first time she'd left the twins and even being away from them for a couple of hours had apparently needed military organisation. Her description of having to express enough breast milk to see them through had made Jess realise that there were a few things about never being able to give birth that didn't seem like such a downside after all. 'Brae's busy with the twins, but he's going to get his cousin to bring the order over and he's asked him to put in a couple of pickled eggs for you, Bobby, as requested.'

'I thought it was me who was supposed to get the pregnancy cravings?' Toni pulled another face.

'Pickled eggs from Penrose Plaice are the food of kings.' Bobby grinned. 'I'll just have to eat them in another room to make sure they don't make my beautiful girlfriend gag.'

'I'd better get another round of drinks poured then, if the food is on the way.' Jess was so happy to see Bobby and Toni openly teasing each other and finally celebrating the fact that they were together and expecting a baby. But Ella's wedding would be next and with so many of the team settling down and starting families, it all felt further away than ever for Jess. Madeline had said there was nothing to stop her adopting by herself, but she wasn't sure that's what she wanted and her mind was still pinging backwards and forwards, trying to work out what on earth she should do about Dexter. Maybe she should just bite the bullet and ask for another perspective, but in the end, even with friends as good as hers, it would have to be her decision. It was much easier just to serve drinks and try not to think about it. 'What about you, Ella? What can I get you to drink?'

'Can you do me one of your famous vodka martinis please?' Ella moved closer to Jess as she spoke, slipping an arm around her shoulders and lowering her voice. Jess clearly wasn't fooling everybody. 'Are you sure you're okay? I know you've had things really hard with Teddy going, but I can't help thinking there's something else.'

'I'm just a bit tired, nothing a cocktail or two won't fix. And I can't wait to see the wedding dress ideas your mum has come up with.' Jess laughed at the look that crossed Ella's face.

'I wasn't joking when I said I'll need to book Truro Cathedral for the wedding if I agree to wear it. The train on Princess Di's dress has got nothing on this.' Ella rolled her eyes. 'I'd still much rather wear her wedding dress and I'm not quite sure what part of *low key* she doesn't understand.'

'She only wants the best for you.' Anna ripped open a bag of kettle chips as she spoke, pouring them into bowls. 'She wants it to be the most amazing day of your life, that's all.'

'That's what all us mums want, I was like that with my Cheryl, drove her half mad she said.' Gwen took another slug of Baileys. 'You can't blame your mum. After all, a mother only gets to organise her daughter's big day once.'

'Gwen!' Frankie nearly dropped her drink, nudging her friend and risking sending the Baileys flying everywhere.

'Oh God, I've got to learn to engage my brain before I speak! I'm so sorry my love.' Gwen put her Baileys to one side and threw her arms around Ella. She'd done it again – not just acknowledged the elephant in the room, but let it out to charge around and trample over everything in its path. But when Jess looked over at Ella, she was laughing. Her first fiancé jilting her on the steps outside their wedding venue probably seemed like a lifetime ago to her now and Ella was proof that second chances really could be the best. Whatever her feelings about the overly elaborate wedding her mother was planning for her, it was obvious she was thrilled to be marrying her childhood sweetheart. But if she hadn't been brave and given both herself and Dan another chance, none of this would be happening.

'I suppose it is the first time I'll actually *get* married. At least I hope Dan's not going to stand me up like Weller did.'

'If he does, we'll hunt him down and make him wish he'd never been born. We can bury him under the patio, with his testicles in a liquidiser, alongside Dom!' Frankie wagged her finger. 'That's if the rest of Port Agnes doesn't get there first if your dad ever gets wind of Dan trying to do a runner.'

'Villagers with pitchforks at the ready.' Ella laughed again. 'I can just picture Dad being behind something like that. It would be like one of the themes he comes up with for the Port Agnes carnival parade and it certainly couldn't be any worse than when he made me and Mum dress up as Cornish pasties.'

'You definitely don't need to worry about Dan doing a runner, he's obviously devoted to you.' Jess would have bet everything she owned on it.

'He really is and so he should be. Everything's been better in Port Agnes since you came home.' Anna looked at Ella. 'Now enough of all this sentimentality, shall I get to the important stuff and grab some plates ready for when the food arrives?'

'I'll come out and show you where everything is and maybe Jess can give us a hand.' Ella turned to Jess, who nodded and followed her friends through to the kitchen, leaving the others to carry on talking; she had a funny feel she might be about to experience an ambush.

'Are you sure you're okay, Jess?' She'd barely got into the room before Anna asked the question. 'You've been through so much lately and you're still waiting on all of us, when we should be looking after you.'

'I like keeping busy.' Jess tried to shrug, but her friends knew her far too well.

'You like keeping busy when you're trying to avoid dealing with something.' Ella looked at her levelly. 'You don't have to talk about it, but you know we're always here if you do.'

'I don't think even you two can solve this one.' Jess smiled at her friends as a wave of exhaustion suddenly swept over her. 'I really like Dexter, more than that, but I've got no idea if I've already blown my chance.'

'So just ask him?' Anna made it sound so easy, but she only knew half the story.

'I could, but even if he feels the same there's no guarantee things will work out.'

'I hate to break it to you, but there's never any guarantee of that.' Ella wrinkled her nose. 'Sometimes you just have to take a chance.'

'Maybe I would if it was just me and Dexter, but what about Riley? I've already had to hand over one little boy I'd fallen in love with and I just don't know if I can do that again if things don't work out, or his birth father takes him away.' Jess plucked at the bracelet of beads she was wearing on her wrist, which Riley had made at school and given to her when he'd last been round to hers with Dexter. 'I'm already at the stage where I can't go anywhere without wearing this bracelet he made me, because it stops me missing him quite as much.'

'Oh, Jess.' Anna squeezed her hand. 'It sounds to me like it's already too late to stop yourself from falling in love with Dexter or Riley. So if you don't take a chance, you lose anyway. But if you risk it all, there's a possibility you might get everything you've ever wanted. Surely that's got to be worth it?'

'She's got a point you know.' Ella wrapped an arm around her from the other side, as Jess's brain scrambled to come up with an argument against her friends' logic. But Anna was right, and now she just needed to find the perfect way and the perfect moment to tell Dexter how she felt, before it really was too late.

* * *

'Jess!' Riley yanked his hand out of Dexter's and ran along the pavement, throwing himself at her – all flailing arms and legs, and a big squeezy cuddle that had just a bit of stickiness thrown in for good measure.

'Hello, sweetheart, this is the best cuddle I've had in forever.' Jess looked over the little boy's shoulder to where Dexter was standing, holding on to Riley's book bag with the hand that was still encased in a plaster cast, and with a very quizzical look on his face. There was no point Jess skirting around the truth. She could hardly say she'd bumped into them by chance, when Riley's school was a good ten miles from Port Agnes and outside of the midwifery unit's jurisdiction, which extended in the other direction to just beyond neighbouring Port Tremellien.

'I missed you both and I'm sorry I didn't get in touch to arrange to get together, but I wondered if now might be a good time?' Somehow she kept her voice steady and stopped short of hurling herself at Dexter with the same sort of enthusiasm that Riley had shown when he'd jumped into her arms.

'I know it's not exactly the weather for it yet...' Dexter paused. 'But maybe we should all go to Romano's for an ice cream. It's just on the high street and it's one of Riley's favourite places.'

'Dexter took me there when I got pupil of the week for my bestest reading.' Riley grinned as he finally pulled away from her and Jess wanted to wrap him in her arms all over again. He was an amazing little boy who'd been through an incredible amount at such a young age. They had so much in common that it felt like she was meant to be part of his life and he was worth risking everything for, just like his stepfather. She just had to persuade Dexter to give her a second chance and let her be part of his life too.

'We always go to Romano's when there's good news to celebrate.' Dexter smiled and Jess had to press her arm into her side to stop herself from reaching for his hand. They'd been careful never to let Riley see them acting in a way that would indicate they were more than friends and, for the most part, that's all they had been. So now definitely wasn't the time to rush in, when she still couldn't be a hundred per cent sure how Dexter felt.

'What's your bestest ice cream?' Riley slipped his hand into Jess's as they headed along the pavement to the high street and some of the tension left her spine.

'Now that's a tough question.' She pursed her lips, thinking for a moment. 'It's got to be between cookie dough and mint choc chip, I just can't decide!'

'Cookie dough, cookie dough!' Riley was almost dancing. 'That's my bestest favourite.'

'Excellent choice, okay, that's decided then. Cookie dough is my favourite too. What about Dexter?'

'His is 'nilla.' Riley wrinkled his nose. 'Boring!'

'Definitely not as good as cookie dough.' Jess winked at Riley, grinning as she caught Dexter's eye. He was smiling that lovely slow smile of his that had put her at ease from the moment she'd met him. If she'd been a gambling woman she'd have put a bet on the fact that Dexter still really liked her too and it made the stakes suddenly feel higher than even. Dexter and Riley could be leaving for Edinburgh any day now and she was nowhere near as certain that he liked her enough to stay in Cornwall, or to ask her if she wanted to go with them. It didn't exactly fit in with the plans they'd made originally to take things slowly.

Jess turned around as they reached the door of Romano's ice cream parlour and that's when she caught sight of Toni, walking along the pavement on the opposite side of the road, hand in hand with Bobby. If she'd been looking for a sign that things could work out against all the odds, then there couldn't have been a clearer one.

As they headed inside, Riley insisted that he absolutely, definitely needed two scoops of ice cream. Predictably, it turned out that his eyes were bigger than his belly and he got distracted halfway through the second scoop. Luckily Romano's had thought ahead and there was blackboard paint all along one wall, with buckets of chalk to keep their youngest customers entertained, and Riley hadn't needed any persuasion to give it a try. He'd told Dexter and Jess that he was going to draw a picture of them all walking here together.

'I just wish my legs were that long.' Jess laughed as she looked across to where Riley was busy with his work of art, his tongue half sticking out with concentration, the way it always did when he was colouring in. 'Although I'm not sure if I fancy having twelve fingers on each hand!'

'I think if anyone could pull that look off, it would be you.' Dexter put his hands on the table and Jess slid hers towards them, like there was a magnetic force. 'How are you doing? It must have been so hard to hand Teddy over to his adoptive parents. I wish I could have been there for you.'

'You would have been if I hadn't been such an idiot. I'm so sorry, Dexter.'

'You haven't been an idiot. I should have been honest when things started to change between us and told you I was worried that you were going to go back to Dom. Not because I don't think you can look after yourself, far from it, but because I'd already fallen in love with you.' Dexter's gaze met hers. 'But I had no idea if you were even remotely feeling the same way, especially when I'd promised to take this slowly. Not to mention how complicated things were for you already, so I thought it was probably the last thing you'd want to hear.'

'What would you say if I told you that it's the nicest thing anyone's ever said to me?'

'I might think you were lying to protect my feelings.' Dexter put his uninjured hand over hers. 'I'm not expecting you to say it back, but I just wanted to put it out there, because once you'd kicked me out of your house for the second time, I realised all the stuff I was worrying about didn't matter because I'd lost you anyway. I promised myself, if I got the chance, that I'd be honest next time and tell you that I love you.'

'That's why it's the nicest thing anyone's ever said to me, because I actually believe it when you say you feel the same about me as I do about you... I'm not sure that's ever happened to me before.' Jess curled her fingers around his. 'I should have been a lot more honest with you too and told you just how important you and Riley were to me, because I do feel the same about both of you. But I think it might be a while before I'm able to say these words out loud. You know, issues and all that!'

'I don't need to hear it. The fact that you came here and put yourself on the line is more than enough for me.' Dexter squeezed her hand and it was all she could do not to lean across the table and kiss him. Public displays of affection were usually her kryptonite, although for Dexter she would have been willing to make an exception. But the best part of all was that she didn't need to; for some reason he loved her just the way she was. Issues and all. There was only one problem now, but it was a pretty big one.

'There's something else I need to tell you first.' Jess tried to swallow, but it was like she forgotten how to.

Dexter reached out and put his hand over hers. 'You don't need to tell me anything you don't want to.'

'But I do.' Forcing herself to look at him again, Jess took a huge breath in, making sure she'd be able to get all the words out without having to stop again. 'When I said during my assessment that Dom and I didn't have kids because we weren't ready, it was a lie. I can't have children and his reaction to that was the beginning of the end for us.'

'I know about the infertility, Jess.' Dexter's eyes never once left her face. 'Dom told me all about it when I followed up the fostering reference he wrote with a telephone interview, but it's never mattered to me. It was always about you from the moment I met you, Jess, even when I was desperately trying to stay professional and just do my job. I don't care about anything we might not be able to have, because I'm so grateful for all the things we've already got, especially when I thought this was never going to happen.'

'Did Dom tell you why I'm infertile, that it's all my fault?' The heat was already rising up Jess's neck. If Dom had used the same words to describe her to Dexter as he'd called Jess to her face, she wasn't sure if she'd ever be able to look him in the eyes again.

'It's not your fault, but if it helps I came as close to slamming the phone down on Dom as I've ever done and it took all I had not to tell him what utter crap he was talking.' Dexter leant forward. 'I love you, Jess, and if we weren't in the middle of an ice cream parlour, I'd show you how much. I know it might take a while, but I'll keep doing whatever it takes until you finally believe me.'

'I don't deserve you.' Jess had imagined this conversation a hundred times and she'd expected Dexter to say her infertility didn't matter, but what she'd never anticipated was that she'd find herself believing him. She hadn't felt this loved in almost twenty years and the heat had moved from her neck to the pit of her stomach. This was what it was supposed to feel like when you loved someone and they loved you back – every bit as much, if not more. It was something she'd never had with Dom and she suddenly realised how right Dexter was. How on earth could she be sad about the things they might never have, when they already had so much?

'Whether you deserve me or not, Jess Kennedy, I'm afraid you're stuck with me.' Dexter grinned, but they were both in danger of forgetting something they still needed to sort out, which could change everything.

'There's just one thing.' Jess looked up at him, his brow creasing in response. 'The tiny matter of a move to Edinburgh?'

'Oh!' Dexter's face immediately lost some of the tension it had taken on. 'We're not going. Riley's dad has gone to live in Germany.'

'Really? How did that happen? I thought they'd have locked him up after what he did.'

'Apparently his band have decided that making it big in Germany is the gateway to Europe.' Dexter rolled his eyes. 'The fact that he's still in the grip of addiction didn't seem to be an issue for him or the rest of his band.'

'I suppose he wouldn't be the first rock star to be a drug addict. I still can't believe he isn't getting charged, though. He could have killed you.' Jess looked over to where Riley was busy creating his chalk masterpiece, Dexter's head twice the size of his body – her heart already racing at the question she was going to ask next. If Riley's father was planning to take him to Germany Jess would be devastated, but it would break Dexter completely. 'What about Riley?'

'Connor's signing full custody over to me. He said if I didn't press charges, which meant he wouldn't lose the chance to go to Germany, that he'd do it. He made the very convincing argument that we both knew it was the best thing for Riley anyway and he was right. So I told the police that the witnesses must have been mistaken and that he didn't push me, the car mirror must have clipped me by accident and that's why I fell into the road.

Luckily the drugs were out of his system by the time they tracked him down. It might seem like the wrong thing to do, letting him off like that, but I'd do anything for Riley.' Dexter stroked her hand again, making her skin tingle, relief flooding her whole body at the same time. 'I know having Riley as a full-time part of my life is an added thing to think about and I understand if that feels like too much, especially as you're missing Teddy so badly.'

'The fact that you've got custody of Riley is the best news I've heard in a long time. Other than not telling you I was infertile, the whole reason I was holding back was because I was terrified of losing both of you, especially as Connor was calling the shots when it came to Riley.' As if sensing that someone was talking about him, the little boy suddenly turned around and came running back towards the table.

'Do you like my drawing?' He tugged on Jess's sleeve and she nodded.

'It's brilliant, sweetheart, I'll take a picture of it with my phone so I can look at it whenever I need cheering up. I love it!'

'Goody, 'cos I love you.' Riley kissed her arm. 'And I love Dexter.'

'I love you too, sweetheart.' Dropping a kiss on top of his head, Jess turned and looked across the table. 'And I love Dexter too.'

In the end, despite all her hang-ups, it had been as easy as that and the little boy next to her had shown her the way: Dexter and Riley loved her and she loved them back. No one could predict if any relationship would last, but it was enough to know that she had love in her life right now and she was determined not to waste another second trying to hide how she felt.

EPILOGUE

Jess's feet crunched across the sand as she headed along the beach towards Ocean Cove. In the end, Toni and Bobby had surprised everyone by jumping ahead of Ella and Dan and organising a June wedding, just weeks before their baby was due.

They'd managed to book St Jude's after another couple had cancelled last minute. The ceremony had been beautiful and it had been a perfect early summer's day, with sunlight streaming in through the gorgeous stained-glass windows.

The reception was taking place on the beach, under a canopy that ran parallel with one of the rows of beach huts which had been rented out for the event. Bobby's father, Scott, was in charge of a series of barbeques and the only challenge for Jess had been keeping Riley away from the flames which seemed to draw him in when no one was watching. Luckily, with Dexter on the case too, they were able to outnumber the little boy and distract him with one of the children's activity packs that had been put on all the bistro tables set out beneath the canopy. It was like a garden party on the beach and the fact that the sun had shone on Toni and Bobby's big day was just one of the reasons why Jess couldn't stop smiling.

'It's great having all this hands-on help with the twins.' Anna turned to Jess and smiled as Ella and Dan walked ahead of them carrying Kit and Merryn.

'They're getting cuter every time I see them.' As Jess spoke, there was a cheer from a group sitting around one of the tables, as a champagne cork was popped into the air. 'I can imagine them getting up to all sorts in a couple of years' time, with Riley as their leader!'

'That would be great and if my two turn out to be anything like Riley, I'll be more than happy. Although I'm not sure who's having the most fun, Riley, Brae or Dexter!' Anna gestured in front of them, to where Dexter and Anna's husband were playing tag with Riley, chasing each other along the sand.

'Hopefully Teddy will get the chance to join in too. I'm babysitting for Toby and Sadie again next week, while they go out to look at venues for his adoption party. Everything seems to be going ahead with the court process and luckily Dom's decided not to try and cause any trouble for once, so they want to get somewhere booked for the celebration when it's all made official.'

'It's so lovely that you get on so well with his parents and that we've got so many little ones between us now.' Anna laughed. 'That'll be Ruth's next project, nagging Ella and Dan about when babies are going to start arriving, as soon as their wedding is over.'

'There's always something to look forward to being a Port Agnes midwife and we'll never go out of business at this rate!' Once upon a time, Jess would have felt a pang of regret that she wouldn't be joining her friends and adding to the unit's own baby boom, but not any more.

Four hours later, it was finally starting to get dark and at nine thirty it was already way past Riley's usual bedtime, but he was determined to stay for the fireworks that Bobby's brother had organised to round off the big day. Jess had been talking to Ella's parents just before the fireworks had started, but she'd excused herself so that she could watch them from down on the sand with her family. It was still strange to hear herself saying those words, but she loved it.

'Here we go, fireworks time.' Jess drew level with where Dexter and Riley were already waiting on the beach at Ocean Cove, smiling as they watched her approach.

'Can you lift me up to see them please?' Riley looked up to the sky, which was already illuminated by a blanket of stars.

'Maybe not all the way up, but let's get you as high as we can.' Dexter hoisted Riley onto his shoulders and they all looked out towards the waves, the tide so far out that Jess couldn't tell where sea began, which meant there was no danger of them getting cut off by the tide. To their right, the lights on the Sister of Agnes Island were shining and it felt like the whole world started and ended within a few square miles.

'I still wish Luna could've come with us.' Riley had become devoted to the little cat and he was the only person she didn't sink her claws into when the mood took her, so the devotion was obviously mutual.

'Grandpa Guy is going in tonight to give Luna her dinner, so she'll be fine and she'll be all the more ready for a big cuddle when we get back.' Jess squeezed Riley's hand, understanding more than anyone just how important the cat was to him. She'd overhead him talking to Luna and telling her all about his mummy dying and his daddy not being able to look after him, which made him sad, but that living with Dexter, and having Jess and Luna had made him happy again.

'Can Grandpa Guy come to dinner soon? I like it when he plays cars with me.' Riley had taken a real shine to Jess's father, and seeing him interact with the little boy and make such an effort to spend time doing the things Riley enjoyed had helped chip away the ice around her heart. It was still early days, but she was already incredibly glad she'd given her father the chance to prove he'd changed.

'I'm sure he'd love that.' Jess moved closer to Dexter as the fireworks suddenly illuminated the sky, marking the end of Toni and Bobby's wedding.

'This is perfect, isn't it?' Dexter stroked her arm and she leant against him in the darkness.

'Thank you.'

'What for?'

'For being the person you are and for letting me into your life, bringing all of my baggage with me. I spent my whole life looking for a family and then I found you. And Riley.'

Along the way she'd picked up friends who were like family too. She'd become an extended part of Teddy's new family and she was even beginning to reconnect with her dad – but the man and the little boy standing next to her on the beach had become her whole world. 'I'm so lucky.'

'We're the lucky ones.' Dexter pulled her even closer, Riley letting out an excited squeal as another firework illuminated the night sky. The family she and Dexter had around them might not be the sort anyone set out to create, but it was perfectly imperfect and most importantly of all it belonged to Jess, so she wouldn't want it any other way.

ACKNOWLEDGMENTS

I hope you have enjoyed the fourth novel in The Cornish Midwives series. Sadly, I am not a midwife, or a social worker, but I have done my best to ensure that the medical and fostering details are as accurate as possible. I am very lucky that one of my close friends, Beverley Hills, is a brilliant midwife and, as always, she has been a source of support and advice. I have also worked with foster carers and social workers for many years and so I have been able to draw upon this experience and their expertise in telling Jess's story. However, if you are one of the UK's wonderful midwives, providing such fantastic support for new and expectant mums, or indeed one of our amazingly dedicated social workers, I hope you'll forgive any details which draw on poetic licence to fit the plot.

The most incredible social worker I have ever had the privilege to work with, Danni Starley, was also an inspiration for Jess's story. Tragically a bright light in the world went out this year when we lost Danni as a result of cancer. Some of the royalties from the sale of this fourth book in the series will be donated to one of the cancer charities that Danni and her brilliant family – Rosie, Oscar and Charlie – tirelessly raised money for and continue to do so in her memory.

The support for The Cornish Midwives novels remains beyond anything I could have hoped for. I can't thank all the book bloggers and reviewers, and Rachel Gilbey, who organises the blog tours, enough for their help. To all the readers who choose to spend their time and money reading my books, and especially those who take the time to leave a review, it means more than you will ever know and I feel so privileged to be doing the job I love. I'd like to give a special mention to Jan Dunham, Debbie Blackman, Ian Wilfred and Beverley Ann Hopper for always being so wonderfully supportive.

Thanks too to all the lovely readers and subscribers to my newsletter, who entered the first name a baby contest for The Cornish Midwife series. Congratulations to Karen Tulley, who chose the name Teddy and will receive a signed copy of this book and some other Cornish themed prizes. There were so many gorgeous names to pick from and some of them will definitely pop up in the next novel in the series, so there'll be more prize winners to come soon.

Another huge debt of gratitude is owed to my lovely friend and beta reader, Pat Posner, who has helped so much in ensuring that this book was ready to go in time for the deadline.

My thanks as always go to the team at Boldwood Books for their help, especially my amazing editor, Emily Ruston, for lending me her wisdom to get this book into the best possible shape and set the scene for the next book in the series. Thanks too to my wonderful copy editor, Cari, and proofreader, Shirley, for all their hard work. I'm really grateful to Nia, Claire, Megan and Laura for all the work behind the scenes and especially for marketing the books so brilliantly, and to Amanda for having the vision to set up such a wonderful publisher to work with.

As ever, I can't sign off without thanking my writing tribe, The Write Romantics, and all the other authors who I am lucky enough to call friends.

Finally, as they always will, my biggest thank you goes to my family – Lloyd, Anna and Harry – for their support, patience, love and belief. A special thank you to Anna and Jack too for bringing a very precious new baby – Arthur – into all of our lives. I'm sure he's going to provide no end of inspiration!

MORE FROM JO BARTLETT

We hope you enjoyed reading *A Spring Surprise for the Cornish Midwife*. If you did, please leave a review.

If you'd like to gift a copy, this book is also available as an ebook, digital audio download and audiobook CD.

Sign up to Jo Bartlett's mailing list for news, competitions and updates on future books.

http://bit.ly/JoBartlettNewsletter

Why not explore the first in The Cornish Midwives series, *The Cornish Midwife*.

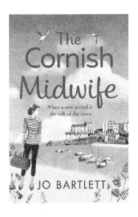

ABOUT THE AUTHOR

Jo Bartlett is the bestselling author of nineteen women's fiction titles. She fits her writing in between her two day jobs as an educational consultant and university lecturer and lives with her family and three dogs on the Kent coast.

Visit Jo's Website: www.jobartlettauthor.com

 twitter.com/J_B_Writer

facebook.com/JoBartlettAuthor

 instagram.com/jo_bartlett123

ABOUT BOLDWOOD BOOKS

Boldwood Books is a fiction publishing company seeking out the best stories from around the world.

Find out more at www.boldwoodbooks.com

Sign up to the Book and Tonic newsletter for news, offers and competitions from Boldwood Books!

http://www.bit.ly/bookandtonic

We'd love to hear from you, follow us on social media:

facebook.com/BookandTonic

twitter.com/BoldwoodBooks

instagram.com/BookandTonic